CHRONICLES OF THE LESCARI REVOLUTION

BLOOD IN THE WATER

ALSO BY JULIET E MCKENNA

CHRONICLES OF THE LESCARI REVOLUTION
Irons in the Fire

THE ALDABRESHIN COMPASS
Southern Fire
Northern Storm
Western Shore
Eastern Tide

THE TALES OF EINARINN
The Thief's Gamble
The Swordsman's Oath
The Gambler's Fortune
The Warrior's Bond
The Assassin's Edge

CHRONICLES OF THE LESCARI REVOLUTION

BLOOD IN THE WATER

JULIET E. McKENNA

SOLARIS

First published 2009 by Solaris
an imprint of Rebellion Publishing Ltd.
Riverside House, Osney Mead,
Oxford, OX2 0ES, UK

www.solarisbooks.com

ISBN: 978-1-84416-841-5

Designed & typeset by Rebellion Publishing

Printed in the US

For Steve

ACKNOWLEDGEMENTS

In another year of change, the invaluable support of friends and family, and of fellow writers and fans keeps me keen to do the very best work I can and to further explore my scope as a writer. Thank you all.

Not for the first time, being married to an old-school wargamer has proved priceless. Thanks, Steve, for marshalling the battles, as well as for all the other things.

Mike and Sue, Rachel, Gill, my thanks for your various perspectives on my work, as well as on life, the universe and everything else, and for prompting me to take a step back and look at the bigger picture when necessary.

Christian and Mark, thanks for everything thus far and I look forward to whatever projects might bring us together in the future, along with chatting over a drink at conventions and swapping news and views. Lisa, you remain copy-editor without equal. I am, as ever, grateful.

Sam, thanks, and it's good to know we're on the same page, even if it does need fewer adjectives as far as you're concerned.

CHAPTER ONE
Thathrin

**The Road from Losand to Carluse Town,
Autumn Equinox Festival, First Day, Morning**

WHEN CAPTAIN-GENERAL EVORD ordered the army to march at first light, he meant just that. The long column had been walking for nearly two leagues and the sun still hadn't cleared the tops of the oak trees.

Tathrin stifled a yawn. At least dawn wasn't so brutally early now the Equinox was upon them. Though that was a double-edged blessing. While the oak trees' leaves were still green, the hedges were showing seasonal gold.

He'd have been up this early at home. On the first day of the Autumn Festival, excitement would have roused him before the sounds of his mother and sisters down in the kitchen. They'd be preparing mutton, fat from the summer's grass, geese plump from gleaning in the wheat fields, succulent mushrooms and puddings sweet with plums and pippins, quinces and pears. His father and brothers by marriage would ensure ale flowed all day, a stronger brew than usual until the five days of festival were done and the year turned to Aft-Autumn.

They'd be joined by aunts and uncles and cousins and any guests still enjoying the hospitality of the Ring of Birches inn—those few who'd suffered some unexpected delay on their journey home. They would all give thanks to Drianon for the bounty of fruit and grain. The motherly goddess's statue was placed by the hearth and every meal concluded with grateful libations.

After sunset, Tathrin's father would set out wine and white brandy, gifts from the merchants who traded along the Great West Road cutting across this country of Lescar. Their mules and wagons carried luxuries and necessities to the wealthy Tormalin Empire in the east and brought different dainties back to the prosperous realm of Caladhria. Some even travelled further westwards to the fiefdoms and city-states that made up the land of Ensaimin. Such men valued clean beds, good food and secure stables and storage lofts. They soon learned that Jerich Sayron hired honest men, found them sound horses and changed their coin without cheating them.

Tathrin's feet mindlessly followed the tramp of the ranks ahead. Banners hung limp from poles slanted over standard-bearers' shoulders, their bright colours muted. Thankfully the dew kept down the dust. It would be a different story by noon, with the recent lack of rain.

Not that they wanted rain. He'd seen a youthful mercenary wishing for a shower harshly rebuked for tempting Dastennin, god of storms. All the experienced swordsmen knew that waging war so late in the year meant the weather could be a foe to equal any enemy.

Tathrin shivered, and not just from the lingering chill after the cloudless night. This was about as far as he could get from a carefree festival. Then again, how often had his family enjoyed a festival of peace and plenty? Only a handful of times that he could recall.

All too often his father had been forced to sell whatever precious liquors he'd garnered to raise the coin for Duke Garnot's quarterly levy. The duke's men would seize livestock and stores from anyone who couldn't pay what the reeve decreed. Tathrin's mother would offer what festival charity she could to those who'd been left destitute. Quarterstaffs and fowling bows to hand, his father and brothers by marriage would keep a nightly watch by the light of the capricious twin moons. Men bereft of home and hope all too often turned to banditry.

Sometimes a dispossessed man or a friendless widow would hammer on the gates of their local lord or lady's manor. They would demand justice, a tenant's rights from this noble who was in turn the sworn vassal of their duke. It never did any good, not that Tathrin heard. A good day saw such appeals fobbed off with insincere sympathy. On a bad day, the suppliant was lucky to escape with a horsewhipping instead of a noose.

And that was in a good year. If Duke Garnot was waging war against one of his neighbours, then his own forces and those of the retaliating duke could lay the country waste between them. Tathrin's mother comforted those mourning brothers, sons or husbands forcibly enrolled in Duke Garnot's militia, already fearing they were as good as dead. His father would retreat to the cellars with the other local guildsmen, grim-faced.

Not that Carluse suffered worse than any other of Lescar's six dukedoms, Tathrin reminded himself.

"Long lad!"

Only two people called him that. Sorgrad and Gren. Sorgrad was away and wouldn't return for a few days. Gren was supposed to be marching with him here at the tail end of Captain-General Evord's retinue. But Gren preferred to range up and down the column, picking up gossip and grumbles, flirting with the women among the mercenaries and cadging whatever he could for the sackcloth provisions bag slung on his hip.

"You look as glum as a man with a three-day cake baking up his arse. Cheer up. Life will look sunnier once you've dropped some prunes in a ditch." Gren held out a rich orange lump flecked with green herbs. "Want some cheese?"

"Thanks." Tathrin had learned to eat whenever the chance arose.

"The scouts reckon they've seen something." Gren's words were muffled by his mouthful, his blue eyes bright with anticipation.

Tathrin considered the thickly leaved hedges flanking the track. They wouldn't be thinned till Aft-Winter. With no work in the fields and their valuable herds penned, farmers could repair the damage done by malice, misfortune or merely the past year's weather. At the moment, half a company of swordsmen could be lurking in the next field and he'd be hard put to see them, even though he was half a head taller than most. Gren barely topped his shoulder.

He frowned at the shorter man. "The captain-general doesn't expect to encounter Carluse forces today."

From the outset, Tathrin had been present for Evord's meetings with his lieutenants and the gallopers who carried his instructions to every one of the eighty-some companies that made up this army's full strength. After all, as far as anyone knew, Tathrin was Evord's personal clerk, his scholar's ring proof that his writing was legible and his reckoning reliable.

Gren ran a hand through his tousled hair, pale as newly sawn wood in the strengthening light. "Could be brave lads from that last village, slipping their leashes to take us on." His grin broadened.

"To save their pretty kittens from a nosing by us dirty dogs."

Tathrin had noted every door and window was shuttered as they'd marched through the village with the sky still darker than a wood pigeon's wing. But it wouldn't be hard for someone who knew the local byways to slip out of a back door and overtake the marching column. Were men and boys hiding out here, clutching mattocks and hoes, believing they must fight to the death to defend their homes and families?

What would Carluse's commonalty know of this army and its true purpose? What would they fear when they saw the companies of blond uplanders like Gren? Mountain Men were rumoured to be brutal savages and marching mercenaries of any stripe only ever brought death and destruction. Until now.

"Arest and his Wyvern Hunters are in the vanguard." Gren had lived a mercenary life long enough to lose every trace of his Mountain accent. He washed down his cheese with a swallow of ale. "Me, I'd kill them all and they can argue the roll of the runes with Saedrin when they reach the door to the Otherworld, but Arest wants you and Reher to come forward, in case we're tripping over farmers. If it's Duke Garnot's militiamen, you two can fall back while we cut them down. All right?" Without waiting for Tathrin's answer, Gren headed for the front of the column.

Tathrin looked quickly around for Reher. Gren wasn't joking when he advocated clearing the road by killing everyone regardless. Arest wasn't so ready with his swords but the Wyvern Hunters would still repulse any attack, determined to be safe instead of sorry. Hapless peasants would be slaughtered.

There. Reher was marching at the rear of Evord's personal guard, the mounted swordsmen who made up the bulk of the captain-general's retinue. That made sense. As a blacksmith, he kept all their horses shod. Would his other talents be called for today? Tathrin fervently hoped not.

Hurrying towards Reher, he felt his armour already weighing him down. Tathrin's leather jerkin wasn't as heavy as Gren's chain mail, even with the steel plates sewn into its linen lining, but its insidious weight still sapped his strength.

Wearing a sheepskin jerkin over his chain-mail hauberk, Reher showed no sign of weariness. He never did and Tathrin didn't think that was just because the man's black beard hid so much of his face. Reher was enormous, taller than Tathrin, who seldom had to look up to anyone, and the smith's arms were as well muscled as most men's thighs. Tathrin's own shoulders had broadened considerably after spending both halves of summer and the first half of autumn being drilled in swordplay by Gren. He still felt a weakling next to Reher. But their common Carluse blood gave them a bond he valued.

They weren't so very far from Tathrin's own home. Could he end up fighting boys he'd challenged to skip stones across a duck pond? Would he find men who'd clipped him around the ear for teasing a chained hound at the end of his sword?

"Reher!" Once he had the smith's attention, he lowered his voice. "There's movement ahead. Arest wants us with him in case it's Woodsmen."

Reher's dark eyes glinted. Like Tathrin and most of the rest, he was dark-haired and deeply tanned after the long summer. "Let's see." He handed the rein leading the mule carrying his tools and supplies to another of the retinue's non-combatants. Surprised, the man accepted it nevertheless. People didn't argue with Reher.

They soon reached the head of the column. Captain-General Evord wasn't a commander to hide away at the tail of his troops. The fields gave way to rough grass dotted with thickets, too far from any village to be safely farmed. Tathrin loosened his blade in its scabbard, tension twisting his gut. This wasn't a high road with the ground cleared for a bowshot on each side to foil bandits. Evord was marching his army along a little-used route to reach their intended foe, all the better to go undetected.

How were locals to know this mercenary army wasn't the usual villainous rabble? It was bad enough when militiamen collected the ducal dues but they were Carluse men at least, even if they'd taken the duke's coin to wear his boar's head badge. Tathrin's father had once slapped him for spitting at a militiaman, and not just to save him from the sergeant's vengeance. Most enlisted to feed their families or because they'd lost all home and livelihood, he'd explained later. Taking what they must to meet the levy, they usually tried to leave a household with enough to survive the hungry winter seasons.

Mercenaries had no kith or kin in Lescar. If they were sent to collect the levy, they descended like ravening curs. All the duke's reeve demanded of a company's captain was the money each household must pay. Whatever else the mercenaries took was theirs to keep. So farmers and craftsmen saw their houses ransacked for hoarded Caladhrian marks or Tormalin crowns.

The mercenaries readily handed over lead-debased Lescari silver for the ducal coffers. They were content to leave the copper pennies that the desperate cut into halves and quarters to make them do twice and four times their duty. The solid coin sent from beyond Lescar's borders would slake the dogs' lust for gambling, whores and drunkenness.

He remembered mercenaries coming to the Ring of Birches just once. Tathrin's father had bought them off with strong liquors saved for just such a crisis. His mother and sisters hid away upstairs. In his farrier's apron, Tathrin's eldest brother by marriage had barred the way, a hammer in one hand, an iron bar in the other. None of the mercenaries had challenged him.

Such men were cowards at heart, that's what his father had said. After these long seasons spent in their company, Tathrin would argue that point. If he ever got safe home and had the chance. He resolutely thrust such thoughts aside as they reached the front ranks of the column.

Men, and not a few women, were marching beneath a grey banner bearing a white gull. Their shields bore white wings with black tips, the paint old and chipped. A new design shone beneath them: a bright yellow quill. Tathrin was still trying to get the measure of such women, all warriors in their own right. Captain-General Evord had decreed no trail of whores and cooks would slow this army.

"There's Gren." Reher whistled a snatch of a flax-finch's song.

It took Tathrin a moment to spot the short mercenary sliding through the tangled undergrowth. Hearing Reher's whistle the second time, Gren glanced over his shoulder and beckoned them onwards.

Tathrin stooped, uncomfortably aware of his height. Reher showed no such concerns as they halted in the lee of a birch tree.

"What's the game?"

"A double handful lurking a hundred paces beyond that twisted thorn." Gren pointed. "Listen and you'll hear their stones rattling in their breeches, they're so scared."

"Where's Arest?" Tathrin couldn't believe the

mercenary captain could hide behind anything less than a full-grown oak. If he wasn't as tall as Reher, he was even more massively built.

"He's playing the swordwing." Gren nodded to his offside. "Zeil and his mates are the corbies there." He jerked his head a second time. "Awn's the tufted owl and we're the spotted thrushes."

Fighting was just a game to these men. Like white raven, where men shifted little wooden trees and carved forest birds around the boards scored into his father's taproom tables. The other player must evade all such traps set for the mythical white bird. Who was going to win today? Tathrin wondered. How much blood would be spilled instead of ale?

Reher nodded, frowning. "We need to know who they are."

"Follow me." Gren darted down a narrow path worn by deer or foresters.

They had reached the edge of Duke Garnot's hunting preserve, where the price of a poached deer was a severed hand. Men living off the woods wouldn't be eager to explain themselves to anyone, Tathrin reflected.

"Stay behind me and stay out of trouble," Reher warned in a low tone.

They all spoke to him like that. Was it because he was still of an age when most youths were just ending their apprenticeships? Or because he wore a scholar's silver ring, bearing the arms of the city of Vanam, far away in distant Ensaimin? Tathrin had soon learned mercenary swordsmen and craftsmen like Reher all assumed a university education eradicated most of a scholar's common sense.

Well, Tathrin knew woods and fields better than any townsman. An autumn morning should be full of birdsong. These thickets were silent, tense. Tathrin fixed his eyes on Gren's mailed back slipping through the bushes ahead. He strained his ears for some hint of anything bigger than a coney making its escape.

Ahead, a man dashed across open ground. Tathrin saw he wasn't wearing the cream surcoat of Arest's mercenaries, the black wyvern lashing its tail. He had no neckerchief of unbleached linen and bold yellow, the colours of Evord's army. He wasn't one of their own.

"Stand and identify yourself!" Reher bellowed.

In the thorn bushes, Gren halted, tense as a hunting hound.

The man stared horrified at Reher and Tathrin. Shouts erupted and someone screamed. Swords clashed in scuffles hidden by the trees. The man fled.

Gren stepped out and extended his arm, chest-high. The man couldn't stop himself. He crashed to the ground, flat on his back, gasping like a stranded fish. Gren barely wavered, his iron-studed boots planted solidly in the leaf litter. Just for good measure, he drove a steel-capped toe into the man's thigh. Tathrin winced. Even before Gren had rebelled to become a mercenary, his muscles had been hardened by boyhood among the mines of the peaks and lakes, on long trips hunting fox and beaver.

The blond man looked down with satisfaction. "Floored like a market-day whore."

The man writhed on the ground, his wheezing pathetic as he struggled to catch his breath. He was a wretched specimen, left bandy-legged by a poverty-stricken childhood, chapped lips drawn back from rotted teeth. Tathrin wondered how long it was since he'd lost everything and taken to the forests.

"So what have we got here?" Reher planted a boot on the fallen man's chest and scowled down. "Not Duke Garnot's cully?"

He wasn't wearing Carlusc black and white. Tathrin bent to rip open his grimy jerkin and the sweat-stained shirt beneath, in case he wore some hidden boar's head pendant. The duke's men might go in disguise but they'd always keep something to prove their allegiance in case they were threatened by one of their own.

"We're just woodsmen, you bastards," gasped the man.

Gren chuckled. "Or do you mean *Woodsmen*?"

Tathrin had been barely breeched when he'd first heard the rumours. Tales of supplies meant for the duke's mercenaries unaccountably seized on the road. An honest family who'd seen their livestock driven off found a flitch of bacon hidden in their woodpile, so the story went. A bag of coin had dropped down a widow's chimney, enough to save her son from the militia's clutches, her daughter from worse. All thanks to the Woodsmen, so the whispers said.

Now Tathrin knew the truth. He knew how much the unfortunate owed his father and his fellow guildsmen. They didn't just drink white brandy and abuse the duke's name when they met in the Ring of Birches' cellar. They did all the good attributed to the Woodsmen and more besides. Who was better placed than an innkeeper to encourage the tavern stories that kept Duke Garnot's men hunting for mythical Woodsmen, and to see a youthful packman or a fresh-faced cook's maid unobtrusively joining a merchant's wagons, heading for sanctuary among those who had long since fled Lescar for exile in cities like Vanam and Col?

But this sorry vagabond didn't look like any of the guildsmen's allies that Tathrin had seen slipping out of the inn's back door in the dead of night.

"How many of you?" Reher took his boot off the man's chest and hauled him up by his collar.

"I won't say." The man spat on Tathrin's boots.

Gren clouted the back of his head. "Mind your manners. He's here to help you."

"Him and the rest of you pissing thieves," the man retorted, unexpectedly bold.

One of Gren's many daggers was already in his hand. He gestured towards the man's crotch. "Do you want to keep your berries on their twig?"

"Don't." Tathrin saw their captive's fingers twitch

towards his own knife. "You've no hope of making a fight of this."

The man subsided, seeing the Wyvern Hunters emerging from the thickets, sunlight glinting on their swords. They walked behind men wearing ragged and dirty clothes, some with bruised faces and shallow wounds to forearms and thighs. Most had their hands prudently clasped on top of their heads. To Tathrin's acute relief, he recognised none of them.

"That's them all flushed out." Arest waved a massive hand, broad as a spade. "Salo, run and tell the captain-general's adjutant."

Reher surveyed them. "Any of you from Carluse Town?"

"I am, and I can hear it in your voice." A man with a broken nose, too furious to be cowed, stepped forwards. "What are you doing with these dogs?"

"Do you know Master Ernout?" demanded Reher.

"Priest at the shrine of Saedrin?" The Carluse Town man was confused. "Of course."

But Tathrin could see he didn't know that the courageous old man was one of those priests conspiring with the master craftsmen to stop the abuse of honest men and women. Along with his niece, Failla. Tathrin allowed himself a moment to wonder how she was. When would he see her again? How long before peace allowed him to pursue their tentative understanding? If she hadn't already forgotten him.

"If you swear, all of you, not to raise a hand against us as we pass, we'll leave you unharmed." The smith looked around the vagabonds, his dark eyes intent. "I swear it by Saedrin's keys. If you doubt me, send to Master Ernout in Carluse Town and ask him if Reher's word can be trusted."

For an instant, Tathrin was horrified. Did Reher want to forewarn their enemy? Then he realised there was no way these men would give themselves up to Duke Garnot. Come to that, the chances were minimal of anyone here reaching Carluse Town before the duke knew exactly what threatened him.

"Will you take his word for it?" Arest enquired genially. "Or do we have to kill you?"

Now the ragged men's eyes were irresistibly drawn to the main track. The first companies were marching past. Tathrin saw the vagrants blanch as the tramp of the approaching column shook the ground beneath their feet. Well, Tathrin wouldn't have believed the army that Evord had assembled if he hadn't seen it with his own eyes.

The vagabonds muttered among themselves as they saw the battle standard fluttering above Evord's retinue. Against the unbleached linen, the circle of hands stitched from cloth of gold shone like a sunburst. Each fist grasped a symbol of honest toil, of learning, of home and family. This army was bringing peace for all Lescari to enjoy such things, or so Tathrin fervently hoped.

"But—" the broken-nosed man gaped at Reher, unable to frame a question.

"You'll know what it means soon enough," the smith promised him.

"Till then, why don't you run off and hide up your own arseholes?" Arest menaced the vagrants impersonally with his sword.

The ragged men swiftly melted into the woods. Tathrin could only hope they had the sense to stay lost.

"Come on." Reher began walking back to the column as Arest reassembled his men for their duties in the vanguard.

The smith glanced at Tathrin. "Your friends need to tell that Parnilesse man, Reniack, to spread his pamphlets and songs towards Carluse as fast as he can."

"Do you think these strays can read?" But Tathrin knew he was right.

"We can't afford delay each time we trip over some runaway." Reher lowered his voice to a rumble. "I could drive them off but I don't want to show my hand."

"No," Tathrin said hastily.

Did anyone suspect the two of them shared more secrets than Carluse blood? If someone did, would explaining that Tathrin's father and Reher both worked with the Woodsmen suffice?

Tathrin didn't relish the thought of anyone else knowing he was the conduit for magical communications between Captain-General Evord and Losand and Sharlac, the towns they had already conquered. Because everyone knew magic was forbidden in Lescar's ceaseless wars. The Archmage Planir was adamant, like all his predecessors. The bold, destructive power of wizardry hadn't been seen on a Lescari battlefield in time out of mind.

Reher would be in more trouble than him, Tathrin thought guiltily. If the smith hadn't studied at the Wizards' Isle of Hadrumal, he was undeniably mageborn with the control over fire that arcane talent granted him. Tathrin was only the passive recipient of information from his friend Aremil. And Aremil was using Artifice, the ancient magic of mind and emotion. Planir had never claimed suzerainty over that.

Few people even remembered this subtle magic existed. It was the scholars of the ancient universities who had rediscovered the lost enchantments. Scholars were still diligently searching for more in the learned halls of Col and Vanam, which was how he and Aremil had heard of it. They had soon seen how it could serve them, as they had sought the best way to truly end Lescar's enduring misery.

Would such arguments convince anyone outraged by Evord's use of magic? Wouldn't the dukes use such an accusation to rally men to their cause?

Tathrin sighed. It had seemed so simple when he and Aremil had discussed all this back in Vanam, merely intent on bringing peace to Lescar.

Chapter Two
Aremil

**Losand, in the Lescari Dukedom of Carluse,
Autumn Equinox Festival, Second Day, Morning**

HE WOULD FEEL much safer with the door locked.
But then he would have to get up and open it when
someone knocked, and they would wonder why
he'd locked it. Anyway, what was he afraid of?
Aremil forced himself to assess the situation as
dispassionately as the scholar he claimed to be. With
the rigorous logic he and Tathrin had both learned
in Vanam's university halls.

Captain-General Evord's men had driven Duke
Garnot's foul-mouthed and vicious mercenaries
clean out of Losand. The town's guildmasters were
recruiting an honest militia under the guidance
of Evord's lieutenant, Dagaran. He was another
mercenary come all the way from Solura, a man of
similar mettle to the Captain-General. Aremil himself

was safely accommodated on the upper floor of this merchants' exchange. How could he admit to feeling imperilled in the heart of this solidly walled town with guards on every gate and the fighting moving further away with every passing day? He couldn't. Not without sounding like an arrant coward, and his pride wouldn't stand for that.

Aremil looked out of the window, at the mercenary army's banner flapping in the wind. He smiled crookedly. It wasn't as bright as Evord's. Only the captain-general's banner bore the insignia in cloth of gold.

Trust Master Gruit to spend his coin on such a flamboyant gesture. The wine merchant had a fine instinct for the dramatic. His impassioned denunciation of his fellow merchants in Vanam, attacking those of Lescari blood who let their kinsmen suffer, had been the first toppling rock that set this whole landslide in motion. When Aremil and Tathrin had trusted Gruit with their own longing to see peace in Lescar, he had proved a staunch ally. Now he was invaluable, organising the astonishing quantities of supplies that the marching army needed.

Aremil's smile faded, his thin face returning to its customary immobility. What would Gruit have to say when the dust had settled? After their careful planning had brought blood and death to Lescar in the name of peace? He would have welcomed the chance to talk to the older man, but Gruit had already left for Abray, the town commanding the crucial junction where the Great West Road crossed from Caladhria into Lescar. Someone had to persuade the merchants and barons of Caladhria to sit on their hands while Captain-General Evord waged this campaign. Gruit was undeniably the best man to do it.

But it was hard on them all, Aremil felt. When everyone's dearest wish was to celebrate festival with family and loved ones, all those who'd united in Vanam to plot this overthrow of Lescar's dukes had scattered to the four winds, even before the fires consuming Sharlac Town stopped smouldering.

Gruit was on the road heading west towards Abray, with Failla and Kerith the dour scholar and aetheric adept. Tathrin and Gren were marching with Captain-General Evord's army. Sorgrad was currently escorting Charoleia and her maid eastwards to Tormalin. The beautiful intelligence broker would use her formidable web of friends and allies there to dissuade the Emperor from interfering.

Branca was with them and Aremil missed her most of all. Did Tathrin know? Aremil felt every pang of his friend's longing for Failla when he wrought Artifice's enchantments to reach through the aether to tell Tathrin all the news from the territory they had already conquered, and to find out all that the captain-general's army was doing.

Aremil missed Branca so sorely. But did she miss him? He couldn't tell. She was so much more skilled with aetheric enchantment, his teacher in the ancient discipline, even if she was a few years his junior. So her innermost thoughts were always wrapped in veils impenetrable to him. Perhaps that was for the best. He was almost afraid to find out what she truly felt.

Which was ridiculous. Had he spent his life schooling his intellect only for the discipline of rational thought to fail him now? Aremil reminded himself how Vanam's university mentors rebuked anyone falling prey to unreasoned emotion. Once the source of any unease was identified, they insisted, it could be dismissed with logical argument.

Aremil decided he didn't mind Tathrin knowing that his respect for Branca was deepening to affection. Though he didn't particularly want the older scholar Kerith to know, nor yet their younger ally Jettin. He barely knew either man. But Aetheric adepts were thin on the ground, and those with Lescari blood, who could be recruited to their cause, were rarer still.

The advantage they offered this rebellion was beyond price. To be able to communicate across countless leagues in the blink of an eye could make the difference between victory and defeat. Artifice's enchantments could reach instantly through the aether, that mysterious medium that somehow linked mind to mind, while their foes' letters were limited to the flight of courier doves or the speed of the fastest horse.

If the price of Kerith's help, and Jettin's, was the two men learning more than Aremil cared to share of himself, it would have to be paid. It was little enough to ask, when so many others would pay with blood and pain.

Aremil only hoped Tathrin would come through unscathed. And Jettin, who was riding with a different contingent of the army, he recalled hastily. At least Branca would be safe, well away from any fighting, enjoying Tormalin's affluent calm. One day, Lescar would benefit from just such prosperity and all this cataclysm would be worth it.

Aremil looked around the room. Losand's merchants had violently evicted the clerk who'd recorded their dealings for the duke's reeve. The shelves were empty of all but a few scraps of ribbon. The chest for his ledgers gaped open, its locks smashed.

A draught played across his neck and Aremil shivered. His sitting room in Vanam had been cosy and warm. Lyrlen, ever attentive, would have lit a fire before he got up. He'd be at leisure to pursue his studies, only interrupted by her bringing his meals or by Tathrin visiting to drink a glass of wine.

Perhaps that was why he felt so uncertain. He was simply homesick. Well, he was in Losand by his own choice, so he had better apply himself to the matters in hand. There was plenty to do without sitting here moping.

Aremil looked at the door. He could find out how both Tathrin and Branca fared using his Artifice.

But Branca didn't expect him to contact her before evening. He wasn't due to send his thoughts in search of Tathrin until the noon chimes, when Evord's lieutenant would guard the door in person. Of all the secrets their plots depended on, aetheric magic was the most closely guarded. They could not risk any duke's spies finding out.

He looked at the timepiece on the wall. The brass arrow seemed to have barely moved down the long scale dividing the daylight into ten equal measures. At least at this season, with both For- and Aft-Autumn bracketing the Equinox, the chimes of daylight and darkness were the same. Summer's long hours would be far greater torment. Winter's short days need not be contemplated. One way or another, Evord had said, their venture must be concluded before any timepiece's faceplate was changed with the turn of For-Winter.

Could they do that? True, they had conquered one dukedom already, but Sharlac had been little challenge. Duke Moncan had withdrawn into his castle seasons ago, to mourn his dead son. His vassals and militias had grown soft and complacent. Aremil didn't think any of the remaining five dukes would be caught unawares, not once news of Sharlac's fate reached them.

He hurriedly smoothed his expression as the door flew open, crashing against an empty shelf.

"Fair festival." Reniack bowed with a flourish worthy of the Tormalin Emperor's court. "What do you think? Not bad for the son of a Carif whore?"

"Fair festival to you." Aremil inclined his head stiffly. "You look more elegant than last night."

Reniack wore a blue doublet with silver buttons over a lace-trimmed shirt. Jewels on the knee-buckles of his breeches might be sapphires, though Aremil thought they were more probably glass. His snowy stockings were immaculate.

The burly man chuckled. "Last night I drank to Duke Garnot's ill-health with the scaff and raff of Losand's gutters. A ragged shirt and a charcoal-burner's jerkin made me a prince among the spigot-suckers."

Aremil refused to react to the vulgarity. "And today?"

Reniack pressed a hand to his barrel chest, his expression lofty, his short beard jutting. "I join the sober elders and goodwives of Losand among the midday rites at Drianon's shrine."

"What do you have to share with them?" Aremil asked sardonically.

Reniack grinned and reached inside his doublet for a sheaf of papers. "I honour Drianon as goddess of harvest but let's not forget her care for hearth and home. Her sacred eagle will always fight for her eaglets."

Aremil studied the crisply printed pamphlet that Reniack laid on the desk. The engraving showed a ferocious and somehow indefinably female eagle clawing at a polecat which was sneaking along a crag towards a nest of anxious chicks.

He looked up at Reniack. "Is it my imagination or does that polecat look like Duchess Tadira?"

"Women hate her more than they fear her husband. They resent their husbands' toil buying her silk gowns to drape her bony buttocks, putting jewels around her scrawny neck." Reniack's voice thickened with his own loathing. "If we persuade the ordinary women that we're fighting for their sake, they'll persuade the men, once the bed curtains are drawn and they're hoping for open thighs."

Reniack's hand strayed to his brown hair, as if to brush it behind his ears. Aremil saw him curb the gesture. The astute pamphleteer wouldn't want the staid folk of Losand wondering at his ragged earlobes. They wouldn't be impressed to learn that the Duke of Parnilesse had ordered Reniack's ears nailed to the wood when he was pilloried for nailing letters to shrine doors in the dead of night, accusing the duke and his brothers of conspiring to poison their father.

The man had spent years stirring up hatred against Parnilesse's duke, concocting inflammatory pamphlets, writing more measured arguments for market-day broadsheets, even turning tavern songs to his purpose, and recruiting a small army of rabble-rousers to help him. His loathing was implacable. That Carluse's Duchess Tadira was Duke Orlin's sister was sufficient to earn her Reniack's spite.

Aremil was glad he had no cause to reach into Reniack's thoughts, to learn what prompted such rancour. He was also glad he was so practised at hiding his own emotions. He really didn't like Reniack, with his coarse language and cynical view of humanity. Though he had no reason to mistrust the pamphleteer. Reniack had proven time and again that he could keep the conspiracy's secrets as close as his own skin. If any duke's spies learned they were using Artifice, it wouldn't be through him.

The pamphleteer had other concerns. "Dagaran said you wanted to see me. What's the latest news from Tathrin?"

"The army is making steady progress through the forest towards Carluse. They've been encountering runaways and vagabonds all through the woods," Aremil explained. "Do you have anyone to send to explain what Evord's army intends? The last thing the captain-general needs is skirmishing delaying his advance."

"Tell Dagaran to give me a handful of fast horses and my men will spread the word all the way to Carluse." Reniack narrowed his eyes. "Can I throw Failla's treachery in the duke's face just yet?"

"No!" Though Aremil didn't know why he was shocked. Reniack never attempted to hide his lack of scruple.

"It might knock Duke Garnot off balance, if everyone knew his whore ran off and faked her own death rather than rub bellies with him any longer."

The pamphleteer chuckled. "If his militiamen are gossiping around their campfires, they're not sleeping or making ready to fight."

"No." Aremil tried to think of some argument to dissuade him. That it would distress Tathrin wouldn't weigh a pennyworth with Reniack. Nor would the pamphleteer much care that Failla was desperate to stay hidden, fearing Duke Garnot's reprisals when he found out she had long since betrayed his secrets to Carluse's guildmasters' plots.

Reniack shrugged. "That's an arrow we can keep in our quiver for another day. When does Tathrin think they'll join battle?"

"Evord expects to force Duke Garnot into a fight tomorrow."

Reniack nodded, eyes distant. "How soon can we realistically have news of the outcome?" He answered his own question. "If we say we had it by courier bird, someone will ask who gave us doves hatched in Losand. How far is it to Carluse? Forty-five leagues? The battle will be closer than that. A man on a fast horse could do it in a day and a half—"

"Only if he didn't mind the horse dropping dead," Aremil objected.

Reniack waved away that concern. "I'll have something ready for the first day of Aft-Autumn. A little shock to wake up the townsfolk after they've slept off their last festival drunk."

"But we don't know what will happen." Aremil coughed on his indignation.

"We'll win, or we'll do well enough to claim we've won. We have to." Reniack nodded at Aremil's crutches, leaning against the side of the desk. "Otherwise we'd all better take to our heels, as best we can."

"I imagine I'll find a seat in a coach," Aremil said curtly.

Reniack wasn't listening, the jerk of the brass arrow on the timepiece catching his eye. "I'll get some of my lads on the road before I head for the shrine. I may even breathe a prayer to Drianon," he added mockingly. "I'll call back tomorrow evening and you can tell me all Tathrin's news."

"Very well." Aremil nodded as the Parnilesse man departed with a cursory wave.

With his broad shoulders and sturdy build, Reniack didn't look as if he'd suffered a day's illness in his life. Was that why he disliked him, because he made no allowance for Aremil's infirmities, the lifelong curse of his near-fatal birth?

But Aremil could hardly complain. He wanted people to see him as more than some cripple with twisted legs, weak eyes and hesitant speech. That was why he had put himself through the torment of the journey here from Vanam. That was why he was so determined to master the secrets of Artifice. If he couldn't take up a sword like Tathrin, he'd serve the cause of peace in Lescar some other way.

Was he more afraid that Reniack would discover his true birth? As long as the pamphleteer thought

Aremil was merely the crippled son of some minor noble, sent to Vanam to live in seclusion, all he had to endure were barbed reminders that humble men's labours paid for his idleness. What would Reniack say if he knew Aremil was in fact the eldest son of Duke Secaris of Draximal? Would he suffer the full force of the man's contempt for all those born to rank and privilege? Or would Reniack condemn Duke Secaris for discarding his own child once it was clear Aremil would never walk unaided, never ride a horse or command an army?

What might Branca learn about his unknown family as her journey took her through Draximal? About the mother and father he couldn't even remember. About Lord Cassat, the acknowledged heir who was so widely praised as handsome and accomplished. Did he even know he had once had a brother?

Aremil shifted in his uncomfortable chair. The cushions he relied on had slipped and there was no one to ease his cramps with warm flannel and relaxing tinctures. Was that why he was so out of sorts? Because he was in such pain? Lyrlen, his nurse since birth, would have known how to soothe his discomforts but she was all the way back in Vanam. He shouldn't have been so ready to rebuke her when she'd warned what tribulations he was bringing on himself.

Reniack said his life had been sheltered. Aremil could hardly deny it. The only Lescari commoner he knew was Tathrin and that friendship was mere chance. They'd never have met if the poorer man hadn't needed to work as a wealthier scholar's servant, to earn his bed and board as he pursued his own studies.

But was he biased as well as uninformed because his knowledge of human nature had been culled from books and plays, as Reniack had once accused? Aremil honestly didn't believe so. With no one to see his drawn face twisting grotesquely, Aremil allowed himself a scowl. He had plenty of reasons to be wary of Reniack that had nothing to do with his personal dislike.

Similarly, he didn't mistrust Failla just because she'd spent the past few years as Duke Garnot's mistress. As Tathrin had said, she'd risked her neck to pass the duke's secrets to her uncle, the Carluse priest. He distrusted her because she'd so thoroughly deceived them all.

She'd borne Duke Garnot's bastard daughter and no one had known that, not even the duke. Desperate to escape and reclaim the girl from the cousin who was rearing her, Failla had told no one when the Duke of Triolle's spy had coerced her into giving up ciphered letters detailing the guildsmen's plots and even hinting at the Vanam conspiracy. There was no telling what damage that might have done, and might still do.

Well, Failla was in Abray with Master Gruit now. With Kerith, who'd used his own Artifice to read her thoughts and uncover her treachery. She could do no more harm and her knowledge of the Carluse guildsmen's plots might still serve their rebellion. They couldn't afford to discard her. If Duke Garnot's men ever caught her, torture would spill out all she knew.

He would continue to trust his instincts, Aremil decided. After all, if he was inclined to blind prejudice, he would never have trusted Branca. She didn't have Failla's beauty to recommend her, and she'd made no attempt to win him with charm. Aremil had had to challenge her scorn for Lescar's endless quarrels. Albeit of Lescari blood, she was Vanam born and bred, in the humblest of circumstances. She'd seen no reason to involve herself in futile strife so far away. Until he had convinced her with scholarly argument, appealing to the intellect that had raised her from a life of toil in Vanam's lower town to studying in the upper town's halls and libraries, even if she had to scrub their floors to pay her way.

Aremil sighed heavily. Failla was in Abray and Branca was on her way to Toremal. Reniack was running loose doing who knew what and Lady Derenna had gone off on some errand of her own, without even telling them when to expect her return. At least he knew where Nath the mapmaker and Welgren the apothecary were. Both were following the army, confident that their different skills would soon prove useful.

All he could do was sit and fret, time hanging heavy on his feeble hands. Could the threads of their plotting possibly hold together long enough for Captain-General Evord to defeat all the dukes on the field of battle?

CHAPTER THREE
Tathrin

**The Road from Losand to Carluse Town,
Autumn Equinox Festival, Third Day, Morning**

WHO WAS IN the vanguard today? Tathrin took a moment to remember Juxon's Raiders. A stern-faced company of men and women with the mongrel accent of those born in the mercenary camps. Lescar's wars had rumbled on for so long, some of the winter encampments in Marlier were decades old. The port of Carif, over on the Parnilesse coast, called itself a free city and enough mercenary companies called it home that Duke Orlin ruled there in name only.

Who would be waiting for news, far away in the Carifate or in some holding on the banks of the Rel? Who would receive some smudged letter, some sad bundle of trinkets, letting them know their loved one lay buried where they had fallen in Carluse's woods?

Tathrin strained his ears. Outraged shouts and the clash of swords drifted through the trees. All around the mercenary companies stood, expectant, waiting for their order to move. Only the banners wavered as standard-bearers shifted their feet. Up on his horse, Captain-General Evord waited calmly for news.

Would a Lescari duke's army even recognise him as the enemy army's commander? Tathrin contemplated the back of the captain-general's armour. It was no different from that worn by any other mounted mercenary. Polished steel back- and breastplates overlaid his chain mail, with more cunningly hinged metal protecting his shoulders, his flanks and thighs. There was none of the intricate engraving and gold embossing that Tathrin had seen on Lord Ricart's armour, when the Duke of Carluse's heir had once ridden past their family's inn along with his personal guard.

Evord himself was wholly unlike the mercenary captains Tathrin had met. The captain-general was a slightly built man of no more than common height, greying too fast for his middle years. He wore a scholar's silver ring, the insignia of the University of Col so abraded as to be almost indecipherable. With none of the obscenities that sullied his soldiers' speech, his accent was as cultured as any noble's. Not a Lescari noble, though. Captain-General Evord was a Soluran, from that vast kingdom in the uttermost west, beyond Ensaimin, beyond the Great Forest.

Solurans defended their untamed borders against

assaults from the brutal tyrants of Mandarkin and incursions by beastmen from the wilderness. Tathrin didn't really know what beastmen were and he wasn't eager to find out. What mattered were the decades of experience Captain-General Evord and his Soluran lieutenants had brought, along with new and unexpected allies. Would their very different strategy and tactics prove decisive, throwing Lescar's dukes into confusion? That's what Sorgrad and Gren and, indeed, all these tens of mercenary companies were wagering. That's what all the coin that Master Gruit had raised to pay the fighting men and women was riding on.

Tathrin's mouth was as dry as a bread oven. Would this first skirmish show which way the runes might roll, now that their vanguard had encountered Duke Garnot of Carluse's scouts? The sounds of fighting were fading. Was it over already?

"There's nothing like swordplay to get the blood flowing after a night out in the open." Smiling contentedly, Gren appeared at his side. Someone else's blood glistened stickily on his hauberk. "You should have come along, long lad, to work some of the stiffness out of your bones."

"What happened?" Tathrin saw a runner wearing the Juxon's Raiders' badge of a spiked warhammer was already at Evord's stirrup. The mercenary lieutenants crowded around to hear what he had to say, their surcoats and badges a myriad different colours.

Mercenary captains sent their most favoured subordinates to ride with the captain-general, and it was a privilege fiercely sought. The younger men would see at first hand how a successful commander ordered his battles, learning the reasons for his decisions. Such lessons would prove vital when they commanded a company themselves. Keeping them some distance from the perils of battle could prove more immediately crucial, if their captain was cut down in some mêlée and they had to take up his standard.

"We killed enough of the arse-lickers to give the rest something to think about," Gren said with callous indifference. "Most of the rest ran off pissing their breeches but we caught a double handful, like the captain-general wanted."

"So the ones who ran off will tell Duke Garnot where we are." Tathrin was still nervous about that.

"We want all Carluse's attention turned this way, don't we?" Gren chided him.

Tathrin nodded, not replying. He was watching Juxon's Raiders bring their ten prisoners to the captain-general's standard. The mercenary companies edged apart to let them through. No one raised a weapon or even a hand but the murmurs of derision grew steadily louder. Then Captain-General Evord urged his horse forwards and silence spread through the forest.

"Good day. Please choose one of your number to speak for you all," Evord invited.

The older men among the captives exchanged a dubious look.

"You're not from round here," a lad younger than Tathrin blurted out. Pale from loss of blood, he clutched a gruesome gash on his forearm.

"Soluran, are you?" a bald man ventured.

"I am," Evord replied courteously.

"Bringing Mountain Men and Dalasorians down on us?" Another of the older men couldn't hide his alarm.

The regular rotation of the marching companies had brought the uplanders to the fore today. Every man was as yellow-headed as Gren, as stocky and as short. Their armour was subtly different, worn over high-necked tunics and leather leggings, their boots reinforced with iron bindings. A contingent of grassland horsemen followed Captain-General Evord, four-score, with bicoloured pennants fluttering on their lances. Knots of cream and gold cord were sewn to the collars of their vividly embroidered cloaks, showing that these riders from the distant plains of the north had sworn allegiance to Evord's cause.

Seeing the Carluse prisoners gaping with astonishment, Tathrin concluded this was exactly what the Soluran captain-general intended.

Evord smiled amiably. "Tell me, boy, what do you make of my standard?"

The youth with the injured arm gazed at the banner with its golden circle of hands each brandishing a different token. "I never seen it before, your honour," he stammered.

"No, it's never been raised before," Evord said kindly. "Tell me what you see."

The boy hesitated, fearing some trick to the question. Tathrin couldn't blame him. The lad had likely never travelled more than a few leagues from the village where he was born. A local priest might have taught him to read and to reckon but he'd never have encountered the measured interrogation of a university mentor, logically drawing him towards a desired conclusion with precisely chosen questions.

Evord glanced at Tathrin. "Well?"

Tathrin fought an absurd urge to laugh. In the midst of these woods, with dour-faced mercenaries ringing the hapless captives, he was irresistibly reminded of Mentor Peirrose's book-crammed study in Vanam, where he and the other students had covered the table with sheets of intricate calculations, the atmosphere stuffy with concentration.

"There's a farmer's hayfork and a sheaf of wheat, a scholar's quill and a goodwife's broom. All tokens of honest labour," he added boldly.

He saw several of the prisoners narrow their eyes, realising he was a Carluse man like themselves.

Evord cleared his throat. "Honest labour by common folk. You also see the priest's handbell, lad. What do you suppose that declares?"

The bald man answered instead. "You claim to be god-fearing?"

Evord looked at him, unblinking. "Poldrion will not refuse me, when I ask him to ferry me over the river of the dead."

Tathrin saw the prisoners looking dubiously at the Mountain Men. Uplanders worshipped only Misaen and Maewelin, maker of all and mother of all, according to their own strange rites. They scorned all the other gods and taproom talk claimed they were capable of anything from raping their sisters to eating their captives.

What about the Dalasorians? Tavern wisdom said the grasslanders had Eldritch Kin in their bloodlines. That's why their hair was as black as the shadowmen who travelled to and from the Otherworld through rainbows and voids in the darkness.

"Piss on Poldrion." A man with a bruised face spat. "Are you going to hang us or cut off our heads?" His voice cracked with apprehension.

"For defending yourselves and your families?" Evord looked at him, apparently shocked. "You see that sixth hand holds a halberd? We believe in every man's right to defend his land and his livelihood. Though not in the right of any duke to force honest men to take up arms and oppress their neighbours in his name," he added forcefully.

Tathrin saw the prisoners didn't know what to think of that.

"Six hands," Evord continued. "One for each dukedom of Lescar. Each one raised against a duke who has beggared his people in vain pursuit of high kingship. A crown as hollow as any victory that might win it. Because we believe any duke so blinded by lust for a trifle, so blind to the suffering born of his selfishness, such a duke has forfeited any right to the fealty of honest men and women."

"So you've come to take the crown for yourself?" the bald man challenged.

Evord smiled, perfectly at ease. "Hardly. Ruling a kingdom I'm not even born to looks like extremely hard work." He waved a hand, encompassing the vast army. "We're mercenaries. We go where we're paid. Would you like to know who's paying us?"

The older men exchanged more dubious glances but it was clear they were desperate to know. The bleeding youth didn't hesitate. "I would."

Evord addressed himself to the boy. "Do you have friends who've fled Lescar for Tormalin, Caladhria or the cities of Ensaimin? Or relatives who live on the charity of such exiles?" He smiled as the boy nodded dumbly. "Never think they've forgotten you, in their peace and safety. Those who have prospered, and plenty have," he assured them, "they're paying us to put an end to Lescar's suffering. All of them, whether they're of Carluse blood, or Marlier, Triolle, Draximal, wherever. We've already taken Sharlac, eight days since—"

That prompted loud astonishment from the prisoners.

"Duke Moncan's defeated?"

"What's become of the Jackal?"

"He's dead."

Evord's blunt declaration silenced them. Only the soft sound of horses champing their bits broke the stillness.

"Jackal Moncan and his heir Lord Kerlin were both slain in the sack of Sharlac Castle." Evord didn't sound overly contrite. "His widowed duchess Aphanie and her daughters are enjoying the protection of certain of Sharlac's vassal lords who have long been outraged by their liege's selfishness."

Tathrin couldn't dismiss that horrific night so simply. He'd seen the slaughter, heard the screams of fear and agony. The stench of blood and bowels had filled his nostrils. He'd choked on the smoke as the castle burned. He'd seen the mercenaries cutting down the Sharlac castle guard. They'd even killed scullions so crazed with fear they snatched up kitchen knives. Gren hadn't lost a wink of sleep over it but Tathrin's nightmares were haunted by what he had seen.

The bald man looked thoughtful. "So what now for Carluse?"

Tathrin guessed he was wondering about Carluse's own disgruntled nobles. These men would have heard the same tales that were whispered in the Ring of Birches' taproom. Last year, or maybe the year before, a lord had rebuked Duke Garnot, protesting over mercenaries' depredations that left his tenants destitute. He had been summarily imprisoned. All accounts agreed on that, even if they disputed his name and estates. His family had been disinherited, everyone knew that too. According to one version, his lands had been granted to the mercenary captain who'd wed the old duke's bastard daughter.

A half-smile touched Evord's thin lips. "Four days ago, we took Losand away from Wynald's Warband. Those we didn't kill were hanged from the town battlements, at the guildmasters' request. Some of our forces still safeguard the town, again at the guildmasters' request, until they raise their own militia. Now we march on Carluse Town and Duke Garnot's own castle. Once we have brought him low," the Soluran concluded calmly, "we will free Draximal and Marlier, Triolle and Parnilesse from similar tyranny."

Some of the prisoners looked appalled. Others couldn't hide their disbelief.

"If you wish to live as free men under just laws, you're welcome to join our army," Evord continued. "Our surgeons will tend your wounds, whether you do so or not."

"You'll let us go?" The bleeding lad stared with desperate hope.

Evord raised his brows. "Who will believe we're intent on freeing Lescar from the dukes' tyranny if we shed innocent blood from the outset?"

Tathrin watched the prisoners conferring in urgent whispers.

"How many do you reckon will join us?" he asked Gren quietly.

"None." The Mountain Man was certain. "They'll run back to their families to bar their doors and hide under their beds until this is all over."

Tathrin had to agree. What honest Carluse man would turn mercenary? Whether they were companies of dusty dogs, fighting for whoever offered most coin, or a duke's hounds, retained with regular payments and granted the right to blend his badge with their blazon, all mercenaries were scum. They stole farmers' and craftsmen's profits and cut down unarmed husbands or sons for sheer spite.

Then there were the women supposedly taken ill. Some girls reappeared, bruises fading, flinching whenever a man came near, even boys they'd known all their lives. Others were laid on untimely funeral pyres with tightly sewn shrouds to hide their injuries. There were broken betrothals or, worse somehow, hurried weddings with the bride's gown girdled above a swelling belly, her beloved grim-faced as he laid her newly cut bridal plait on Drianon's altar.

That's what mercenaries were to the common folk of Carluse. That's what Tathrin had believed, after the battle the year before last when Duke Moncan's army had attacked the town of Losand. He had watched weeping mothers carrying urns of ashes to Misaen's shrine, the closest sanctuary since Wynald's Warband had ransacked Trimon's temple on the Abray Road. He had seen his friends and their fathers nailing coins or scraps of cloth to the shrine door in token of silent vows of vengeance.

Yet he had helped start a war that would sweep across all of Lescar. He had helped summon up an army of mercenaries brutal and callous enough to win that fight. Tathrin was going to have a great deal of explaining to do, whenever death took him to stand before Saedrin, to account for all he'd done with his life. Could he possibly satisfy the god, so he'd unlock his door and allow Tathrin to pass through to rebirth in the Otherworld?

He hadn't been able to justify his actions to his family, when he'd snatched a day after the fall of Losand to ride home and make certain the Ring of Birches still thrived. He had barely begun explaining why he had abandoned his promising apprenticeship in Vanam before his father had berated him for taking up with cut-throats and thieves. It made no odds who waged a war, he bellowed. Innocent blood turned earth to mud regardless.

His mother had wept as if Tathrin were already dead. Why had he come back, a mercenary cur, when they had sacrificed so much to send him to safety in Vanam? His intelligence had won him a scholar's silver ring. Why hadn't he stayed to better himself and rise above his despised Lescari birth? Tathrin heaved a sigh.

"Cheer up," Gren said genially. "This lot'll soon take to their heels and we'll be on to the next fight. You'll soon get your chance to blood your sword properly."

Tathrin just grunted, watching the Carluse prisoners nodding as they reached their decision.

The bald man stepped forwards, apprehensive but resolute.

"If your honour pleases, we'll have our wounds tended and be on our way."

"Very well." Evord nodded.

Tathrin saw their decision came as no surprise to the Soluran captain-general. Then he saw Evord beckoning and ran forwards.

"Tell Aremil that Reniack and his friends must spread their songs and pamphlets as widely as possible, as speedily as they can. He must convince the Losand guildsmen to send word to their fellow craftsmen in Carluse Town, to promote our cause in every village and hamlet. We cannot win this war merely by winning battles. Tell him to tell Dagaran to stay vigilant."

Evord looked down from his saddle, his grey eyes shadowed. "Tell him to warn Lady Derenna and our allies in Sharlac. The commonalty there and the undecided vassal lords will keep their heads down as long as the smoke from Sharlac's fall still drifts across the skies. They're all waiting to see which way the wind blows next. If they hear the common folk of Carluse are fighting us, if Duke Garnot can claim his vassals and tenants are rising up to support him, those who don't want us holding Sharlac any more than they loved Jackal Moncan will start snapping at our heels. Lady Derenna must be ready to counter any hint of disaffection."

"I will make sure he tells her," Tathrin assured him.

Lady Derenna would still be defending their cause in Sharlac. After all, she had spent the summer travelling the length and breadth of the dukedom, arguing in favour of the need for change with those nobles as opposed to arbitrary rule as she was. Though Tathrin wasn't necessarily convinced her sympathies lay with the commonalty. Lady Derenna's objections were the intellectual reasoning of a Rationalist, focusing on the resentments that tyranny prompted. That and the fact Duke Moncan had sentenced her husband to house arrest. Given the choice of joining him or exile, she had fled to Vanam.

Evord was watching the Carluse men being led away to Juxon's Raiders' surgeon.

"Still, this skirmish counts as a little triumph to begin this campaign, doesn't it? Let's hope it's as easy to strike Duke Garnot a decisive blow when we catch up with him tomorrow. If we can't manage that, unrest in Sharlac will be the least of our problems. And of course, the Dalasorians must play their part at Ashgil."

He surprised Tathrin with a sudden smile. "Who knows? Perhaps we haven't fought the first battle of this campaign after all. Let me know as soon as you've spoken with Aremil." He spurred his horse into a brisk trot away.

Tathrin sighed again. He might feel more useful if he were actually able to use Artifice's enchantments himself. But all he could do was wait for Aremil to reach out and touch his mind. And that was a very different experience from what he'd expected. Tathrin shivered despite the warmth of the unseasonal sun.

No one had told him Aremil would be able to pluck what he liked out of his innermost thoughts and feelings. If he'd known, would he have agreed to serve as the link between the other conspirators and Evord's army? That was a pointless question. He could no more refuse now than any of them could turn back.

Not now the army they'd raised was marching to overthrow Duke Garnot. Not now the Dalasorians were riding across the open vale to the east, the other prong of the fork they hoped to impale him upon.

CHAPTER FOUR
Aremil

**Losand, in the Lescari Dukedom of Carluse,
Autumn Equinox Festival, Third Day, Noon**

DAGARAN OPENED THE door. "Good day, Master Aremil."

"Good day to you." It occurred to Aremil that the Soluran lieutenant had never once wished him fair festival. Belatedly, he realised he knew nothing of Soluran customs, not even which gods they worshipped.

"I have no more news from the forest." He tried to straighten in his chair. "Not since that skirmish with Duke Garnot's scouts."

He knew there were wizards in distant Solura, but did they know anything of Artifice? Aremil had no idea. Perhaps they did. Dagaran took their enchanted communications in his stride. Then again, Aremil hadn't seen anything perturb the saturnine man. He went about raising the militias to defend Losand and Sharlac as placidly as a merchant totalling his ledgers.

"I'm more interested in events at Ashgil." Dagaran came to adjust Aremil's cushions with impersonal efficiency. "If you could contact Jettin?"

"Of course." Aremil felt embarrassment colour his cheekbones. He should have thought of that himself. He drew a steadying breath. It was getting easier to work this enchantment. Branca had been quite correct, saying practice would help.

"*Al daera sa Jettin sast elarmin as feorel.*"

Though he had only met Jettin a few times, the other scholar was a far more experienced adept. That made the task easier.

"*Al daera sa Jettin sast elarmin as feorel.*"

He wondered how soon he'd be able to contact anyone unschooled in Artifice by focusing his thoughts alone on the enchantments. At present he could only reach close friends like Tathrin and he still had to speak the ancient charms aloud.

"*Al daera sa Jettin sast elarmin—*" Stumbling over the words, he rebuked himself. "*—sast elarmin as feorel.*"

He must focus his thoughts on Jettin. Youthful and lightly built, olive-skinned with curly black hair. Hot-tempered, always ready to argue with any Vanamese dismissing the Lescari as beggars and fools.

"*Al daera sa Jettin sast elarmin as feorel.*"

Jettin was no fool. He wore an advocate's ring, not easily won. Nor was he a beggar. Since fleeing Triolle in his own youth, his father had traded in spices to become one of Vanam's wealthiest men.

"*Aremil!*"

Jettin's exultation made his head swim.

"*We did it!*"

Aremil felt as if he was being swept clean out of the room. His eyes and ears told him he stood in a crowded marketplace. Aremil understood Tathrin's ambivalence over Artifice far more clearly these days. It took a distinct effort of will to feel the chair beneath his thighs, his hands resting on the desk.

"You've taken Ashgil?"

Aremil heard the scrape of Dagaran's boots. He couldn't see the Soluran. His mind's eye was filled with Jettin's jubilant memories of the morning's adventure.

That didn't outweigh Aremil's exasperation. Jettin had been told to stay well clear of danger. He'd still decided to ride with the lancers. Left to his own devices, he'd have been in the front rank; Aremil could see that clearly in his thoughts.

But the Dalasorian clan lords were among the few admitted into the secret of Artifice. Like Captain-General Evord, they had only agreed to join this army once they saw how such hidden advantage could tip the scales in their favour. Evord had told them how few adepts served the exiles, so Sia Kersain had sent Jettin to ride in the rear. Tall, lean and hatchet-faced, the Dalasorians' highest clan lord wasn't a man to be argued with.

Aremil felt the jolting of the trotting horse beneath him and the sharpness of Jettin's irritation. The young adept hadn't stayed ill-tempered for long, though. It was a bright, clear morning and the Vale of Ashgil lay open ahead. The fields were empty, a chequerboard of stubble and ploughed black earth after the harvest.

They saw the coloured tiles of Ashgil's shrine roof first. Aremil recognised Ostrin's loyal hound, russet against the black, and the god of hospitality's bunch of grapes in red as bright as blood.

Rega Taszar led his forces away over the fields to the east. Hedges dividing the vassal lord's fields from his tenants' gave Dalasorian horses scant pause. Pata Mezian's regiment stayed on the high road, nine troops each of four-score riders. Two of his troops were armed with the recurved bow of the grasslands, cunningly wrought from bone and sinew for the lack of trees. Rega Taszar had four such troops of archers under his command and eight of lancers.

Sia Kersain rode with only a few score shy of a thousand horses. Now they quit the high road for the westerly flank. Aremil's stomach lurched as Jettin's horse leaped. Dust rose as their hooves pounded the hard, dry ground.

Ahead, the market town came clearly into view. He saw tiled roofs above the ragged battlements. He couldn't see much of the town's walls. Well inside

Carluse, not threatened by war within a generation, the guildmasters of Ashgil had permitted all manner of building beyond their gates. Houses with grey shingled roofs stretched along the high road.

At some signal that Jettin missed, every horse shifted from the trot to a canter, pennants streaming from the riders' lances.

He could see people now, where the fields met vegetable gardens. There must surely be shouts of alarm but he couldn't hear them. The thunder of hooves, the rattle of harness filled his ears as the canter became a gallop. He gripped the saddle with his thighs, the reins digging into his gloved hands. The morning chill was a distant memory amid the heat rising from the horses.

How by all that was holy could the Dalasorians ride one-handed, managing lances at such a breakneck pace? Aremil realised Jettin was shamefully relieved that he wouldn't be called on to fight. He needn't risk making a fool of himself, or worse, injuring his own mount as he fumbled his sword

The Dalasorian riders swept on. He glimpsed women fleeing towards the town's walls, their aprons fluttering white. Men threw aside hoes and ran. Some fool opened a sty, desperate to save his pig. The beast disappeared into an orchard.

None of Sia Kersain's archers wasted their arrows on such targets. They were heading for the town's western gate. The reports from Evord's scouts had been clear. Duke Garnot's militia were guarding the roads. They were going to fight them for control of the western gate, for the road leading to Thymir and Carluse Town beyond. Rega Taszar's forces were circling to capture the gate on the Tyrle Road heading south. Pata Mezian's regiment would smash through the north gate, coming straight down the high road from Sharlac.

He didn't have time to think about that. There was the Thymir Gate still standing proud of the crumbling wall. Duke Garnot's white flag with its black boar's head flew from the topmost coign. Down on the ground, the militiamen on guard were being overwhelmed by panicking people desperate to force their way through.

Incredibly, the horses drew still closer together. Dalasorian boots jostled his own as they rode stirrup to stirrup. He was seized with sudden terror lest a spur dig into his ankle. But there was no time to be afraid. They were wheeling around, charging up the road. Would the militia drop the portcullis and deny them at the last gasp?

His mount snorted, the bit clamped between its teeth. If he'd wanted to stay clear of the fray, he had no chance now. This horse was going to charge with its herd mates and there was no way he could hold it back.

He had no idea where the archers were but he saw militiamen fall from the battlement, pierced by arrows. The first horses were charging through the gate's arch, bodies disappearing beneath their hooves. Lancers broke away on either side, pursuing anyone in ducal colours still outside the walls.

A few militiamen swung their swords. One frantic blade cut a lancer's hand clean off at the wrist. The rider stuffed his reins in his teeth. Snatching a thrown lance from the air, he ran the Carlusian through.

Aremil lost sight of the maimed man in the mêlée. His own horse finally slowed, along with the riders around him. Once they could see daylight through the arch of the gate they entered the town. Their horses picked a careful path through liveried bodies, snorting at blood trickling in the gutters. A dog howled when a dismounted Dalasorian used the flat of her blade to beat it away from a corpse it was sniffing.

We did it. We took Ashgil, and so easily. The dukes won't know what's befallen them; we'll win this war so quickly.

Jettin's exultation rang through memories so vivid they could be Aremil's own. He was acutely aware of the contrast with Tathrin's recollections of Sharlac's fall. He looked around to reassure himself all the dead men wore militia colours. To his relief, the townsfolk were clustered in alleys and doorways. Ashgil had fallen and there had been no massacre, not this time.

"*Count what's left before what's lost, once the storm's passed by.*"

Behind the old proverb, he could feel Jettin's irritation at his anxiety. Why couldn't he just celebrate their success? If innocents had died, such tragic accidents were unavoidable. Didn't he want to see Lescar free?

"Master Aremil?" It was Dagaran.

Aremil gritted his teeth. He concentrated on feeling every crease and scuff in the leather-topped desk with his fingertips. He even welcomed the cramps in his wasted legs as he wrenched sensation and emotion free of the younger man's Artifice.

"Is the town secure?" he demanded.

"*Tied up tighter than a miser's purse!*"

Now Aremil saw the marketplace again, as clearly as if he stood next to Jettin. Cowering Carlusians were approaching the mounted clan lords, their hands spread wide to show they carried no weapon. He could see the numb shock on their faces.

Militiamen faced mounted mercenaries from time to time. But if Lescari rode into battle, such companies would dismount after the initial clash, to fight hand to hand with sword and mace and shield. That was how such encounters went, as far as these Ashgil men knew. They had never faced mounted lancers, mounted archers, with horses as skilled in battle as their riders.

Aremil fervently hoped all Captain-General Evord's innovations were going to prove so successful in this campaign.

Then he saw Dalasorians in their brightly embroidered tunics going in and out of houses, carrying sacks and barrels.

"The town isn't to be plundered," he said sharply. "Remember the captain-general's orders!"

"They're only replenishing supplies used on their journey."

Was Jettin telling the truth? Aremil had no hope of reading his innermost thoughts now his exultant recollections of the battle were over.

"Very well, as long as that's all they do."

Aremil heard a rattle of parchment as Dagaran sorted through the maps piled up on the desk.

"Please ask him to find Rega Taszar. Ask how many troops he will need to keep with him to hold the town until I can organise a militia."

Aremil dutifully relayed the Soluran lieutenant's request. Now he was more fully in control of his own Artifice, he could see Jettin clearly. The youth was filthy with sweat and dust, still flushed with the thrill of the charge.

Aremil's own hands were still trembling. He'd never imagined he'd enjoy galloping on a horse. When he hadn't known how it felt, his inability to ride was merely one mild regret among many. Now he struggled to curb his frustration with the infirmities that denied him such delight. Artifice proved a double-edged blessing once again.

"I see you need a moment to gather yourself. I'll tell you what Rega Taszar says at the next chime."

With the faintest echo of distaste, Jettin swiftly withdrew his enchantment. As the weaker adept, Aremil had no hope of holding him. The vision of distant Ashgil faded. Dizzy, Aremil screwed his eyes shut. When he opened them, Dagaran was leaning on the far side of the desk, looking intently at him.

"Master Aremil, are you all right?"

"I will be." Aremil hadn't anticipated the shock of breaking such an intense aetheric link. Tremors wracked him and he blinked. He so disliked seeing the world through his own inadequate eyes after enjoying Jettin's crystal-clear vision.

Dagaran stood upright, still looking concerned. "If we're to hold Ashgil there are things I must set in motion, but I shall call back as soon as I can manage it. Can I send anyone to you in the meantime?"

"No, thank you. I'll be fine." Aremil cast around for something else for Dagaran to focus on. "May I know what the rest of the Dalasorians will be doing, while Rega Taszar holds Ashgil?"

It was an even roll of the runes whether Dagaran would tell him or not. Captain-General Evord prized discretion above almost all other virtues.

The Soluran hesitated and then drew a finger across the map he had spread out on the desk. "They will ride west, as soon as their horses are rested."

"To Thymir?" Aremil was confused. That was one of Duke Garnot's personal manors, but it commanded no more than a large village.

Dagaran allowed himself a brief smile. "To take control of the road running north from Carluse Town into the forest."

"But Duke Garnot and his army have already reached the forest." Aremil knew that from Tathrin's reports.

Dagaran nodded. "And the Dalasorians will be ready, whatever the outcome of tomorrow's battle. If the captain-general routs the Carluse forces, or if they manage to retreat in good order, the Dalasorians must cut them down. Victory means little if your enemy can rally and come back to fight another day." He looked graver. "If the day goes against us, as is always possible, we'll need the lancers to strike at Duke Garnot's men from behind, so Captain-General Evord can withdraw without losing too many men."

"I see." Aremil felt a chill that had nothing to do with the draughts in the room.

"Make sure Tathrin knows he must tell us at once, if the tide of battle turns against the captain-general tomorrow." Dagaran rolled up the map and bowed briefly. "Till later."

"Till later," Aremil echoed.

The door closed behind the Soluran and Aremil was left alone with his apprehensive thoughts. He really didn't think this war would be won as easily as Jettin imagined.

CHAPTER FIVE
Litasse

**Triolle Castle, in the Kingdom of Lescar,
Autumn Equinox Festival, Third Day, Evening**

THE GREAT HALL's flagstones had been scoured white and the panelling glowed with polish. Garlands of leaves had been fashioned from scarlet silk and gold brocade. The harvest's fruits had been cunningly crafted from glossy wax. Up in their gallery, the musicians wove every horn's voice, each viol's thrill into seamless harmony.

Those disinclined to dance, too old or too replete with roasted venison, capon and goose, sat at tables in the side aisles. Dishes of candied fruits flanked platters of wafer cakes and marchpane fancies. Lackeys offered goblets of wine or cups of barley cream dusted with Aldabreshin spices.

No one could accuse her of dereliction in her duties as duchess this festival. Which was just as well, because no one had suggested, with her father and brother newly dead, her mother and sisters' fate unknown, that she might be spared the burden of ensuring everyone else's enjoyment, of providing all their guests' entertainments.

Litasse paced out the next measure of the dance, her fingertips touching those of Duke Orlin's brother. Lord Geferin stepped deftly around as she sank into a curtsey, her rich maroon skirts rustling. His gaze lingered on the low-cut neck of her gown before meeting her eyes with unmistakable invitation.

She rose from her curtsey, her smile as meaningless as she could possibly make it. Unable to stop humiliation colouring her pale cheeks, she consoled herself with a glance around. All those dancing were just as flushed, thanks to the heat from the tiered candle-stands that made the hall with its coloured glass windows a jewelled lantern in the castle's dark courtyard.

No one would be discussing her choices for the banquet or the decorations, though. Litasse knew all the whispers were debating her choice of bedfellows. How could she have deceived her handsome husband with someone as undistinguished as Master Hamare? She had heard Lady Erasie asking Lady Mazien just that, not realising she was within earshot.

Even more deliciously scandalous, what lovers' quarrel could possibly have ended with Litasse stabbing the spymaster? Was it true the castle guards had broken down a locked door to find the Master Intelligencer dead at her feet? It was. They had found her with his blood on her skirts and the dagger that killed him in her hand.

Litasse matched Lady Erasie's steps down the hall. What would the empty-headed gossip say if she explained how Master Hamare's interest in her daily pleasures and trials had warmed her lonely heart? Was it any surprise that she'd welcomed his discreet adoration and soon yielded so gladly to his ardour? When Duke Iruvain paid her less heed than his hounds and his horses. When his visits to her bedchamber were as selfish as his daily routine. If everyone were so scandalised by her failings as a wife, what of his failings as a husband?

What would any of them say, as they murmured behind their hands, if she told them she hadn't stabbed Hamare at all? That he had been murdered by two Mountain Men, who'd appeared out of nowhere thanks to some foul wizardry. Then that same magic had carried them away, leaving her trapped in the locked room with no one else to be blamed.

No, no one would ever believe that. Because magic was the one weapon that no duke dared wield in their endless skirmishes and periodic campaigns, testing another dukedom's strength, encroaching upon their borders. Far easier to believe that Litasse, once of Sharlac, now of Triolle, was just a faithless whore.

Reaching the end of the hall, she spun around to walk elegantly back outside the lines of dancers. From the corner of her eye, she could see Duchess Sherista of Parnilesse doing the same on the opposite side. She moved as lightly on her feet, despite the four children and twelve years' advantage she had over Litasse. While every other woman wore autumn hues in honour of the festival, Duke Orlin's duchess wore a sumptuous emerald gown in tribute to her husband's livery colours. That had the happy effect of drawing every eye to her, Litasse thought tartly.

Had Sherista ever taken a lover? Had she found the marriage arranged for her parents' advantage and a dukedom's gain as cold and lonely as Litasse had? Or had she grown to love her husband and found that love returned, as Litasse's mother had assured her would happen?

There was no way to tell. Sherista's face was as serenely unreadable as ever as she slipped past Lord Geferin. Did he keep brushing against her, Litasse wondered? Did she have to endure him caressing her shoulder, even her rump if they encountered each other on some narrow stair? Or did he only take such liberties with a known adulteress? From his manner this festival, he seemed to assume Litasse would open her knees to any man. How dare he? Litasse stifled her irritation and walked on, head high, shoulders back.

· She reached the head of the hall. Behind the high table on the stepped dais, Duke Orlin of Parnilesse still sat in his place of honour, his eyes shifting from his duchess to his brother as they made their way through the dance. Was he a jealous spouse or a fond one? Did he suspect his own brother's intentions? Or did he fear what Lord Geferin might let slip? The rumours they had conspired to poison their father persisted.

This was no time for such idle thoughts. Her own husband approached, his arms outstretched. When they had first met, Litasse had admired his broad shoulders, his strong hands. As their wedding renewed the alliances between Triolle and Sharlac, Duchess Aphanie had promised her tender companionship in her marriage. That promise had proved hollow indeed. Now Litasse merely wondered what might provoke Iruvain to hit her again.

Stepping into his embrace, she linked her hands behind his head. His doublet matched her gown. The garnets studding his gilt collar echoed the rubies glittering on her breast. They were the most handsome couple in the gathering, even if that wasn't why all eyes were on them.

"Smile," he ordered.

"I don't—"

He lifted her off her feet, whirling her around. Their cheeks brushed, his rich brown curls tickling her neck. His dark eyes were stony. "I said, smile."

"My lord, I grieve—"

"Shut up."

As he lifted her again, Litasse ended the dance with elegantly pointed toes and a flourish of her skirts. The long knife's scabbard pressed against her thigh. She wouldn't be caught unarmed again, even if she didn't know who she feared most: her husband or the men who'd slain Hamare.

The musicians concluded with a triumphant chord. All around, husbands and wives returned to each other's sides.

Duke Iruvain bowed low, brushing his full lips against her jewelled rings. In public at least, he was doing all he could to still lively expectation that he'd repudiate his slut of a wife. He still insisted Litasse had merely defended her honour. She didn't know why. Who could possibly believe that loyal Hamare would force himself on his own duke's wife?

"Your rouge is smudged."

He wouldn't want anyone seeing the fading bruise left by his furious blow.

"I'll see to it."

"Your Grace." Her elderly waiting woman was already on hand, her lined face disapproving. "You are unbecomingly flushed."

"That will do, Pelletria," Litasse said sharply.

Iruvain walked away with a hint of satisfaction on his face. If he wouldn't punish Litasse by setting her aside, he'd quickly made sure she was as friendless as possible. He'd dismissed all her waiting women, even hapless Valesti who'd known nothing of Litasse's deceptions.

A solitary lutenist sang up in the gallery. The other musicians were ringing a steward carrying a tray of horn cups and a flagon of ale. On the dais Sherista of Parnilesse embraced her husband, her burnished tresses ebony against his silver beard. His mossy doublet was just a shade darker than her gown. As he caressed her milky shoulder, the jet of his rings reflected dark fire from the candlelight.

Pelletria led Litasse to a tapestry-hung corner. "No need for *you* to hide a dyer's bottle in your baggage." With her back to the gathering, her thin lips curved in a confiding smile.

"That's gratifying to know, but have you discovered anything more immediately useful?" Litasse tucked an errant wisp into the golden net confining her own black hair.

"This Soluran and his mercenary army are marching through the forest to Carluse." Pelletria's lips barely moved. "They'll join battle today or tomorrow."

"How soon will we know the outcome?" Litasse searched the great hall for Iruvain.

How much did he know? Now that Hamare was dead, all the dukedom's couriers brought the news they'd once carried to the Master Intelligencer straight to their duke instead. But Litasse had seen how Iruvain scorned so many of the other reports, from merchants and those who served them on the road, who collected the tolls on the dukedom's bridges. The intricate web of informants that

Hamare had so carefully woven was in danger of falling apart.

"I left three courier doves with a trusted man in Carluse Castle." Pelletria dabbed the fine gloss of sweat from Litasse's brow with a scrap of powdered muslin. "We'll know how Duke Garnot's army fares half a day after Duchess Tadira."

Iruvain would never have allowed Pelletria to serve her if he suspected her tirewoman had been one of Hamare's enquiry agents. Still less if he knew the crone had been unobtrusively searching out Carluse secrets this past half-year. She need not fear that he'd guess Litasse was defying him and gathering her own reports, making good use of Hamare's legacy, even if Iruvain wouldn't.

"What will Duke Garnot do, once he's whipped these curs?"

A frown deepened Pelletria's wrinkles. "That depends whether he crushes them or merely puts them to flight."

Litasse watched Iruvain smiling. Lady Mazien laid a flirtatious white hand on his arm. The duke's rich laugh echoed around the hall, louder than the lutenist's ballad.

"Do you think he'll take a mistress?" Litasse wondered aloud. "To pay me back with my own base coin?" If he was dipping his middle finger in some vassal lord's purse, would she be any safer?

"Perhaps. He'll only believe you're innocent if we can find proof that these rebels have suborned magic." Pelletria searched the purse on her girdle for a pot of rouge.

Litasse watched Iruvain escort Lady Mazien to a shadowed side table. "Some are saying it was him who cut Hamare's throat." And no one who whispered that condemned him.

"Then they'll choke on their words, when we prove it was foulest sorcery." Pelletria carefully blurred the lingering marks of Iruvain's fingers.

Litasse closed her eyes to curb prickling tears. She would have utterly despaired if Pelletria hadn't believed her. But the old woman knew Hamare could never love a woman capable of killing him. More, Pelletria had loved Hamare like a son. She had been Hamare's first confidante, when he'd returned from Col's university to serve Iruvain's father.

Duke Gerone had known information could protect his vulnerable fiefdom better than armies. Triolle was surrounded by all Lescar's other dukedoms and in battle was a match for none. Iruvain could deny that all he liked and diligently drill his brightly liveried militiamen, but sticking feathers on a bantam didn't make it an eagle.

Pelletria stepped back to survey her handiwork. "Duke Orlin has been asking why Iruvain doesn't dissolve your marriage. Your husband tells him he's intent on securing Triolle's claim to Sharlac's succession. He can hardly press your claims as Duke Moncan's eldest daughter if he sets you aside." She screwed the lid tight on the rouge pot. "Once you bear him a child, he'll think again. But he won't want you pregnant until there's no possible chance you might carry Hamare's baby."

Litasse had wondered why Iruvain hadn't chosen to punish her in their bed. "Everyone would start counting back on their fingers."

Pelletria nodded. "Especially those with their own claim on Sharlac lands. So I don't think you have much to fear until you bear a child of undisputed Triolle blood and we know that it will thrive. After that?" She tucked the cosmetics back in her purse. "Some poisons mimic a wasting disease. Never fear, Your Grace. We'll make sure that doesn't happen to you."

Her faded eyes glinted with ruthlessness that both reassured and unnerved Litasse. She saw Iruvain had abandoned Lady Mazien and was heading for their corner.

"Send a courier bird to Hamare's man in Draximal," she said quickly. "I want to know what Duke Secaris plans, and see if we've had any word from Marlier."

"As you command, Your Grace." Pelletria withdrew, her expression as stern as ever, no hint of indulgence for her mistress.

"You're neglecting our guests," hissed the duke.

"Forgive me."

She followed him onto the dais, eyes modestly downcast, every measure the dutiful wife. He drew her chair back, as attentive a husband as a woman could wish for.

Duke Orlin smiled. "You have entertained us so lavishly; it will be hard to tear ourselves away."

"So courageous." Duchess Sherista leaned forward to lay her hand on Litasse's. "Is there still no word of your lady mother and your sisters?"

She must have found twenty occasions to make that solicitous enquiry these past two days. Litasse knew Parnilesse's servants were asking her attendants the selfsame thing.

"Sadly not." Litasse's pleasure at denying the answer Sherista craved was only spoiled by the anguish the truth brought her.

"We are most anxious to know how Duchess Aphanie fares." Duke Orlin was all sympathy. "Even if our ties to Triolle are merely those of affection rather than blood."

"I will be sending Lord Roreth north to make enquiries now the festival's done." Iruvain nodded towards his brother, deep in conversation with some simpering maiden.

Litasse had heard of no such plan. She couldn't help her start of surprise, her fingers jerking beneath Sherista's. "Forgive me." She covered her eyes with her hand, feigning distress. It only took a moment and genuine tears glistened on her lashes.

"Perhaps Duke Secaris will discover some news for you on his return to Draximal." Duchess Sherista reached for her wine. "That would be some consolation for ending his visit so abruptly."

That was another lure she kept throwing out, fishing for any dissent between Draximal and Triolle.

"He could hardly leave Lord Cassat to face this crisis alone." Litasse dried her eyes with a napkin, careful not to smudge her rouge.

Iruvain nodded. "We're honoured that he delayed his departure even a day."

Did he think he was fooling Duke Orlin or was he merely fooling himself? Duke Secaris had needed to rest his horses before heading northwards again, otherwise Litasse was convinced he would have turned for home as soon as the Draximal courier had reached him with news of Sharlac's fall. While his heir was widely admired, Lord Cassat was barely nineteen.

Duke Orlin stroked his silver beard. "Do you think these villains will head eastwards to threaten Draximal?"

Litasse gave him his due. Duke Orlin had learned of Sharlac's fate and then Losand's fall sooner than he would have if he'd been celebrating the festival in Parnilesse. On the other side of the scales, he was cut off from all his own sources of intelligence. He betrayed no hint of frustration.

Iruvain brushed that aside. "Duke Garnot won't leave one in a hundred alive to plague anyone."

Duke Orlin raised his wine glass. "Talagrin send him swift victory over these blackguards."

As Iruvain and Sherista echoed his invocation to the god of the hunt, Litasse barely let the wine touch her lips.

Carluse's duke was as much to blame for Sharlac's fall as these curs of mercenaries. Garnot had waged war on Sharlac only a few years since. His own bastard son had killed her beloved brother Jaras. If her father hadn't been so unmanned by that crippling grief, this cowardly attack would never have taken him so unawares.

"We must see where these dogs run, once Garnot has whipped them," Duke Orlin mused. "They're mercenaries, so someone must pay them. If they hide behind Duke Secaris's midden, much becomes clear."

Iruvain was genuinely perplexed. "Draximal and Sharlac have long been allies."

Duke Orlin's lip curled. "Duke Secaris covets any land that adjoins his own."

"Your Grace, you know the attacks that you suffered this summer were deceits." Iruvain looked troubled. "Intent on setting you and Duke Secaris at odds, to distract us from this army gathering above Sharlac."

Litasse drank her wine. Now Iruvain was taking credit for all that Hamare had discovered. After he had mocked the spymaster, when he'd first warned of intrigue among Lescar's exiles in Vanam. If only Iruvain had let Hamare pursue his suspicions, this vile plot could have been unmasked and forestalled.

She took a second mouthful, to stop herself telling Duke Orlin that the foul mercenaries who'd attacked Parnilesse's militia and burned that bridge crossing his border to Draximal had been using magefire. The wizard who'd murdered Hamare had admitted it to her. But no one would believe it if she said so. She set down her glass and the lackey quickly refilled it.

"We shall stay watchful till Draximal's good faith is proven." Duke Orlin shrugged. "What do you know of Duke Ferdain's response to this upset?"

Did he want to know what Ferdain of Marlier was doing, or did he want to know how swiftly and accurately Triolle got news from the west? Probably both, Litasse decided.

Iruvain scowled. "I watch Marlier as closely as you watch Draximal. We're raising militia to guard our borders to north and west alike."

"That's wise." Orlin nodded. "Duke Ferdain allows these curs of mercenaries far too long a leash in his lands."

Whereas Master Hamare had been adamant that Triolle had no reason to suspect Marlier. All Duke Ferdain wanted from the mercenary camps was his share of their gold. So what advantage did Orlin seek by ensuring Iruvain was looking west to Marlier instead of east to Parnilesse?

Litasse folded her hands in her lap so no one could see her knuckles whiten. Hamare would have seen what lay behind all this so clearly. Anguish twisted her heart.

The musicians struck up a new dance and Duke Orlin rose to his feet.

"Your Grace, please honour me as my partner."

"The honour is mine." Litasse flattered him with a dazzling smile.

Iruvain promptly offered his hand to Sherista. "Then I have the good fortune to escort Your Grace."

"Let's look forward to dancing at Solstice," she said pertly, "with all this unpleasantness far behind us."

Her hand on Duke Orlin's arm, Litasse walked down from the dais to join the sets forming for the dance.

What might Hamare suspect? First he'd want to be certain Parnilesse wasn't allied with this mercenary commander who had slaughtered her family. Parnilesse had its own enclave where these ragged dogs were for hire, in the port of Carif. Parnilesse and Carluse were allies thanks to Tadira, Parnilesse born, Orlin's sister and Duchess of Carluse these twenty years past. Duke Garnot had found a true love there and Carluse had been Sharlac's foe for time out of mind. Litasse had learned that much at her dead father's knee.

Things should become clearer once Duke Garnot won his battle. If Pelletria's courier birds flew straight and true, Litasse should know how he'd fared within a few days. She would know before Iruvain did.

CHAPTER SIX
Tathrin

The Forest Road to Carluse,
Autumn Equinox Festival, Fifth and Final Day,
Afternoon

THEY'D LEFT THE dense timber behind. Ahead, bright tangles of gorse dotted heath brown with bracken. Less danger of attacks by lurking assailants. More chance of arrows harrying them from a distance. One way or another, blood would soon be shed. At the retinue's dawn meeting, Evord had announced they'd bring Duke Garnot to battle today.

But now the day was fading fast and evening drew on. Surely Evord wasn't planning a night attack? Tathrin looked up anxiously. The Lesser Moon was still short of its half circle and though the Greater Moon was only a few days from full, these unbroken high clouds would shroud its light.

His dun horse whickered and shook its head

irritably. Tathrin smoothed a hand down its neck. He knew how the beast felt. The day had seen an exhausting series of alarms that came to nothing.

Several times a galloper brought news that Duke Garnot was drawing up his forces to fight. Word spread through the army, making ready to advance. Then another rider arrived on a lathered horse saying the Carlusians were in retreat. The mercenary army had pushed on more quickly, until a frantic horn signalled imminent attack. Evord's regiments assembled in a flurry of standards, amid a commotion of weapons and shouts. But no Carluse assault ever came.

Tathrin licked dry lips and his hand strayed towards the water bottle slung on his saddle.

"I shouldn't," the man riding beside him advised. "Not till you're drier than a widow's tuft. Who knows when you'll get a chance of a refill?"

"Of course." Tathrin had learned that lesson the hard way when Evord was still mustering his army far away in the high wolds above Sharlac. The long, hot summer had dried up so many of the springs.

That felt like half a lifetime ago. Now the nights grew steadily colder. Sleeping in the open as they advanced through the forest, the men huddled together wrapped in their cloaks, still booted, their weapons to hand. At least it hadn't rained. Not so far, anyway. Tathrin wondered if they could possibly take Carluse Town before the first serious storm of autumn.

Could he sleep in a real bed there? A yawn seized him, so fierce he felt a twinge in the angle of his jaw. These past few nights, every time he was dozing off, the sentries changed or a mercenary captain arrived to confer with the captain-general. It was hard to believe the Soluran had had any rest. But Evord's face showed no sign of weariness, the visor of his plain helm raised as he talked quietly with the mercenary captain in overall command of their foot forces.

He was a tall man, shaven-headed with unblinking eyes as black as pitch. Tathrin only ever heard him called the Hanged Man. His company marched under a black banner, a corpse swinging from a gibbet for their blazon. The Gallowsfruit, they called themselves, or so Gren said. The Mountain Man always knew what was going on, even if he wasn't officially included in the captain-general's counsels.

Tathrin frowned and looked around. He hadn't seen Gren since shortly after noon. No, there was still no sign of him.

Emerging from the forest, the army spread out across the heath, hundreds upon hundreds of foot soldiers, sober in their leather and chain mail. Here and there companies who favoured surcoats broke the monotony in colourful lines. Standard-bearers brandished each banner, bright despite the dull day.

Tathrin turned in his saddle. While almost all the Dalasorians had been sent to attack Ashgil, the rebellion's army still boasted a double handful of mounted mercenary companies, currently riding as the rearguard. More heavily armoured than the lancers, they were used to fighting in Lescar's varied terrain, readily accustomed to dismounting once the first force of their charge was spent.

Where were the Mountain Men? As the last riders emerged from the shadow of the trees, Tathrin realised he couldn't see any of the yellow-headed warriors. Gren had told him they were keen to fight.

Though these uplanders didn't share the uncomplicated relish for carnage that Gren never bothered to hide. In their smaller companies of fifty or sixty men all linked by blood, they were fighting for gold, pure and simple. Gren had explained how their women were the Mountains' custodians, living out their days in the valleys where they were born. Like their mothers before them, their word granted access to the mines and forests to their husbands, sons and brothers. Those Mountain laws and customs were enforced by their priests and priestesses, the *sheltya*, who had some shadowy Artifice all their own, from what Aremil had told Tathrin.

The measure of a Mountain Man was the wealth he amassed digging ores, trapping furs and trading. In recent years, fighting for lowlander coin had become an accepted means of filling their purses. Out to raise an army with no interest in claiming Lescar itself, Evord had recruited nearly a thousand uplanders eager to prove their worth.

Tathrin wondered how many would change their

minds and take to the mercenary life like Sorgrad and Gren. Some, doubtless, but most seemed intent on going home to win a willing bride. The more he saw of the uplanders, the more Tathrin realised how unusual Sorgrad and Gren were. Whatever remote valley had reared such changelings must have echoed with sighs of relief once they'd departed.

Seeing the Hanged Man ride away, Tathrin kicked his horse into a trot. "Captain-General, if you please!"

"Tathrin." Evord acknowledged him with a nod.

Horsemen, ready to gallop wherever Evord sent his orders, eased aside to allow Tathrin in close.

"My lord," he asked in low tones, "what should I tell Aremil when we next speak?"

Evord smiled briefly. "Tell him we'll be bringing Duke Garnot to battle before Losand's next chimes."

"We will?" Tathrin couldn't help his surprise.

"I think we've had enough of this inconsequential skirmishing," Evord said drily. "Duke Garnot's spies will have told him that our Dalasorians rode down the Vale of Ashgil rather than risk the woods where they cannot use their speed and lances to any great effect. He won't have heard they've taken the town, not yet, so he'll expect them to be riding right around the forest hoping to catch his troops exposed on open ground as he retreats to Carluse Town. He knows he can't risk that. So he's looking for the best possible ground to bring us to battle in these southern fringes of the woods, where he thinks he can secure the advantage."

"Why did he venture out of Carluse Town in the first place?" Tathrin wondered.

Evord smiled more widely. "He's the duke. He must be seen defending his right to rule. Moreover, if he sits tight in Carluse Castle, that begs us to besiege him and he won't have prepared for that. It's only twelve days since Sharlac fell, after all. He'd soon be starved out."

Not soon enough. The duke and duchess would be the last to go hungry and only after all their household and the innocent folk of Carluse Town had suffered horribly.

"Why hasn't he attacked us sooner?" Tathrin was still curious.

"At the moment, we have more men than he does." Evord glanced sideways at Tathrin. "Not many more but enough to give him pause for thought. If Duke Garnot can avoid a decisive battle until Duke Secaris of Draximal sends reinforcements, the balance unquestionably tips in Their Graces' favour. Duke Garnot sent Draximal an offer of alliance on the first day of festival." He chuckled. "It's a shame he didn't know Duke Secaris was on the road to Triolle, only thinking of eating and drinking at Duke Iruvain's expense."

"Halcarion favoured us there." Tathrin only hoped the goddess of luck and light continued to look on them so kindly. "But a Draximal courier will surely have caught up with him by now." He swallowed a qualm. Of course he'd known their rebellion would challenge Aremil's unknown father sooner or later. "What do you suppose Duke Secaris will do?"

"Hard times make for strange bedfellows. Draximal and Carluse will make an alliance once Duke Secaris learns of Sharlac Castle's fall and Duke Moncan's death." Evord had no doubts. "He and the Jackal were long-standing allies, and you told me yourself that Draximal's heir ordered a general muster of militia on the very eve of festival. Lord Cassat knows his father's mind."

"You don't think that's to defend their own borders?" That was what Aremil had believed, when he had told Tathrin the news that Branca had learned. "What about Draximal's quarrels with Parnilesse?"

"Duke Secaris will make peace with Duke Orlin for the sake of avenging Sharlac, ostensibly at least," Evord assured him. "More importantly, Duke Secaris won't want Duke Garnot defeating us unaided. Then Garnot would be free to claim whatever he might like of Sharlac's unguarded territory." He shrugged. "Duke Secaris will want to share in any victory so they can carve up the dead Jackal's dukedom between them. That's a price Duke Garnot will be willing to pay. In the meantime, he'll weaken us as much as he can. All the while, he knows Triolle, Parnilesse and Marlier will be raising their own forces to weight the scales against us."

"How soon can Draximal's muster reach us?" Tathrin asked apprehensively.

"Not soon enough to help Duke Garnot," Evord said calmly. "I've sent our upland friends around to menace his rearguard. Duke Garnot cannot risk being surrounded or cut off from the road back to Carluse. Now he has to stand and fight. If he picks the right ground, he'll think his chances are better than even."

Tathrin nodded, his throat dry. "What do I tell Aremil?"

"He must be ready to tell Master Jettin to convey my new orders to Rega Taszar. Just as soon as I know what those orders might be." Evord raised a hand to forestall any more questions. "Now, if you'll excuse me."

Tathrin saw banners shimmering as the marching ranks yielded to gallopers from several directions, all heading straight for Evord's banner. He let his dun mount fall back as the captain-general's personal guard drew up around the cream and gold standard, ready to attack any rider who might be a foe. Such deceits were hardly unknown.

"Eagle's claws! Eagle's claws!" The first man shouted out the word of the day and brandished the cream and yellow kerchief at his wrist. One of Evord's Soluran lieutenants rode forwards, raising a reassuring hand.

Tathrin watched the great mass of the army slow as word spread that their commander had news. Banners nodded towards each other, as if they conferred like the company captains beneath them. The murmur of conversation among the foot regiments rose to an expectant hum.

"Now would be a good time to wash the dust out of your throat." It was the mercenary who'd warned him against drinking his water earlier. Gren had introduced them but for the life of him, Tathrin couldn't remember the man's name. Only that he rode with a company called the Tallymen and had been wounded at Sharlac. He was serving his time as a messenger until his gashed thigh healed.

A second galloper arrived with a blond Mountain Man riding on his horse's rump. Tathrin's momentary hope was disappointed. Not Gren, this man's words were far more heavily accented.

"Over that rise, east of the main track." He turned to point. "Open ground and then a ridge with trees. The duke's men on the high ground."

Evord nodded. "What are the foremost banners?"

The horseman answered. "Mercenary regiments hold the right and left flanks and are gathered in the centre. Militia regiments fill the gaps between them, two on our left hand, just the one on our right."

Evord's hand stilled a murmur of contempt for militiamen among his guardsmen. "And their mounted mercenaries?"

"To the rear of the militia, flanking the duke's standard," the Mountain Man said carefully.

"They'll stop the militia routing." The horseman scowled.

"No matter." Evord's pale eyes glinted. "What banners are on the flanks?"

The Mountain Man's gaze lengthened with recollection. "On their left hand, I saw four damask roses on a green banner, and pails on a yoke, black against brown."

"The Moonrakers are on the far right, with the Red Hounds between them and the militia." The horseman was more familiar with the mercenary companies who swept to and fro across Lescar, riding the profitable tides of ducal ambition.

That didn't stop one of Evord's lieutenants making certain. "A black banner with moons and stars between them? A mastiff's head inside an oak wreath?"

"Both moons at the half and Halcarion's Crown." The horseman shot him a sardonic look. "I couldn't say exactly what leaves made up the dog's wreath."

Evord's look silenced them both. "Then we move Longshanks to our left flank and bring Juxon's Raiders forward to our centre. Tell the Hanged Man." He nodded at a galloper who promptly spurred his mount away.

"Tell the rest of the regimental captains that my orders from this morning still stand. Now let's get this done before we lose the light." Evord urged his horse onwards as riders scattered to relay his instructions.

The army marched on with fresh purpose. The companies taking the lead were already skirting the hillock the Mountain Man had pointed out.

Above the pounding of marching feet, Tathrin heard faint shouts and horn calls from the far side. The Tallyman rode close to Tathrin at the rear of Evord's retinue. Bracken brushed his stirrups as they left the track and began climbing the slope of the hillock themselves.

Apprehension gathered in the pit of Tathrin's stomach. They didn't have the solid ranks of mounted mercenaries behind them any more. Those men were riding a still more distant arc around this rise in the land.

His horse seemed to pick up his nervousness. It jostled the Tallyman's mount, which snapped back with long yellow teeth. Shying away, Tathrin's horse fought him all the way up the hillock. By the time he had it in hand, he was sweating under his heavy armoured jerkin. Flushed with embarrassment as well as exertion, he forced the horse to the edge of the guardsmen gathering around Evord.

He found he had an excellent view over the open ground the Mountain Man had described. Banners jaunty, Evord's men were drawing up in three solid regiments where the slope below met a wide grassy chase. Movement snagged the corner of his eye and he saw their mounted mercenaries were mustering far away to their right. Somewhere away to their left, beyond where he could see, the rest of their horse companies would be doing the same.

He remembered how the horsemen had waited in the darkness outside Sharlac. When Duke Moncan's men had got the upper hand over the Tallymen, disaster might have followed. Then Evord's signal brought the mounted reserve into the fight, cutting Duke Moncan's guard to pieces.

On the far side of the sward, the ground rose to a ridge thick with trees. Duke Garnot's army was ready and waiting. Six distinct regiments held the lower ground. Mercenaries held the centre and each flank, their massed banners colourful. The militia companies in their midst looked like clusters of pied crows in Carluse's black and white livery, the blades of their halberds bright.

As the ridge curved around, so did the entire Carluse line, threatening Evord's men with a murderous embrace. Up on the highest ground, just below the trees, mounted mercenaries were massed behind the militia. In their centre, Tathrin could see Duke Garnot's black and white flag. One of those men beneath the boar's head standard must be the duke himself.

Desultory arrows were already coming from the Carluse archers. Why weren't Evord's men retaliating? Then Tathrin saw the Carluse missiles falling short. So their bowmen had no chance of striking Evord's retinue, he realised with guilty relief.

But the rebellion's mercenaries would be stuck full of arrows as they crossed that open ground. After that, they'd be toiling uphill, the enemy coming at them from all sides. How could they possibly prevail?

CHAPTER SEVEN
Tathrin

The Battle of Carluse Woods,
Autumn Equinox Festival, Fifth and Final Day,
Afternoon

"DON'T FRET." THE Tallyman grinned. "The captain-general knows what he's doing." He pointed to the left end of their own battle line.

Tathrin craned his neck to see a mercenary standard of a black topboot on a light blue ground. A second standard hung beneath it, soiled white. A gust of wind smoothed it out to show a red horse's head, nailed to the pole upside down.

"That's Wynald's Warband's standard!"

"In the hands of the Longshanks." The Tallyman chuckled. "See how the Red Hounds like that."

Tathrin could hear anger curdling the shouts from men under the mastiff banner in Duke

101

Garnot's line opposite. The Longshanks repaid them with their own coin.

"Mangy curs deserve a kicking!"

"Feel our boots up your arses!"

"That's how they like it!"

"Got arseholes slacker than a drunkard's purse, they do for each other so often!"

As the taunts became still more obscene, Tathrin slipped off a glove and licked a finger to test the wind. How could he possibly hear individual voices all the way up here? There was barely any breeze. So how could gusts keep flaunting that captured flag in the Red Hounds' faces?

"You think that's bloodstains?"

"Nah, we used it to wipe our arses!"

Suspicion hollowed Tathrin's stomach. Where was Reher? He'd thought the smith was still safely far to the rear, with the rest of those supporting the army and waiting to tend the wounded.

"Here we go." The Tallyman's fists clenched on his loose reins.

The Longshanks moved forward, clashing their swords on their shields. The rest of the regiment followed. Arrows arced through the air, lethal volleys loosed by the Carluse archers safely drawn up behind their black-and-white-liveried militiamen.

Tathrin winced. How could the mercenaries keep walking onwards, when an arrow might skewer them at any moment? How could they ignore friends on either hand, yelping and clutching at a piercing shaft, or worse, falling silent and still, remorseless boots stepping over them?

He saw the advancing men and women raising their shields. No, not shields, but the panels of crudely woven laths that Tathrin had seen them making a few nights ago. He'd thought they were in case of rain. Now they were sheltering the foot soldiers from a very different storm, soon bristling with arrows they'd foiled.

Evord's army had archers too and they had marched forward with the mercenaries. Protected by those panels, they sent their own murderous arrows into Carluse's ranks. Tathrin saw men falling, dragged backwards by urgent hands. As gaps opened up, he could see the Carluse archers exposed.

Keen-eyed crossbowmen from Evord's line advanced, each with a companion sheltering him. Men were knocked clean off their feet across the Carluse ranks. Tathrin caught his breath as the duke's own crossbowmen pushed forward amid the militia and levelled their weapons. But their bolts didn't fly nearly as far or as fast as Evord's did.

"Please make sure Aremil conveys my thanks to Master Gruit. Those steel crossbows are worth every gold crown."

Captain-General Evord's words startled Tathrin. He hadn't noticed the Soluran approaching to get a clearer view of the battle.

Before he could say anything, the Tallyman stood

in his stirrups with a muted cheer. "See? Longshanks are drawing the Red Hounds out!"

"Captain Siskin has always struggled with his temper." Evord smiled with discreet satisfaction. "The Red Hounds have faced the Longshanks twice in recent years," he explained to Tathrin. "Both times they've been soundly beaten. The last time, Longshanks captured the Hounds' captain and ransomed him back."

"They sent Dandy Siskin back stripped naked and shaved bare as a baby boy." The Tallyman chuckled. "He'd better not trip over his feet today. His sergeants won't buy him back a second time."

The Red Hounds were racing forwards, screaming with fury. The Moonrakers had no choice but to follow. Left exposed, they'd be at the mercy of the rebellion's mounted forces on that flank. Mercenary companies all along the line of Duke Garnot's army began to move, their banners flying.

Below Tathrin, Evord's second and third regiments began moving forward; more slowly than the one led by the Longshanks but no less belligerent, yelling their scorn and defiance.

"Watch the Carluse militia," Evord said quietly.

The companies in black and white livery drawn up between the mercenary regiment on the duke's right flank and the hired companies in the centre were edging forwards. A flurry of irate horn calls slowed them. Their standards wavered, irresolute. Some began to return to their places, only to halt in confusion. The mounted forces drawn up at the duke's right hand had already moved to hold the ground left unguarded by the Red Hounds' intemperate advance.

The Red Hounds had very nearly closed with the Longshanks. Only Evord's mounted mercenaries weren't waiting in reserve on that side of the battlefield. They were charging right into the Red Hounds' flank. Even above the din, Tathrin heard screams of agony cut short by merciless swords.

As the Red Hounds stumbled backwards, the riders wheeled away. Tathrin recalled Captain-General Evord insisting that this time the mounted mercenaries stay horsed as long as they possibly could.

Now the Longshanks charged forwards, more banners following. Evord's left-hand regiment cut through the scattered Red Hounds to lay into the other Carluse mercenary companies opposite across the grassy ride. Carluse's archers gave up their volleys. The risk of killing their own men was just too great.

The rebellion's archers had no such problems, still raining lethal shafts down on Duke Garnot's waiting regiments. In the centre Juxon's Raiders now led a steady advance, all the following banners still in disciplined ranks.

Tathrin wondered who Juxon had been. Now the company was led by a disconcertingly handsome woman called Jifelle.

"Here they come." Evord's satisfaction was tinged with something Tathrin couldn't identify. Sorrow? Regret?

Duke Garnot's army was advancing, unwilling to endure any more of the rebellion's arrows. Counting their standards, Tathrin tried to guess at their numbers. More than three thousand? Then Carluse had as many foot soldiers as Evord and the militia were armed with halberds. Could the polearms' greater reach give the Carluse men a decisive advantage over more experienced swordsmen?

Battle was now well and truly joined between the rebellion's mercenaries and the Carluse militia in the centre. Carluse's men were learning that their halberds only served them as long as they kept the enemy beyond the point of the vicious blade. As the mercenaries dodged and stepped inside the flailing poles, their swords ripped into leather and flesh.

Meaningless insults taunted foes who couldn't hear, intent on their own killing and survival. Banners swayed and shifted, warriors gathering around them before charging shoulder to shoulder. As the slaughter ebbed and flowed, voids came and went, briefly revealing trampled grass stained with blood, corpses motionless among fallen weapons and severed limbs, the wounded writhing.

A gust of wind swept up the stink of slaughter. Tathrin gagged on the acrid mix of blood and sweat, piss and shit, crushed greenery and churned-up mud. Then the breeze shifted and all he smelled was spicy gorse. Where did that come from?

"Those bastard Spearmen need a kick up their arses." The Tallyman glowered at the right flank of the rebellion's army. "Shall I ride to warn the captain of Nyer's?"

Tathrin saw a green standard with a broken spear retreating. Captain Vendist had formed his new company only that spring, Gren had said, and the other captains were trading wagers on how long his standard would fly.

"Hold your ground," Evord told the Tallyman.

It was too late to warn Nyer's Watchmen. Tathrin saw their blazon, a grey tower on a black flag, forced back, lest they get cut off. He caught his breath. The Wyvern Hunters' creamy flag with its black-winged beast came up behind the Spearmen.

"Captain-General!" A galloper hurried up, his horse tossing its head. "Your orders for the reserve on the right?"

The anxious man pointed at Duke Garnot's horsemen. They were moving slowly down from the ridge. Tathrin looked at the wavering line below, then glanced back over his shoulder and his apprehension turned to sick certainty. Evord's reserve was too far away.

If Duke Garnot's riders charged into battle, they would hit the Spearmen before the rebellion's reserve could reach them. If Evord's mounted force moved first, trying to reach the mêlée to reinforce the Spearmen, their path would be blocked by Duke Garnot's riders. Whoever moved first, Carluse had the advantage.

Tathrin counted the mounted companies' banners drawn up around Duke Garnot's standard. Ten of them, just the same as the captain-general. He swallowed, his throat dry as ashes.

Evord smiled. "The captains of horse have their orders. I see no reason to change them."

The only horsemen that Tathrin could see fighting were on the far side of the battlefield. Evord's second mounted regiment, re-formed after breaking the Red Hounds' advance, were now laying into the duke's horsemen there as they tried to hold their army's flank behind the Moonrakers.

Once again, Tathrin smelled freshly cut gorse and could see no reason for it.

Then, as the duke's horsemen were forced back, Mountain Men erupted from the trees on the ridge. They thrust rough-hewn poles and lacerating gorse boughs between the horses' legs, under their tender bellies. Dodging around their hindquarters, they slashed mercilessly at their hocks.

"That's a good use for the shortarses," the Tallyman murmured with approval.

Tathrin swallowed bile burning his throat. Horses were collapsing, hamstrung, gutted, screaming with agony. Tears stung his eyes. Men had chosen to be in this battle. Those poor beasts hadn't.

Carluse's riders twisted and hacked at their blond assailants. Some leaned perilously out of their saddles. Others jumped down to fight hand-to-hand, ready to take on the Mountain Men with their greater height and longer swords.

Now horses were stumbling on grass suddenly slick beneath their hooves. Some riders fell with their mounts. Those trapped by a pinned leg were swiftly killed by Mountain swords. Others died crushed by their hapless steeds' death throes.

Tathrin's chest tightened. There'd been no rain for days and he could see no sign of a spring on the slope.

Yellow-haired men lay dead on the ground, some cleanly decapitated by a rider's deft sword. Others were felled by some horse's brutal kick, faces crushed, ribs shattered.

Evord was issuing brisk orders, writing on scraps of paper, sending gallopers hither and yon. His whole army was advancing across the grassy sward now, driving the entire Carluse line back.

Tathrin saw that the Spearmen had rallied, marching shoulder to shoulder with the Wyvern Hunters. Behind the advance, the rebellion's archers were already busy among the fallen. Wounded comrades were swiftly carried somewhere to the rear of Evord's retinue. Any enemy still breathing had his throat cut, his body looted.

"Militia," the Tallyman said with contempt. "Soft as shit and twice as useless."

Carluse's black-and-white-liveried ranks were breaking in utter confusion. Men were fleeing the battle, casting halberds and standards aside. Evord's mercenaries, led by Juxon's Raiders, let them run. Guiltily relieved, Tathrin hoped some of those husbands and fathers might get safely back to their families.

Then he realised Evord's army wasn't particularly interested in showing mercy. With the militia fled, they could concentrate their wrath on the Carluse mercenaries still holding the centre of the line. As he watched, he saw several of Duke Garnot's paid companies break and run after the routing militia.

Hooves thundered. Captain-General Evord's mounted reserve who'd been waiting so patiently were charging the mercenaries now exposed on the far left of the duke's line. Tathrin caught his breath. The duke's horsemen were still poised below the ridge. Surely they would charge to save their comrades?

Perhaps they might have, if the second regiment of Mountain Men hadn't appeared to attack them with all the ferocity their countrymen were famous for. As Evord's horsemen rode unopposed to cut down the Carluse mercenaries Tathrin winced, expecting slaughter worse than any he'd yet seen.

"They don't call them the Slippery Eels for nothing." The Tallyman chuckled. "Old Dorish will be ruing the day he took Carluse's coin though."

The main battle standard amid Duke Garnot's mercenaries was leading a measured retreat. Tathrin had thought the writhing black shape on the pale green ground was a snake. The Tallyman clearly knew better.

"Doesn't it bother you?" he asked abruptly. "Fighting men you know?"

The Tallyman shrugged. "Safer to surrender to someone you can trust if the battle goes against you."

He pointed to the centre of the battlefield and Tathrin saw mercenary standards dipping. Men held up empty hands to show they'd sheathed their swords.

The Tallyman tensed. "The bastard's running!"

Duke Garnot's personal standard was disappearing into the trees on the ridge. His retinue had drawn up close around him, reinforced by his remaining mounted mercenaries.

"New orders for the Tallymen!" A galloper trotted towards them, slapping a scrap of paper into Tathrin's companion's hand. "Escort prisoners to the rear."

As the man cantered away Tathrin felt singularly useless. All he could do was wait till Aremil's Artifice touched him, to relay the battle's outcome.

Was it a victory? Duke Garnot had got away. However many men had died on both sides, that meant more fighting. If they defeated Duke Garnot next time, they must still overcome Draximal,

Marlier, Triolle and Parnilesse. He looked at the carrion birds already wheeling above the carnage, their cries mingling with injured men's curses and weeping.

Were there fewer dead on their side than on Carluse's? Tathrin hoped so. But how could they sustain any losses and still wage battle after battle against freshly drafted militia and new-mustered mercenaries eager for ducal gold?

"Tathrin!"

A galloper was returning with a yellow-headed man clinging to his waist.

Gren leaped down from the horse's rump, exultant. "We said Evord was the man for this campaign!"

Tathrin's horse snorted with disquiet. Gren's chain-mail hauberk was spattered with blood, while a gruesome smear clotted his hair into spikes.

"Are you wounded?"

"Not hardly," Gren said scornfully. "I told you. The soothsayer said I was born to be hanged."

Tathrin's horse tossed its head and tried to back away. As he got the animal in hand, a second messenger arrived with a passenger.

"Sorgrad!"

Gren embraced his older brother. Sorgrad was a little taller and somewhat broader, his blue eyes more gentian than cornflower. Like most Mountain Men, he wore his years lightly. It had taken Tathrin some while to realise both were ten years or more his senior.

Gren pulled the leather thong out of his hair to retie it more securely. "Where've you been?"

Even knowing Sorgrad's talent for staying well groomed in the least promising circumstances, Tathrin didn't think he'd been in battle. He was wearing a plain grey doublet and a short riding cloak rather than armour. His fine yellow hair, cropped shorter than Gren's, was combed and his boots were polished.

"Draximal." Sorgrad shot him an amused glance. "Among other places."

Gren chuckled. "You should have seen the Longshanks twisting the Red Hounds' tails."

"I did," Sorgrad assured him.

"And Alrene and his boys from the Teyvasoke?" Gren demanded.

Alrene was one of the two Mountain captains that all the rest deferred to, though Tathrin wasn't sure why. A *soke* was a valley in the upland tongue, he'd learned that much.

Sorgrad nodded. "The captain-general knows we're fastest over rough ground."

Something in his satisfied smile hardened Tathrin's suspicions. "You were helping them?"

Sorgrad raised blond brows in innocent query. "How, exactly?"

Tathrin scowled at him. "If anyone learns what you did—"

"What I've been doing is escorting Lady Charoleia and Mistress Branca along the Great West Road towards Tormalin. Why would anyone think different?" Sorgrad looked at him, a sapphire glint in his eye. "What would anyone suspect? Everyone knows there are no mageborn in the Mountains."

Which was merely one of the mysteries around Sorgrad. Tathrin subsided. He could only hope no one else had wondered at the sudden breezes waving Wynald's captured flag in the Red Hounds' faces, carrying the Longshanks' taunts so clearly to them. Hopefully no one would wonder at the churned-up ground beneath the dead Carluse horses. Men and beasts could slip on blood and horseshit just as readily as water seeping unbidden from a dry slope. At least no one would have seen Sorgrad anywhere close. Tathrin would wager good coin on that.

Gren slapped his brother on the shoulder. "Let's get down to the field, before all the dead are picked clean."

"Go ahead." Sorgrad nodded. "I'll find you after I've reported to Evord."

"Don't be too long." Gren sauntered down the slope, whistling a taproom tune.

Tathrin was torn between his misgivings and relief that Sorgrad was back. It was the older Mountain Man who'd seen him safe through that first terrifying battle, when they had used the night and deceit to set Parnilesse and Draximal fighting over Emirle Bridge, along with so much more than ordinary trickery.

"Just what are you going to report to Evord?" he asked pointedly.

Sorgrad's smile widened. "Everything the captain-general needs to know." He walked towards the men gathered around the Soluran.

Tathrin wondered what would happen when Sorgrad's secret was discovered. He knew that Aremil was not nearly as sanguine as he pretended. If the enchantments let his friend see more deeply into his thoughts than he liked, Tathrin was repaid in kind.

He knew Aremil and Branca, and the scholars Kerith and Jettin, uneasily anticipated the day they would be summoned to defend their use of Artifice in Lescar's wars. The aetheric adepts doggedly assured themselves that Archmage Planir had no claim on their magic. Besides, they had done no harm, merely passing information more swiftly and more securely than any courier or messenger dove. True enough, but Aremil still feared the Archmage's wrath.

What could Sorgrad possibly say in his own defence? That he'd harmed no one directly, by using his influence over the air to display Wynald's captured banner? That he'd merely summoned a little water to aid his countrymen, not attacked the Carluse horsemen himself?

What good would that do, when the Archmage's ban on wizardry was absolute? And Sorgrad could hardly claim such innocence if it was ever proved that his magic had set Emirle Bridge ablaze, not the arcane alchemy of sticky fire that everyone had blamed.

Tathrin grimaced. Sorgrad might argue he was no true mage. He'd never studied in the island city of Hadrumal or bent his knee to the masters and mistresses of elemental air and earth, fire and water. What of it? The slightest proof that he'd used magic in Lescar would condemn him before Planir the Archmage. Tathrin burned to know if Sorgrad's reluctant accomplices would be condemned too. There was no one he could ask that.

How many people knew Sorgrad's secret? To Tathrin's knowledge, only Gren, himself and Reher in the army marching with Evord. Beyond that, there was Aremil, Reniack and Gruit, Branca and Charoleia. Surely they would all keep their mouths shut for fear of the Archmage's wrath?

CHAPTER EIGHT
Branca

The Toremal Residence of the Princely House of Den Souvrian,
Autumn Equinox Festival, Fifth and Final Day, Evening

"So that's another *victory to add to our tally!*"

Jettin was exultant, Kerith less so.

"*Duke Garnot lives to fight another day.*"

Branca looked more closely at the tall, stern-faced scholar, leaning against a stone pillar, his arms folded across his chest. He was Carluse born after all, his accent still clear after all the years he'd lived in Vanam. What was troubling him? If it had been Aremil, she'd have known but Kerith was so much more adept. No hint of his innermost thoughts floated through the aether to her.

"Do you have family near to the fighting, or friends?"

"*No.*"

Kerith's brief reply offered no clarification.

Jettin's eager thoughts still pursued Duke Garnot. He paced back and forth across this echoing hall that existed only in Aremil's imagination.

"*We could bring him to bay all the sooner if we knew what he was planning—*"

"*No!*"

Kerith's adamant refusal echoed around the shadowy aisle.

Branca didn't need to see into the older man's mind to know how much he detested what he had done to Failla, when he'd forced her to reveal just what she'd betrayed to Pelletria, the Triolle spy. Failla had told Branca herself, shuddering with tears and halting words. She would suffer any violation of her body rather than endure that again, her every thought laid bare. If that was how she felt, what must Kerith think of himself?

"*We cannot even contemplate doing something like that.*"

Seated in his high-backed chair, Aremil's voice was firm, with none of the hesitation that afflicted him when they spoke face to face.

"*We would never be able to argue that we're using no magic to materially affect the outcome of this war.*"

Branca knew how often he rehearsed his defence against such an accusation.

Not for the first time, Jettin wasn't ready to yield.

"*Mentor Tonin spoke of enchantments so subtle the victim doesn't even know their thoughts have been read.*"

"Mentor Tonin is in constant correspondence with Planir the Black," she said tartly. If the Archmage didn't claim suzerainty over Artifice, he had rapidly forged links with all the most advanced adepts. "The less contact we have with the mentor, the more likely we are to escape censure."

Branca made sure to hide her own regret. She would dearly have loved to ask their old tutor how Artifice might be used in defence of herself and others. She had already been attacked once since embarking on this conspiracy, escaping crippling injury by the merest chance. She didn't want to ever be so defenceless again.

A torch in a bracket behind Aremil's head flared briefly in response to his irritation.

"*We're straying from the point. What news do you have for me?*"

"We only reached Toremal today," she said quickly. "I should be able to tell you more tomorrow."

"*It will be some days before news of this battle reaches Abray. For the moment, the Caladhrians are telling themselves it's hardly surprising that someone took advantage of Sharlac's lack of a leader and attacked. They're waiting to see what happens next.*"

No hint of reservation shadowed Kerith's words. Branca was content to rely on his assessment.

"Everyone in Ashgil was keeping their head down when we left. As long as the guildmasters are running things, they're willing to go with the run of the runes. Of course, if Duke Garnot prevails, they'll swear on all that's sacred how they were only taking care of his rights and dues."

For an instant, the clouds around Jettin's thoughts thinned. Branca caught a glimpse of Dalasorian lancers riding down the Carluse boar's head, the duke's standard toppling, every man dying pierced by several lances.

Was she the only one to see that? Kerith seemed to be still wrapped in his own concerns. Aremil was looking towards the far door.

"Forgive me. I must go."

And with that, the stately hall dissolved like mist on a sunny morning. Branca was back in her silk-hung bedchamber. Her body had never left and she'd always been aware of the stool she sat upon, the closed door she faced, even the noises beyond. Adept as she was, she needed only a fraction of her mind to reach through the aether to the others. Though she was still striving to increase her awareness of everything around her while she was working enchantments. She wasn't ever going to be caught unawares again.

"Don't you want to ask Mentor Tonin why Aremil can only meet us in that made-up sanctuary?"

Jettin was increasingly torn between curiosity and irritation at this quirk of Aremil's Artifice.

Branca could see him clear as day in her mind's eye, ostensibly knelt in prayer by a roadside shrine to Trimon. She blinked and saw the red velvet drapes of her room instead.

"*Does it matter? It's convenient enough.*"

Kerith sat by a writing desk in a library walled with books. Sheets of paper at his elbow were screwed up in exasperation.

Before Branca could sense any reason for that, Kerith abruptly withdrew from this shared enchantment.

"*Good day to you both.*"

"*Till next time.*"

Jettin was gone as well. She could tell he was simply eager to embark on his next adventure. But something was troubling Kerith. Back in Vanam, he'd have been intrigued by Aremil's imagined hall, searching the libraries for any reference to something similar amid the most ancient enchantments.

Branca sat for a moment to recover from the light-headedness that lingered after balancing the thoughts of three other adepts with her own. Taking a deep breath, she rose, unlocked the door and went into the adjoining chamber.

The luxuriously appointed dressing room held more gowns than Branca would ever own in a lifetime. It was bigger than her whole lodging back in Vanam, where she struggled to rent a small parlour with a still smaller bedchamber.

"Captain-General Evord has won a significant victory over Duke Garnot but not secured a decisive victory."

"Good. Tell me the details later." Charoleia was painting her lips at the dressing table. "You had better get ready."

"I have a headache." Branca glanced dubiously at the blue gown hanging on the tall mirror. It looked uncomfortably close-cut for her generous figure and was far too striking a colour.

"Trissa will make you a tisane."

"My lady." Her obedient maid headed for the door. Brush poised, Charoleia turned. "You'll enjoy yourself once you get there."

"I very much doubt it," Branca said with feeling.

"Men and women determined on one last night of fun can be wonderfully indiscreet." Charoleia set down the brush and opened a pot of rouge. "Some will be brooding over infelicitous encounters with friends and rivals over festival. Some will be regretting unfortunate indiscretions." She added an infinitesimal blush to her flawless cheekbones. "What's not to enjoy?"

Branca smiled at her arch tone. "Won't some just take pleasure in the music and dancing?"

"We're hardly interested in them." Charoleia rose and smoothed her gossamer petticoats. "Now, let Trissa see to your face and put on that gown."

Branca sighed. "I don't see why you want me to come. These are your friends."

Charoleia was amused. "The Sieur Den Souvrian and his charming wife are hardly my friends."

"Is it wise to say so when we're enjoying their hospitality?" Startled, Branca looked around. Who might have an ear pressed to a keyhole? She disliked being constantly attended. Servants were a luxury for Vanam's wealthy households on the slopes between the lower town by the lakeshore and the university citadel on the heights.

"Any servants within earshot know my open purse depends on their closed mouths." Charoleia adjusted her garters. "As to Messire Den Souvrian and his lady, I'm of use to them and they're of use to me and those are the steps danced at the Tormalin Imperial Court."

"Who am I of use to?" Branca demanded with some asperity.

Charoleia considered the question judiciously. "Well, you're so remarkably plain that even the tediously undistinguished Demoiselles Den Souvrian will look charming beside you. Madam their mother will thank me for that."

Branca laughed. "That's something, I suppose."

"Don't underestimate the value of going unregarded." Charoleia stepped carefully into her gold silk gown. "You're of considerable use to Aremil sitting listening to people who don't notice you."

When had Charoleia last entered a room without immediately drawing all eyes? Branca had never known anyone with such glorious hair, such perfect features, so shapely a figure and such elegant poise. Fortunately Charoleia was also one of the most intelligent people she'd ever met, who valued Branca's wit and scholarship just as highly as her own beauty.

Charoleia would never scorn any tool that might help achieve her own ends. She made a handsome living buying and selling information and on occasion concealing it and misdirecting those who sought it, for the proper payment from those with something so crucial to hide.

Branca watched as Trissa put down the tisane she had fetched and went to settle the gown on her mistress's hips. She laced it mercilessly tight as Charoleia stood, back straight, shoulders back, her eyes distant as she contemplated the evening ahead.

It was a very good thing this formidable woman was supporting their attempts to bring peace to Lescar rather than opposing them. Was it because she was Lescari born? Branca really had no idea. Charoleia could change her accent as easily as she changed her gloves. Trissa, her maid, sounded Relshazri but Branca wasn't necessarily inclined to believe that either.

She frowned at a new concern. "Won't people wonder at seeing you here? When you were in Vanam so recently? And then in Draximal?"

Few people knew Charoleia had been in Losand, so there shouldn't be awkward questions about how she made a three- or four-day journey to Draximal overnight. But taking a boat down the Drax to the River Asilor and then a carriage from Solland to Toremal would ordinarily take eight or nine days. It only needed someone to speculate that some mage had helped them. Then all their secrets could be guessed.

"Lady Alaric has travelled to Selerima for festival." Charoleia adjusted the swell of her bosom within her bodice. "Mistress Horelle paid that brief visit to Draximal." She nodded and Trissa began buttoning the gown. "Lady Rochiel has been in Toremal all through festival."

How did she keep all her various guises straight? She must have a mind like those Aldabreshin cabinets, full of separately locked boxes.

Branca pinched the bridge of her nose. She really did have a headache. "Remind me who Lady Rochiel is?"

"The younger daughter of a minor Sharlac noble. She mostly lives with exiled cousins in Tormalin's northern provinces. For reasons no one's quite sure of, she never made a suitable marriage. Some say she's an adventuress, given her unexplained absences. Others would certainly hope so." Charoleia smoothed the saffron lace framing her exquisite cleavage and looked more closely at Branca.

"Drink your tisane, my dear. We'll see how you feel then. I can always make your excuses." She shook her head, tumbling chestnut curls shimmering in the candlelight. "Wizards find it impossible to master Artifice. I'm beginning to think aetheric adepts should avoid any dealings with magecraft."

Branca pressed a hand to her mouth. Even mentioning it brought back nauseating memories of Sorgrad's magic, the iridescent light and unexpected heat carrying them first from Losand to Draximal and then from Draximal to Toremal.

"Sit down." Charoleia guided her to the dressing table stool. "You're a ghastly colour."

Branca saw her reflection was indeed ashen. Charoleia found her a smelling bottle of vinegar and fragrant herbs amid the clutter of cosmetics.

"Here, try this."

She looked up to meet Charoleia's violet eyes in the mirror.

"He's gone back to Lescar, hasn't he? We needn't use his magic again?" She took a deep breath of the spiced vinegar and felt a little better.

"From now on, we travel by boat and carriage," Charoleia promised.

"Will we be going back to Draximal?"

"Who knows?" Charoleia shrugged.

Aremil knew they'd stayed in an inn beneath the very walls of his father's castle. While Sorgrad trawled the taprooms to learn what the common folk thought of Sharlac's fate, Charoleia had waited for her own spy among Duke Secaris's intelligencers. Branca could only pace the floor of their private parlour.

They'd learned everyone was confident Carluse would soon put these attackers to flight and retake Losand. Then Draximal would claim its share of Sharlac's heirless domains. There was widespread approval of Lord Cassat's actions, mustering the dukedom's militia and sending the castle's fastest courier after Duke Secaris on his leisurely progress to Triolle.

Tavern sages agreed they must also show Parnilesse that Draximal was not to be trifled with. With Duke Orlin's sister wife to Duke Garnot, Carluse and Parnilesse would be working hand in glove. Only a cautious few considered the possibility that Carluse wouldn't prevail, leaving Lord Cassat to lead Draximal's army against the exiles.

Branca had told Aremil all that. She'd waited for him to ask what Charoleia's web of suborned servants could tell him about Duke Secaris's household, about the parents he didn't remember, the brothers and sisters who believed he'd died as an infant. But he hadn't asked. Either he'd overcome his curiosity about his unknown family or he'd decided they couldn't afford such distraction.

Aremil wasn't stupid. Branca had admired his intellect from their first meeting. She'd seen his courage, as she challenged him to test his afflicted body's capabilities. He would never have mastered Artifice without coming to a fuller understanding of his infirmities. And now her admiration for him was turning inexorably into affection, no matter how unwise that was.

She'd looked deep into his determination to solve Lescar's woes. She wasn't going to help some wealthy invalid indulge fever dreams that would just get better men killed. Hotheads in the lower town's inns sometimes proposed taking up swords to reclaim what they'd lost. Branca's father always condemned such folly. He'd abandoned any thought of returning to Triolle along with the arm and the leg he'd lost to a wagon's crushing wheels and a surgeon's knife.

Lescar was no place for a cripple, of base or exalted birth. Which was why Duke Secaris had sent Aremil away, first to a remote manor and then to Vanam when he inconveniently failed to succumb to childhood illness.

The sound of Charoleia unlocking her jewel coffer recalled Branca's wandering thoughts. She watched her don a flamboyant necklace of amethysts and citrines. The amethysts were the same shade as her eyes. The woman Branca saw now looked most unlike the modest Lady Alaric she'd met back in Vanam. Lady Rochiel favoured audacious necklines and clinging skirts that invited any man old enough to shave to admire the line of her thigh. And why was she wearing such frivolous garters if there wasn't a chance they'd be seen?

Trissa brought the glass of tisane in its silver holder over to the dressing table. "Drink it before it gets cold."

Branca took up the glass and rolled the pierced silver ball around in the hot water to encourage the steeping herbs. She sipped and found the aromatic warmth soothing. "What do you hope to learn tonight?"

"News of Sharlac's fall will have been circulating. We want to know what everyone makes of that." Charoleia considered her reflection in the long mirror. "We want to know what these lesser Tormalin lords think their noble princes should do. Will they advise sending gold to Duke Secaris so Draximal can hire mercenaries to crush this outrage? Or should Tormalin interest back Parnilesse?"

"Do we want to divide opinion?"

Branca knew that would be easy enough. The dukes were bitter rivals for the lucrative trade with Tormalin's noble princes and their vast estates. It ensured the ducal families' luxuries, whatever the poverty blighting lesser Lescari lives.

"Insofar as we can without attracting attention." Charoleia turned with a swish of her skirts. Lady Rochiel even moved differently from Lady Alaric. "The more the great houses debate, the longer they'll stay out of Lescari affairs. In the meantime, we gather whatever information will bolster our arguments, when the time comes to convince the Emperor to hold himself aloof. Now, my dear, do you feel up to coming out?"

Branca hesitated. "Oh, very well."

Trissa swiftly found her comb and pins. "If you could lift your chin."

Branca closed her eyes. She had no desire to see herself being primped and painted.

"I want to know who's heard rumour of Losand's fall," Charoleia continued. "The fastest couriers will only just have brought that news to the Emperor and the foremost princes. Anyone who hints at it is very well informed. I don't imagine we'll hear much beyond insincere sympathy," she added tartly. "Carluse has precious few friends in Tormalin."

Branca nodded as Trissa wiped something cool and moist across her forehead. "So no one will weep for Duke Garnot's latest misfortune?"

"If you hear the slightest whisper about the battle in Carluse's woods, let me know at once." Charoleia paused, thoughtful. "No one here can possibly know about that unless they have magic to call on, whether it's elemental or aetheric. That would be a whole new roll of the runes. I'm also interested in any opinions of Triolle," she continued briskly.

Branca stiffened as Trissa's brush tickled her cheek. "Duke Iruvain has friends in Tormalin?"

"Master Hamare had spies in Toremal," Charoleia corrected her. "We need to know if Duke Iruvain has the wit to continue using them. Or if he even knows who they are. I may be able to buy some of his people's allegiance," she said thoughtfully. "Duke Iruvain doesn't command anywhere near the respect his late lamented father did."

Branca swallowed, grateful she wasn't looking at Charoleia. "Won't Triolle's spies want revenge on whoever had Master Hamare killed?"

Strictly speaking, Sorgrad had wielded the knife. But he'd done so on Charoleia's instructions. As composed as she was ruthless, the woman had made no secret of that. Wasn't she in the least apprehensive that suborning Sorgrad's wizardry to encompass such a murder would attract the Archmage's wrath?

Charoleia smiled serenely. "Hamare's accused of forcing his affections on Duchess Litasse. Duke Iruvain would have been entitled to his blood, if Litasse hadn't been found with it on her hands and her skirts." She raised a warning finger. "Not that we know any of that."

"Who do you think will take Master Hamare's place as Triolle's chief intelligencer?"

Branca would have bitten her lip but Trissa was painting it.

"If he's still alive, it'll be Karn."

Charoleia's answer wasn't what she wanted to hear. Branca shivered at the memory of her encounter with the Triolle spy. "Master Welgren hoped that wound would prove mortal."

Trissa clicked her tongue. "If you could keep still."

"Sorry." Branca tried not to flinch as a brush coloured her eyelids.

Even with that suppurating gash in his side, thanks to an attempt on his life at Charoleia's instigation, Karn had traced their plot through Sharlac. Had he survived to carry word to Triolle that Lady Derenna was persuading disaffected lords to wait out any forthcoming upheavals, travelling far and wide with Branca meekly playing her maid? Thanks to Derenna, not one vassal had ridden to the imprisoned duchess's aid or sought revenge for Jackal Moncan's death. Not yet, anyway.

"I'll only believe Karn's dead when I see his body," Charoleia said tersely.

Branca had never believed she could desire a man's death. But Karn's attack on her, Lady Derenna and Welgren the apothecary who'd been serving as their escort, that had truly terrified her. In her few quiet moments, she was doing all she could to recall whatever enchantments might defend her. Her old teacher, Mentor Tonin, would disapprove but he was safe in Vanam. Even in Toremal Branca didn't feel much safer than she had in Lescar.

"Open your eyes," Trissa invited.

Branca regarded her reflection with some surprise. No artistry with powder and paint could alter her round face and blunt features. All the same, Trissa had smoothed her clear complexion to porcelain. Sooty lashes and subtle shades enhanced her dark brown eyes while plum-coloured gloss lent her lips unexpected fullness.

She'd already submitted to Trissa's curling tongs, as her mousy locks grew to her shoulders. Branca normally cut her hair a good deal shorter to fit neatly under a cap but Charoleia had forbidden such dowdiness. Now Trissa had pinned her tresses back, leaving just a few ringlets to frame her face.

"This gown is an excellent colour for you, and you should borrow my garnets." Charoleia cocked her head, a faint frown marring her brow. "Though you don't look plain enough to let Den Souvrian's daughters shine. Perhaps you should stay at home."

Branca laughed. "No, I'll risk disappointing our hostess. Thank you, Trissa."

She studied herself in the mirror. What would Aremil make of her transformation, if she reached through the aether to tell him what they'd discovered before they retired that night? No, that would risk waking him and he needed his sleep. She shouldn't be so selfish.

Aremil would contact her soon enough, once Tathrin and the captain-general's army caught up with Duke Garnot.

CHAPTER NINE
Tathrin

**The High Road from Abray to Carluse,
1ˢᵗ of Aft-Autumn**

GREN WAS AMUSED. "Is someone you owe money to following us?"

"I'm wondering how far behind the foot soldiers are."

All Tathrin could see was the first company of their mounted rearguard, trotting briskly as they left the rutted forest road for the broad gravelled highway.

Sorgrad was looking ahead. "What we need to know is where the Dalasorians are."

At least Tathrin knew that. "Jettin told Aremil they passed Thymir at first light."

Rega Taszar's troops were holding Ashgil while Sia Kersain and Pata Mezian's regiments rode on towards Carluse Town.

Sorgrad shook his head. "It's going to be a cursed close-run thing."

"We should have pressed on through the night," Gren remarked. "We won't get a brighter pair of moons this side of Winter Solstice."

That was true. In their transitory camp, Tathrin had seen the Greater Moon a day closer to its full and the Lesser Moon rising nearly at its half in the clear cold night. But Evord had insisted they halt.

"The captain-general said the risk wasn't worth the reward."

Sorgrad agreed. "Duke Garnot can lame his horses and commandeer fresh ones at the next farm. We can't afford delays and we'd have to pay even if we could find remounts. On the other hand, the duke won't want to get too far ahead of his foot regiments. We'll catch him." He had no doubt about that.

"The sooner the better." Gren smiled with anticipation.

Tathrin didn't feel nearly so sanguine. The array of standards looked impressive but their mounted companies totalled maybe seven hundred and fifty men and women, less than a quarter of their full muster of horsemen as long as the Dalasorian lancers were still absent.

After the serious losses he'd suffered in the woods, Duke Garnot had around the same number of mercenary cavalry and around two thousand men on foot.

In his guise as Captain-General Evord's clerk, Tathrin had been tallying the Carluse figures: the muster rolls of the mercenaries who'd surrendered, those who'd retreated in good order, along with estimates of the militia fled or rallied. Then there was the count of the enemy wounded, roughly bandaged and dismissed to fend for themselves, and the final grim total of corpses. It was probably safe to assume Evord now had a thousand more foot soldiers than Garnot, he had concluded. Until some other duke managed to send reinforcements.

Sorgrad was looking more closely at him. "What's the weevil in your bread this morning?"

Tathrin cleared his throat. "I don't like seeing the dead burned in common pits." That was true, if not the whole truth.

"Can't fight battles without burials." Gren waved a dismissive hand.

"I don't expect you to understand," Tathrin said shortly.

"Because we're savage uplanders who throw our own dead into holes in the ground?" Sorgrad narrowed his blue eyes. "I understand your customs. I was shaking the dust of these roads off my boots when you were still in leading strings."

"Arest's lads would rather be burned than left for carrion crows," Gren asserted.

"Never mind."

Tathrin would have thought mercenaries would want to delay their arrival before Saedrin, not hasten it with the dissolution of fire. As long as their mortal remains endured, they didn't have to answer for their evil deeds or suffer the torments of Poldrion's demons until Saedrin judged them worthy to pass through his door to the Otherworld.

Regardless, he was more concerned with living mercenaries than the dead. He fought an urge to look back over his shoulder again. Where were the Carluse mercenaries who'd abandoned Duke Garnot's cause and surrendered after the battle?

Captain-General Evord had promised them a swift death on a gibbet if he ever saw their faces again. They'd given him their oath they'd quit Lescar entirely. But what was the word of someone fighting for the richest paymaster worth? If they were heading away, what destruction were they wreaking as they went?

The road ran down towards a dip between two low hills and he squinted into the bright morning sun.

"Horse!" Gren's eyes were keen, despite his idle demeanour.

Sorgrad recognised the Dalasorian dapple galloping towards them. "There's one of Sia Kersain's girls."

Regardless, Captain-General Evord's retinue closed up until several of the gallopers identified the young woman as one of those skirmishers who'd ridden ahead through the night.

Evord glanced swiftly at Tathrin. He knew what the Soluran was asking and shook his head. No, there was no fresh word of the lancer regiments who had seized Ashgil.

Gren was reading a stone waymark by the roadside. "Forty-six leagues back to Abray. Thirty leagues to Dromin off yonder." He gathered up his reins and nodded forwards. "That means we're within a league of Carluse Town."

The brothers knew these roads as well or better than Tathrin. He'd only made the journey through the forest a few times, with his father and a few other guildsmen covertly trading white brandy without paying Duke Garnot's tariff. Tathrin's father only ran such a risk when he was desperate for coin to pay the festival levy. The forest road was perilous for anyone not riding with forty-some mercenary companies and nearly half as many again made up of Mountain Men. Even with the three regiments of Dalasorian lancers currently absent, Evord's army was a daunting force.

He saw the captain-general clap a congratulatory hand on the girl's shoulder and look round at all his gallopers. "Duke Garnot is just ahead of us. Now we make him stand and fight!"

Evord's retinue spurred their horses to a canter. Gallopers headed up and down the line, spreading the word. As the pace quickened, dust rose to obscure mounts and men alike. Tathrin settled himself in his saddle, apprehension crawling up his spine. How could they possibly win a decisive victory until their marching regiments caught up?

Hooves loud all around him, they reached the dip between the low hills. Ahead, the Vale of Carluse offered placid grazing and a few copses separating ploughed fields. It was deserted. No one worked the fields or drove a wagon. Stock was penned in barn and byre and every building within sight was shuttered close.

The highway ran towards the silver thread of the little river that watered this stretch of the vale. A bridge carried the road over towards the market town of Tyrle, three days or more further south. On this side of the water, a broad fork headed for Carluse Town. Tathrin's eyes followed the road to the hill where the first duke had built his castle while the Old Tormalin Empire crumbled to ruins around him.

It stood alone on the grassy plain. High on the summit, the castle's towers flaunted Duke Garnot's flag. Below, a lattice of streets spread down the flanks of the hill, finally curbed by the solid bulwark of the town wall encircling the bottom. Ashgil's disastrous sloth wasn't tolerated here. Carluse Town's battlements were in fine fettle.

As they cantered, the horses shoulder to shoulder, Tathrin saw sunlight glinting on armour up on the town's gatehouse. This formidable bastion was the only way into the town. Fighting up through all the houses and workshops was the only way to reach the castle. There was no matching incline on the far side . Anyone approaching on the highway from

Ashgil would see Duke Garnot's stronghold perched atop a sheer crag.

The duke's forces were marching swiftly along the road. From this vantage point, Tathrin could see the six regiments clearly: three with black and white militia banners, three with many-hued mercenary standards, one at the front and two at the rear. The army didn't look appreciably smaller, even though Tathrin knew their numbers should be reduced by a quarter or so. Could Duke Garnot have summoned up some new muster of militiamen, some mercenaries he'd kept in reserve?

Gren chuckled and patted his bay gelding's neck. "It's a race to the gates."

"We'll win it," Sorgrad promised grimly, shortening his reins.

If Evord's force didn't currently have the advantage in numbers, they certainly had it in speed. Duke Garnot had only one mounted regiment, riding close behind the duke's retinue. Everyone else, mercenaries and militia alike, marched along the gravelled road.

"What's that?" Tathrin sat up straight in his saddle.

"Horn calls," Sorgrad said with satisfaction.

The leading companies of Evord's horsemen accelerated to a gallop as they reached level ground. Tathrin's own horse plunged forwards, eager to follow. He curbed the beast with firm hands. The captain-general was still holding his retinue to a placid canter.

Even with his greater height Tathrin could see little beyond the shifting riders ahead. Where were those brazen cries coming from? Was it encouragement from Carluse Town's battlements? Then the curve of the road gave him a clearer view.

There was nowhere for the highway proper to go beyond the castle so it didn't enter the town. Skirting the town wall, it disappeared in the shadow of the crag. Now Tathrin saw Dalasorian lancers appearing from behind the outcrop, their horns singing. Flags waved frantically from the Carluse Town gate.

Gren chuckled. "His Grace won't know whether to piss or shit himself."

Sorgrad hissed between his teeth. "It's too soon."

Tathrin didn't understand him. There was no way Duke Garnot could reach Carluse Town now without fighting the Dalasorians. The horsemen were spreading out, the forest of lances lowering to menace each side of the beleaguered Carlusian column. Tremors shook the assembled banners. Surely their victory over Carluse was complete?

At the captain-general's signal, Evord's retinue left the road to assemble where the incline still afforded a clear view. The mounted companies of the rearguard cantered past.

The Carluse column was breaking up. The foremost companies were at a standstill, those at the rear edging backwards.

Tathrin frowned. The Dalasorian troops were still riding along on either side of the road. "Aren't they going to charge?"

"Not while their archers still have arrows," reproved Gren.

Bodies already lay scattered along the verges. As the Carlusian regiments fragmented, the mounted bowmen deftly picked off stragglers. To the north of the road Tathrin saw individual Dalasorian troops break off from Pata Mezian's regiment to gallop towards the widening gaps. Militiamen hastily presented a ferocious palisade of halberds. The Dalasorians wheeled away, their assault a mere feint to distract their foe.

Because Sia Kersain was attacking from the south. Militiamen and mercenary companies alike broke and ran as the clan lord's lancers ripped through their ranks. Banners waved frantically to recall those made of stern stuff, but before the Carlusians could reunite effectively, Pata Mezian's regiment attacked in earnest.

Carluse men huddled together, halberds bristling. That saved them from the lancers' charge but Dalasorian archers scarcely needed to aim to find a victim in such close-packed ranks. Mercenary bowmen rallied sufficiently to loose their own ragged volleys. Too late. Their mounted assailants were already well beyond bowshot.

"Skewered like festival fowl," said Gren with satisfaction.

"Not yet." Sorgrad pointed. "I said they attacked too early."

Duke Garnot's remaining mounted regiment knew attacking the Dalasorians was folly. Giving their horses full rein, they abandoned the battle for the road to the west. The duke's own banner was right in their midst.

"They're heading for the bridge," Tathrin realised.

"They are," Sorgrad agreed grimly.

The Carluse mounted regiment quickly reached the village divided by the fast-flowing little river. The foot soldiers saw their duke was making a stand. Some were unable to follow, those knots of men surrounded by circling lancers. Others saw no hope of reaching the bridge, throwing down their swords and raising empty hands. The rest sought safety in re-forming as best they could, pressing close together and retreating down the road. Mercenaries wearing the boar's head flanked black-and-white-liveried militiamen and refused to let them flee. Faced with this impenetrable defiance, the Dalasorians turned their horses for the Carluse Town gate, cutting down any lingering unfortunates as they went.

"Where are they going?" Tathrin demanded.

"To stop Duke Garnot's garrison coming to lend a hand," growled Sorgrad.

Gren was watching Evord's cavalry. "Have they been feeding those horses plum pudding?"

Despite their best efforts, Tathrin saw their own mounted mercenary regiments couldn't stop the Carluse column making haste to the sanctuary of the village by the bridge.

Tathrin's stomach churned with sympathy for his countrymen. How scared they must be, so weary after the battle in the woods and the long march they had just made. Every man must be suffering with bruises and festering scrapes, so thirsty from the dust of the road.

The mercenaries were jog-trotting along, still in their companies, banners disciplined. Tathrin recognised the black eel on the green flag. Slippery Captain Dorish was leading another resolute retreat.

"Shit," Sorgrad spat with disgust.

The first Carluse ranks reached the shelter of the village. The foremost riders of Evord's army were just reaching the tail-enders, drawn swords bright in the sunlight. Men fell dead in the dust but the riders could do scant damage before arrows from the village forced them back. There was no way they could mount a charge amid the stone houses and narrow lanes. Horns called as Evord's mounted company captains drew their men back to a safe distance.

Gren loosened his sword in its scabbard. "When do we get to fight?"

"We don't," Sorgrad said grimly. "Not if Duke Garnot has half the sense he was born with. He'll leave a rearguard to hold the bridge and head for Tyrle to regroup."

Tathrin looked at him, aghast. How was he going to tell Aremil their hopes of defeating Duke Garnot had vanished a second time?

He looked at Evord, to see the captain-general talking to a swarthy Dalasorian galloper, both men fluent in the Old Tormalin that was the fallen Empire's legacy to all their erstwhile conquests. It was the language of scholarship too, enabling Tathrin to understand them.

"No, he cannot abandon his castle. Duchess Tadira is in residence there."

"You wish to lay siege?" the weather-beaten rider demanded.

"With Duke Garnot's men at our backs to harass us?" The captain-general looked grimly towards the bridge. "No, we must break him once and for all today. We must cross the bridge and take that village before the Carlusians can rally and march south."

Gren turned to the west. "Do you hear that?"

Tathrin looked back up the high road. Faint in the distance he heard a swift rhythm.

"That's better," Sorgrad allowed. "Once our foot regiments and the Mountain Men arrive we'll have five men to every two of theirs."

A pock-faced lieutenant raised a hand. Tathrin recognised him from a company called the Shearlings, who marched under a ram's head banner. "Can we get over the river anywhere else? To strike them in the flank."

Evord shook his head. "The next nearest bridge is half a day's march."

The Shearling looked at Sorgrad. "Can Mountain Men swim?"

"If we must." He looked dubious.

The swarthy Dalasorian laughed. "Our horses swim. Few bridges on the plains."

Tathrin reluctantly cleared his throat. "There's a ford, not too far away."

Evord looked at him with a steely interest. "Where?"

Tathrin knew the Soluran had pored over their maps so long he could have drawn them out blindfold. There was no ford marked this close to Carluse.

He hesitated. "It may not be safe with the river so high."

"Who cares about safe?" Gren chuckled. "Halcarion favours the bold."

"Show me." Evord snapped his fingers. "A map!"

One of his Soluran lieutenants was already unfurling one.

"It's a secret, to avoid the duke's tolls on the bridges." Tathrin urged his horse to the captain-general's side. "My father showed me once." He pointed to a bend in the river hidden from the town by a shallow knoll. "There, I think." He paused. "Maybe a little further."

"Right under Duke Garnot's nose?" The Shearling was openly sceptical.

"I crossed it with my father." Tathrin set his jaw.

He'd never been so frightened, not till he'd marched with this army anyway. If Duke Garnot's personal guard had caught them, they'd all have been hanged. His father made no secret of that.

Mercenaries would take the precious white brandy for themselves and maybe let them live. As it was, the Lesser Moon's crescent had been Halcarion's smile and they'd gone undetected.

Evord looked at him. "Would you recognise the place again?"

"I think so." Tathrin nodded. They'd crossed in the last chime of the night. It would surely be easier to find in full daylight.

"Then go with Astamin Ikar." Evord nodded to the Dalasorian, writing swiftly. "Give my compliments to Sia Kersain and will he please take his troops over the river while Pata Mezian's regiment keeps the Carluse Town garrison penned. Sia Kersain is to seize the Tyrle Road and strike Duke Garnot in the rear. As soon as he does that, we'll launch our assault from the front. That should break them."

"As you command." Taking the written copy of the orders, the Dalasorian urged his horse into a gallop.

Tathrin spurred his own mount to follow. Sorgrad's horse sprang forward beside him, eager to outstrip the rival steed. Gren pressed close on his other side.

"You're coming too?" Tathrin didn't know whether to be relieved or concerned.

"I don't want to have to tell Charoleia we let some Carluse militiaman skewer you." Sorgrad's smile widened. "Or Failla, come to that."

CHAPTER TEN
Tathrin

**The Battle for Carluse Bridge,
1ˢᵗ of Aft-Autumn**

THEY SOON CAUGHT up with Astamin Ikar. It took longer to reach Sia Kersain's lancers, circling below the walls of Carluse Town. Troops distinguished by their clan colours were racing in all directions. Flags waved urgently from the gatehouse, answered by signals from the castle's lofty towers.

"What are they saying?" Tathrin shouted to Gren, gesturing up at the walls.

"It's a feint to draw them out," he yelled back.

Tathrin slowed to let his horse catch its breath. Astamin Ikar was explaining their new task to Sia Kersain, his gestures animated. The clan lord nodded and intricate horn calls immediately summoned his troop captains. They meant nothing to Tathrin but he knew the Dalasorians had no trouble distinguishing them. Each child grew up with the horns' voices as familiar as their mother tongue, by far the best way of communicating across the grasslands.

Dalasorian children rode as readily as they walked, following the herds of cattle and horses across the boundless plains. Boundless but not trackless: roads cut through those northern lands. Traders' packhorses brought metals and furs from the far Gidestan Mountains to Tormalin, to Caladhria and the towns of Ensaimin. Merchants' wagons carried fine goods crafted by the smiths and tanners of distant Inglis. Since empty carts offered no profit, those same merchants took luxuries from southern climes back to the remote north-eastern city, along with Aldabreshin spices and jewels from the perilous Archipelago.

Merchants had no interest in cattle. Dalasorians needed coin to buy the luxuries that proved their status among their clans, the gifts that cemented alliances. Evord had promised them good Tormalin gold along with the pick of whatever horses they captured.

Tathrin saw Sia Kersain's troop was now riding towards them. As they galloped the Dalasorians shouted eagerly in their own tongue.

"What's got them so excited?" Tathrin called out to Sorgrad.

"Sia Kersain says those who distinguish themselves get first pick of Duke Garnot's stables."

As their horses joined the galloping Dalasorians,

the wind snatched away whatever Gren said about that. Tathrin caught a glimpse of Jettin as they rode on, but soon lost the youth amid the throng of riders.

He looked briefly at Carluse Town as they passed by. Failla had friends and family behind those walls, even if those who didn't know of her valour as the guildsmen's spy had disowned her as Duke Garnot's whore. If he could save them from a siege or worse, that was some small service he could do her.

Sia Kersain led them onwards, the rangy Dalasorian horses unflagging. Tathrin forced his horse close to the clan lord, Sorgrad and Gren close behind.

"My lord!" He pointed as he shouted. "We must follow that defile, so we can't be seen from the walls."

They could only cross the river safely if the Carluse sentries believed the Dalasorians had ridden right around the crag, in some vain hope of finding another way into the town.

Sia Kersain waved an acknowledgement and turned down the crease in the land. His riders pressed close behind, horses jostling through the stunted trees.

Was the knoll between the town and the river tall enough to hide them as they cut across to the river? Tathrin couldn't worry about that now. He searched desperately for the markers his father had shown him on that night so long ago. Where was the scar of that quarry where the hills rose from the fertile plain? Saedrin save him, why had he ever opened his mouth? Then he saw the notch in the northern horizon.

"Stop!" He reined in his horse and looked across the river.

"So where's the ford?" Gren scanned the flourishing undergrowth on the far bank. "No one's passed this way lately."

"We have to draw a line from that quarry right across the river to Trimon's shrine over there." Among the drab roofs clustered around the bridge, Tathrin easily found the white tiles, even if the travelling god's harp was merely an indistinct smudge of brown.

"We must hurry." Sia Kersain rode up. "They will see from the castle as soon as we cross."

Sorgrad nodded. "They'll risk fifty men to slip one through to warn the duke."

Five hundred or more lancers, more than half as many mounted archers and they were all looking at Tathrin. Some exchanged doubtful remarks in their own tongue.

He drew a nervous breath. "May I have a lance?"

Even with the lack of recent rain the dark waters were flowing higher than they had in the height of the summer he had last been here.

A skirmisher handed over his weapon. Tathrin dismounted to probe the water. Mud sucked at the pole and he had to wrench it free. A second attempt had no better result and the drag of the water was stronger than he expected. Too narrow and awkward to be profitably navigable, the river was nevertheless deep enough to be perilous.

On foot he couldn't see the shrine. With the Dalasorians gathered so close, he had no clear view of the horizon. He stabbed at the water and nearly lost his precarious footing. The lance saved him, striking something firm.

He looked up at Sia Kersain. "I think this is it. There are flat stones on either side of the ford, to stop the gravel being washed away."

The Dalasorian shouted and three men and a couple of women hurried forwards with ropes and lance poles.

Sorgrad led Tathrin's horse up. "Well done."

"Thanks." He scrambled back into his saddle, breathless with relief.

The Dalasorian horses plunged into the water, trailing ropes. Others followed to mark the hidden path with poles. A chestnut gelding staggered, water frothing white around its chest. Sia Kersain was shouting orders in his own tongue again.

"Once we're across, we form up before heading for the bridge," Sorgrad translated.

The first troop begin crossing, four abreast. One horse jibbed. That disconcerted the one beside it. Those following close behind slowed. A black mare stumbled, its rider nearly losing his seat. Those waiting to cross shouted a warning.

Sorgrad glanced at Tathrin. "Cross too slowly and the river could take you."

He nodded. "I see that."

Now the horses faced the challenge of the far bank. The first to scramble out trampled the yellowing vegetation. Those who followed found the crushed leaves treacherously slick. The edge of the bank was soon crumbling into muddy smears snatched away by the river. The first Dalasorians across were shouting, waving from the far bank.

"We need to start as close to the upstream edge of the ford as we can." Gren indicated the ropes now slung between the poles.

Tathrin chewed his lower lip, trying to judge how long each troop was taking to negotiate the ford. The procession waiting to cross the turbid river seemed endless. He counted the pennants on the far bank. Two troops of mounted archers had already crossed and four of lancers.

But the captain-general must have judged they could make the crossing and still turn the battle against Duke Garnot. He would never have sent them here otherwise, not just on Tathrin's word.

Sia Kersain and his skirmishers plunged into the water. Gren urged his horse forwards. Sorgrad forced his mount close to Tathrin's side. "Our turn."

The water rose up his thighs, bitterly cold. His horse shuddered, searching for a foothold. He tried to kick the reluctant beast on. It was astonishingly difficult with the water pressing on his legs. Someone screamed. Tathrin couldn't tell who. Shouts erupted all around, incomprehensible Dalasorian fury.

"Down!" Sorgrad's hand smacked the back of his neck.

Tathrin banged his nose on his horse's mane. "What—?"

"Arrows!" Sorgrad shoved him again.

Tathrin heard their vicious chirrup. A man screamed and fell from his horse to vanish beneath the water. The masterless horse floundered. Other horses tried to move away, resisting their own riders' authority.

More men and women were falling victim to the archers, knocked into the maelstrom of thrashing hooves. Tathrin saw a woman grab desperately for a drowning man, his life's blood streaming into the water from a gash on the side of his head.

"Come on!" Gren lashed his horse mercilessly with a looped rein.

There was a momentary lull in the arrows. Tathrin heard swords clashing up on the bank. Clinging desperately to his saddle, he forced his horse up the pitted slope, flanked by Gren and Sorgrad. Up on the grass, Dalasorians were locked in combat with a mounted company of mercenaries.

"The slack-arsed Locksmiths!" Gren drew his sword. "I'll have that bastard Iverac!"

"Follow Sia Kersain," Sorgrad shouted, "or I'll tan your hide for a waterskin!"

Tathrin felt sick. How could he have been so stupid? If he knew about the ford, other folk were bound to. Someone, mercenary or militiaman, must have told Duke Garnot and he'd sent the Locksmiths here to hold it. Where was Jettin? Could he use his Artifice to send word back to the captain-general?

Tathrin searched frantically for the Vanamese youth's curly head but couldn't see it anywhere. Was he dead or fallen? He looked back to see horses and riders still crowding each other in the water. The drowned were now hindering the living until the corpses broke free to be swept downstream.

Sia Kersain was shouting, standing tall in his stirrups. Tathrin saw a troop of vengeful riders skirt the Locksmiths' line to bear down on the archers at the waterside. The bowmen saw death coming for them and ran back to the mounted men holding their steeds. As they fled, the rest of the Locksmiths began extricating themselves from the mêlée. The Dalasorians weren't letting them go without a struggle. Lancers and swordsmen fell to the ground, screaming and bleeding, horses bolting in all directions.

Gren was swearing in the Mountain tongue, murderously angry. Sorgrad was silent, pale hair sleek with water, his blue eyes darkly opaque. Tathrin's horse followed its stablemates after Sia Kersain. The clan lord's troop was already galloping away from the chaos, intent on the battle at the bridge.

Hands numb inside his slippery gloves, Tathrin clung desperately to his reins. He couldn't stop shivering. The padding of his armoured jacket was saturated with cold water and his boots squelched in his stirrups.

Locksmiths, archers and swordsmen were all racing towards the village. He could hear horses pounding behind him. How many Dalasorians had been lost in the crossing? He didn't dare look.

Sia Kersain's troop found a lane. Sorgrad followed, then Gren and Tathrin. Dust rose to turn the horses' foaming sweat to mud. On either side, Dalasorian riders came crashing through the hedges, more lost as their weary horses stumbled.

Houses appeared sooner than Tathrin expected. Sia Kersain's pennant swerved violently as horns sounded and the Dalasorians divided. Tathrin's horse reared and tried to charge after those who were heading south towards Tyrle.

Sorgrad's horse blocked his path. "Head for the bridge," he bellowed.

Tathrin's horse bucked and kicked, confused and frustrated. He knew just how it felt.

"Where's the Locksmiths?" yelled Gren.

A sudden wave of Dalasorians swept Tathrin towards the river. He saw the village, the hump of the bridge ahead. Men in Carluse livery dashed between the houses, amid mercenaries in leather and chain mail. Were they Duke Garnot's hirelings or had Evord's men already made their way across?

He could feel the weight of his sword on his hip but he made no effort to draw it. Sorgrad's lessons hadn't included fighting from horseback. The best he could hope for was not getting killed till he could push clear of the slaughter and find his way back to Evord's retinue.

Limp bodies lay ungainly in the gutters, just as they had in Emirle Bridge. Innocent men and women, like the dead of Sharlac and Losand and Ashgil. All for the sake of freeing Lescar from warfare. The bitter irony threatened to choke him.

Then Tathrin saw mercenaries throwing down their weapons. Banners dropped too fast for him to see their blazons. Who was surrendering? Had Evord's men won the day? Or Duke Garnot? All around Dalasorian lancers slowed, equally uncertain.

An instant later Tathrin wrenched out his sword. Carluse militia were charging across the bridge towards them. Those Dalasorians still carrying lances levelled them and Gren whooped with delight, crouching low on his horse's neck. Sorgrad spurred his mount towards the oncoming foe and Tathrin's horse galloped with them.

But Tathrin saw the liveried men were tossing their halberds aside. They fled in all directions, faces twisted with terror. Blood and muck already stained the white quartering of their tunics. Those too injured to run any further collapsed in the futile shelter of doorways, their faces blank and hopeless.

Tathrin sheathed his sword as his horse slowed, its head drooping, finally exhausted.

"Where's the captain-general?" Gren shouted out to someone.

Tathrin didn't catch the reply. Where was Duke Garnot? That was more to the point.

They turned a corner and he saw the white roof of Trimon's shrine, the village's marketplace overlooked by the travelling god's statue.

Evord sat on his horse, nodding as a burly mercenary captain wound his green banner around its staff and laid it down in surrender.

"That's the Slippery Eels," Gren said, irritated. "Where's the bastard Locksmiths?"

More mercenaries marched into the square. Men wearing yellow and cream kerchiefs guarded men with their hands on their heads. Duke Garnot's black and white tokens were trodden underfoot.

"Tathrin!" The Tallyman riding with Evord's retinue came running over, grinning. "The captain-general wants you."

"Go on, lad." Sorgrad reached for his reins.

"Have we won?" Tathrin slid from his saddle. He could hardly believe it.

"For today." The Tallyman nodded. "They made a better fist of holding off our foot regiments than I would have expected. More of their column got across the bridge than we hoped. But when they saw your Dalasorians coming, the mercenaries had to split to cover that flank. The militia lost their nerve and began running. The duke said he was going to get help from Tyrle but only a fool would believe that." He gestured towards the surrendering captain. "Dorish knows his men won't see a payday as long as Garnot's locked out of his castle so he decided to cut their losses."

"I wonder who's read the same as him in the runes." Sorgrad surveyed the captured men sitting down on the dusty cobbles.

Tathrin was astonished to realise some of them were already casting handfuls of the three-sided runes. Did every mercenary carry a set of the nine triangular bones? Could any of them truly believe the future was predicted in the fall of the angular symbols, one face down, the other two upright or reversed on each game piece? Back in Vanam, Tathrin had heard that these primitive customs persisted in the distant forests beyond Ensaimin. He hadn't expected mercenaries to trust such superstitions.

No, they must just be gambling, an inveterate habit among companies of men who hazarded their own lives so readily.

It wasn't as if any consistent logic underpinned the runes. True, the Sun, the Greater Moon and the Lesser made an obvious trio. One could see a certain sense in the Deer, the Oak and the Forest sharing a bone, like the Salmon, the Reed and the Sea; the Wolf, the Pine and the Mountain, and the Eagle, the Broom and the Plains. Who could argue the Wolf was stronger than the Deer, the Eagle stronger than the Salmon?

But Air, the Storm and the Chime? Calm, the Earth and the Drum? Why should the Mountain Wind be linked with Fire and the Horn? The Sea

Breeze with Water and the Harp. Why was the Harp stronger than the Horn? The Reed stronger than the Broom plant? It irritated Tathrin nearly as much as the irregular divisions of the seasons. No one could argue over either Solstice and Equinox but the turns from each aft-season to the next for-season were arbitrarily determined by priests in Saedrin's biggest temples. Did they roll a rune to decide?

"Hey, did you take a clout to the head or something?"

Tathrin blinked as Gren snapped his fingers right under his nose. He hastily gathered his wandering thoughts. This was no time to take refuge in the academic debates he'd enjoyed in Vanam, however much he might wish he was back there.

"Yes. I'm listening."

The Tallyman shrugged. "From what we can tell, Duke Garnot's got a scant cavalry regiment left and twenty-some companies of foot still following."

"Will these men be hanged?" Tathrin asked with misgiving. He remembered the stench lingering around Losand when the prisoners from Wynald's Warband were executed.

"When we need reinforcements?" The Tallyman was startled. "You don't waste a mind as sharp as Dorish's."

Tathrin saw the stocky man bend to retrieve his company's standard.

"I'll gladly accept your service." Evord's words rang around the marketplace as his lieutenant returned Captain Dorish's sword.

The mercenary brandished it boldly. "We'll gladly pay Duke Garnot back for his cowardice!"

That won a cheer from Evord's men and those who'd just abandoned Carluse alike.

Tathrin was astonished. He was even more surprised to see a few cautiously opened shutters around the marketplace, as men from all the different companies knocked on doors, offering Tormalin gold for bread and ale. Then he saw the captain-general beckoning and hurried forwards.

"In here, I think." Evord led him into Trimon's shrine. "Find Jettin and tell him to send word to Aremil. Duke Garnot is beaten."

"You've captured him?" Tathrin's heart leaped.

"No, but I'll settle for what we've won today." Evord smiled thinly. "Duke Garnot has fled for Tyrle with the remnants of his army. Tell Aremil I want Reniack to set every tavern in Lescar buzzing with the news that Duke Garnot has abandoned both his castle and his duchess."

"We've taken Carluse Town?" Then Duke Garnot was surely beaten.

"No." Evord blighted Tathrin's hopes once again. "But Pata Mezian has the town garrison securely penned."

Tathrin stripped off his sodden gloves and ran a filthy hand through his hair. "I thought we couldn't risk a siege."

"Besieging Duke Garnot with all his mercenaries and militia safely inside the town would be one thing. Camping at Carluse's gates while we wait for Duchess Tadira to see she's no choice but to yield the castle is quite another. We need to rest the horses and tend our wounded regardless, and we must deal with all these prisoners."

"You're paying Duke Garnot's mercenaries to turn their coats?" Tathrin couldn't help the doubt in his voice.

"Only those we agree we can trust," Evord assured him. "All our own captains must say yea or nay before any company joins us."

"What happens to the ones you don't want?"

Evord understood what Tathrin was asking.

"The men of Wynald's Warband indulged their every base lust while they rode under Duke Garnot's protection. They paid the penalty." Evord looked at the statue of Trimon. "If anyone here accuses these men, they will stand trial according to Lescari laws. But most are honestly fighting for hire. I want whatever companies march with Draximal and Parnilesse to know they can surrender to us safely.

"That said," the Soluran continued, "there will be plenty we've captured who we don't want and plenty who'll scorn our offer. Far too many to let loose this time. Duke Garnot may be a broken spear but Marlier and Draximal will be recruiting all the swords they can. Our prisoners must be escorted to Abray under guard. Tell Aremil that Master Gruit needs to prepare the Caladhrians for their arrival. Master Reniack should send some of his songsters and storytellers along to persuade them to keep walking westwards."

"What about the Carluse militia?"

"As long as they give us their oath not to raise arms against us again, they can go home—with a full belly," Evord added, "and their wounds tended and all their autumn levies excused. That's another task for Reniack, to spread word of our clemency as widely as he can. As soon as we take the castle, anyone who's already paid Duke Garnot's levy will get their coin back."

Tathrin was surprised into a grin. "You will be popular, my lord."

"My rank is captain-general," Evord reminded him. "Make sure your countrymen know it. Everyone must believe I'm not looking to rule in Duke Garnot or Duke Moncan's stead. Now, once you've told Aremil everything that's happened here today, I need all the latest news that Dagaran has gathered from Sharlac, Losand and Ashgil. We must make sure all our gains thus far are garrisoned. We have to secure Carluse Town as soon as Duchess Tadira surrenders."

"How soon will that be?" Tathrin wondered.

Evord looked thoughtful. "It could be all the sooner if we can get word to Failla's uncle the priest. Tell Aremil to ask if she knows any hidden ways in through the walls."

CHAPTER ELEVEN
Failla

**Abray, on the Border of Lescar and Caladhria,
4th of Aft-Autumn**

"MY LADY." THE grey-gowned maid bobbed a
curtsey as she opened the door.

"Thank you, Courra." Entering the house, Failla
handed the girl her painted silk shawl and her
bonnet, a frivolous curl of woven straw adorned with
iridescent feathers from the wild isles of Aldabreshi
warlords. "Where's Master Gruit?"

"He's with Master Cardel and Baron Dacren."
The girl bobbed another nervous curtsey at the
mention of those formidable men. "They've sent
for their coach so I'm sure they'll be leaving
soon."

Failla checked her reflection in the mirror and
smoothed her apricot silk dress. "Is there a fire in
the honeysuckle salon?"

165

Though the days continued bright and clear, more like Aft-Summer than Aft-Autumn, the afternoon sunshine had been deceptive. That elegant shawl hadn't been nearly enough to keep her warm, even on the short carriage ride from Baroness Lynast's house.

"Yes, my lady." Thin-faced and ginger-haired, the maid curtseyed yet again. "Shall I bring you some almond cordial, my lady?"

"Yes, please." Failla smiled. "And spiced wafer cakes?"

She longed to tell the girl there was no need to go in awe of her. To explain she'd known the biting poverty that had robbed Courra of most of her teeth. But she had her role to play here, so she must act like a lady who'd been pampered since birth. Still, she'd insist the girl accept a cake when she brought them.

"I can open the salon door myself." She smiled to take any sting from her words. "Just take my hat and shawl to my dressing room and then fetch the cordial and cakes."

As Duke Garnot's mistress, she'd been tacitly ignored by most of his servants, covertly scorned by those loyal to Duchess Tadira. If she played the queen at the duke's high table whenever the duchess was absent, everyone knew that was as much an illusion as a juggler's tricks. Her rich gowns were all bought for the duke's pleasure, and every stitch of lace beneath. If he tired of her, Garnot could throw her out naked, everyone knew that. Anyone who imagined she had traded her virtue for wealth and influence would have agreed they'd been sadly mistaken.

Now she pretended she was Master Gruit's niece, a merchant whom Garnot would disdain as lacking any rank. Yet all these gowns and jewels were hers to keep, along with the daily allowance of small silver that the old wine merchant pressed into her hand. She smiled as she headed for the honeysuckle salon, halting only as the main door to the street opened a second time, unheralded by the knocker.

"Here's Mama!" The nursemaid ushered in a little girl wearing a lemon linen gown in much the same style as Failla's. Though the child was spared the rigour of a boned bodice and her hems prudently ended above her ankles. A cream wool wrap saved her from the season's chills.

"Mama?" The child's soft brown eyes searched the cobalt-tiled hall.

"Here I am, my love." Failla sank down, her arms outstretched. "Anilt?"

"Go to Mama." Untucking her wrap, the nursemaid encouraged her charge with a gentle push.

The little girl's rose-petal lips twisted with disappointment. "Mama?" She advanced uncertainly.

"Little chick." Failla embraced her.

Her heart ached as she felt Anilt stiffen, resisting. She hid her face in the child's soft black curls. As dark and curly as Duke Garnot's hair. She didn't imagine these servants wondered about Anilt's father, though. They'd be gossiping about the way the child barely seemed to know her own mother.

"She needs her nap, my lady," the nursemaid apologised. "We have had a long walk."

"Walk," Anilt agreed brightly, looking up at the woman.

"Of course." Failla relinquished her daughter. Lessons in hiding humiliation learned in Carluse Castle proved useful in this household. "But join me when she's rested. We'll play with your ducks, shall we, chick?"

She smiled hopefully at Anilt and was rewarded with a giggle. "Ducks!"

It would take time. Drianon save them both, it wasn't even twenty days since she'd reclaimed her child. But it was hard, and harder still not to resent Lathi's hold on Anilt's heart. And that was unforgivable, when all her cousin had done was help hide Failla's pregnancy and save Anilt from life as a duke's bastard, her only value as a game piece in Duchess Tadira's petticoat diplomacy.

Before the nursemaid replied, a door across the panelled hall opened and three men emerged from the library.

"Upstairs, young lady." The nursemaid took Anilt's hand to hurry her.

"Madam Sibetha," pleaded Gruit. "Indulge an old man after a long day's business."

Anilt was already twisting free of her nurse's restraint. She ran towards Gruit, her arms upraised. Failla hid the pang that cost her. Anilt had known Gruit for ten days and adored him from the first.

"Here's my favourite little chick." Gruit swept her up with an ease that belied his wrinkles and snowy white hair. "Now, Anilt, say good day to these fine gentlemen."

The three men laughed as she hid her face in the furred collar of his grass-green mantle.

"Good day to you, my little lady." His midnight-blue gown as old-fashioned as Gruit's, Baron Dacren bowed stiffly, leaning on his cane. His indulgent smile told Failla he was as fond a grandsire as any little girl could wish for.

Anilt looked around shyly. "Good day," she said with endearing precision.

"Your great-niece will be a beauty to equal her mother." Master Cardel, as yet showing only a touch of white at his chestnut temples, glanced across the hall to Failla. Pressing a hand to his red velvet paunch, he made her a polite half-bow.

"You are very gallant." Failla made sure her smile was no more than common civility. That gleam in Cardel's eye suggested he had more than compliments in mind. After all, she was supposedly the favoured niece of one wealthy merchant, and the widow of another, whom she'd honoured with a child thus proving her fertility.

Well, Failla had no intention of encouraging any man's advances, save perhaps one, but he wasn't here nor likely to be so any time soon. Did Tathrin think of her, she wondered?

"Ah, my friends, here's your carriage," Gruit said with honest regret.

They all heard the rattle of wheels and harness outside.

"We must bid you farewell, Mistress Failla," Baron Dacren apologised. "It's no weather to keep horses standing."

"Assuredly not," she agreed.

Courra hastily set Failla's hat and shawl on a side table and hurried to open the door, revealing a warmly caped coachman.

"Good day." Baron Dacren held out a wrinkled hand to Gruit. "Please congratulate your cook for serving such an elegant meal. And thank you for the food for thought."

Failla saw a shrewd glint in the old man's eye. What had they been saying in such privacy? Master Gruit had opened the library door himself, so they'd had no servant inside to fill their wine glasses, tend the hearth or overhear their conversation.

"A good deal to mull over." Master Cardel offered the older man his arm and helped him down the steps. The coachman closed the door behind them.

Gruit looked from Failla to the nursemaid. "Let's all take some cordial and wafers, shall we?"

"Cakes?" Anilt piped up hopefully.

"Just one," Gruit warned. "Otherwise you won't eat your supper and Madam Sibetha will scold me."

"Don't think I won't," the nursemaid agreed, amused. "Ring for me if she gets fractious." She curtseyed impartially to Gruit and Failla. "Master. My lady."

Still carrying Anilt, Gruit headed back into the library. "So tell me about your afternoon."

Failla longed to hold her daughter herself. Anilt would surely come to love her better if they could spend more time together. But Master Gruit had established this household in the pattern he'd known back in Vanam, when his wife had still lived and his two daughters ran around in short skirts. As far as he was concerned, children always had nursemaids to relieve women of the burden of motherhood.

Hopefully his daughters would soon present him with a covey of grandchildren. It wasn't that Failla begrudged the affection Master Gruit lavished on Anilt. She just wanted the chance to win her daughter's love, to go to her when she woke in the night. She'd missed so much that even such trials appealed.

She closed the door to the hall. "Baroness Lynast invited Mistress Bohad, Lady Kishote and Lady Vapanet to view this particular dressmaker's designs. It seems the woman is very particular whom she sews for. She would have been visiting at least one Lescari duchess if the situation there wasn't so uncertain."

"Who?" Gruit asked with interest.

"That she wouldn't say, out of professional courtesy." Failla didn't hide her scepticism.

"Did you discuss more than the latest Toremal fashions?" Gruit set Anilt down on a cushioned settle.

"Thankfully, yes." Failla sat down beside her daughter. The little girl folded her hands in her lap and contemplated the petticoats frothing around her knees. "Though the dressmaker did show us some beautiful gowns."

"If it serves our purpose, buy some." Gruit lowered himself into his preferred chair. "What do their ladyships make of recent events in Lescar?"

"They're remarkably indifferent," Failla said frankly. "If Duke Moncan and his heir are truly dead, then some other Sharlac lord will simply take his place. Trade along the Great West Road will go on as it always has. If Duke Garnot is unable to return to Carluse Castle for the moment, that's of no great concern. He will soon secure whatever forces he needs to raise the siege." She stroked Anilt's hair as the little girl began playing with the fringe on the cushions.

"In the meantime, Baroness Lynast is delighted her husband will get such handsome prices for the meat and grain raised on their lands. Every other duke will be hiring more mercenaries, so their quartermasters will be busily buying provisions. She hasn't the least interest in which mercenary companies these goods will be sold to or whoever might be leading this army attacking Carluse." Failla raised her hand as Anilt twisted away, intent on her cushion.

"Lady Vapanet's husband tells her the fighting will continue until the bad weather arrives. Then there'll be money to be made feeding the armies in their winter camps. Once the battles resume, sometime around the turn of Aft-Winter to For-Spring, there'll be the usual profits outfitting them. Caladhrians will prosper as they always have done, until this current conflict burns itself out, as such squabbles invariably do."

Anilt looked up, startled by Failla's tone. She tried to moderate her contempt but it wasn't easy. At least her whore's bargain with Duke Garnot had been a straightforward one. Rather than starve in the gutter with her aged mother, she had given her body in return for his favour, and she'd discreetly turned its tangible expressions such as gowns and gifts into coin. Her true self had remained untouched no matter how he used her, kind or cruel according to whim. These women seemed to have slavishly adopted all of their husbands' greed and prejudices.

"All the while, as Lady Kishote agrees, their husbands can buy up ore and timber and whatever else the dukes will sell at prices born of their desperation for coin. Merchants like Mistress Bohad's gracious husband will sell the peasants who've fled Lescar the cheapest possible goods for their last cut coppers. The ladies all look forward to buying splendid festival gowns next year," she concluded waspishly.

Tathrin had told Failla how the Lescari habit of cutting up pennies was mocked in Ensaimin. How the other students had laughed at him when he'd first opened his purse. Now she realised she hadn't truly appreciated his humiliation, not till she'd seen these fine ladies' amusement.

Gruit's snowy brows drew together in a frown. "They don't scruple to say such things to you, when they know you're Lescari born?"

"Of Lescari blood, not Lescari born," Failla corrected him. "They're careful to express their admiration for yourself and my supposed father, wise enough to leave the chaos of Lescar to those too stupid to haul themselves out of the mire."

"What did you say to that?"

The opening door interrupted Gruit. Failla waited until the lackey had set down the tray of silver-mounted goblets and a jug of cloudy cordial. A prosaic horn beaker stood beside the crystal dish of cakes.

"Thank you, we'll serve ourselves." Gruit waved the youth away.

The lackey cleared his throat. "Madam Sibetha sent the little miss's milk."

"So I see." Failla rose to fetch it, along with the linen napkin the nurse had thoughtfully provided.

"So," Gruit continued as the door closed. "What did you say?"

"That Vanam's wealthiest merchants see more profit to be made from peace." Failla tucked the napkin into Anilt's lace collar. "As do those with Lescari blood all across Ensaimin."

"I take it you had to explain?" There was little humour in Gruit's smile.

"Such a notion would hardly have occurred to them." Failla held the beaker to Anilt's lips.

"Cake?" the child asked hopefully.

"When you've had your milk." Failla smiled as Anilt obediently drank. "Mistress Bohad thinks peace would only give Lescari smiths and potters the leisure to make goods for themselves rather than buying such things from her husband. Lady Kishote is none too keen on Lescari peasants spinning their own linen instead of selling their flax for a pittance and having to buy back finished cloth from her husband's tenants."

Gruit scowled more fiercely. "You pointed out that the Lescari in Ensaimin will put far more silver in Caladhrian coffers if they aren't sending every coin they can spare to keep their kith and kin from beggary?"

Failla tipped the beaker for Anilt. "These ladies assume Ensaimin's merchants will get first call on that coin. Only Baroness Lynast might consider peace worthwhile, if it means travel to Tormalin isn't so disrupted by battles and bandits. She gets terribly seasick," Failla explained sardonically. "Travelling downriver to Relshaz and taking a ship across to Solland is such a dreadful trial."

"My heart bleeds." Gruit heaved himself out of his chair and poured two glasses of cordial.

"At least they see no profit in Caladhrians getting involved in Lescar's troubles." Failla sighed. "It's nothing to them who calls himself duke of wherever. Mercenaries can't be trusted beyond a blind man's bowshot, so only a fool would try to influence them. Until this storm blows over, their best course is to stay well clear. At least I could agree with that and hint they'd serve their husbands best by offering such advice behind their bed curtains."

"Master Cardel and Baron Dacren should be saying the same around the merchants' exchanges." Gruit's lip curled. "I explained just how badly Abray will suffer if Ensaimin's merchants see Caladhrians hindering their efforts to bring peace to Lescar. We can always send our goods to Toremal via Hanchet and the Dalasor Road."

"Did they believe you?" Failla found that hard to credit.

"Probably not, but who would have believed Lescar's exiles would fund an army to bring down the dukes?" Gruit chuckled. "I pointed out how many Dalasorians are riding with Captain-General Evord. I may even have mentioned how eagerly the clans would welcome such new trading opportunities." He shrugged. "Even if they think that's the remotest roll of the runes, Caladhrians won't want to take that chance."

"Halcarion willing." Failla still wasn't convinced. "The important thing is that they stay out of this fight. Is there any sign of their parliament reconvening?"

"None," Gruit said with relief. "Evord was quite right. The news of Sharlac's fall had barely reached Abray by the start of festival. By the time the barons hereabouts had agreed on a message to send to Trebin, even their fastest courier couldn't get their dispatch to the parliament before the turn of Aft-Autumn. All the barons who attended the parliament are still heading home along a score of different routes. Recalling them would take an age and a half and most of them would only start arguing about such an affront to their hallowed traditions. I don't see them reassembling before the Winter Solstice parliament in Ferl."

Failla hoped he was right. "So the fighting should be done before they can reach a decision."

"If all goes to plan, and Evord's schemes prosper." Gruit brought her glass of cordial. "Let's hope Lady Charoleia and Branca are having as much success keeping Tormalin's princes from sticking their noses into Lescar's affairs."

"We'll find it harder to stop interference once we have thrown down the dukes." Sipping her drink, Failla didn't dare contemplate any other outcome. "Did Baron Dacren ask what happens then?"

Perhaps they should follow Caladhria's example and institute a parliament. Giving every landed lord a voice in lawmaking hereabouts meant the nobles were far too busy debating and divided into too many factions to ever resort to open warfare.

"I imagine he will soon ask what we intend. Emperor Tadriol will certainly want to know," Gruit said frankly.

"They don't call him 'the Provident' for nothing." Failla recalled eavesdropping on conversations between Duke Garnot and his advisors. They all respected the Tormalin Emperor, despite his comparative youth.

"Kerith had better warn Aremil that we will need some convincing answers, and soon." Gruit straightened the fronts of his gown. "By the bye, Master Cardel had a rather unexpected question."

Failla had soon realised Master Gruit fussed with his clothing when he had something unpalatable to say. Curiously he didn't seem to betray himself like that to anyone else but her. "He wants your permission to court me?"

"I thought it safest to say you were spoken for." Gruit smoothed the fur trimming his collar. "So I said you had an understanding with Kerith."

Failla was so taken aback she sat open-mouthed for a moment. "You said what?"

Before Gruit could answer, the library door opened on a brief knock.

"Master Kerith," the lackey announced.

It was like some child's tale of the Eldritch Kin. Mention the shadow-men and they'll appear. It was bad enough she had to sit at the same table as the Artificer. The thought of being asked about Kerith's intentions the next time she viewed a dressmaker's wares with the noble ladies of Abray was enough to make her stomach rebel. For an instant, Failla tasted the bitter almond cordial rising in her throat.

CHAPTER TWELVE
Failla

**Abray, on the Border of Lescar and Caladhria,
4th of Aft-Autumn**

KERITH CLOSED THE door as the lackey departed.
He looked at the merchant, his eyes hooded. "Am I
intruding?"

"No, not at all." Gruit covered his confusion by
picking up the crystal dish of cakes. "Can Anilt have
her treat? If she's drunk all her milk?"

"Please?" The child looked up at Failla, dark eyes
wide with appeal.

"Just one," Failla reminded her.

Gruit offered Anilt the dish. She promptly took a
cake in each hand.

"One," Failla reproved.

The child's mouth tightened obstinately. She made
no move to put either cake back.

"Anilt!" Failla's stomach hollowed. If Sibetha

rebuked Anilt, the little girl immediately behaved. She had no such respect for her own mother.

"Oh dear." Gruit shook his snowy head, disappointed.

"Your mama said one cake," Kerith said sternly.

Anilt immediately dropped both cakes in the dish and hid her face in Failla's lap.

"Hush, chick, don't be silly." Failla held her tight, her reassurance light with feigned amusement.

At least the child had turned to her rather than running to Gruit for protection. But why was Anilt so afraid of Kerith? Grudging, she had to admit Kerith had never been anything but kind to Anilt, within the bounds of his habitual reserve.

Was it just his appearance, so stern in his long black tunic and breeches? Reared on Lathi's remote farm, Anilt would never have known a man who dressed in such a fashion, with his cropped dark hair and beard, his only adornment the silver ring that Vanam's university granted its scholars.

The child couldn't possibly know how unspeakably cruel he had been to Failla.

Gruit set the dish down, cakes forgotten. "What's the news from Carluse?"

"Duchess Tadira is adamant. She tells the townsfolk that Duke Garnot has withdrawn only to regroup. She will hold Carluse Castle until he returns. He will come back to save them from this army of mercenaries who have plundered Sharlac and Losand, and are now laying waste to Carluse, raping and murdering wherever they please."

Kerith addressed himself to Gruit, avoiding any possibility of meeting Failla's gaze. Well, he knew all she had done, all that she was, better than anyone else alive. She should just be grateful he didn't voice his contempt, she told herself coldly.

"The townsfolk cannot possibly believe her." But doubt undercut Gruit's protest.

Failla could believe it. She knew just how convincing Duchess Tadira could be, and how ruthlessly she would turn on anyone who gainsaid her.

"What else do they have to believe? There's no news reaching the town to contradict her." Kerith shook his head. "The castle guard have been seizing food and fuel from every household. They're barely leaving the common folk enough to feed themselves. Anyone living by the town wall has been thrown into the streets, to find shelter as best they can. Their houses have had their lower doors and shutters nailed up and archers keep watch from the upper rooms. Some of the cellars have been undermined, so the houses can be brought down to block the roads if there's a successful attack on the gate and the enemy gets a foothold inside the walls."

"How long can Evord maintain the siege?" Failla demanded.

Kerith addressed his reply to Gruit. "According to Jettin, the captain-general is content to wait her out for another ten days. It will take at least that long for Draximal, Parnilesse and Marlier to satisfy themselves that news of Duke Garnot's defeat can be trusted. Then they must decide how to respond. Meanwhile our army can make good use of the time to rest their horses, tend the wounded and repair their gear. After that, though, he says they must move on and that means taking Carluse Town, even if it costs us dearly. Evord says not breaking Carluse could lose us the entire campaign."

"How does he propose to enter the town?" Gruit wondered.

"It will have to be an all-out assault on the gates." Kerith grimaced. "For the moment, though, he says not to look for the worst roll of the runes."

An all-out assault, Failla thought, her stomach hollow. Then the mercenaries would plunder the town. That was always the price of such defiance. But Duchess Tadira wouldn't pay it. It would be the ordinary folk, like her Uncle Ernout, her Aunt Derou, cousin Serafia and her little boy, Kip. No Carluse militia would defend them, all safely garrisoned in the castle.

"A great many captured mercenaries are being sent here under guard," Kerith continued. "The captain-general asks that you warn the local barons and encourage them to do all they can to keep these men walking westwards. For our part, we should expect Reniack today or tomorrow."

Failla wondered if the rabble-rouser's pamphlets and rumours could really persuade such men to abandon their hopes of money to be made in Lescar. She felt Anilt shift in her lap, turning her head to look suspiciously at Kerith. Failla reached for a cake and offered it to her. The little girl sat up and nibbled it.

Gruit was nodding. "I will call on Baron Dacren and Lord Vapanet first thing tomorrow. They won't want underemployed mercenaries lingering hereabouts any more than we do." He raised a gnarled finger. "You told Evord that the next supply wagons will arrive in Losand tomorrow? I have sent everything he asked for."

"I have told both Jettin and Aremil," Kerith assured him. "Lieutenant Dagaran will send troops of his skirmishers out from Losand to escort all the wagons safely along the high roads." The scholar gestured towards the untouched glass of cordial on the tray. "May I?"

"Of course," Gruit said impatiently. "Now, what does the captain-general think Draximal and Marlier will do, once they're sure Duke Garnot's truly a broken arrow?"

Kerith hesitated before drinking. "Jettin says Evord refuses to speculate. We should all wait and see what Mistress Charoleia can discover from her web of informants. Aremil agrees."

"Do all Solurans keep their counsels so close?" Gruit vented his exasperation in a hissing breath. "Can we not send out some enquiry agents? What about Sorgrad and his brother? Surely their talents could be put to better use than swinging a sword?"

"A spy using elemental magic would bring down the Archmage's wrath on us all," Kerith said sharply.

"He need not use his wizardry," Failla objected. "He has far more talents than that."

Kerith was startled into looking directly at her. "You think so?"

Failla was surprised at what she read in his eyes. Did the scholarly adept really think she bore Sorgrad and Gren a grudge? Granted, they'd kidnapped her when Garnot had sent her to await his pleasure at Thymir Manor. But she'd been looking for a chance to flee the duke's protection, to reclaim the daughter no one knew she had borne him.

She hugged Anilt close, heedless of cake crumbs. If she had fled on her own, they wouldn't be nearly so safe. Thanks to Sorgrad's ingenuity and Gren's casual grave-robbing, duke and duchess alike believed she'd been kidnapped for profit and the ransom they'd paid had only bought them burned fragments of bone and fabric. As Garnot had so often told her, one could never really trust mercenaries. She was still surprised he'd paid up though.

"What about Parnilesse and Triolle?" Gruit demanded. "Do we have any news from there? Duke Orlin and his duchess celebrated the festival with Duke Iruvain."

"Whatever Parnilesse decides, that's the most distant dukedom," said Kerith, a trifle irritated.

"We'll have plenty of time to make ready once Mistress Charoleia tells us what Duke Orlin intends. She and Branca will return to Losand by way of Parnilesse and Triolle, once they've concluded their business in Toremal," he explained, seeing Gruit's perplexity. "They can tell the captain-general everything they've learned on their way.

"As for Triolle," the scholar continued, "Evord is satisfied that Master Hamare's death has drawn their teeth. Now Duke Iruvain lacks information as well as his best advisor. The dukedom has little enough coin to hire worthwhile mercenaries at the best of times. There's no one to lead their militia effectively in battle since the duke and his brother are so young and untried."

Gruit nodded slowly. "Isn't there still a fair chance of Duke Garnot returning with some significant force? Marlier's full of mercenary camps. How do we know that's not where he's headed?"

"Most of the mercenaries camped on the banks of the Rel take their cue from Ridianne the Vixen," Kerith reminded him, "according to Sorgrad anyway and Captain-General Evord agrees. Neither of them thinks any company captain will be keen to trust Garnot's promises of coin while his coffers are still besieged in Carluse. His Grace doesn't exactly have a record of successes in this campaign. Sia Kersain's scouts report that Duke Garnot is retreating towards Tyrle with his mounted companies. The foot regiments and militia have been left to make shift for themselves." Kerith smiled with measured satisfaction. "Our scouts say tens, scores of men are drifting away with every night that passes."

"Can't we get that news into Carluse Town?" the white-haired merchant asked with sudden hope. "Couldn't Sorgrad and Gren sneak in? If we can give the lie to Duchess Tadira and her promises of Duke Garnot's return, maybe the townsfolk will open the gates to Evord?"

"Why should the townsfolk believe unknown upland mercenaries instead of Duchess Tadira?" Failla demanded. "Even supposing they manage to open their mouths before they're hanged from the castle gates. You know all the tavern tales about Mountain savagery. As soon as they show their yellow heads, there'll be a hue and cry that Evord will be able to hear outside the walls."

Gruit yielded with ill grace. "Surely Duchess Tadira will surrender inside a handful of days. She has to know what's befallen Duke Garnot. He'll have taken courier doves from their castle loft to send her dispatches."

"Perhaps, perhaps not." Failla shook her head. "Regardless, she'll hold out till the last drop of water and crumb of bread. Even if she believes Duke Garnot's so thoroughly beaten that he no longer commands respect, she'll just set up Lord Ricart in his father's place. She'll look to Duke Orlin of Parnilesse to support her and he'll be delighted to have his nephew as Carluse's duke, so thoroughly beholden to him. You can be certain she has courier doves hatched in Parnilesse ready to hand."

She had more immediate concerns. "I take it my uncle is sending letters out to tell Evord what's happening in the town?" Uncle Ernout, Saedrin's priest, who knew so many secrets and held them all close, her own deceits included. And not just her deceits.

"The boy bringing the last one said he'd been told not to return." Kerith answered her reluctantly. "Master Ernout warned us not to expect to hear from him again, not for some time."

"Why?" Failla's demand outstripped Master Gruit's.

Anilt shrank from her mother's raised voice. Failla stroked her hair to soothe her, still intent on Kerith nevertheless. "What don't you want to tell us? What else have you learned?"

Kerith set down his half-drunk cordial, his expression more dour than ever. "Duchess Tadira will not countenance talk of surrender or even of negotiation. When the castle's sergeant-at-arms asked permission to send a courier to Evord, to ask for the return of any wounded captives, she had the man hanged from the castle's gate."

"What?" Gruit was horrified.

"Sergeant Banel?" Appalled as she was, Failla knew Duchess Tadira's heartlessness of old.

"Jettin didn't know the man's name." Kerith looked unwillingly at her once more. "A double handful of

189

men in the castle have been flogged or imprisoned. No one's seen your cousin Vrist since the first night of the siege. Your uncle has no notion what's become of him."

"He's only a boy," Failla protested. "What could a groom possibly know?"

Gruit looked troubled. "He knows who he's been carrying letters for even if he doesn't know what they say."

Failla blanched. But surely if Tadira knew Vrist had been carrying word from the castle, she'd have hanged him for all to see. "Perhaps he's hiding." She could only cling to that hope.

"It turns out that Duchess Tadira has known since For-Autumn that certain guildsmen have been plotting against Duke Garnot." Kerith cleared his throat and gazed out of the window. "It seems Duke Iruvain of Triolle discovered their conspiracy and sent word to prove his good faith as Carluse's friend. One of the guildsmen has already been hanged. Master Settan, the brewer."

Perhaps now they'd believe her. Failla had told them Master Hamare's spy had already known about the guildsmen's plots. She had only confirmed what that vile old woman had said. She'd only done that because Pelletria had threatened to betray her and Anilt alike to Duke Garnot. Even then, and she'd sworn it on Anilt's life, even then she'd only told lies to the crone.

But Master Gruit and his friends had still feared she was lying, so they'd sent her away from

Abray. None of them trusted her now, except Tathrin. Because he knew just what Duke Garnot and his duchess were capable of.

Kerith couldn't look at her now. He might well be ashamed of himself, Failla thought fiercely. Whatever anyone else's doubts, Kerith knew the truth. He had used his Artifice to wrench it from her, deaf to her pleas, her tears. He had violated her memories, her fears and desires, more thoroughly than any rape could abuse her body. He could at least have argued her case. But he'd all but ignored her ever since that appalling night.

Agitated, Gruit paced in front of the fire. "If Master Ernout thinks he's under suspicion, he must leave by the same route as his messenger."

"He won't." Failla was certain.

Twisting his scholar's ring around his finger, Kerith glanced at her. "Would Duchess Tadira truly have Saedrin's priest hanged?"

"Yes." She held his gaze. He must surely understand Tadira's ruthlessness. He had felt her terror lest the duke and duchess learn of Anilt's birth. Bastard children were merely game pieces like little wooden birds. If their loss could serve Carluse, they would be discarded without remorse. Garnot's bastard son Veblen had died for his father's quarrels with Sharlac. Failla had seen the duke's base-born daughters married to mercenary captains merely to save the dukedom's silver. That was the fate Pelletria promised Anilt, if Failla didn't let her read the guildsmen's letters.

She was surprised to see Kerith growing pale. Even more, to recognise the pain and fear in his eyes. Somehow he was reliving her memories, all the agonies she'd suffered, all she'd risked for the sake of her child. He knew why she'd hazarded her life and Anilt's, Aunt Derou's perilous herbs bringing her to childbed half a season early. Because Duke Garnot had recalled her, just when she'd allowed herself to believe Duchess Tadira had contrived to make her exile permanent. There'd have been no concealing the pregnancy she'd been unable to end when it might still have been safe to do so.

Very well. That should convince him of Carluse's rulers' utter ruthlessness. Failla let no hint of forgiveness soften her gaze. Serve him right if he couldn't forgive himself.

Anilt stirred beside her. Failla saw her little girl had fallen asleep, her black curly head on her cushion. She swallowed the lump in her throat. Whatever Kerith's offences, she had more immediate concerns, more important debts to repay. If Captain-General Evord let his men loose on Carluse, the sloping streets would run with blood. The blood of her kinsmen.

"Is there any news of my cousin Lathi?"

Lathi, who'd taken Anilt from her, still wet with birth blood, who'd nursed her at the same breast as her own recent child. Lathi, whom Anilt had looked for when her nurse had said Mama was waiting. As far as anyone had known, Lathi was the little girl's mother. Only she, Failla and their Aunt Derou knew different. Aunt Derou, who was trapped inside Carluse Town, along with Serafia and her little boy Kip, left fatherless by Duke Garnot's wars.

Gruit answered, visibly pleased to have some good news. "She and all her children are on their way here." His face creased with some concern. "Her husband insists he stay to defend their farm. Who knows what marauders might come their way?"

"True enough." And Failla was as responsible as the rest of them for letting marauders loose in Carluse. "You will see them safely provided for, when they arrive?"

"Of course." Gruit looked surprised she had to ask.

"Let Lathi look after Anilt." She caressed her daughter's head, hiding her anguish. "While I go to Carluse."

"What?"

Gruit's shock was only outdone by Kerith's.

Failla looked at the white-haired merchant. "I can get inside Carluse Town. The people know me and I know who I can trust."

"But they think you're dead," he protested.

"I can convince the guildsmen to defy Tadira. She's only one woman. They fear her, but only because of Duke Garnot's power. If I convince them he's beaten, that's as good as a key to the gates." She forced a smile. "Her Grace has already done half the work for us by hanging Sergeant Banel and Master Settan."

"The captain-general will never agree," Kerith snapped.

"Let's ask him and see," Failla shot back.

Gruit looked troubled. "He might think of some less hazardous way to use Failla's familiarity with the castle and its servants."

"You'll abandon Anilt a second time?" Kerith challenged her.

"This has nothing to do with you, whatever you may think you know of me." Fury at his presumption saved Failla from the urge to weep at the thought of doing just that. "All you need to do is tell Jettin to tell Evord what I'm offering. You swore to use your Artifice without fear or favour, didn't you?"

Kerith reddened with anger to equal her own. "Do you question my word?"

"Enough, please." Gruit hurried to stand between them, his hands beseeching. "Kerith, no one doubts you. Failla, yes, we will make your offer to the captain-general. But I cannot imagine he'll let you place yourself in such peril."

Failla brushed a curl from Anilt's soft cheek. "When we have his decision, we will all abide by it."

Kerith couldn't have seen so deeply into her mind after all if he thought she would ever risk losing Anilt again. She wouldn't have made this offer if she didn't think she could get in and out of Carluse

Town uncaptured. Uncle Ernout and all his allies would protect her. She would come back, and if Anilt would be happiest in Lathi's care while she was away, that was how it must be.

She had the rest of her life to win back her daughter's love. But Failla didn't think she'd be able to live with herself, if one day she had to tell Anilt she'd shrunk from doing all she could to save the rest of their family.

Uncle Ernout held more than her secrets safe inside his shrine. He still had the gold she had hoarded, as she sold as many of Garnot's gifts and gowns as she could without risking suspicion. Once she had borne Anilt, she had lived for the day she could flee the castle and reclaim her daughter from Lathi. That gold was to have carried them far away to a place where nobody knew them. It wasn't too late to put that coin to good use.

If she couldn't take up a sword to help win this war, a woman always had other more subtle weapons to use.

Chapter Thirteen
Litasse

**Triolle Castle,
6th of Aft-Autumn**

"I DIDN'T SEND for you." Iruvain didn't look up from the map spread across the table.

"My lord husband, I was wondering if you've any news from Sharlac."

Outside, Litasse noted, the man-at-arms who'd opened the door to the audience chamber drew it close without the latch quite catching.

"No," Iruvain said dismissively.

So, as Litasse had suspected, he hadn't made good on his promise to send Lord Roreth north.

"Is there news from Carluse?" she asked diffidently. "The castle is rife with rumour. Some say that Duke Garnot has crushed these exiles in Carluse's forests. Others claim he's been defeated himself. Or are these mercenaries truly nowhere near Carluse but plundering Ashgil instead?"

"Your only concern should be silencing such gossip." Iruvain was still scowling at the map.

"The best counter to hearsay is truth." Litasse itched to read the ciphered parchments piled up beside the chart. Even more beguiling, she could see the translucent slips of paper brought by courier doves.

"Your devotion to truth rings hollow." Iruvain finally looked up, his eyes shadowed.

He had been up all night, Litasse realised. He'd worn that maroon doublet with the purple-slashed sleeves when they'd dined together last evening.

"My lord." She tried for humility. "Your people are afraid. Ashgil is mere days' march from our borders. Perhaps if your people saw you strengthening Triolle's defences with proven warriors—"

"I will not spend coin recruiting mercenaries." Iruvain thumped the table with his fist. "I wonder at you advising such profligacy when you've so often lamented Triolle's poverty. Or do you want me to invite Marlier's spies right into our counsels?"

Litasse tried not to show her fear. "My lord, there are mercenary companies in Relshaz owing no allegiance to Duke Ferdain—"

"Tend to your own duties, my lady wife! I will manage my responsibilities as I see fit!"

As the duke shouted angrily, the man-at-arms in the hallway threw open the door, one hand on his sword hilt.

Iruvain turned his wrath on the hapless man. "What do you want?"

"Your Grace—"

"My lord husband, I will leave you to your correspondence." Litasse hurried out past the man-at-arms, her gold brocade skirts rustling.

"Get out!" Iruvain bellowed at the gaping man.

As the door closed, Litasse heard a muffled thud against the wall. Iruvain had presumably thrown something in a typically useless gesture. She hurried away.

The audience chamber was on the lowest level of the castle's mightiest tower, reserved for the duke's apartments. Litasse went out into the open bailey, her hands modestly clasped at her waist, so no one could see them trembling.

She had no option. Only the open battlements offered a route between the ten towers rising from the massive grey curtain wall. Even that lofty route offered no shelter. All Triolle's dukes and their households must endure whatever weather Dastennin decreed if they wanted to cross from one apartment to another. All for the sake of their boast that any attacker must fight a separate battle to claim each one of the castle's turrets.

With no high ground for Triolle's dukes to build on, even with a deep ditch on one side and the stream dammed to make a mere on the other, determined attackers would soon surround their castle. The best they could do was present sheer walls to the outside world, pierced only by arrow slits so each tower's defenders could kill anyone attempting to scale its neighbour.

Litasse shivered, then assured herself no one could read anything into that. The skies remained clear but each day grew cooler. Had her mother and sisters found shelter somewhere warm? Autumn came sooner to the high wolds of Sharlac than to this dismal bog of a dukedom. Tears pricked her eyes and she sniffed. Hamare would have discovered her family's fate by now.

"Your Grace." Pelletria approached, walking with the stiffness she feigned around the castle. "I have your shawl."

"Let's see how the roses are faring." Litasse smiled for the benefit of three scullions hurrying past. They hastily doffed their caps. So she still commanded some respect.

She was doing her very best not to give Iruvain cause to doubt her or to prompt any more tittle-tattle. With Pelletria in constant attendance, she was never alone with any man but him. Since Duke Orlin and their other Parnilesse guests had departed, she'd only worn her most decorous gowns, her jewellery as modest as any dowager's.

Did the various servants busy around the bailey even care? She watched a maid with an armful of linen hurrying to the laundry in the White Tower's basement. Swordsmen in Triolle's green and yellow livery leaned against the gatehouse, swapping jokes. Several guildsmen from Triolle Town waited, irresolute in their finest mantles. They must have come to ask Iruvain about the threat looming in Carluse.

"Do you suppose they'll be reassured to see me tending Duchess Casatia's garden?" she wondered under her breath. "Do you suppose Iruvain's temper might improve if he goes out and kills a few deer?"

Discreet amusement lit Pelletria's faded eyes as she draped the embroidered shawl around Litasse's shoulders. "Is he very out of sorts?"

"I think he's scared," Litasse said thoughtfully. "He's had a double handful of letters. See if you can get hold of some before they end up in the fire. Be careful."

"I've been careful since before you were born," Pelletria reminded her.

"There are courier dove despatches too." Litasse forced herself not to look up at the Messenger Tower. Its turret held the courier bird lofts and Master Hamare's rooms were a few floors below.

They had shared such exquisite, silent passion there. How soon would she have to feign noisy ecstasy when Iruvain came to rut? How soon would some unloved child's birth cord tie her to Triolle's future? Either prospect left Litasse hollow with dread.

They reached the neatly trimmed hedge surrounding the little garden in front of the Duchess's Tower. Iruvain's mother had stocked it with the rarest herbs and flowers, now all sinking into autumn torpor. Was that how she had escaped the tedium of her life?

"I hope you know how to prune roses," Litasse said frankly. "It would be a poor omen if the wretched things die."

Pelletria pulled a short, sharp knife from a hidden sheath as they approached a tangled arbour. "Let me save Your Grace's hands from the thorns."

"Have you had any answer from Hamare's man in Relshaz?" Litasse glanced around to make sure no one was within earshot.

"He's spreading the word among trustworthy mercenaries." Pelletria carefully cut a spray of leaves.

"That should save some time, if we can only make Iruvain admit we need them."

Litasse longed to kick at the gravelled path, to relieve her frustration. No mercenary captain would order his company north without a parchment sealed with Triolle's green grebe. Only the duke could put his signature to that.

"Some hired swords are already offering their services to Triolle," Pelletria said calmly. "I don't imagine His Grace will turn them away, if only for fear of them wreaking havoc by way of revenge."

"What do you mean?" Litasse was bemused.

"Duke Garnot is fleeing Carluse." Pelletria pared another shoot back to weathered wood. "This Soluran's army fought his forces to a standstill south of Losand and then blocked his retreat to Carluse Castle. Duchess Tadira is besieged inside Carluse Town."

"How long can she hold out?" Litasse wondered. Was it too much to hope the bitch would starve to death?

Pelletria shook her head. "I can't say, Your Grace."

Litasse scowled. "How long before their wizard reduces Carluse's walls to rubble?"

"I doubt they'll do anything so obvious to incur the Archmage's wrath," Pelletria pointed out.

Litasse couldn't argue with that. She sighed. "So where's Duke Garnot now?"

"He retreated to Tyrle in hopes of regrouping. But nearly all his mercenaries decided against throwing good coin after losing runes. They're on their way to Triolle. Duke Garnot has no choice but to follow."

"He's coming here?" Litasse's hatred nearly choked her.

"Within a few days." Pelletria paused to look sternly at her. "Didn't Master Hamare teach you to face ill news as resolutely as good? Talking of good news, I've had word of your mother."

"Where is she?" Litasse sank onto the arbour's bench as her knees gave way. "What of my sisters?"

"Do you know a manor called Nolsedge?" Pelletria briskly stripped away stray fronds. "Home to Lord Rousharn?"

"I think I've heard of it." Litasse was breathless with relief and then fear. "My father confined Lord Rousharn to his lands for objecting to some decree." She suddenly remembered. "That anyone paying an overdue levy would gain title to the defaulter's property."

Her mother had argued against such a measure but her father had been obdurate. Since her brother Jaras died, he'd listened to no one.

"Lord Rousharn had a wife, Lady Derenna." Pelletria resumed pruning.

"She fancied herself a natural philosopher?" Litasse had some vague recollection of a stern-faced woman in an outmoded gown and tarnished jewellery.

"That's her. Well, your lady mother and your sisters are now her guests." Pelletria contemplated her handiwork. "Insofar as they're guests who cannot leave or send letters or receive visitors."

"On whose authority?" Fury warmed Litasse.

Pelletria shrugged. "When your father confined Lord Rousharn, Lady Derenna fled to Vanam."

Litasse stared at Pelletria. "She's part of this plot that Hamare uncovered?"

The old woman nodded. "It seems she's been travelling among her friends, among Sharlac's nobles, who share her scholarly inclinations. She was persuading them all to keep to their own demesnes even if calamity befell the duke."

"She should be whipped at a cart's tail for such treachery," spat Litasse.

"Maewelin make it so," Pelletria agreed.

To Litasse's eyes, blurred with tears, the old woman seemed the very embodiment of the vengeful winter hag, guardian of widows and orphans.

"Who told you this?" she demanded. "How can I

get a message to my mother?"

Pelletria looked towards the half-wall sheltering the castle's narrow back gate. "That will be difficult. She has managed to smuggle some letters out but only because her captors permit it."

"Hush!" Litasse stiffened as a servant approached, sullenly hunched in his faded livery.

Pelletria continued regardless. "They want to read her appeals to Sharlac's vassal lords, and to know who replies, and how."

"Don't look at me, Your Grace." The servant bent to pick up the prunings.

It took all Litasse's resolve not to spring to her feet. "Karn?"

Just as Hamare had been Pelletria's apprentice in the covert service of Triolle, so Karn had been her lover's protégé. But Hamare had gone to his funeral pyre thinking the younger man was dead.

Stricken, Litasse looked at Pelletria. "Have you told—?"

"I know," Karn growled.

"Where have you been?" Litasse twisted her shawl around her hands. "He sent you to Vanam—"

"I was in Marlier trying to find Duke Garnot's whore when someone tried to kill me. Which proved I'd caught a promising scent." Beneath his hood, Karn's voice was harsh with amusement. "Once I was recovered enough to ride, I followed some mercenaries who were quitting the Marlier camps to go north. I found this Soluran's army gathering. I was trying to find out more. Forgive me, Your Grace. I couldn't get word to Master Hamare in time to warn of Sharlac's peril."

As Karn looked up at her, Litasse drew a shocked breath.

She'd always thought Karn was much her own age. Now he looked ten years older. When she'd last seen him, summer sun had lightened his sandy hair to dark gold. Now his head was shaved to stubble. His eyes were sunken, his cheekbones painfully prominent. Once she had thought him handsome. Hamare had traded on those good looks, sending Karn to seduce women and men, for the sake of their pillow talk. Who would want to bed Karn now? He looked like a death's head.

"What happened to you?"

"My wound festered repeatedly." His face twisted with remembered pain. "I had to come down from the hills."

Pelletria broke in. "Which is how he discovered Lady Derenna's treachery."

"They knew I was on their trail." Frustration sharpened Karn's words. "These people, who hatched this plot in Vanam, they have their own intelligencer, Your Grace. A woman called Lady Alaric."

"She has a handful of other names that Master Hamare knew and doubtless more besides," Pelletria hissed.

"I fell into fever." Karn was gripping a thorny stem so hard that blood oozed between his fingers. "When I came to my senses Sharlac was already lost."

"Can we find her? Can we kill her?" Litasse asked with sudden savagery.

"Her loss can't help but hinder them." Karn's red-rimmed eyes were implacable. "And we owe them Master Hamare's death, don't we?"

"We have more immediate concerns," Pelletria interrupted. "What's to be done with Duke Garnot?"

"I've stripped him of his mercenaries." Karn smiled with gaunt satisfaction. "It wasn't hard to persuade them to come and serve Triolle instead. I knew that's what Master Hamare would have wanted."

"I wish I knew what else he'd advise." Litasse couldn't help glancing up at the shuttered windows of the Messenger Tower. "But all his papers were burned, when their wizard came to kill him." She choked on the awful memory.

"Not all." Karn shook his head. "Hamare had a ciphered ledger that he always kept hidden."

"What?" Litasse stared at him.

"No one must know of it, Your Grace." Pelletria raised a green-stained finger.

"Where is it?" Litasse found she'd wound the end of the shawl painfully tight around her fingers. She ripped herself free.

"Hidden in the Oriel Tower." Pelletria looked around the bailey.

"Duke Orlin and his retinue lodged there over festival," Litasse said with alarm.

Pelletria chuckled. "His man was too busy trying to get into Hamare's rooms to tap the panels in hopes of secrets there."

"Did he succeed?" Litasse was appalled.

"No, but I made sure he got enough chances to keep him out of other mischief," the old woman said serenely.

Karn wasn't amused. "You should have cut his throat."

"Never mind that," Litasse said impatiently. "Let's find this secret ledger."

"If you'd care to lead the way." Pelletria nodded towards the Oriel Tower.

Litasse walked as casually as she could across the open bailey. At least inside the castle, the original one-roomed levels of each tower had long since been divided into comfortable apartments lit by generous windows. Triolle's dukes could accommodate noble guests in all the luxury they were accustomed to. As long as they didn't mind getting wet if it happened to rain on their way to dinner.

As they approached the steps to the Oriel Tower's door, Litasse turned to Pelletria. "What's my excuse for being here?"

She knew Iruvain's sneaks were constantly watching her, even if he didn't always listen to what they told him. More fool him. She and Pelletria sifted every scrap of gossip swirling around the back stairs, discussing how to make best use of it.

"You're seeing if guest linens need renewing," Pelletria suggested.

"Indeed."

Litasse went up the steps and allowed Pelletria to open the door. A startled lackey emerged through the parlour door. "Your Grace—"

"Don't let me disturb you." With a charming smile, Litasse continued to the stairs.

"I'm not saying the laundry mistress can't be trusted," Pelletria protested in querulous tones.

"A chatelaine has a duty to be certain." As they reached the next floor, Litasse looked a silent question at her.

The old woman nodded upwards, so they climbed the next flight of stairs and the next. Karn followed silently at their heels. The topmost floor was gloomy, only one inadequate window shedding light on the closet doors.

"In here." Pelletria found a key among the modest bunch hanging from the chain around her waist and unlocked one.

Litasse's heart was pounding.

Only a single arrow slit lit the panelled storage room. Karn picked his way carefully through heavy chests stacked three deep. He reached up to the moulding beside the window and gasped. Sinking down, he pressed a hand to his side.

"Let me see that injury," Pelletria demanded.

"No." Karn glared at her.

"I need you fit and well," Litasse said bluntly, "if the three of us are to defend Triolle as Master Hamare would have wanted."

Karn grimaced with something between pain and anger. "As you command, Your Grace."

He hitched up his tunic and the shirt beneath. All Litasse could see in the dim light was a dark, angry scar. And she could count every one of his ribs.

Pelletria stooped to look more closely. "It's barely healed. If it breaks open again, it could be the death of you." She shook her grey head with misgiving.

"I'll risk a third roll of those runes." Karn let his clothing fall and reached up to the moulding again. Pushing it up revealed a small hole.

"Here." Pelletria passed up her bunch of keys.

"You carry such a secret with you?" Litasse stared.

Pelletria smiled. "Where better to hide a leaf than a forest?"

Turning the key, Karn opened the panel like any other cupboard door. Reaching inside, he took out a thick leather-bound book. "These are Master Hamare's most dangerous secrets."

Taking it, Litasse found only pages of close-written nonsense. "It's ciphered. Where's the key to that?"

Pelletria shook her head. "We don't have it."

"Master Hamare said you were an apt pupil." Karn looked at her, unblinking.

Litasse stared at them both. "It could take until Solstice to break it. We don't even know if this can help us."

"There'll be something we can use in there." Karn's sunken eyes were pools of darkness. "Master Hamare knew there are always some mages whoring their wizardry around Caladhria and Tormalin. If anyone else ever used magic against Triolle, he was ready to fight fire with fire."

"They sent a wizard to kill him," Pelletria agreed. "We can only avenge him if we suborn one ourselves."

Litasse hugged the heavy book close. The smell of leather and paper was a bitter reminder of her times with Hamare. The pressure of the scabbarded knife against her thigh was a constant reminder of his death. It was the one the wizard had used, which he'd pressed into her hand. Iruvain had never taken up her challenge to find anyone who could identify it as hers, let alone anyone else's in the castle. He'd just discarded it. But Pelletria had found it for her.

Iruvain would never avenge Hamare. He wasn't even defending Triolle adequately, never mind taking the fight to these vile conspirators, making them pay for destroying Sharlac. There was no way she could do anything of the kind herself, even with Pelletria and Karn to help her.

Could a wizard level the balance? Wasn't that only fair? These exiles had been the first to bring magic into Lescar after all. Besides, she needn't make any decision just yet. She had to learn how to read the ledger first. "We need to make sure I can work on this undisturbed."

"I have an idea about that, Your Grace," Pelletria assured her.

Until she managed to decipher the ledger, there were things to be done in the meantime, especially with an extra pair of eyes and ears. Litasse looked at Karn. "How well does Duke Iruvain know your face? Does he know you were an enquiry agent for Hamare?" Even if he did, would he recognise the younger man now?

Karn shook his head slowly. "I was only one among a hundred men-at-arms, as far as His Grace was concerned."

"Good." Litasse nodded. "Can you get yourself into his retinue? We need to know what his letters say, what reports he is receiving."

He smiled thinly. "I can do that, Your Grace."

"Start thinking how we can get a letter to my lady mother." Litasse turned to Pelletria. "And I want to know all you can tell me about Sharlac and this treacherous vassal Lord Rousharn."

CHAPTER FOURTEEN
Aremil

**Losand Merchants' Exchange,
6th of Aft-Autumn**

"WE'VE RAISED TWO companies of militia in Sharlac.
The Shearlings we have convalescing there will give
them some backbone, so the Sundowners' wounded
can rejoin Captain-General Evord outside Carluse
Town." Relaxed in the window seat, Dagaran turned
a page in his ledger. "We've mustered one company
of militia hereabouts and the Tallymen are knocking
them into shape."

"So much for their furlough from the battle lines,"
Aremil said wryly.

Hobnailed boots marching up and down the square
had drowned out the noise of the fountains all morning.
They only ever paused for pungent observations from
the mercenary sergeants. Aremil had been amused by
the inventive obscenity of their insults.

"The Wheelwrights march south this evening." Dagaran turned another leaf. "With that troop of Pata Mezian's lancers, now that they're satisfied with their remounts."

Aremil swallowed. "Are they still so resolute, after their clan suffered such grievous losses at Carluse Bridge?"

How could the Soluran lieutenant calmly total so many men's deaths in his neatly inked columns?

"They are." Dagaran's raised brows betrayed his own surprise. "Now, do you have any news for me from Ashgil?"

"Jettin tells me Rega Taszar's regiment still holds the town securely. His scouts are keeping track of the Draximal army." Aremil stiffened to curb a tremor in his words. "Lord Cassat is definitely marching south, though Rega Taszar won't swear he's going to Carluse to relieve the siege."

"We'll know more once they cross into Carluse territory." Dagaran pursed his narrow lips. "If I were inclined to wager, I'd say Lord Cassat will head for Triolle as soon as he hears that's where Duke Garnot has fled."

That was good enough for Aremil. He'd heard the mercenary sergeants mocking Dagaran for his refusal to bet on a roll of the runes. The Soluran said he only ever laid his money down on certainties. He played white raven though, and Aremil found him a challenging opponent. But this was all rather more serious than a strategy game.

"How substantial a force have Draximal mustered?"

"They have around thirty companies of mercenaries, mounted as well as marching. We suspect more will join them." Dagaran frowned. "Lord Cassat is drafting townsmen and farmers into the militia at every halt. Draximal will field at least as big an army as Carluse first mustered, quite probably bigger."

"Every man fresh, while our forces have already been fighting and marching for twenty hard days." Aremil couldn't help a shiver of misgiving.

Dagaran surprised him with a grin. "They've been sitting with their feet up outside Carluse for the last handful."

Only those who weren't dead or so badly wounded that they could no longer stand. Aremil refused such consolation. "They won't sit and wait for Draximal to arrive." Captain-General Evord had told Tathrin that often enough. The thought rang through his mind every time Aremil reached through the aether to him. "Not when there's every chance we'll see an army coming from Marlier too."

"Is there?" Dagaran sat up straight.

"Kerith has been paying close attention to the gossip coming up the River Rel on the barges ferrying goods to Abray," Aremil said heavily. "The talk along the wharves is that Duke Ferdain has ordered a general muster. So many reports can't all be wrong, so Kerith says."

"They won't all be militiamen drafted at the point of a pike," the Soluran observed thoughtfully. "Ridianne the Vixen's hand-picked mercenaries will make that a force to be reckoned with."

"That's what the captain-general said," Aremil agreed. "So we must put an end to this siege, and quickly." He searched the Soluran's face. "I don't suppose you have any idea what the captain-general might be planning?"

Dagaran shook his head. "I couldn't venture a guess."

Aremil only hoped his expressionless face hid his foreboding. Tathrin hadn't actually told him but Aremil heard echoes of conversations that his friend recalled. Hot-headed as ever, Gren had advocated a night assault with a chosen band of mercenaries. They would scale the walls and kill the sentries before opening up the gate for their allies.

Tathrin had expected Sorgrad would mercilessly crush such idiocy. The older Mountain Man had just shrugged and allowed they'd succeeded in something of the kind before. Aremil knew exactly what Tathrin feared when he heard that. Only Sorgrad's magic could ensure such a raid's success.

"I'm sure the captain-general will let us know exactly what we have to do to assist." Dagaran closed his ledger and stood up. "Shall we dine together this evening? I believe you owe me a game of white raven?"

"I would be delighted." Aremil allowed a smile of genuine pleasure to twist his face.

Dagaran could be relied on to order a meal that Aremil could eat unaided despite his tremulous hands.

A knock at the door interrupted them and a mercenary sergeant stuck his bandaged head around it.

"There's two Sharlac nobles to see Lord Aremil. Some puffed-up cock and his hen." He grinned. "Shall I convince them to take no for an answer?"

"I'd prefer to know their names," said Aremil.

"Lord Rousharn of Nolsedge and his wife Lady Derenna," the man replied promptly.

"Please show them up." Aremil pushed against the arms of his chair in an effort to sit up straight. To his relief Dagaran resumed his seat in the window.

He heard the sergeant go back downstairs, his words indistinct. Heavy boots hurried up the wide oak stairs, lighter footsteps following. There was brief whispered conversation outside the door before Derenna strode into the room.

"Good day, gentlemen." She turned with a swish of crimson skirts. "My lord, may I make known Master Aremil, a student of various disciplines in Vanam. Master Aremil, I have the honour to make you known to my husband, Lord Rousharn of Nolsedge."

Aremil didn't recall Derenna being such a stickler for etiquette when they had first met in Vanam.

She'd shown no great care for her appearance either. Today, however, there were no frayed hems on this smart gown. Instead of mismatched silver combs, hairpins tipped with tiny enamelled lilies secured her dark braids.

He inclined his head. "Forgive me if I don't rise—"

"No, of course, your infirmities." Lord Rousharn was looking at his withered and twisted legs, not his face. Then he looked at Aremil's hands. "A student but not a scholar? Well no, naturally. Forgive me." The burly man's eyes drifted to his crutches.

Derenna's husband could justifiably claim to still be in his prime. His dark hair was barely receding; his shoulders were broad beneath his belted buff jerkin, his waist trim and his legs muscular in his close-fitting breeches and riding boots. He was at least the same height as Tathrin, who was the tallest man Aremil knew.

Rousharn also had a remarkably eloquent face. No wonder he'd fallen foul of Duke Moncan. Aremil saw both his curiosity and his instinctive revulsion for a cripple. He clenched his weak hands. He wasn't about to explain just why they were still bare of a silver ring boasting Vanam's blazon. Not when claiming one would have meant either lying on his oath to the university's archivists or revealing his own true birth.

He cleared his throat of the spittle that so often beset him. Drooling would hardly make a good impression. "My lord, my lady, the honour is all mine. May I also make known to you Dagaran Esk Breven, lieutenant of Evord Fal Breven?"

"Forgive me, I'm not familiar with the conventions of Soluran names." Lord Rousharn stripped off his gauntlets to offer Dagaran his broad hand.

Dagaran clasped his forearm in mercenary fashion. "Breven is the district of my birth. The distinction is that my family owns no land in our own right. The captain-general is lord of a broad demesne."

"Is that so?" Lord Rousharn nodded with interest.

"You can discuss it some other time. We do have more pressing matters to address." Derenna sounded more amused than exasperated.

Aremil couldn't recall seeing her smile before. He'd heard from various friends in Vanam's learned halls that shared intellectual curiosity had first drawn this couple together. Mutual respect for each other's intelligence had kept them devoted through the birth of their five children and their trials under Duke Moncan. Now it looked as if genuine affection also blessed their match.

"Indeed." Lord Rousharn continued to address Dagaran. "Duchess Aphanie has made a request of us and we feel we should refer it to the captain-general, my wife and I."

He glanced at Derenna and she spoke up. "The bodies of Duke Moncan and Lord Kerlin were naturally brought to Duchess Aphanie, as we sheltered her and her daughters at Nolsedge."

Lord Rousharn interjected. "Their pyres were lit with all deference and every rite that she wished for was duly observed."

Why did he feel the need to stress that, Aremil wondered? Did he think he'd be accused of ill-treating his unwilling guests? True, Rousharn was a noted Rationalist, and so many inclining to that philosophy derided religion as outmoded superstition. Aremil was inclined to agree.

Derenna continued. "Duchess Aphanie wishes to dedicate the urns of their ashes in the shrine to Poldrion within Sharlac Castle. She also asks if anyone knows what became of her son Lord Jaras's ashes, when the castle was sacked."

Her disapproval of that destruction was clear. Usually Aremil found it hard to tell what she was thinking, her features were naturally so severe. Being reunited with her husband was revealing new facets of her character. Aremil wasn't entirely sure what to make of that.

Dagaran bowed politely and withdrew a step. "Master Aremil will relay such questions to Captain-General Evord's retinue."

"Naturally." Now it was Lord Rousharn's turn to clear his throat. He turned towards Aremil but still didn't meet his eyes. Despite his best efforts, his expression betrayed his disdain.

Aremil reminded himself to rule emotion with reason. As a Rationalist, Lord Rousharn was doubtless dismissive of any magic, elemental or aetheric. His own scholar's ring was from Col, after all. He hadn't had the benefit of tutors like Mentor Tonin, explaining that dismissing the undeniable reality of magic was the height of irrationality.

"Though Sharlac Castle was extensively damaged once the fires took hold, I am assured the sanctity of the shrines was respected." Aremil glanced at Dagaran and was relieved to see the Soluran's nod. "Dagaran, please make enquiries about the urn."

"Lord Jaras's ashes weren't safely stowed in Poldrion's shrine," Derenna said testily. "Duke Moncan kept them in his own apartments."

"I see." That wasn't good news. Aremil knew every room save the Sharlac Castle shrines had been extensively plundered.

Still, if Lord Jaras's urn was anywhere, it would be in Sharlac or Losand. Captain-General Evord had decreed the advancing army wasn't to be burdened with booty, not when it could be safely left with friends. Aremil could only hope the seals were intact and no mercenary had dumped the former Sharlac heir's ashes to use the urn as a spittoon or worse.

"How soon can you provide Duchess Aphanie with a fitting escort?" Lord Rousharn turned to Dagaran again.

Aremil felt his irritation with this overbearing man turning to outright dislike. Was he one of those Rationalists so rigorous in their logic that they believed afflicted children shouldn't be supported through their infirmities, living or dying as nature intended?

Once again, Dagaran deferred to Aremil. "We must refer such a request to the captain-general, don't you think?"

"I quite agree," Aremil said as firmly as he could. "I'm quite sure he'll tell us any such visit must wait until peace is restored to Sharlac and all of Lescar."

That wasn't what Lord Rousharn wished to hear. "I'm sure I can muster some of my own militiamen, if you're unwilling to spare us your swords."

"Don't you think you might spare Duchess Aphanie the grief of seeing the ruin of her home, at least for a little while longer?" Aremil retorted. He paused as if to gather his thoughts. Talking clearly became a trial when he was annoyed, and he'd be bitten by Poldrion's demons before he'd give this man any more excuse to despise him. He continued with careful precision.

"Do you fully understand the hazards the duchess and her daughters would face on such a journey? Some of those mercenaries who've abandoned Duke Garnot will have turned to banditry. There are other perils besides. What if some enterprising vassal lord seizes the duchess with a view to marrying her daughter by rape? That would secure a claim on the dukedom, wouldn't it?"

"None of Duke Moncan's vassals would do such a thing." Lord Rousharn was outraged.

"No?" Aremil challenged. "What about his erstwhile mercenary captains? Have they no ambitions?"

"Let's set that aside for the moment," Derenna interrupted. "What are Captain-General Evord's plans for Sharlac, when peace has been restored?"

"What will become of Carluse when Duke Garnot is driven out for good?" Lord Rousharn quickly added.

Those weren't casual questions. Aremil saw they'd come here seeking those very answers. This business with Duchess Aphanie was just a convenient excuse.

"Captain-General Evord is focusing all his efforts on securing that peace," he said curtly. "There's time enough to decide what comes later."

"Not if you want calm to continue in Sharlac," Lord Rousharn asserted. He turned to Dagaran. "I have sounded out the most clear-headed and reasonable noblemen. We are agreed. The dukedom needs a regent, not least to defend Duchess Aphanie from any who seek to exploit her."

Somewhat to his surprise, Aremil saw the man was wholly sincere. But why should that surprise him? Once again he reminded himself reason must rule emotion. When he had first met Lady Derenna back in Vanam, her integrity had impressed him, balancing her abrasive character. She would only have married a man of similar resolve. Even if he did despise cripples.

This time he didn't wait for Dagaran to refer Lord Rousharn for his answer. "I will put your suggestion to the captain-general."

Derenna looked Aremil straight in the eye. "Kindly tell him all the vassal lords of Sharlac agree my husband is by far the most suitable regent."

Rousharn hastily demurred. "My wife does me too much honour."

He wasn't even being falsely modest, Aremil had to acknowledge that.

Not that it altered the facts. This unwelcome development promised to be a considerable headache. Derenna had many influential friends throughout Sharlac, nobles who shared her scholarly inclinations. These men and women had devoted their energies to natural philosophy, mathematics and the like precisely because they were intelligent enough to scorn the squabbles of Lescar's dukes and their toadies. They had accepted her arguments that the most rational course was to wait out this war and see how the final runes fell.

Derenna was still speaking. "The captain-general cannot take his campaign forward if he has to worry about chaos at his back. A regent in Sharlac can rescind Duke Moncan's most loathsome decrees, and that will win more nobles to our cause. The commonalty will be reassured as well. Those who might well exploit the current uncertainties will see we're determined to secure good governance."

Lord Rousharn nodded. "If Draximal sees unity among Sharlac's lords, Duke Secaris will be less inclined to attack us in order to threaten the captain-general on two fronts." He bowed briefly to Dagaran. "Forgive me. I know from my wife that Captain-General Evord has no intention of seizing Sharlac or Carluse for himself, still less Lescar's crown. But many will fear just that and Parnilesse and Draximal will swear he has kingly ambitions. A regent in Sharlac, of Sharlac blood, will do much to negate such alarm."

Did he think Aremil was incapable of understanding such concerns? Because he was crippled or because he was supposedly of modest birth? Lady Derenna had no notion that he was Duke Secaris of Draximal's son, so she could hardly have told her husband.

Aremil briefly considered letting saliva trickle down his chin or yielding to the cramps that were tormenting him, so his feet jerked awkwardly. That might drive Lord Rousharn out of the room. Not Derenna though. She was made of sterner stuff.

Yet again, Dagaran declined to answer, looking to Aremil instead. How long would it take for Lord Rousharn to get that message?

"I will certainly put your arguments to Captain-General Evord." Aremil nodded politely to them both. "In the meantime, would you use your evident influence with Sharlac's vassals on our behalf? Clearly no ducal levies have been gathered this Autumn Festival, not in Sharlac Town or anywhere our writ runs. I'm not sure what noble lords have done in their own demesnes. Could you see who might agree to support Captain-General Evord with solid coin as well as good wishes? Sharlac's lords can help secure their freedom from coercion by dukes or by anyone else by helping us pay off our mercenaries as soon as their job is done." That should give them something else to argue about.

"That's something a regent would be well placed to do," Lord Rousharn said quickly.

"Quite." To his exasperation, Aremil was unable to stop a tremor shaking his hand.

To his profound relief, Dagaran walked over to open the door. "It has been an honour to meet you, my lord, my lady." He bowed to them each in turn. "Please leave word where you're lodging with my clerk. If there's anything we can do while you're here, you only have to ask."

"Thank you." With a brisk nod to Aremil, Lord Rousharn strode from the room.

"Till later, gentlemen." Derenna followed more slowly, her expression contemplative.

Dagaran closed the door behind her. "Those two seem very well suited," he commented softly as they heard them descending the stairs.

Aremil grimaced, shifting in an effort to ease his aching back. "Derenna is a formidable woman. I'm just glad Reniack is away in Abray."

Dagaran was quick to catch his meaning. "You think we'd see popular feeling rise up in favour of a regent for Sharlac?"

"Derenna didn't scruple to use Reniack's talent for rabble-rousing to stir up resentment when Jackal Moncan kept her husband locked inside his own house."

However unlikely it seemed, Aremil knew the Sharlac noblewoman and the Parnilesse whore's bastard had been working together long before Master Gruit introduced them both to him and Tathrin.

The Soluran retrieved his ledger. "Why send them chasing the vassal lords' spare coin?" He was curious, not critical. "It's not as if we need the gold, not yet anyway, and that'll just give them more opportunities to enlist support for this regency."

Aremil shrugged in his ungainly fashion. "They'll argue in favour of it regardless. At least this way it might look as if Derenna and Rousharn are out to enrich themselves. Someone else may decide they'd like their own cows drinking at that pond."

Dagaran laughed. "What will we do if a handful of hopefuls present themselves?"

"Invite them to decide among themselves?" Aremil suggested. "That should keep them talking in circles for a good while."

"That always keeps the Caladhrians out of mischief," Dagaran allowed.

"Kerith was saying we'll need answers for Caladhria, when their lords start asking what becomes of Lescar with no dukes." Aremil sighed. "The sooner Evord can break though this siege of Carluse Town the better. As long as he's marching and fighting, everyone else is too busy watching and waiting for news to come up with all these inconvenient questions and initiatives."

"Perhaps Mistress Charoleia will have some interesting suggestions to put a spoke in Lord Rousharn's wheel." Dagaran headed for the door. "You and I can discuss it all over dinner."

"I look forward to it."

As the Soluran departed, Aremil swiftly turned his thoughts towards Branca. There was no one's advice he would rather seek.

CHAPTER FIFTEEN
Branca

The House of Caprice, Toremal,
6th of Aft-Autumn

"WE REALLY NEED *to think about Lescar's future when all the fighting's done. We don't have that much time, not if Evord makes good on his promise to finish this campaign by mid-winter.*"

"Kerith said the same."

"*Did you get the feeling there was something he wasn't telling us?*"

Aremil's instincts were becoming more finely tuned.

"Yes, I did." But Branca had found no way to pierce Kerith's mental armour.

"*In the meantime, do you think Charoleia could find something to Lord Rousharn's discredit?*"

Aremil's dislike of the Sharlac noble seared the aether like acid. Branca found that troubling.

229

"I doubt he had much opportunity for mischief locked up at home. Shall we leave slinging muck from the gutters to Reniack? To counter Parnilesse and Draximal's slanders here?"

"*How are their appeals being received in Tormalin?*"

"There's a great deal of outrage, but as yet, no princely house seems ready to advocate the Emperor dispatch the legions." Branca hesitated before continuing. "Lord Cassat is well known in noble circles, and much admired."

She half-expected to feel Aremil's resentment of this unknown boy enjoying the rank and privilege that should have been his. She'd seen the intractable bitterness in the back of Aremil's mind, that any crippled child should be discarded so readily.

To her surprise, she saw instead that Aremil was guiltily relieved to be spared the burden of defending a dukedom. He wouldn't be called on to risk life and limb while his unknown father stayed safe in his castle. He only envied Lord Cassat his fine horses, as he envied Tathrin and Jettin their mounted adventures these days.

Branca quickly cast around for something to say before Aremil realised what she was seeing. "Tell the captain-general to keep a weather eye to the west. Charoleia says the Duke of Triolle is recruiting mercenaries in Relshaz."

"*She does?*"

Aremil's surprise was twofold: firstly, that Iruvain of Triolle was finally taking some initiative; secondly that Charoleia had news from Relshaz when she herself was in Toremal.

Branca heard the flutter of wings. For the first time in this conversation, she yielded and allowed herself to be drawn into Aremil's echoing stone hall. Looking up, she saw courier doves fluttering amid the fanned vaults.

"*A line drawn straight across the map between the two cities must measure more than two hundred leagues.*"

A chart table appeared by Aremil's chair, showing how Caladhria and Tormalin framed the Gulf of Lescar.

"*Can courier birds fly so far over open water?*"

"I've no idea," Branca admitted.

Aremil smiled at her, as crookedly as always. His thin body, painfully twisted, was confined to his chair as usual.

Branca looked past him to the shadows. Aremil might think he had no illusions about his infirmity but sometimes she saw a different reflection of him in the distance, confident and straight-limbed. Not today. Was that thanks to Lord Rousharn?

"*That dress is very becoming.*"

"Thank you." She curtseyed, her blue skirts whispering on the flagstones.

"*Where are you? Can I hear voices?*"

Yes, his aetheric senses were definitely strengthening.

"See for yourself," she invited.

The more she could draw him out of that imagined hall the better. She'd be doing him no favours if he became as much a recluse there as he had been in his house in Vanam.

"*It's a playhouse?*"

"For marionettes. The Tormalins adore them. Charoleia says it's an ancient and honoured art."

She turned her attention to the figures frozen on the stage below the private balcony box where she sat. Each one was half as tall as an adult, their wooden faces lifelike, their clothes finely tailored. The painted backdrop was a work of art, framed by a gilded facade that hid the puppeteers. The opulence wasn't limited to the stage. Every seat was cushioned with scarlet velvet and the walls were hung with painted silk.

She could sense Aremil beside her. Closing her eyes, she recalled the marionettes' intricate dance for him, their fluent gestures and the eloquent melodies of the flutes and viols.

"It's very different from tavern puppets' cavorting, isn't it?"

She immediately wished the thought unspoken as Aremil wistfully answered.

"*I wouldn't know.*"

He had never seen the stuffed cloth caricatures waved in the inns along Vanam's lakeshore, the bawdier the fable the better. He'd never even enjoyed the decorous plays preferred by the scholars in their walled citadel on the heights.

Too late. Branca felt him withdraw as he sensed her pity. A stray thought could be as deadly as a loose arrow, and as impossible to recall. That's what Mentor Tonin had always said.

"*I must see if Tathrin has any news. I'll tell him what Charoleia says of Triolle.*"

Then he was gone, only his guarded apprehension lingering in her thoughts. Aremil admired Charoleia but couldn't hide his unease at the way she manipulated so many people as deftly as any puppeteer. What would happen if she got all those strings in a tangle?

Was that his distaste, or her own? Where was Charoleia? The second performance was about to begin. Branca looked over the balcony, down to the floor of the playhouse. The noise rising from the beautifully dressed crowd rivalled any tavern clamour in Vanam.

A few moments later, a quick knock sounded on the door. Branca hurried to unlock it.

Charoleia didn't enter. "Have you got your wrap and your reticule?"

"Where are we going?" Branca quickly gathered up her warm shawl and the ribbon-tied purse.

"Duke Orlin of Parnilesse has persuaded rather too many of his Tormalin friends to present his pleas the Emperor." Today Charoleia's hair, her jewels, her ochre gown, were all as demure as any matron's. "They're saying it's time to send in the legions, while the Soluran's army is still besieging Carluse."

Branca's throat tightened. "Will Emperor Tadriol agree?"

They walked swiftly along the dimly lit corridor.

"Let's see if he'll listen to some counter argument. Then we will have to leave, quickly and unseen. Be ready to use whatever Artifice you see fit."

Before Branca could worry what she meant by that, Charoleia knocked just once on a closed door. A man a handful or so years older than Branca opened it.

"Lady Alaric of Thornlisse. Good evening to you."

As they went in, he locked the door behind them. Though there were a handful of chairs in the dimly lit box, he was quite alone. Elegant in a dark full-skirted coat over pale breeches and an embroidered waistcoat, his only jewels were a collection of heirloom rings.

"A chaperone, my lady?" He looked quizzically at Charoleia.

She smiled. "I doubt you wish to provoke undue speculation."

"Everyone's still debating who I danced with at every festival ball," he said sardonically. "I gather the tavern wagers on my empress's birth are divided between four princely houses."

"My money rests with D'Istrac," Charoleia said serenely.

The man's good humour vanished. "Does it?"

Branca stood silently, as a good chaperone should. So this was the Emperor of Tormalin. Tadriol, acclaimed as "the Provident" by the ruling princes of Tormalin's noble houses when they had approved his nomination to the throne. A reassuring title for a man entrusted with all their dealings beyond the Empire's borders, and with ensuring impartial laws were enforced within them. He was unremarkable in appearance, of middling height with wavy brown hair and mild eyes. Though his voice held a note of command to equal Captain-General Evord's.

"Sit, please, and tell me why you've requested this audience."

Charoleia sank elegantly on the chair he indicated. "You know what's happening in Lescar, Your Highness."

He swept back the skirts of his coat to stick his hands in his breeches' pockets, incidentally revealing an elegant small sword. Branca didn't think it was just there for show.

"I hear your long-running sore of a country is plagued with a fresh outbreak of bloodletting. I cannot decide who's more blameworthy. Those of your countrymen who follow their noble dukes so blindly into battle, or those who flee to safer lands once they have begged, borrowed or stolen enough. I gather it's such exiles who hired this Soluran and his mercenaries?"

Branca stiffened. Tadriol's contempt stung all the more as she heard the echo of her own disdain, before Tathrin and Aremil had enlightened her ignorance.

Charoleia was unruffled. "You'll be glad to learn we've come to our senses. The dukes will soon be thrown down, Your Highness, and wiser heads will prevail."

"Soluran heads." Tadriol was clearly displeased. "Well known to King Solquen."

"Captain-General Evord is an honourable man," Charoleia assured him. "He will return to his own lands when the fighting is done."

"Will he?" Tadriol was sceptical. "And the thousands of men he has under arms? They'll all march meekly away?"

Charoleia nodded, confident. "We will pay them handsomely to do so."

"You think such treacherous hirelings will stick to their bargain?" Tadriol shook his head. "I will not see King Solquen establish his own man as ruler of Lescar, getting a stranglehold on the Great West Road so that he may crush our trade any time he chooses."

"That will never happen." Now Charoleia was amused.

Tadriol wasn't smiling. "You have some flight of birds to show me, or some concatenation of the stars? You think I'm some credulous Aldabreshi to be swayed by such predictions?"

Charoleia answered his sarcasm calmly. "No, but I can promise that you will see Lescar free of all Solurans, mercenaries and ducal militias. As long as you send in no legions. That will only drag out the bloodshed."

"Not according to Duke Orlin of Parnilesse," he said curtly.

There was a moment's silence, all the more potent for the hum of conversation beyond the balcony.

Charoleia angled her head. "Don't you think His Grace is as culpable as any other Lescari duke for his people's suffering? They've all indulged their petty quarrels and foolish ambitions by bleeding their vassals and the commonalty dry these past ten generations."

"I agree," the Emperor assured her, "and you're gracious in not accusing me and my fellow princes of aiding them in their folly. Let's not forget it was the rivals for Tormalin's throne who first encouraged the governors of Lescar's provinces to call themselves dukes in the days of the Chaos. It was my predecessors who promised the High King's crown to whoever brought Lescar back to the Imperial fold." Tadriol looked at her, unblinking. "One swift way to make amends would be to make good on that promise. Our legions could impose a single ruler. Given the choice between that and a Soluran overlord, even the most fractious duke should see sense."

"You think so?" Charoleia mused. "With a legionary's boot on their neck? You don't think those who've lost out will simply unite against both you and your chosen king?"

Emperor Tadriol smiled. "We will make it clear that the kingship will be shared among all their houses, just as the Imperial Throne passes from one princely house to another. I would propose passing the crown from one dukedom to the next as each ruler goes to answer to Saedrin. That should curb any ducal tendency to abuse such a privilege. Every noble house in Tormalin succeeding to the Imperial Throne knows full well that excesses will be punished with the other princes' displeasure and a new dynasty acclaimed to replace them."

"You accused King Solquen of undue ambition." Charoleia shook her head in wonder. "I would have thought Tormalin's princely houses had more than enough to occupy them in the new lands across the ocean."

"All the more reason to see peace in Lescar." The Emperor was unmoved. "All the more reason to forestall even the remote possibility of Soluran forces threatening our western border."

Even a thousand leagues away in Vanam Branca had heard of the untamed lands far away across the wild waters of the Eastern Ocean. The far continent had first been discovered in the days of the Old Empire, when Tormalin rule extended all the way to the White River and the Emperors contended with the Kings of Solura for rule over Ensaimin. Artifice had enabled the Emperors to govern such vast domains. Aetheric magic had enabled them to cross the raging deep.

But that had been a step too far and the Empire had collapsed into the Chaos. Almost all knowledge of Artifice had been lost. But now Mentor Tonin said all the princes of Tormalin were searching their houses' archives for scraps of aetheric lore, enlisting scholars such as himself from Vanam and Col.

Had Tormalin's princes erred in calling this young emperor "the Provident"? Wouldn't he be better called "the Bold"? What did that mean for Lescar?

Charoleia sat pensive in the stillness. Branca had never known anyone so impossible to read. What was she thinking?

"Who would you crown first?" the beautiful intelligencer asked with interest.

Tadriol pursed his lips. "The Duke of Parnilesse's lands are closest."

"That would be a bold move," Charoleia observed. "To entrust your honour to a man who poisoned his own father."

"That has never been proven." Tadriol spoke too quickly.

"It can be proven," Charoleia assured him. "You could well find such Parnilesse nostrums ensuring that the Lescari crown passes from hand to hand like a hot coal until it comes right back to Duke Orlin's heirs."

"Then perhaps I shall honour Duke Secaris of Draximal," Tadriol retorted.

"When he has suborned sorcery against Parnilesse? You heard how arcane fires burned Emirle Bridge this summer?" Charoleia frowned. "You have always insisted wizardry has no place in governance, Your Highness."

"I agree with the Archmage that wizardry has no place in warfare," the Emperor said swiftly. "His Grace of Draximal won't be tempted to such folly again if such a law is backed by Tormalin's legions, as well as by Planir's strictures."

"True enough." Charoleia sounded as if she entirely agreed. "And you'll have the leisure to give such a bold undertaking all the attention it requires?"

"What do you mean?" Tadriol was as puzzled as Branca.

Charoleia smiled. "Semarie D'Istrac is a beautiful girl, but your courtship would become so sadly complicated if her brother's indiscretions were to come to light."

Tadriol's face darkened. "Explain yourself."

Branca glanced sideways at the locked door. Was the key still there?

"Mud sticks. The whiter the gown, the more impossible it is to remove stains." Charoleia sighed. "Gossips will believe the worst of even the most innocent girl."

Tadriol took a step towards her. "Madam—"

"Touch me and I will scream." Charoleia sprang to her feet. "So will she."

Tadriol retreated, appalled. "As if anyone would believe—"

"Do you want to take that wager?" Charoleia crossed swiftly to the door and twisted the key. "Good night, Your Highness."

Branca scurried after her, struggling for words. Charoleia opened an unexpected door in the corridor's curved wall. Branca followed her down a plain staircase lit with tiny lamps. She finally found her voice as they reached the bottom.

"What now?"

Charoleia was listening at the lower door concealing these servants' steps. "We're leaving Toremal," she whispered. "Your Artifice must hide us as we leave the playhouse. Then you must blur all trace of us until we're well beyond Tadriol's reach. Can you do that?"

Branca hastily searched her memory. Mentor Tonin had once shown her an enchantment, not to vanish into thin air as a wizard might, but to ensure anyone catching sight of an adept immediately forgot they had done so. She nodded reluctantly.

Charoleia smiled. "You needn't fear a beating. But Tadriol would keep us as his closely guarded guests until one of his own Artificers went looking between our ears."

"So Tadriol does use magic to rule?" Mentor Tonin insisted that forcibly reading another person's thoughts was only permissible in the direst of circumstances. Branca wondered if he knew how little heed these Tormalins were paying to his principles.

"He doesn't use wizardry," Charoleia corrected her, "but he's as keen as any other Tormalin lord to see what advantages Artifice might offer."

Branca ran a hand through her hair, heedless of ruining Trissa's handiwork. "So what happens once we've escaped?"

"All Tadriol's efforts will be turned to finding the truth," Charoleia said softly, "about D'Istrac, about Parnilesse poisoning his father and about Draximal suborning wizardry." She smiled. "And how his beloved's brother might have erred."

"What has he done, this D'Istrac?" Branca wondered.

"Nothing that I know of." Charoleia shrugged. "But he's a wealthy young man in the Empire's biggest city with every temptation at his elbow. He'll have some guilty secrets."

"You were bluffing?" Branca realised she shouldn't be so surprised.

"Let's not risk an Artificer discovering that." Charoleia smiled. "If Tadriol's looking for something that's not there to be found, he'll be too busy to make mischief for us."

Branca was still worried. "Unless he sends Tormalin's legions into Lescar regardless?"

Charoleia shook her head. "He's not convinced he should intervene. Didn't you hear that in his voice? But if the captain-general's campaign grinds to a complete standstill, he might be persuaded. Evord must end that siege at Carluse and press on."

"How long will that take?" Branca had no idea.

"He's had five days so far. It could only take another handful or he could still be sitting there at

Winter Solstice, if nothing shakes Duchess Tadira loose. Even if that does mean Sorgrad using his... ingenuity." Charoleia wrinkled her nose. "If we could spare a few days, I'd like to find out which princes are so keen to see Duke Orlin made High King. But Lady Alaric is going to have to disappear." She shrugged. "A great shame, but she was the only one of my guises whose path had crossed Tadriol's. We'd never have got an audience otherwise. Well, it's time we were heading for Parnilesse to see what scents we can pick up there."

She opened the door to the entrance hall. "Now, make sure that nobody sees us."

For a panic-stricken moment, Branca couldn't recall the incantation. Then she reached for Charoleia's hand, whispering, "*Fae dar ameneul, sar dar redicorlen.*"

Fingers laced together, they walked towards the playhouse's double door. They had to step sideways time and again to avoid maids carrying dishes of sweetmeats and trays heavy with glasses of wine. Noblemen and -women were slipping away from the entertainment for their own illicit purposes, with eyes only for each other. They wouldn't have noticed a marching legion, Branca thought wryly.

"*Fae dar ameneul, sar dar redicorlen.*"

They reached the floridly carved doors opening onto the steps to the street. Branca took a quick breath of the cold night air.

"*Fae dar ameneul, sar dar redicorlen.*"

"I hope those shoes are comfortable." Charoleia cross-tied her shawl like the humblest peasant. "We've a fair amount of walking ahead."

Branca broke off the incantation. "We're not taking the carriage to Den Souvrian's house? What about Trissa?"

Charoleia lifted her hem as she went down the steps. "She's spending her evening off at an alehouse in the shadow of the law courts. We'll meet her there."

Branca balked. "But our baggage?"

"Don't worry. She'll have everything you wouldn't want to lose." Charoleia chuckled. "There was always every chance we'd have to do a flit."

Branca followed, murmuring the aetheric enchantment.

"Fae dar ameneul, sar dar redicorlen."

Though it seemed these women were perfectly adept at making rapid departures without any magical assistance.

CHAPTER SIXTEEN
Litasse

Triolle Castle,
8th of Aft-Autumn

"YOU'D THINK HE was High King, the way he carries himself."

From the windows of the music room in the Duchess's Tower, Litasse watched the Carluse ranks passing through Triolle Castle's gatehouse. Their horses were groomed, their harness polished, their surcoats quartered in dense black and spotless white. A brazen fanfare echoed around the stone walls as the boar's head banner snarled.

Beneath it, Duke Garnot's armour was polished to a mirror shine, the brass embellishing his shoulders as bright as the sun, even as the shadows deepened around the bailey.

"When he's not even cock of his own dunghill any more," Litasse added with contempt.

Karn was counting. "He's riding with a hundred and ten men. Three companies of militia are still trailing after him though. They'll arrive in three or four days, if they don't think better of it."

Litasse sincerely hoped they did. "I wonder what he'll make of that."

"You won't see him acknowledge doubts, or even grief." Pelletria stood at her shoulder. "Even when his bastard Lord Veblen died, no one saw him shed a tear or voice the least regret at sending the lad into battle."

"He is an arrogant swine."

All the same, Litasse couldn't help a treacherous thought. A little heartlessness might have served Sharlac better than her father's endless mourning for Jaras. Triolle certainly needed Iruvain to start making some tough decisions.

She watched her husband emerge from the Duke's Tower and extend his hands as Duke Garnot dismounted. Iruvain gestured towards the Oriel Tower. His meaning was plain: Duke Garnot should take his ease after so long in the saddle.

Duke Garnot shook his head, stripping off his gauntlets. He handed them backwards, confident someone would be there to take them. One attendant obliged as two more stepped forward to remove his surcoat and unbuckle his armour. In buff breeches and a grimy padded tunic, Duke Garnot strode towards the Duke's Tower. Iruvain hesitated then followed.

Litasse took a deep breath and smoothed her sage gown, the precise shade of Triolle's green grebe up on the yellow flag. "How do I look?"

"Tired," Pelletria said frankly. "But we can always blame your grief and fear for your family."

Litasse nodded. Hamare always said the best lies bordered the truth.

"Karn, go and fetch and carry and overhear whatever you can while his men are being settled. Pelletria, let's make our honoured guest welcome."

She was careful not to hurry across the bailey to her husband's door. Haste would be noticed by Duke Garnot's spies and she certainly didn't want to draw his attention in her direction.

"Your Grace." The man-at-arms attending the Duke's Tower door clearly had his doubts about admitting her.

"Good day." Litasse smiled sweetly as Pelletria deftly stepped past to open the door.

She could already hear Duke Garnot's commanding voice in Iruvain's audience chamber.

"Their commander is a Soluran with a formidable reputation among the mercenaries. For once, that's not drunken exaggeration. But I have him tied down. When you and I unite all true-born Lescari, we will crush him."

Iruvain's reply was lost as Pelletria opened the door.

"My lord husband." Litasse curtseyed gracefully. "Your Grace."

Duke Garnot was by the window. Much of a height with Iruvain, he was similarly muscled from long years of riding and practice with sword and bow. Unlike Iruvain he'd used those skills amid the perils of warfare, not merely for the pleasure of hunting. If his dark hair was threaded with silver and his features were weather-beaten, that only emphasised his experience.

Iruvain's face twisted like a petulant boy's. "My lady wife—"

"Your Grace, we are so concerned about Duchess Tadira." Going swiftly to Iruvain, she tucked her arm through his. "Is there news?" Now he couldn't shake her off without looking a lout.

"My lady wife continues to hold Carluse Castle as resolutely as ever." Duke Garnot bowed stiffly.

So he was feeling his years, Litasse noted, after riding so far and so fast.

"I expect Triolle's aid in relieving my duchess of that onerous duty." Duke Garnot looked pointedly at Iruvain.

"Naturally."

Litasse wanted to kick Iruvain. If their situations were reversed, Duke Garnot would screw every possible concession out of Triolle, up to annexing land on their common border, before making the least, most evasive promise that he would later disown.

"What have you mustered by way of an army?" Garnot asked impatiently. "Make no mistake—if we don't put a stop to these invaders, they'll overthrow every dukedom!"

Was that fear underneath his urgency?

Litasse nodded, all earnest concern. "We have seen their vile threats."

Pelletria had shown her some of the broadsheets circulating round Carluse's markets, the night letters nailed to shrine doors. The lurid ones detailed every brutality visited upon Carluse's commoners by mercenaries in the duke's pay. Some hinted at debauches involving Garnot's heir Lord Ricart.

The more sober publications detailed the high-handed way Duke Garnot wielded his power. They sighed over Duchess Tadira's arrogance. Not that Carluse suffered worse than any other dukedom. They stressed as much, with illustrative detail. All the dukes had broken their compact with their vassals and the commonalty. Though towns across Ensaimin ruled themselves unburdened by fealty's yoke, they observed. The honest men and women of Lescar should strive for such a future.

Iruvain squared his shoulders. "We have mustered militia from every district."

After screwing the broadsheets up and throwing them back in her face, saying he had no time for such nonsense.

Litasse wondered when he'd admit he had hired the mercenaries who'd abandoned Duke Garnot, when they'd offered their service in return for Triolle's coin. As Karn had said, Iruvain had been too fearful of the havoc the disgruntled companies could wreak to refuse.

"It's been six days since my lord sent word to Relshaz." Litasse pressed close to Iruvain, every measure the dutiful wife. "There will be mercenary companies ready to march north as soon as we send a courier dove."

"Send it today," Duke Garnot ordered.

Iruvain's furious gaze accused Litasse. "You—"

As Litasse had gambled, he choked on revealing to Duke Garnot that she'd gone behind his back.

"Curse a cat for stealing milk before you scold a woman's loose tongue," the Carluse duke growled. "How many companies have you retained? Foot or mounted? How many archers? We need crossbowmen to bring down those cursed Dalasorian lancers."

Iruvain found his voice. "That depends how much coin you can contribute to this venture."

"Coin?" Duke Garnot stared at him. "All the gold we need is safe inside Carluse Castle. In the meantime, we have your silver to call on."

Litasse felt Iruvain stiffen. He had accused her of belittling his dukedom when she warned against boasting that Triolle's mines were richer than they'd proved in many long years. Now that crow had come back to peck at his eyes.

Duke Garnot's thoughts had moved on. "Relshaz is a cursed long way from here and we need to move swiftly. Have the mercenaries take ship to the mouth of the Dyal and barges can bring them upriver after that."

"The cost will beggar us," Iruvain protested.

No, Litasse thought, *it will beggar Triolle. We can't spend Carluse gold when it's locked up with Duchess Tadira.*

"The cost of miserliness now will be more than you or I wish to pay later." Garnot's gaze drifted towards the windows. "This Soluran is as fine a commander as I have ever faced. Even Duke Moncan couldn't stand against him. Saedrin grant him peace," he added with insincere haste.

Litasse hid her face in the mossy sleeve of Iruvain's doublet and hoped Duke Garnot took her grimace for sorrow. She would rather spit in his face. Infuriatingly, though, he was right. Triolle had no hope of standing alone against this Soluran's army.

"We can pay them something on account and promise richer rewards once the campaign is won," Iruvain said unwillingly.

"Promise whatever you want," Duke Garnot said impatiently. "Just get them here to march for Carluse before this Greater Moon turns dark." He scowled ferociously. "I'll have no one saying I've abandoned my dukedom."

That latest accusation nailed to shrine doors really goaded him, Litasse saw. She hoped her smile didn't betray her satisfaction.

"We will have coin to spare once we've reclaimed all that these scum looted from Sharlac," she remarked artlessly.

Iruvain had better make sure her claims came first. She wouldn't wager a copper cut-piece on Duke Garnot ever settling his debts.

He looked at her, sharply curious. "Do you know where Her Grace your mother is being held? Where your sisters may be?"

"Sadly not," Litasse lied.

She wasn't going to tell Garnot, so he could concoct some scheme to snatch one of her sisters to wed his damp-handed, lecherous son. Thankfully, she, Pelletria and Karn were the only ones sharing that secret.

Duke Garnot let that go. "What do you know of Draximal's muster? Or Parnilesse's?" he asked Iruvain.

"Draximal has mustered at least five thousand men." Iruvain's face cleared. "A thousand mercenaries and four thousand resolute militiamen, as of Lord Cassat's most recent dispatch."

Duke Garnot snapped his fingers. "Send a courier and have Lord Cassat ride on ahead of his men. We need to take counsel together before relieving Carluse's siege."

Indignation coloured Iruvain's cheekbones. "Might you be a little less peremptory inside my castle, Your Grace?"

Duke Garnot was unimpressed. "Do you want this Soluran's army camped at your gates and threatening your lovely wife? What of Parnilesse?"

"Duke Orlin is raising militia." Iruvain betrayed

his own doubts. "But he talks of unrest within his own borders."

Duke Garnot grunted. "He'll be facing open revolt if we don't put a stop to this Soluran. I'll send a courier to Lord Geferin myself. If that pair don't send aid for Tadira's sake, she'll make sure they regret it," he added ominously.

Could she prove her brothers had murdered their father? Doubtless, since Litasse had always been convinced she'd shared in the plot.

Duke Garnot was pacing back and forth. "What about Marlier?"

"What about Marlier?" Iruvain retorted.

Garnot halted. "You've sent no word?"

"I don't trust Duke Ferdain." Iruvain was as sullen as a schoolboy.

"Nor do I," Duke Garnot spat, "but if I'm going to be whipped, I'll take five strokes from a nettle rather than one from a thorn stick!"

When had he ever been offered that fabled choice, Litasse wondered contemptuously?

"That ageing whore Ridianne commands more than half the mercenaries camped on Ferdain's land. You tell him to send them north just as fast as he can!" Garnot thumped the table. "We must crush this Soluran while he's still intent on Carluse. Victory will be ten times harder if we have to meet him in the field again."

His face turned ugly. "Tell Ferdain if we don't relieve Carluse, Marlier will be the next domain ransacked. Then tell him if we do break the villain and Marlier hasn't helped us, we will march on his castle ourselves to take whatever recompense we think fit!"

His wrath hung in the air like the threat of thunder.

"My lord husband, you are the only one who can secure Marlier's forces." Litasse looked up at Iruvain, wide-eyed and trusting. "Whatever your suspicions of Duke Ferdain, he cannot accuse you of ever openly attacking his interests."

Unlike Duke Garnot. They all knew the truth. Duke Garnot had fought along Carluse's border with Marlier as a young man. He had encouraged Duke Orlin to attack Duke Ferdain's ships as they sailed along Parnilesse's coast to Tormalin.

"Very well," Iruvain said slowly. "I will send a courier to Marlier."

Duke Garnot nodded, satisfied. "Tell him to send his whore on ahead as well, so she can learn what we decide in council with Lord Cassat and Lord Geferin."

Litasse made very sure she hid her true feelings. Iruvain deserved no such credit for Triolle's peace with Duke Ferdain. With Master Hamare's assistance, it was Iruvain's father who'd avoided provoking either Marlier or Parnilesse into a quarrel that would be Triolle's ruin. After his death, Iruvain was merely too awed by his new responsibilities to cause offence. Master Hamare had barely been able to persuade him to look beyond his own borders.

If her fool of a husband had only listened to the intelligencer, this whole vile plot hatched in Vanam could have been stifled at birth. Then her father would still be alive.

She smiled adoringly at Iruvain before making a polite curtsey to Garnot. "I see you have so much to do. I will make certain your accommodations are ready whenever you seek them, Your Grace. Should I delay dinner, my lord?" she asked meekly.

Iruvain looked at her with faint suspicion. "No, let's not inconvenience the kitchens."

"Very well." She curtseyed and departed.

Pelletria followed, silent and unnoticed. They didn't speak until they were safely in Litasse's boudoir.

"You may have overdone the humility." Pelletria was amused.

"He can hardly accuse me of being too modest a wife." Litasse had more important concerns. "We need Karn. He must find a way to make sure he's the courier taking Iruvain's letter to Duke Ferdain." She paused. "I think we had better rewrite that letter ourselves."

Pelletria nodded. "I don't suppose Duke Iruvain will point out the advantages of confronting this Soluran in Carluse territory instead of inside Marlier's own borders."

Litasse nodded. "Once he's delivered that, he can ride on to Relshaz."

"To summon the mercenaries we've had waiting

there?" Pelletria frowned. "A courier dove will be faster."

"And now Iruvain will send one." Litasse nodded. "In the meantime, we will secure more certain aid than Marlier's boldest whore. Lock the door."

As Pelletria complied, Litasse searched among the keys hanging from her own girdle and unlocked the heavy chest beside her writing desk. "Have Iruvain's sneaks told him how diligently I'm keeping the household accounts?"

"Naturally." Pelletria helped her stack heavy ledgers on the floor.

Once the chest was empty, they could turn it over, laying it quietly on the hearthrug.

Litasse pressed the hidden slip of wood that freed the bottom panel. "How many hidey-holes did Hamare have round the castle?"

Pelletria took the intelligencer's ledger from the hiding place. "Duchess Casatia had this chest made, Your Grace. She kept one set of household accounts to show Duke Gerone and a second ledger for her own purposes."

"Saedrin save us!" Litasse would never have thought that of Iruvain's beloved mother.

She shook off her surprise. Righting the chest, Pelletria set out the castle's accounts on the table, along with paper and ink. She'd been doing the calculations while Litasse had wrestled with Hamare's cipher late into these past few nights.

Some day Litasse was going to ask just when, and why, Pelletria had learned to copy her handwriting so accurately she was hard put to tell it from her own. She turned to a page she had dog-eared in the ledger.

"What have you discovered, Your Grace?" Pelletria looked at the list below the writing. All but three of the words were scored through with black strokes of ink.

"These are wizards whom Hamare believed could be bought." Litasse's hand strayed to the reassurance of the knife strapped to her thigh. "We know this Soluran and the plotters from Vanam use magic. Karn's right. We must use magic against them."

"Are you sure?" Pelletria's frown deepened her wrinkles.

"Garnot of Carluse said '*if* we don't crush this Soluran'. Litasse took a sheet of paper and began writing. "He's twice faced the man in battle and lost both times. My father hated Garnot but he never denied that the swine's the finest commander of all Lescar's dukes."

She looked up, her pen paused. "Garnot said '*if* we don't crush this Soluran' because he's not at all sure we can. That's why he has no hesitation in allying with Draximal when they've always been at daggers drawn over the Great West Road. That's why he'll send Iruvain cap in hand to Duke Ferdain and forget the bad blood between Marlier and Carluse just as long as they can secure Ferdain's mercenaries. Duke

Garnot's even ready to threaten Orlin of Parnilesse with whatever it is that Duchess Tadira knows about their father's death. Uniting all the dukedoms is the only way Garnot believes he can defeat this Soluran. And he still says 'if', even though he has no idea that they can call on a wizard."

She wrote, swift and decisive. "I won't shed a tear if Carluse falls but if the Soluran looks our way next, we will need more than mercenaries to defend us. If Duke Garnot prevails, well, I won't stand to see him crown himself High King on the strength of that victory, even if I have to suborn wizardry to stop him."

Her voice shook despite herself. It was all very well coming to this shocking conclusion alone in the night, staring at the canopy of her curtained bed. It was quite another to say such a thing out loud.

But what else could she do, friendless as she was, to avenge her dead father, to see her mother and sisters rescued? To salvage Triolle from the wreckage of Iruvain's indecision? Desperate times called for desperate measures.

What could Archmage Planir of Hadrumal do to her anyway? She was Duchess of Triolle. He could hardly lock her in some island dungeon. He would rebuke her, certainly, and she would weep prettily, begging his forgiveness. She would plead ignorance and grief, whatever it took to placate him. The thought of doing so soured her stomach, but what other weapons were left to her?

Pelletria watched her triple-sealing the letter. "This wizard's in Relshaz?"

"So Hamare's ledger says." Litasse gazed at the letter, her hands trembling. "Let's just hope he's still there to be found."

Chapter Seventeen
Tathrin

The City of Relshaz,
13th of Aft-Autumn

"Just look big and dangerous." Sorgrad threw back his cloak to free his sword hilt.

"He can manage big," offered Gren.

"Shut up," Tathrin growled.

"Better," Gren approved.

The merchants who paused at Tathrin's father's inn reminisced fondly about this city of canals embraced by branching channels of the River Rel as it met the sea. They recalled the glittering fountains, the perfumes of the flower-hung balconies, the white-painted buildings and the wild salt scent of the breeze. They spoke of the myriad exotic wares that Aldabreshi galleys brought up from the Archipelago: pungent spices, enamelled bronzes, fabulous glassware, ceramics fine as eggshell and rainbows of silks from gossamer to heaviest damask.

They didn't mention the reek of stagnant drains in filthy slums like this or taverns like the Sea Serpent with its obscene sign, stinking of unwashed bodies and smoking tallow. The windows were so dirty that candles were lit barely halfway through the afternoon.

As they entered, conversation slowed and everybody stared. Tathrin was getting used to this by now and they all looked at home here after three days of not shaving, barely washing and no clean clothes since they had left Carluse. Gren looked if he'd rolled out of a rag-picker's cart.

Sorgrad led the way through the scarred tables and skewed benches. Men hunched around a table, casting rune bones. Tathrin saw a trio land: the Sea Breeze, the Reed and the Chime. The next man's hand threw the Deer, the Horn and Calm.

"Moons uppermost." He pointed to the heavenly rune, where the Greater and Lesser Moons showed on either side, the Sun hidden face down. "Lesser runes rule."

"Do we have time for a game?" The younger Mountain Man cracked his knuckles hopefully.

"There's no skill in runes." Tathrin was careful to mute his scorn. "I laid out all the odds for you, remember?"

It had been something to do while they endured nine tedious days of the lengthening siege of Carluse.

Tathrin absolutely agreed with Gren. Sieges were really boring.

Then he'd discovered the younger Mountain Man had as much of an aptitude for numbers as his brother. So Tathrin had found paper and pen and run through every possible permutation of the nine bones with their twenty-seven runes, to prove that wagers on which three symbols might land upright was betting on nothing but chance.

Gren nodded. "But what makes you think I give the drip from a trollop's—"

"Hush." Sorgrad frowned over his shoulder.

They followed Sorgrad to the rear of the dimly lit room.

That summed Gren up really, Tathrin mused. No matter how clear the facts might be, if they didn't suit him, he simply ignored them.

No matter how disastrous it would be for Sorgrad to use his magic to overcome Carluse Town's defiance, Gren still urged his brother to act. He had the sense not to suggest wizardry to Evord himself, but he was just as ready with madcap schemes for overcoming sentries or even scaling the murderous cliff face on the far side of the castle crag.

Tathrin wondered if Evord had decided to send them to Relshaz, to pursue Charoleia's warning that Triolle was recruiting mercenaries, just to get rid of Gren's pestering. Though as it turned out, everything they'd discovered today suggested Charoleia was right. How many mercenary companies had left the city in the past few days? Eleven? Twelve?

"Klare." Sorgrad tapped a man on his oiled-sailcloth shoulder. He was deep in conversation with three others all dressed like watermen. "You're a hard man to find."

"Only when it suits me," the man replied, unsmiling.

His dusky skin might just be the accumulated grime of years but Tathrin doubted it. He knew that plenty of Relshaz folk had mingled mainland and Aldabreshin blood, though he'd seldom seen such faces in Vanam, Caladhria or Lescar. Most slaves who bought their freedom from their Archipelagan warlords rarely left the trading cities of the coast.

"Do you know where I might find Dandren Quicksilver?" Sorgrad asked amiably.

"Wrong side of the city, runt," Klare sneered. "He took ship up the coast this morning."

"Just him or the whole company?" wondered Sorgrad.

"The whole company."

Tathrin couldn't see what warranted Klare's satisfaction.

Sorgrad frowned. "Where do you suppose they're going?"

"The Carifate." Klare seemed to think that was obvious.

"Sorry to have troubled you." Apparently chagrined, Sorgrad headed back to the noisome street.

As he followed, Tathrin wondered why two of the other men had betrayed the same smugness as Klare. The third merely looked bemused.

The door slammed behind them. "What now?" Tathrin asked.

"Klare was too pleased with himself to be lying, so the Quicksilver Men have definitely taken ship up the coast." Sorgrad walked towards an alley offering a path through the crowded buildings.

"He was too quick to say they're heading for the Carifate," Gren insisted.

"He was." Sorgrad nodded. "Well, Charoleia's heading for Parnilesse. Tathrin, have Aremil ask young Branca to find out what they can about goings-on in Carif."

"I will." Tathrin wondered briefly if that port city infested by mercenaries was as unsavoury as Relshaz. "So the man who told us earlier that Dandren was taking a barge upriver was lying?"

"Egil the Toad?" Sorgrad looked thoughtful. "It seems so, but he's not usually one to piss in another man's ale. Do you suppose he was lying to us in particular, or just to anyone looking for the Quicksilver Men?"

"Let's beat some answers out of him." Gren cracked his knuckles again. "If I can't get a game of runes, I may as well break some heads."

The appalling thing was Tathrin knew he wasn't joking. Either prospect entertained Gren equally.

"Give me a moment." Sorgrad was still thinking.

"That was Capale the Sailmaker with Klare."

"Looking like a hound that can't catch the scent?" Gren shrugged. "Yes, it was."

"Capale's a crook but once he's bought he stays bought." Sorgrad smiled. "We'll see what a few silver crowns can buy from him later. I don't think we'll trouble Egil the Toad again. Let's go and see Downy Scardin instead."

Gren was surprised. "You're ready to pay his prices?"

"We can spend coin or we can spend time," Sorgrad said tersely. "We don't have time to waste."

Tathrin didn't recall them mentioning this other man before. He just knew this new scheme meant more traipsing along the flagstoned roads and muddy alleys. His legs were already aching viciously. Sitting outside Carluse Town's gates might have been boring but it hadn't been nearly so hard on his feet.

He sighed and followed the two Mountain Men. He had no idea where they were going now. Despite criss-crossing the city from the docks that opened onto the Gulf of Lescar back to the wharves that served the River Rel, Tathrin still had little idea of its overall layout.

After a little while, though, he noted the streets were getting wider. The air was sweeter as the open gutters ran with water to sluice the refuse away. He could smell cooking and hear voices hinting at normal life behind the blank walls lining the street. The Relshazri didn't seem to favour windows looking outwards.

Soon clean paving underfoot lifted his spirits further, as did fresh whitewash on the plastered brick houses. Then he realised their dirt and dishevelment were attracting ominous looks from the porters at the doors of the increasingly opulent dwellings.

"How much further?" he asked quietly.

"Not far." Sorgrad met a door-ward's glower with a cheery grin.

They turned down a cobbled lane where fruit trees overhung garden walls. Gren stopped by a gate and gave a bell pull a swift tug. Somewhere over the white wall, Tathrin heard a chime.

They stood waiting for a few moments. There was no sound within, no opening door, no steps coming to open the gate. Gren rang the bell a second time. There was still no response. Frowning, Sorgrad looked around. Satisfied no one else was in the lane, he tried the gate's iron handle. It turned and the gate swung inwards.

Gren drew his sword. "Downy Scardin doesn't leave his gate unbolted."

"Quick." Sorgrad shoved Tathrin's shoulder.

Gren bolted the gate as soon as they were in the garden. It was smaller than Tathrin expected, the patterned paving overshadowed by the thrusting fronds of plants he didn't recognise.

Seeing Sorgrad ready his blade, he drew his own. "What now?"

Gren was looking at a half-open door with coloured glass panes. "Downy?"

Sorgrad took a silent step towards the house. "It's Maspin, from Ambafost."

There was no reply. More crucially, Tathrin couldn't hear a sound to hint at anyone within, hiding or lying in wait.

"Downy Scardin?" Gren moved closer to the door, stooping, tense as a hunting cat. Then he stood up, his sword hanging loose. "We're really behind the fair today."

"What is it?" Sorgrad slipped past him to pull the glass-panelled door fully open.

Tathrin saw a fat man in a silk tunic and trews sprawled across a cushioned daybed. He had copper-coloured skin, long black hair and a beard plaited with gold chains. A dark stain spread from under his beard all over the breast of his ochre tunic.

"Watch that gate." Leaving Tathrin on the steps, Sorgrad went for a closer look. "Has he been robbed?"

"Hard to say." Gren was by a desk piled high with letters, sealed and unsealed, ledgers and papers of all descriptions. He tugged at a drawer and found it locked. So was the one beneath.

"He's been dead since early this morning, I'd guess." Sorgrad was leaning over the corpse, prodding at the bloodstain with the tip of his dagger and sniffing. "Throat cut by someone who knew exactly how."

Gren contemplated the locked desk. "If you kill a man for some secret he won't hand over, why don't you search for it afterwards?"

"Maybe they just found it easily?" As soon as Tathrin spoke up, he regretted it.

"Anything worth killing for, Downy would have it secure." Sorgrad studied the dead man. "And I can't think of any secret he wouldn't sell, not for the right price."

Now Gren was looking at the desk with keener interest. "What kind of price do you think we'd be talking?"

"Maybe his killer didn't want to pay?" Tathrin hazarded.

"We haven't got time to go into all his business." Sorgrad gestured at the littered desk. "Downy had his fingers on threads stretching all the way to Selerima and Col, looping through every town between here and there."

"Charoleia would know what's worth our time," Gren persisted.

"She's not here." Sorgrad's tone made it clear the discussion was over.

Tathrin looked around the room. Everything else appeared undisturbed: the lacquered table and wooden chairs, the vase of rich red blooms, the framed portraits on the wall. The desk was cluttered with paper but the piles were neat enough. "Wouldn't things be all over the floor if someone had been searching?"

"True enough." Sorgrad sheathed his blades. "Well, there's nothing for us. Let's go and see Egil the Toad again."

"I wonder if anyone's cut his throat," Gren mused on his way to the door.

"There are enough folk who'd like to." Following, Sorgrad grimaced. "Maybe Downy just fell foul of the wrong man."

Tathrin looked at the corpse. "What are we going to do about him?"

Gren chuckled, amused. "He's not our problem, long lad."

Sorgrad was heading for the gate. As he lifted the latch, a burly man shoved it from the other side, barging through. He launched himself at Sorgrad, intent on wrestling him to the ground. The Mountain Man stepped deftly aside and drove his assailant off with a punch to the short ribs.

Before Tathrin could take a relieved breath, more men forced their way through the gate.

"Boots and fists and a knife if you must," Gren warned, "but slice, don't stab."

Tathrin saw one of their would-be attackers settle brass knuckles across his fist. That punch could stun him, if it didn't kill him outright. How were they supposed to win this fight without their swords?

"Leave one of them conscious." Sorgrad retreated to stand beside him. "We want answers."

Tathrin saw such confidence didn't deter the dirty and ragged men. He frowned. They looked like bargemen from that foul tavern, the Sea Serpent.

Whoever they were, they made the first move. One rushed forwards, his eyes glittering with more than liquor. He punched at Gren. Dodging the blow, Gren seized the man's fist in his own crushing grip, swiftly using his free hand to punch his assailant's shoulder. That deadened the second blow the man launched. Before he could recover, Gren hooked a boot behind his knee. As the man fell back into a stand of ferns, Gren kicked him in the face.

Another bargeman came straight for Tathrin, his arm swinging up and around. Instinctively raising his forearm, Tathrin felt agony and numbness shooting down to his fingers. The bargeman was using a lead-weighted cosh.

Tathrin threw all his weight behind a punch to the man's jaw. The pain in his knuckles was worth it as the man stumbled back into the green-stained wall. But the bargeman quickly pushed himself off the plaster, swinging his cosh at Tathrin's head. Tathrin remembered Sorgrad's lessons in avoiding a knife. Stepping forwards, he blocked the man's forearm this time so the cosh only struck empty air. He smashed his fist backhanded into the man's nose. The bargeman's answering blow glanced off Tathrin's cheekbone.

As his assailant staggered backwards, blood streaming from his nose, Tathrin saw Sorgrad had already knocked one bargeman onto his hands and knees. The man whined, spitting teeth onto the patterned paving.

Then he saw the dull sheen of a blade. Another man had recovered from whatever blow had sent him reeling, ready to stab Sorgrad's unarmoured back. "Behind you!"

Sorgrad whirled around and knocked the knifeman's arm sideways. Before the attacker could react, Sorgrad kicked him hard in his groin. The man doubled up, retching. Sorgrad stamped on his knife-hand, the crack of bone audible.

Whatever Gren had done to the fifth attacker, it left him huddled on the ground, his bloodied face twisted. The man with the cosh took to his heels. Fleeing through the gate, he left only a bloody handprint on the plastered wall.

"Let's get out of here." Sorgrad kicked the knife under a trailing vine.

Gren was rubbing his grazed knuckles. "So who were they?"

As they went out into the lane, he fell silent.

"Keep your hands where they can see them." Sorgrad displayed his empty palms.

"Who do you suppose called the Magistrates' Watch?" Gren followed his brother's example. "Now's a good time to look big and foolish, long lad."

Tathrin wasn't sure what he looked like. He could feel his cheek swelling where he'd been punched. His arm ached horribly where the cosh had struck it.

The men carried halberds but any resemblance to Lescar's militias ended there. Their polearms weren't tipped with plain cleaving blades but bristled with spikes and curved hooks. They all wore the finest chain mail that Tathrin had ever seen, each steel ring so small the hauberks hung like cloth.

"We've none of us drawn a sword," Sorgrad said calmly.

"Just defended ourselves." Why did Gren's virtuous statement sound so like a lie?

One man walked forwards. This must surely be the sergeant. He wore a long sword and, Tathrin noticed uneasily, had a barbed lash coiled in his belt.

"Defended yourselves?" He looked inside the garden gate. "That's as may be."

His tone was neutral. He drew Sorgrad's sword a handspan out of its scabbard. It slid easily out and back in. With a friendly smile, Gren allowed the man to check his own blade.

The sergeant turned to Tathrin. "Your sword?"

"I never touched it." Tathrin stood still as the man satisfied himself it hadn't been thrust bloodied back in the sheath.

"You're wearing armour." The Watchman flicked the front of Tathrin's jerkin, audibly striking the metal plates beneath the leather.

"That's hardly forbidden," Sorgrad said peaceably. He and Gren had shed their hauberks though. Openly going armoured in Relshaz could be taken as proof they were looking for a fight, he'd told Tathrin.

The man shrugged. "You can explain yourselves to the Magistracy. Come on."

Sorgrad meekly followed the sergeant, Tathrin at his side, Gren close behind. The Watchmen surrounded them, fore and aft and two deep to either side. They walked swiftly through the streets in silence.

Tathrin's blood was running cold. Relshazri Magistrates were only concerned with the smooth operation of Relshaz's trade. That's what the merchants said, who passed through his father's inn. Natural justice need not prevail, if it proved inconvenient. What else could you expect in a city where the wealthiest men got themselves elected to unquestioned authority by buying up the votes of the rest?

"Don't fret, long lad," Gren said cheerfully. "Relshazri Magistrates don't hang, not even killers. You'll just end up in the slave pens and be sold to some warlord's wife with a taste for pale sausage."

Tathrin wasn't amused. He knew the Relshazri slave trade brought considerable wealth to the city but it had nothing to do with him. At least, it never had done before. What were they going to do now?

He tried to resist the obvious answer as they took a turn, another and then another. Eventually, he couldn't help a sideways glance at Sorgrad. Just now, he'd gladly suffer the nauseating sensations of being carried away by magic.

Sorgrad's eyes met his. The Mountain mage smiled, amused. "Cheer up. Every bone rolls one good rune. If we're arrested in Relshaz and the Magistrates can swear to it, no one can accuse us of anything in Carluse."

"What do you mean?" Sudden apprehension put all Tathrin's current fears to flight. "They're not going to do it, are they? Failla and Reher? But the captain-general forbade it!"

A sudden halt interrupted him.

"Ah." Sorgrad's expression lit with understanding. "I see."

"Stopping for a break?" Gren asked brightly.

"Round the back." The Watch sergeant headed for an alley.

Sorgrad followed, Gren at his side. Tathrin had no choice but to trail after them. The sergeant knocked on an iron-studded door and someone opened a peephole. As the door opened, Sorgrad went to step through.

The sergeant held him back. "She says we can trust you. If not, if she doesn't kill you, I will."

"Fair enough." Sorgrad nodded, unperturbed.

Bemused, Tathrin watched the sergeant and his men depart.

"Come on," Gren said impatiently. "The day's finally looking up."

Going inside, Tathrin blinked. It was a kitchen, of sorts. A marble bench against the back wall supported shallow charcoal braziers where young women were frying meat and fish. More girls sat around a well-scrubbed table eating bread and cheese and pickles. They were all young and pretty and their complexions ran from buttermilk to burnished ebony. None wore much by way of clothing.

Gren already had an arm around the waist of a willowy brunette. She wore a skirt of red ribbons hanging from a belt of brass links and a twist of the same silk wrapped around her breasts. The fabric was so sheer Tathrin could see the dark circles of her nipples.

Gren's hand slid down to finger the ribbons on her hip. "Is there space on your dance card for me?"

She looked at him through sooty lashes. "Is it true what they say about an uplander's stamina?"

Tathrin realised several girls were looking speculatively at Sorgrad and a few were gazing at him.

One lass caught his eye and grinned, her teeth white against copper skin. "You're a tall boy, long hands, long feet. Are you made to the same measure everywhere?"

Gren chuckled. "No, he'd be three handspans taller, sweetness."

"Excuse me." Tathrin managed a tight smile as he grabbed Sorgrad's shoulder and forced him around to face him. "What's happening back in Carluse?" he demanded furiously.

CHAPTER EIGHTEEN
Failla

Carluse Town,
13th of Aft-Autumn

FAILLA HUDDLED IN her sable cloak. The fur offered wonderful warmth as well as concealment. She only wished she'd asked Master Gruit for fur-lined boots as well.

The captain-general looked up at the last paring of the Greater Moon. The Lesser had waned to a gibbous oval. Stars glittered in the vast darkness and frosty grass crunched underfoot. The soldiers surrounding them faced into the night even though it was ten days since anyone had escaped the town's locked gates.

"You're sure about this?" Evord kept his voice low, despite the distance to the nearest mercenary tents.

"I am." Failla fought not to shiver. It would only

be the bitter cold but she didn't want the Soluran doubting her.

"I would never have asked this of you, but since you have offered..." Evord shook his head. "We cannot delay any longer now the dukes are showing this common purpose."

"I know." Failla had told him as much, as soon as she'd arrived from Abray.

Captain-General Evord's eyes reflected torchlight from the camp. "Tell your uncle I will send a herald to the gate at midday tomorrow. If the town does not surrender, we must attack."

If that happened, innocent blood would be shed. Even Reniack's talent for twisting the truth would be hard pressed to show Evord's mercenaries as heroes fighting for Lescar's freedom if that came to pass.

"I'll tell them," Failla promised.

"Are you sure you don't want an escort?"

She shook her head. "Reher knows the way and he's strong enough."

The blacksmith was exchanging a few quiet words with one of the mercenary lieutenants. Hearing his name, he looked around, expectant. With a black sheepskin over his leather jerkin, his shoulders were twice as wide as the mercenary's. If they were seen from the walls of the town, if any of the Carluse garrison pursued them, Failla was betting Reher could defend them both till her screams brought the mercenaries' sentries running.

"Then I wish you success," Evord said softly, "and commend your courage."

"It's my home." Failla raised her hood to hide her pale face. "My family are trapped."

Leaving the circle of soldiers, Reher at her side, Failla glanced back just once. The men were already marching away, towards the camp, ranks closed to protect their commander.

"Don't look at the lights." Reher's voice rumbled in the darkness. With his black hair and dense beard, there was little enough of his face for the moons to betray. "Your eyes must get used to the darkness."

"I know."

Stubble crackled beneath Failla's boots. Assuming Carluse sentries would be watching the road, they were keeping to the fields. Reher stooped to stay below the spindly hedge stirring in the night's breeze.

He had family and acquaintances inside Carluse Town. The captain-general knew that. Once they were inside, anyone who knew Reher, friend or foe, would surely think twice before attacking him. Evord couldn't deny that. So Failla was more than justified in seeking out the blacksmith among the artisans supporting the army.

She fervently hoped Reher wouldn't need his other talents. They'd agreed magic was only excusable in the direst emergency, to save his life or hers. The last thing Reher wanted was to fall foul of Hadrumal. He was convinced the penalty would be imprisonment

on the Wizards' Isle, until his magic was trained as
the master mages saw fit.

Failla wouldn't have asked for his help if she'd had
any other choice. But that would mean betraying
the guildmasters' secrets and the one hidden path
into Carluse. Reher already knew about it and he
was a man of Carluse, first and last, even though
he was mageborn. Uncle Ernout always swore that
Reher's grasp of fire had only ever served his craft or
furthered the guildmasters' endeavours.

They were following the river towards the hidden
ford where the Dalasorian lancers had suffered such
grievous losses. An earthen mound rose dark against
the night sky. They hadn't buried their dead, not
like the Mountain Men. Reher had explained their
custom was to build pyres for all the fallen together,
surrounded by their dead horses. When the flames
died down, they had raised this mound to cover the
whole.

Their campaign was leaving its mark in Lescar
in more ways than one, Failla thought. So many
deaths. There'd been death for as long as she could
recall. Could this season of slaughter truly end the
relentless bloodletting?

"This way."

Reher left the rustling river for a line of twisted
trees. They followed a rocky crevice up towards the
castle crag, water whispering in the depths.

Struggling to pick out a path in the darkness,
Failla was nevertheless relieved to see no sign of

Reher raising even a glimmer of magelight. He was also impressively stealthy for such a big man, forging through the fresh drifts of leaves making no more noise than the animals rustling through the undergrowth.

Did Reher realise, Failla wondered, that she knew he had killed Lord Veblen? It hadn't been Aldabreshin alchemy that burned Duke Garnot's bastard son to a blackened husk. She wouldn't say anything though. Not unless the Archmage threatened Reher. Then she'd tell how Carluse's guildmasters had decreed that both Jaras of Sharlac and Veblen of Carluse must die on the same field of battle. Reher had just been their tool.

Were they wrong, the old men, when Carluse had seen two years of what passed for peace after that? Neither commander was left to carry forward that summer's warfare in their father's name. Would Uncle Ernout have done any different, if he'd known she had been fond of Veblen? Not loved him, nor desired him as she knew he desired her, but Failla had liked him well enough. She'd planned on seeking his protection when Duke Garnot tired of her. But Veblen had died and Anilt was born and everything had changed.

Failla was struck with sudden longing to know how Tathrin fared in Relshaz. After all the shams of Abray, it had been such a relief to see him again. He knew the worst of what she had done and still never condemned her. He understood the realities of life in Carluse, the agonising choices she had faced.

She hoped he'd understand when he returned and found she'd gone into Carluse Town. He had been adamant he and Reher should be the ones to run such a risk, when she'd first proposed her plan. But Captain-General Evord had refused to allow anyone to attempt it. Until Aremil's messages and those from Kerith and Jettin brought such ominous news of the dukes' machinations. Once Tathrin, Sorgrad and Gren were safely gone to Relshaz, Evord had turned to Failla and Reher. The Soluran wasn't so different from the guildmasters, choosing the right tool for each task without compunction.

They reached the edge of the trees. Grazing stretched between the road and the town walls, cropped and trampled by the town's cattle, the weather too cold and dry for the grass to recover.

Reher was studying the ramparts. Failla could see the evenly spaced torches burning by the watchtower doors. A few lighted windows showed as the hilly streets rose towards the castle. The black outline of the keep blotted out the stars.

Tadira would be saving every last candle to fuel her defiance. *Much good will it do her*, Failla thought savagely. The duchess would have no choice but surrender when the townsfolk opened the gates. But to secure that, they must get inside.

She pressed close to Reher, her whisper the barest breath. "Can you see the sentries?"

He grunted deep in his barrel of a chest. "Stay close."

She had no option when he seized her arm and ran across the grazing. She snatched at her sable cloak, bundling it up so she wouldn't trip. They dropped down behind a weathered statue of Ostrin, god of grape and grain, of hay and harvest.

Her heart pounding, Failla wondered why Duke Garnot had never rebuked the guildsmen for leaving such an eyesore on the road, when they took such pains to maintain other shrines. Presumably such things were beneath his notice.

"Keep watch." Reher ran his hands around the base of the plinth.

Nothing stirred along the road save a hunting owl. A fox barked, answered by a vixen. The torches on the watchtowers burned steadily, unshaken by any suddenly opened doors.

Reher grunted and straightened up. His massive hands were lifting the plinth. Stone grated on stone, so loud Failla feared the sentries on the wall must hear. With no one using the passage since Uncle Ernout's final messenger, no one had greased the hinges so cunningly wrought by the master stonemason. She stood frozen with apprehension.

"I can't hold this forever," Reher growled through gritted teeth.

She wasted no time with apology, slipping into the stone-lined hole. Her hands frantically searched the darkness. Where was the oak post she had to drop into the socket in the top step? Stubbing her fingers on it, she ignored the pain, swiftly securing its foot. Looking up, she saw Reher already lowering the statue. She held the post steady so its top slid into the hollow in the plinth's underside.

"Out of the way." Reher's boots nearly kicked her down the steps as his bulk blotted out what little light there was.

She heard a tearing sound and a hiss of pain. "Are you all right?" The hole was a tight fit for a man of his heft.

"Nothing that won't heal." Hobnails scraped on stone. "Move the post when I lift the statue."

Taking the weight on his shoulders, he forced it up. Failla wrenched at the heavy oak. It came free so easily she nearly fell backwards. Saving herself by letting it fall, she heard it clatter down the steps as the plinth thudded back into its stone surround.

Failla pressed against the wall in the absolute blackness. Her fingernails scraped the masonry, muck slick beneath her fingers. Her sable cloak would be filthy, she thought inconsequentially.

"Let's get on without breaking our necks."

Failla was surprised to hear the scrape of steel and flint. A shaving of kindling flared and she saw Reher's massive hand reaching for a lantern on a stone shelf. He lit the stub of candle and shut the pierced tin front, heading down the steps. "I'll go first."

The lamp shed enough light to show Failla that the passage was dry underfoot, the walls stone-lined, oak lintels supporting the roof. How long had it taken the guildsmen to construct it? How had it been done without the duke's men knowing? Without someone betraying such a secret for the gold and the favour it would win? How many barrels of white brandy, brought to the tunnel from the hidden ford, had bought someone's silence?

At first, the tunnel looked endless. Then it seemed no time at all before Reher stopped at more steps and handed her the lantern.

"Wait here."

"No." Failla spoke quickly to forestall whatever Reher might say. "I can hardly go back and get out on my own if they catch you. If they send someone down to find me, I'll be trapped like a rat in a drain. If we're taken above ground, we can both raise a riot that might just save our lives."

"Stay close then." He didn't sound pleased.

This stair was roofed with floorboards. At the top, Failla lifted the lantern to give Reher more light as his blunt fingers searched the planks. Finding some cunning latch, he raised a silent trapdoor.

Every nerve strained to snapping, Failla emerged into a cellar, empty but for discarded sacks stained with grease and two grain tubs hoarding a handful of husks. The air tasted of rancid pig fat.

Reher noiselessly lowered the trapdoor and moved to the room's main door to listen. He lifted a finger to his bearded lips.

Failla scowled. Did he think she was such a fool?

Reher lifted the latch. Failla followed close. This second cellar was as barren as the first. One hogshead remained on its curved rest, lacking bung or spigot. The other two stands lacked even empty barrels.

Reher opened the far door as cautiously as the first. They both heard a steely slither.

"I have a sword."

The lantern went out so fast only Reher's magecraft could have snuffed it.

Failla spoke first. "Milar?"

The unseen man was astonished. "Who's there?"

"It's me, Failla."

"What?" Disbelief rang through the darkness.

Reher chuckled. "What kind of inn do you keep, if you can't offer a working man ale?"

"Reher?" The sword slid back into its sheath. "Wait a minute."

The exasperated voice faded and a wiry man returned with a candle in a brass stick. His nightshirt hung loose over hastily donned breeches and bare feet. He stared at Failla, gaunt with shock. "They said you were dead."

She flinched at the pain in his voice. "I'm sorry. It wasn't my choice."

"It wasn't, truly." Reher's support was as welcome as it was unexpected.

"What are you doing here?" Milar brushed hair out of his eyes with the back of his other hand. It was useless for more than that, the bones crushed, broken fingers knitted all awry.

"We need to see Ernout." Reher looked at the stairs leading out of the cellars. "Do the duke's men patrol the streets all night?"

Milar was still looking at Failla. "Serafia wept for days, as stricken as when she lost Elpin."

"I'm sorry." Tears pricked Failla's own eyes. "Uncle Ernout knew—"

She couldn't go on. Her cousin had known enough grief, her betrothed lost in the same battle that had crippled Milar's hand. Elpin's body had never been found, leaving Serafia to raise a fatherless son when she should have been a joyous bride.

"If the priest didn't tell her, he had good reason," Reher said firmly. "Milar, we're sorry to rouse you but we've no time to waste. How hard will it be to get to the shrine unseen? Or can you get Ernout to come here without the duke's men sniffing around?"

"He's not at the shrine," Milar said reluctantly. "They took him to the castle two days since."

Reher grimaced. "We'd better talk to Master Findrin."

Milar cut him short with his ruined hand. "The duchess's men beat him senseless, when he tried to stop them taking Ernout."

Failla was too shocked to speak. What could they do now?

"Come on. I need a drink." Milar led them up to the tavern's kitchen.

Reher managed to smile. "You've kept some bottles safe from the castle guards?"

"Behind the plinth of the dresser. I can't rouse the fire," Milar apologised. "We've little enough fuel to cook on, never mind warm the room."

"It doesn't matter." Failla wrapped her cloak close and sat on a stool by the table.

No wonder the guardsmen hadn't found the wine. Even Reher had to stretch on tiptoe to reach the hidden bottles.

Watching Reher drawing a cork, Failla gathered her wits. "What happened to Uncle Ernout?"

"He went up to the castle to ask after young Vrist." Milar looked helplessly at her. "Your Aunty Derou, she's frantic with worry."

Reher sloshed wine into three goblets. "We never thought Tadira would lay hands on the priest."

"Nor did we." Milar gulped wine as he sat. "But why are you here? When you could be safe anywhere!"

"We came to tell Ernout that the townsfolk must open the gates." Failla fought to stop her voice trembling. She didn't dare lift a glass. "We can tell everyone the truth of what's happened at Losand, what's happened at Ashgil. That will surely convince them."

"The guardsmen say both towns have been sacked and burned. Hundreds put to the sword." Milar looked from her to Reher.

"That's all lies," the smith assured him, leaning against the chimney breast beside the empty hearth. "The commander keeps his companies on a tight leash. The Guilds are managing each town's affairs now, sworn to keep the peace. All the militiamen who sued for mercy when Duke Garnot was beaten in the woods, they've all been allowed to go home once they laid down their arms."

"Duke Garnot's been beaten?"

Failla saw hope, or possibly the wine, stirring colour in Milar's drawn cheeks. "His Grace fled to Triolle," she told him. "Those few men with him are falling away."

"That's not what Her Grace says," Milar assured them.

Failla reached for her goblet. "Seeing me alive should prove she doesn't know all she claims."

"She still holds the castle. Her men hold the town gates." The spark in Milar's eyes died. "With Ernout gone, and Findrin senseless, there's no one to rouse men to defy her. She had Master Settan hanged." He drained his drink. "Whatever you might say, folk are afraid. Duke Garnot may be gone today but if he ever comes back, anyone standing against Tadira will be flogged till their bones break. Then their bodies will be tossed to the dogs."

"If the gates don't open by noon tomorrow, the army outside will attack," Reher countered.

"Whatever orders the captain-general gives about sparing innocent folk, some will surely die," Failla said urgently.

Milar shook his head, despairing. "I think folk would still rather answer to Saedrin instead of Duchess Tadira."

"We must make them see sense." The blacksmith slammed his goblet perilously hard on the table. "How soon can we bring the remaining guildmasters together?"

"About half a chime before you're dragged off in chains and hanged," retorted Milar.

Failla gazed into the candle flame. Milar was no coward, nor a fool. Uncle Ernout would never have drawn him into the Guilds' conspiracies if he had been. If he said the townsfolk were too cowed to act, he was right. Reher could loom and glower and nothing would change.

"Who's commanding the castle guard?"

"Why do you ask?" Milar looked at her with misgiving.

"If we won't persuade the townsfolk to open the gates, we must make Tadira's guards see sense." Failla concentrated on the candle flame. "She's only one woman. If the garrison won't back her, what can she do?"

Reher nodded slowly. "I'll bet my anvil they want to live to see the turn of the year just like anyone else."

"Half of them, maybe." Milar shook his head. "The rest will sit tight and count on Duke Garnot rescuing them before they've eaten the food they stole from the town."

Reher was undeterred. "If only half decide to surrender, they can beat sense into the rest."

"How are they to know who else feels the same?" Milar demanded. "Do you think any man will stand up to be counted just because you bang on the castle gates and demand they lay down their arms?"

Failla closed her eyes. The candle's lingering image glowed against the darkness of her vision.

"I know which men we would need to persuade, to turn the rest against the duchess. I can get inside the castle if you two will help."

She had come too far to give up now.

CHAPTER NINETEEN
Tathrin

The Silk Scarf, Relshaz,
13th of Aft-Autumn

"So WHO ELSE knows about this?" he demanded.

"Will you let it drop?" Sorgrad stared at him, exasperated. "I've told you all I know."

"All you know, or all you think I need to know?" Tathrin challenged.

Sorgrad's grin taunted him. "Who knows?"

"Enough!" An older woman with milky skin and dyed scarlet hair clapped her hands. Concealing more than it displayed, her rose-silk gown was at least as seductive as the younger girls' dresses. "You two have been bickering all evening. Either shut up or go outside and settle this quarrel with your fists. Or I'll have one of my boys shut your mouths for you."

The girls, who'd been coming and going all evening, halted in their various tasks to exchange wide-eyed glances. That was clearly no idle threat.

Sorgrad's smiled widened as he glanced at Tathrin. "Want to see what you can beat out of me?"

"No." He wasn't fool enough to imagine he'd even land a blow on the Mountain Man.

Why by all that was sacred and profane were they wasting their time in a whorehouse? Did Aremil know what was happening in Carluse? Tathrin couldn't decide what made him feel more betrayed— that Failla would do this without him, or that Aremil could let him travel to Relshaz in ignorance of the plan.

He folded his arms, shoulders hunched, brooding on the bench by the brothel's kitchen door.

"So who's guarding your doors?" Sorgrad rose and went to the table, taking a seat beside the scarlet-haired woman. "Anyone I might know?"

She looked at him, unsmiling. "Where's your brother?"

"Up to his ears in ribbons, probably." Sorgrad shrugged.

Before the woman could reply, one of the doors on the far side of the kitchen opened. A heavyset man with an oddly twisted face looked in. "She'll see them now."

"Finally." Sorgrad was instantly on his feet. "Come on."

Tathrin followed. What else could he do? Steal a horse? Stow away on a barge sailing up the Rel? He couldn't get back to Carluse inside a double handful of days without Sorgrad's magic. He went mutinously up a plain wooden staircase.

"Gren!" In the hall above, Sorgrad shouted. "Sheathed your favourite sword yet?"

A door opened to reveal Gren, stripped to the waist, a glass of wine in his hand. "Say hello to Semila," he invited.

Tathrin caught a glimpse of the brunette girl reclining naked on a bed, content as a well-stroked cat.

Sorgrad spared her an appreciative grin before snapping his fingers at his brother. "Get your shirt and your sword. She's ready to see us."

As Gren ducked back into the room, Tathrin followed Sorgrad to the door at the far end of the hall. He was taut with apprehension. The Mountain mage hadn't answered any of his questions about this place or who they'd be meeting.

The door opened into an elegant boudoir, the air heavy with perfume. A handsome woman took her ease on a daybed. Her hair was beautifully dressed but no dye hid the white amid the chestnut, while cosmetics enhanced her beauty without seeking to conceal her wrinkles. Her sea-green gown was expertly cut to accommodate her generous curves, though clearly she had not always been so stout. Amid the lace of her petticoats, her feet were dainty in satin slippers.

Sorgrad swept a courtly bow. "Mellitha Esterlin, may I present—"

"Tathrin Sayron, I know." She greeted him with a smile. "Please don't think too badly of Relshaz. These two have a lamentable taste for the gutters."

"I—" Tathrin settled for a bow. "Madam."

Appearing behind him, Gren chuckled. "She's not the draper in this button-shop."

"I mean no offence." Tathrin's bruised eye throbbed as he blushed.

"No, dear, I'm one of the city's tax-gatherers," the woman said calmly. "Since I assess this house's earnings, the owner accommodates my private meetings. Now, 'Grad, explain yourself."

Sorgrad satisfied himself that the door was closed. "We're seeing which mercenary companies are leaving the city and where they're headed."

Tathrin didn't know which he found more unnerving: the woman's air of authority or Sorgrad's ready acquiescence. He sat on a cushioned loveseat and just hoped he wasn't making it too dirty.

"You're working with Mistress Charoleia? In this Lescari scheme?"

There was enough of a question in Mellitha's tone to deepen Sorgrad's frown.

"I'd like to know why you might think different."

Mellitha wasn't impressed. "Did you kill Downy Scardin?"

"No," Sorgrad said flatly.

That was true but would this woman believe it? Tathrin had seen both brothers tell outrageous lies without turning a hair. If she knew them, presumably she had too.

Mellitha turned a motherly smile on him. "Tell me, where've you been today?"

Tathrin didn't have a hope of explaining where they'd been in the city, so he settled for telling her what they'd done.

"We've been trying to trace the Quicksilver Men. A man called Egil said they were going upriver but it seems they went by sea."

"As you know full well, Mellitha." Sorgrad gestured to a shallow silver bowl on a side table. "How long have you been scrying after us?"

Gren paused in buttoning his shirt. "So that's how the Watch knew to come and stop us getting our heads kicked in. I'm obliged to you, madam mage."

"My pleasure." Mellitha's smile was as pert as a schoolgirl's.

Tathrin would rather have faced those brutal men again if this woman had been scrying, using elemental magic to follow them through the city. What could that mean?

Sorgrad had other concerns. "What's Downy Scardin's death to you?"

"We'll get to that in good time." Mellitha pursed her full lips. "Now that Master Hamare is dead, who do you suppose gives Triolle's enquiry agents their orders?"

Did this magewoman know Sorgrad had killed Hamare? Blood pulsed in Tathrin's temples.

"Duke Iruvain." Sorgrad saw no mystery. "We keep tripping over his men's tracks."

"All the way to Egil the Toad's door," confirmed Gren. "Iruvain's calling up mercenaries and we want to know where they're mustering."

Mellitha raised a manicured finger. "I mean Master Hamare's personal agents, not the folk gathering gossip on street corners for Triolle."

"I don't know what you mean." Sorgrad's eyes glinted, hard as sapphires.

"Would it surprise you to learn that Duchess Litasse directs them now?" Mellitha's dark eyes were impenetrable. "I don't believe her husband has any notion that she's doing so."

"I wouldn't have imagined it before I met the lady." Sorgrad's gaze was opaque with recollection. "Now I could be persuaded."

Whatever had happened, after Sorgrad's magic had carried himself and Gren right into the heart of Triolle Castle and safely out again, Sorgrad had withdrawn into his own thoughts for days. Tathrin hadn't dared ask for any details.

"Bright as steel on flint, she was," Gren said cheerfully. "Blood and magefire all around and she wouldn't let us see her frightened."

Tathrin's blood ran cold. If Mellitha didn't already know Sorgrad's secret, she did now.

Gren saw nothing amiss. "You've always liked fiery girls, haven't you?"

"You know nothing about it." Sorgrad's reply

was just a little too swift.

Gren was right, though. Tathrin had seen Sorgrad's respect for Failla, when she had defied the three of them, even as they were busy kidnapping her. How would that courage serve her now, if she were captured in Carluse?

"Don't fret, my dear."

He realised Mellitha was looking at him. What had his face given away?

"Wizardry's no crime in Relshaz," Mellitha explained. "Sorgrad and I know where we both stand."

The Mountain Man demurred. "That remains to be seen."

"Let's see if we can clarify matters." Mellitha rang a silver bell on the table at her elbow.

The room's second door opened. This place must be an absolute maze. Then again, so were Vanam's brothels, in Tathrin's admittedly limited experience.

He knew enough to be sure that the young woman who entered was no whore. Her luminous hazel eyes were striking but she had none of the prostitutes' superficial prettiness. Her neat grey dress sought neither to display nor to conceal her figure, and her self-possession convinced Tathrin she neither required nor desired any man's admiration.

"May I introduce Jilseth, recently arrived from Hadrumal? As you might imagine, she enjoys Archmage Planir's confidence." Mellitha's hand swept around. "This is Sorgrad and his brother Gren, and Tathrin, who finds himself in uncomfortably deep water through no fault of his own."

Tathrin knew his face betrayed his dismay. A second magewoman—and worse, one with personal ties to the Archmage?

Mellitha smiled serenely. "Tathrin, Gren, fetch that table so we can all see more clearly."

He quickly helped Gren do as she asked, careful not to spill the water filling the shallow silver bowl.

Sorgrad looked at Mellitha. "Who are we scrying for?"

"This is a little different." Jilseth took a small vial out of a purse at her waist and poured viscous oil onto the water. It wasn't green oil pressed from olives, or anything else that Tathrin knew from his mother's kitchen. Yellow scum spread across the water with an acrid odour that caught in the back of his throat.

"What's that?" Sorgrad growled.

He didn't mean the oil. Jilseth was unwinding a scrap of muslin to reveal a bloody bone, fresh shreds of meat clinging to it.

"A joint from Downy Scardin's forefinger." She dropped it into the bowl.

"Necromancy."

Gren's revulsion startled Tathrin. Gren, who'd gone digging in an ancient battlefield to find the bones to fake Failla's death.

"Gentlemen, if you could pay attention." Mellitha gestured towards the bowl.

Amber light bubbled up from the bone, consuming the floating oil. Wisps of bitter smoke rose from the seething bowl. Jilseth gathered them with her hands, coaxing them into a ball. Golden light flowed from her fingers, weaving a net among the smoky tendrils.

This wasn't like a scrying, seeing a flat image floating on water. Something coalesced inside the sphere of light and shadow hovering above the bowl. A miniature vision of a room, like the doll's house Tathrin's sisters had played with. The figures inside weren't fashioned from clothespins and scraps of cloth, though. He desperately stifled a cough.

A fat black-haired man in tunic and trews sat by a desk piled high with papers. He was nodding as he spoke to another man, taller, thin, with a shaven scalp. Dressed in riding boots and breeches, his long-sleeved jerkin hung unbuttoned over his shirt. The thin man handed over a heavy leather purse. The fat man stowed it in a drawer and turned the key. He began writing, pausing several times to gesture.

The thin man nodded and waited patiently. When the fat man concluded his letter, the thin man drew a dagger hidden beneath his tunic and swiftly cut the fat man's throat to the bone. Taking only the letter, and reclaiming his purse, he cautiously opened the glass-paned door. But he didn't leave the garden by the gate. Tathrin saw him climb onto the windowsill outside, presumably reaching for the balcony above. His boots disappeared from view as the vision in the smoke dissolved.

"There's not a Watchman born thinks to track a man over rooftops," Gren mused. "Not unless he sees him climbing, and even then they don't like following."

"As any decent thief will tell you," agreed Sorgrad.

"Do you know who he is?" Jilseth demanded.

"No." Sorgrad answered for them both. "Do you know what he wanted with Downy Scardin?"

Mellitha shot him a hard look. "Downy Scardin helps evil men find each other. Would you care to tell us your business with him?"

Jilseth's gaze was equally penetrating. "Of late, Scardin's been taking coin from the corsairs who lair in the Archipelago's fringes and raid the Caladhrian coast."

Gren shrugged. "We know nothing about that."

"We're busy enough in Lescar." Sorgrad smiled.

"Are you?" Jilseth raised an auburn eyebrow. "When the corsairs are offering a fortune in gold and gems for any wizard willing to dirty his hands?"

"No fortune's worth Archmage Planir's enmity," Sorgrad assured her. "As you're well aware, if he's sent you to dissuade any mages tempted to turn mercenary."

Jilseth looked intently at him. "You've never been approached, on your own account, or by someone asking if you know any other renegade mage?"

"I'm no renegade, madam," Sorgrad assured her. "How could I be, when I owe no allegiance to Hadrumal?"

Staring into the bowl, Tathrin noticed that the finger bone was parboiled. He swallowed queasily.

"Then what was your business with Downy Scardin?" Mellitha demanded.

"None of yours," said Gren caustically.

Tathrin's tongue was stuck to the roof of his mouth. He cleared his throat. "That man, who killed the fat one, his name is Karn. He's a Triolle spy."

"The man who attacked Branca and Lady Derenna?" Sorgrad's face hardened.

Gren looked as menacing. "When they were travelling in Sharlac with the apothecary?"

"It's him," Tathrin insisted.

When Aremil had told him of that assault, he'd seen every detail of Branca's recollection. Aremil's fear for the woman he loved had laid his mind wide open. Tathrin had been stunned to realise the depth of Aremil's feelings for the plain and sturdy Artificer. And he remembered this spy Karn's face, no question.

"Kindly explain," snapped Jilseth.

Sorgrad looked at Mellitha. "Charoleia said Karn was Master Hamare's closest confidant."

"Other than Duchess Litasse." She glanced at Jilseth. "So Triolle's suborning magic to strengthen their cause?"

Gren was as quick as Tathrin to pick up her meaning.

"You thought someone else was trying to find a renegade mage? You thought it was us?"

Jilseth wasn't about to apologise. "Archmage Planir knows you have few scruples and no respect for his authority or Hadrumal's laws."

Mellitha folded her beringed hands in her lap. "You have already used magic in Lescar's wars," she observed mildly.

Tathrin tensed. What now? Would Sorgrad try to fight both magewomen? Tavern tales of magical duels back in the days of the Chaos told of such battles causing wholesale devastation. Surely they wouldn't do anything so destructive here?

What about Gren? Tathrin stole a sideways glance, fearful he'd see the Mountain Man reaching for some blade. Was a knife any use against a wizard? He realised he had no idea. Even if it was, how could Gren hope to fight his way out past the brothel's armed guards? Assuming he was thinking that far ahead. Then he realised Gren was smiling.

Sorgrad was too. "You know about that?"

"Archmage Planir is not impressed." Mellitha might have been scolding them for stealing butter from her pantry.

Jilseth was far more stern. "You're fortunate that punishing you risks bringing the truth of Emirle Bridge into the light. Then Draximal will insist the magic was Parnilesse's doing, while Duke Orlin claims just the opposite, regardless of what Planir says."

"The other dukes won't care who's at fault." Mellitha shrugged. "They'll just want to secure magic for their own purposes as swiftly as possible, now the Archmage's prohibition has been broken."

"Planir would find that inconvenient." Sorgrad was grinning. "But what's this got to do with us?"

Mellitha gestured towards the bowl, rank fumes still rising from the water's surface. "This man Karn is already a thorn in your side. Why don't you pursue him, and make sure he doesn't hire any wizard, for your sake as well as ours?"

Jilseth nodded. "That should settle your account with Planir over Emirle Bridge. As long as you use no more magic in Lescar."

Sorgrad waved that away. "What does Triolle want with magic? Do you know who Downy Scardin wrote that letter to?"

Jilseth paused for a moment before answering. "To a wizard called Minelas. Don't concern yourself with such scum. I'll make sure he sees the error of his ways."

Gren chuckled. "I wouldn't like to be in his shoes."

Tathrin tried to hide his relief. They might just escape the Archmage's wrath, if Planir had a worse offender to punish.

The younger magewoman stood up. "Find Karn and tell me what you learn."

Sorgrad pursed his lips. "Only if you let us know what you find out when you catch up with Minelas."

"That sounds like a fair exchange," Mellitha said firmly, before the younger magewoman could answer. "Now you two have met, you can bespeak each other."

"I can scry on you any time I want now." Jilseth looked at Sorgrad, unblinking. "Don't be tempted into follies like Emirle Bridge again."

"That would be foolish," he admitted with a charming smile. Jilseth was unmoved.

"Then I believe that concludes our business," Mellitha said briskly. "Jilseth, will you go and summon our carriage, please? Can we offer you three a ride somewhere?"

Gren chuckled. "And miss out on the ride I've been promised here?"

Sorgrad ran a hand through his blond hair. "This is as good a place as any to listen for talk of Scardin's death. Whores hear useful rumours. One could get us a sniff of this Karn's scent."

"True enough." Mellitha nodded, rose and made her way to the door. Jilseth followed, her expression still disdainful.

As the door closed behind them, Tathrin drew a shuddering breath. "What now?"

Gren looked towards the hallway. "I fancy ruffling that long lass's ribbons a second time."

Sorgrad nodded. "Let her know we'll pay the girls handsomely for any pillow talk about Scardin. With any luck we'll have a trail to follow by the morning."

"What happens now the Archmage knows you're using your magic?" Tathrin demanded.

"Planir's lass told us more than she intended." Sorgrad was unperturbed. "She knew about Emirle Bridge but she didn't mention anything else we've done. So either she doesn't know or Planir doesn't think it warrants his attention. She said nothing at all about Reher and if they knew of him, she would have. Planir doesn't let untrained mages escape Hadrumal's instruction.

"Mellitha said nothing about us walking back to Lescar," he continued. "I reckon we can still use my magic for our own purposes, as long as we're discreet. As long as we find this man Karn and put an end to Triolle's hunt for a mage." His face hardened. "Subtle wizardry could cause no end of trouble while the army's besieging Carluse, delaying Evord while the dukes unite."

Tathrin's fears for Failla redoubled. "But we have to get back there. We can't go chasing this spy."

"We don't want to miss all the fun," Gren agreed. "Either way, if Evord sacks the town, or if Failla and the smith get the gates open. That Jilseth looks as if she can take care of whoever's twisting Planir's nose."

"I wouldn't want to cross her." Sorgrad shrugged. "Let's see what Aremil says, and the captain-general."

"So we're going back to Carluse?" Tathrin stood up, bracing himself for the shock of the wizardry.

"Not yet." Sorgrad unbuckled his sword-belt. "Not till we know if Evord wants us chasing Karn."

"Right." Gren rubbed his hands gleefully. "Call me when you know."

Before Tathrin could protest, he disappeared through the doorway into the hall.

"Why don't you find a nice girl to clear your head while you're waiting for Aremil's call?" The Mountain Man grinned and followed his brother.

Tathrin sat down again. If only he could let Aremil know he needed to talk to him. But no, all he could do was wait, yet again. He sighed and tried not to listen to the sounds of the brothel's commerce along the hallway. After a while, he began wondering if he could go back to the kitchen in hopes of some supper.

Then the door opened. "Gren said you needed something for your face?" A pretty Caladhrian girl in a lace shift came in. She carried muslin and a bowl of warm water fragrant with herbs. Before Tathrin could say anything, she sat on his knee. The lacy shift rode up her thighs. She clearly wore nothing at all beneath it.

She looked critically at his blackened eye. "Poor boy."

Closing his eyes as she bathed the bruise, Tathrin felt the cloth catch on his bristles. "I haven't shaved—"

"Hush." She pressed a finger to his lips. "Would you like some white brandy to take the sting out of that? Or something sweeter?" She kissed him. "Yes, that's better, isn't it?" She took his hand and cupped it around her breast, kissing him again.

So soft, so warm, so fragrant. Tathrin couldn't help his rising ardour and knew the girl must be feeling it too. Would it be so wrong? Tathrin couldn't decide. His tired mind in turmoil, he found himself responding to her kiss.

"That's better." The girl deftly unbuckled his belt and tugged his shirt free. "Not so shy now."

Unresisting, he let her lead him to the daybed. As he lay back, he thought she was going to unlace his boots. She unlaced his breeches instead. Tathrin wound his bruised hands in the girl's soft hair and closed his eyes. Why not take a little pleasure for himself? It wouldn't mean anything, after all.

He was so weary, so confused, still a little afraid, still more than a little angry with Sorgrad, with Gren, with Aremil and Failla for keeping such secrets from him. If he could lose himself in physical sensation, maybe that would stop him worrying about her.

CHAPTER TWENTY
Failla

Carluse Town,
14th of Aft-Autumn

"BRING US OUR priest!" Milar's shout was a plea.

Reher's bellow was a full-throated accusation. "How dare you detain Master Ernout?"

Failla had left them in the cobbled marketplace overlooked by the castle's gatehouse. She was walking swiftly along the wide rocky ditch that separated the town's most prized houses from the castle precincts. In the pre-dawn light, everything was grey: the garden walls down the slope to her left, the path worn in the turf ahead, the forbidding battlements across the gaping chasm to her right.

"Bring us our priest!"

That roar must have rattled the windows. She heard lesser voices. Reher's shouts were rousing outraged householders. Milar had already knocked on plenty of doors as they marched up the long main street.

"If Ernout committed some crime, let him answer at the shrine of Raeponin!" he demanded.

Failla had kept her head down and her hood up for fear of being recognised, so she had no idea how many townsfolk were braving Duchess Tadira's anger for Ernout's sake. Fewer than his kindness and generosity merited, she wagered. But saving those who deserved it meant saving cowards and ingrates too.

She hurried on, clutching the hood under her chin. Faint amusement lightened her apprehension. Plenty of folk would recognise Reher, and they'd want to know where he'd been and how he'd evaded the besieging army to get back into the town. The castle guards wouldn't be able to tell nosiness from insurrection as the crowd swelled. So they'd send for reinforcements and men at more tedious posts would hurry to see what was afoot.

The ditch curved and Failla saw the castle's lesser gate. To her relief, its narrow wooden bridge was intact. Either Duchess Tadira refused to countenance preparation for a last stand or the garrison commander knew a few men with axes could bring it down before any assault reached this far.

Other voices drowned out whatever Milar and Reher were shouting now, though if they were raised in agreement or protest, Failla couldn't tell.

She looked covertly at the slit windows on either

side of the lesser gate. Sentries would be watching her. But they'd just see an unknown woman hoping something remained of the castle's leavings, which were set out every evening for the hungry poor. Only Failla saw no sign of the usual baskets. There were no scraps on the dusty ground, no footprints.

Had Duchess Tadira abandoned that customary charity? Failla cursed under her breath. She should have asked Milar. But she'd have had to explain her plan. Both men would have instantly forbidden it. If she'd stopped to reflect, she might even have changed her own mind.

"Open up and answer for your misdeeds!"

How long could Reher keep up such bellowing? How long before some sentry here wondered what this black-cloaked woman was doing, if there was no food to be scavenged?

She hurried across the narrow bridge, drew a deep breath and knocked. Saedrin send she knew at least one of the sergeants on guard. One of those who didn't enjoy Duke Garnot's favour. If not, well, whoever was on the night watch would be sluggish and heavy-eyed, ready for his bed. Failla was ready to promise to join him, if that's what it took to get into the castle.

But her knock prompted no answer. She tried again, frowning. The peephole remained blind, the door locked. Had the commotion drawn all the sentries to the main gate? Scores of voices were now demanding their priest.

Well, this wasn't the only way in. She had come too far to give up now. If she did, all she'd have achieved was getting Milar and Reher clapped in chains.

Failla unclasped the sable cloak and let it fall to the broken bottom of the ditch, twice a tall man's height below. Regardless of the chill, she couldn't risk the fur's weight dragging at her shoulders. Pressing her face to the castle wall, she began edging along the sloping turf, towards the empty sky where the rocky ditch met the cliff.

The wall continued around, above the shattering drop. It was only at the very pinnacle of the crag, on the far side of the inner keep, that gardens had been laid out between the defences and the unguarded drop. Failla wasn't attempting to go that far. Sentries manned the garden's gates and even the Mountain Men had shaken their heads at the thought of scaling such lethal heights. She just had to round this first corner and make her way to the sluice chute. Step by tiny step, she continued.

The sun was rising on the far side of the castle. As soon as she rounded that first corner, she'd be hidden in the dense shadow falling across the broad vale below. Bigger and heavier men had done this and more than once. She'd never heard of one falling to his death.

Her creeping fingers found the angle of the wall. Despite herself, she gazed out across the dizzying emptiness. Distant hills were shadowed with trees. The insistent breeze tugged at her skirts. No. She wasn't going to look down. Failla pressed her face against the unyielding stone and edged along the narrow ledge between the wall and the calamitous drop.

The sluice chute wasn't far and her nose told her when it was close. Failla took as deep a breath as she could without gagging and halted. She wasn't going to fall to her death on some slick of night soil. Maidservants would already be emptying the chamber pots.

Sure enough, she heard the sluice room door open. Pots rattled and noisome contents slopped through the chute. A bucket clanked and water rushed out to wash the ordure down the cliff.

How soon before she heard a voice she could trust? There were few enough of those. She shivered, her hands going ominously numb.

Halcarion be thanked, excited voices followed the next rush of waste.

"He was Findrin's journeyman!"

"What's happened to the priest?"

Not the woman Failla would have chosen but trustworthy enough.

"Zarene!"

The clink of earthenware stilled.

"What's that?"

Failla breathed more easily. The startled girl must be new to the castle, so she wouldn't recognise Failla.

"Zarene, it's me, Failla!"

"But you're—" Zarene choked.

"Where—?"

Failla spoke swiftly to stop the new girl's questions. "It was the only way I could get safely away."

"Saedrin save us." Zarene's curiosity overcame her bewilderment. "What are you doing out there?"

Failla chose her words carefully. Zarene was too timid to trust with the truth.

"What you don't know can't get you whipped. Just open the upper window and throw out the rope."

"What window? What rope?" the new girl demanded.

"I don't know—" Zarene wavered.

"Drianon's my witness, I'm here to help. All of you and your families. When did you last see your mother, Zarene?" Failla guessed the duchess was keeping the castle servants confined, so they didn't learn how harshly she was treating the town.

"They won't let us—" Zarene whimpered.

"Who is that?" the new girl persisted.

"You stick to your own stitches!" Zarene spat with all the fury of a victim unable to confront her true tormenters.

"I'm a friend, truly," Failla promised, suddenly terrified the girl would retaliate by betraying them both.

"I'll open the window," Zarene said abruptly. "But no more."

Failla heard rapid feet and the door slam. The new girl's life must be free from love and lust, if no one had told her about the knotted rope hidden behind the shutters above the sluice.

Dalliance between the castle's maids and the garrison was strongly discouraged. Any unwed woman found pregnant was ordered to name the father and he was obliged to marry her. Refusal meant dismissal and loss of all ducal favour. Few men seeking riches through fealty to Carluse colours risked that.

Few maidservants wanted to be shackled to a swordsman at Duke Garnot's disposal. The town had enough widows. They favoured courtships with honest craftsmen. Long since, some ardent swain and his bold girl had decided market-day meetings weren't enough. He'd risked the cliff ledge so they could exchange loving words through the smelly chute.

Was she the first to secure a rope to the storage room window? Failla didn't care. Halcarion just send that none of the sentries privy to the secret had cut it down. Hopefully being able to slip out unseen to the town still outweighed the risk to the castle's defences. After all, who but the castle's loyal inmates knew of it?

The window creaked. She risked a careful look up. The rope slithered down and she grabbed at it. Her foot slipped and her blood ran cold. But she was safe, a knot digging into her palm.

She climbed as quickly as she could. It would have been easier with her skirts tucked up but she dared not stoop on that narrow ledge. When she finally reached the sill, she hauled herself inside, her hands and arms burning. The upper room was empty. Good. Failla didn't have to explain herself to the new girl.

The chest beneath the window held darned sheets salvaged from the laundry's rag pile to save lovers' knees and buttocks from the floorboards. Failla gathered up an armful. Her dress was plain enough for a maid's and dangling linen hid her lack of an apron.

She slipped through the door and down the stairs. As she'd wagered, there was no one around. Everyone was occupied with the uproar at the gates.

Easing the door to the castle's outer ward open, Failla saw sentries up on the battlements exchanging shouts and gestures with men-at-arms inside the castle. More distant, she heard shouting outside the main gate. Reher's booming voice was unmistakable.

She scurried past the great hall, at the heart of the range of buildings dividing these outer precincts from the castle's inner ward. No one shouted incredulous recognition. Before anyone wondered why a maid carrying sheets went straight past the laundry, she threw the musty linen down some cellar steps and hurried on.

Between the main gate and the stable yard, the pale stone of the riding school shone in the strengthening daylight. Whatever folk had guessed, when Duke Garnot ordered the old bastion demolished, no one had expected a new hall built solely for exercising horses. Why not, when Carluse's famed stables won him so much gold and admiration? The horsemasters answered to no one but the duke. Crucially, Horsemaster Corrad had scant respect for the duchess.

But the arched gateway into the stable yard was choked with grooms, all nudging elbows and wide-eyed conjecture. She recognised Parlin, the lad who'd been burdened with telling the duke she'd been kidnapped that spring. She couldn't possibly get past him unnoticed. Shading her eyes as if the rising sun dazzled her, she thought furiously.

Beneath the riding school's costly windows a narrow door enabled the duke to take his guests inside to watch his horses display their paces. It was seldom locked and she could reach the yard through the riding school. She began walking.

Someone cried out. Failla heard outrage and accusation. Whether or not it was flung at her, she broke into a run. She wrenched the door open, dashing inside to slam it behind her.

"Who—?" Horsemaster Corrad's famed ill-temper foundered on astonishment. "Failla?"

She pressed her back against the door, sick with apprehension but determined to make him listen.

"Master Corrad, who can you trust among the garrison sergeants? You have to persuade them to open the town gates."

There wasn't a man in the castle who didn't trust Corrad. They might not like him but everyone knew he was honest.

He gaped at her. The handful of mounted grooms were just as dumbfounded. Even the horses pricked curious ears.

"If Carluse doesn't surrender, that army will attack at noon. They've been told to give quarter but the guards will fight, you know that. Who knows what will happen then? But if the gates can be opened, no one need die!" She took a step forward, beseeching. "They're not here to rob us or seize the High King's crown. They want to throw down the dukes to bring us all peace."

"Seize her!"

Failla looked up to the balcony where Duke Garnot's guests were wont to enjoy wine and sweetmeats. Lord Ricart, Carluse's heir, looked down. His face, finer featured than his father's but with that same strong jaw, twisted with hatred.

He jabbed a finger at the closest groom. "Tell my mother we have a spy in our midst!"

The youth looked desperately at Corrad. The horsemaster visibly hesitated.

"You take your orders from me," Ricart spat, "or I'll take a whip to you!"

He turned to come down from the balcony. The panicked boy slid from his saddle and fled through the riding school's entrance.

"Master Corrad. Duke Garnot is defeated. He's been driven out of the dukedom. His mercenaries have deserted and he's begging for shelter in Triolle." Failla seized the man's unresisting hand.

"All the militiamen who surrendered have been sent back to their homes and farms. This army doesn't attack the innocent. They've spared Losand and Ashgil. Whatever Duchess Tadira has told you is lies!"

Lord Ricart threw open the door at the bottom of the balcony stairs. "We expect my father's army any day!"

Failla saw Corrad's expression harden. The horsemaster had spent enough years dealing with youthful grooms to know a frantic lie when he heard one.

She lowered her voice. "I have gold hidden in the town, three hundred Tormalin crowns. Promise whatever you need to open the town gates and all that's left is yours."

Corrad was honest, respected and he hoarded every copper cut-piece he could.

He searched her face for falsehood. "Where is it?"

"Saedrin's shrine." There was no point in holding back. "In the urn with my grandfather's ashes."

Lord Ricart strode towards them, incensed. "I told you to seize that lying whore!"

Failla saw a flash of the lust she had always discouraged, then Ricart's realisation that she was now at his mercy.

"She's going nowhere, my lord."

As Corrad grasped Failla's upper arm, she allowed herself some hope. His grip was firm yet gentle, as he was with his horses.

"She's going to be flogged till her bones break!" Lord Ricart's knuckles smashed into her cheekbone, knocking her off her feet. "Traitorous whore!"

With a heart-rending scream, Failla sprawled on the sand and sawdust. The unnerved horses jostled and stamped.

"Get them back to the stables!" Whatever else, Corrad wouldn't risk injury to his charges.

Satisfied, Failla lay limp and tried to ignore the dizzying ache in her face. Lord Ricart was a strong young man, even if he lacked his father's breadth of shoulder.

"Get Sergeant Haddow! Now!"

She cried out as he wound his hand in her hair and hauled her upwards. He didn't let her stand, her feet slipping on the sawdust as he dragged her towards the door. His excruciating hold meant tears blurred her vision. She had no notion where Corrad had gone. Once outside, she shivered in the shadow that the riding school cast across the outer ward.

"Scared, bitch?" Viciously satisfied, Lord Ricart twisted his hand still tighter.

"Help me! Help me!" Failla wasn't feigning terror. Haddow was loathed and feared in equal measure by the garrison's men. "Save yourselves! Surrender! Garnot is beaten!" She fought against Lord Ricart's hold, screaming at the top of her voice. "The duchess is lying! She'll see you all dead if you let her! Open the town gates and save yourselves!"

Lord Ricart tried to beat her into silence. She fended off his blows as best she could. Through her tears she saw consternation spread through the gathering crowd and heard breathless gasps of recognition, of her name.

"Silence!"

Duchess Tadira's voice cut through the noise like a whipcrack.

Lord Ricart let Failla fall. "This whore bids us surrender!"

"I said *silence*."

The duchess's cold fury stilled every voice inside the castle. Outside the gates, Failla could hear Reher still leading insistent demands for the priest. She lay still, her breast pressed to the cobbles, her hands braced, covertly looking around.

Duchess Tadira descended the Great Hall's steps. Had Ricart's messenger reached her or had she been on her way to confront the townsfolk at the gate?

"Sergeant, cut that slut's throat." The duchess indicated Failla with a contemptuous gesture. "Then go about your duties." She raised her voice with implicit threat. "All of you."

In the half-year since Failla had last seen her, the slender duchess hadn't altered. Her silver-blonde hair was perfectly restrained by a gold crescent set with moonstones. The breeze barely stirred the gossamer veil hanging to her shoulders, a shade lighter than her grey velvet gown. Her eyes were paler still, cold as winter ice. She could pass for ten years younger than Duke Garnot, unless one were close enough to see the fine wrinkles where her skin had dried against her sharp features.

At the bottom of the steps, a garrison sergeant whom Failla didn't know reluctantly drew his sword. "Your Grace—"

"Cut her throat," Duchess Tadira ordered with slow precision.

Failla found she felt oddly calm. At least it would be quick. At least Anilt was safe and Lathi would love her. Her death might even be enough to provoke the townsfolk into open defiance. Would that save Uncle Ernout, young Vrist and the rest?

The garrison sergeant still didn't move. "If she's guilty—"

"Guilty?" Lord Ricart's brutal kick numbed Failla's thigh. "Of course she's guilty!"

"What of?"

An unseen voice prompted an uneasy stir among the swelling crowd of servants.

"Who said that?" Furious, Lord Ricard rounded on them.

No one identified the dissenter.

"She is guilty of treason against our duke." The duchess calmly surveyed the gathering. "As is anyone who doesn't return to their duties at once."

No one moved and Failla realised the hubbub beyond the gates had subsided.

"Where's Haddow?" raged Lord Ricart.

"Here, my lord."

Failla saw the bully striding from the gatehouse. The dislike of servants and castle guards alike was palpable.

"Cut that bitch's throat and then cut his!" Lord Ricart jabbed a trembling hand at the disobedient sergeant. "Let that be a lesson to you all!"

"Your Grace?" Loathsome, not stupid, Haddow looked for the duchess's affirmation.

Tadira nodded. Haddow drew his sword.

"No." The troubled sergeant moved between Haddow and Failla.

"No?" Incredulous, Lord Ricart drew the ornamental sword at his hip. "No?"

"This isn't right," the sergeant protested desperately, his blade held low in defence.

"Let Master Ernout judge her!" someone yelled, a different voice from the first.

There was a stir of agreement.

"In Duke Garnot's absence, I hold all power of life and death." Tadira walked briskly down the steps.

Lord Ricart didn't understand until she took the slender sword from his unresisting hand. The courageous sergeant tried to block her path. Haddow seized his chance and the man had to meet his slashing stroke or lose his leg. Their swords locked. Neither could move without freeing the other to slay him.

"She wants to murder me but she can't kill the truth." Failla tried to stand as Duchess Tadira advanced. Her leg wouldn't support her. Had Ricart's kick crippled her? "Duke Garnot has abandoned you. Carluse Town will fall before sunset. Open the gates and you save yourselves." Her words rang through silence inside the castle and beyond.

She held Tadira's gaze with her own. "Killing me won't change that."

The duchess spat in her face as she drew the sword back. Failla closed her eyes. If Anilt never remembered her, perhaps that was all for the best.

The thrust through her throat never came. Tadira gasped. Failla opened her eyes to see the duchess fall backwards.

"Mama!" Ricart shrieked.

Tadira raised herself on one elbow and stared incredulously at her grey velvet midriff. A crossbow bolt pierced her breastbone. She choked, blood trickling from her mouth. Ricart reached her as her bubbling breath faded and she slumped back onto the cobbles.

"You!" Maddened with hate, his eyes fastened on Failla.

He stooped to the unsullied sword. Before he could snatch it up, an arrow struck his shoulder, spinning him around. As he fell, the shaft snapped beneath him, driving the head deep into his body. He screamed as blood pooled beneath him.

In the next instant Haddow collapsed to the ground, bloody hands clutching his belly as he yelped. The sergeant's swift sword had disembowelled him.

Failla was still looking at Ricart. An arrow had felled him, not a second crossbow bolt. At least two of the castle's defenders had abandoned their fealty to mother and son. She looked up at the battlements to see men fighting, the sun striking fire from their swords and daggers.

Maids and lackeys fled. The gatehouse was in chaos as half the garrison turned on the rest. Daylight flooded into the outer ward as the great gates opened. The combined wrath of the townsfolk and the defiant garrison was overwhelming those loyal to Duke Garnot's badge.

"Please, let me help you." The sergeant offered his hand.

Failla took it, struggling to her feet. Despite the agony in her thigh, she exulted. The exiles had taken Carluse. Nothing could stop Captain-General Evord now.

CHAPTER TWENTY-ONE
Litasse

**Triolle Castle,
16th of Aft-Autumn**

"CAN YOU SMELL rain?" Atop the Duchess's Tower, Litasse contemplated the overcast sky.

"I don't believe so, my lady." Pelletria glanced at the southern horizon. No thicker clouds there presaged a downpour.

"How long will the wells hold out?" Litasse looked at the mere between the castle and Triolle Town's walls. Weeds flourished on the cracked mud ringing the dull water.

"Longer if His Grace orders the town gates barred to mercenaries, so the brewers need only supply our own folk," the old woman answered tartly.

"He can hardly do that with Marlier's whore and her bastards taking over the best tavern." Though at least Duke Ferdain's brindled bitch kept her companies on a tight leash. Litasse wrapped her shawl around her shoulders as she turned to survey the tents and pennants beyond the White Tower and the Oriel Tower. "Iruvain says we have three thousand paid men following Triolle's flag now?"

Was he deluding himself, just as he fondly believed he was still in command?

"Nine companies of cavalry turned their coats from Carluse colours to Triolle's, and eight of foot." Pelletria contemplated the dust stirred by hooves and boots. "However, all the mercenary muster rolls are under strength following their losses in Carluse. Even with the guards in Duke Garnot's retinue, and Duke Iruvain's personal troop, the tally isn't quite that."

"Fewer mouths to feed and horses to water." Litasse frowned. "Are the militia bringing their own supplies? How many have obeyed Iruvain's summons?"

"Over a thousand men, and they're bringing corn for bread and ale and animals for slaughter," Pelletria reassured her. "Eighteen mercenary companies have come upriver from Relshaz. Though Karn says not to expect any more, not yet awhile."

Litasse was caught between hope and dread. "He's back?"

"A courier dove," Pelletria said apologetically.

"What has he learned in Relshaz?" Litasse steeled herself.

"The Soluran is promising handsome rewards to the mercenary companies, while he sits out this siege of Carluse." Pelletria folded her wrinkled hands at her waist. "Many prefer the more solid offers that Duke Iruvain and Duke Garnot can make but Karn doesn't like to see so many waiting to take the highest bid. We don't know how much coin these exiles have."

"Hamare would have found some way to undermine the Soluran's hold on his hirelings." Grief, frustration and fear provoked Litasse. "They would have been turning their coats from these rebels' colours to serve Triolle."

"Maybe so, Your Grace." Pelletria paused, contemplative. "Regardless, it's clear it will take every resource we can muster to stop this Soluran and save Triolle, and to reclaim Sharlac."

Meaning they had no choice but to enlist a wizard. Litasse looked towards the Chatelaine's Tower and the Steward's Tower flanking the gatehouse. "What news of Lord Cassat and Lord Geferin this morning?"

Like Ridianne of Marlier, Draximal's heir and Parnilesse's brother had responded promptly to Iruvain's invitation to this council of war, riding on ahead of their armies with only a swiftly mounted detachment of personal guards.

"Both their lordships have breakfasted," Pelletria assured her.

The gusting wind brought a snatch of distant horn calls.

Pelletria stiffened. "An alarm?"

Litasse pointed at urgent colours waving from the town gate. "A summons for all the captains." She'd insisted the old woman teach her to read battlefield signals.

Pelletria pursed her lips. "Ah, Ridianne of Marlier is riding this way."

Litasse saw the red and silver standard leading the horsemen galloping out of Triolle Town. "So there's news." She began walking quickly along the battlements.

"Not too fast, Your Grace," reproved Pelletria. "You're merely taking the air."

"Of course." Litasse curbed her pace with some effort. She stole a glance at the bastion, seeing one of the sentries there quickly disappearing down the stairs. Off to tell Iruvain what she was doing or warning him to expect Ridianne?

They reached the Grebe Tower, where Triolle's heirs and daughters were traditionally housed. The nursery's dustsheets wouldn't be coming off any time soon. Iruvain still hadn't visited her bed. The sentry doing his best to find a spot sheltered from the wind bowed hastily. Litasse acknowledged him with a meaningless smile.

Now she saw a liveried man-at-arms running across the open bailey, heading straight for the Duke's Tower. Two more were hurrying along the battlements to take the news to the Chatelaine's Tower and the Steward's Tower.

The man on the Messenger Tower was one of

Iruvain's own. He bowed curtly to Litasse. Litasse didn't even meet his gaze. Let him think he was doing his duty, still forbidding her access to Master Hamare's rooms as Iruvain had decreed.

They reached the Duke's Tower. The man guarding the turret opened the door to allow Litasse and Pelletria inside. They hurried down the spiral stairs, skirts inelegantly hitched.

Litasse wondered whereabouts in the castle's accounts Pelletria hid the sums she was paying these suborned men. No matter. Iruvain had no interest in details as long as the ledgers balanced. Apparently nothing drew his attention to his guards' divided loyalties.

They reached the ground floor and Pelletria hurried towards the duke's private servery. In the shadows behind the stairs, Litasse took a steadying breath. The other dukes would soon be here to discuss this news. Would Pelletria's plan to insinuate her into the audience chamber work?

It seemed an age before they arrived. At long last the door to the bailey opened to admit exclaiming voices. The slam of Iruvain's audience chamber door silenced them all.

"Your Grace, here." Pelletria was at her elbow with a tray of cordials and cakes.

"Make sure no one knocks." Litasse straightened her shoulders, took the tray and stepped forward. The old woman opened the door, brushing aside a lackey's protests.

The chamber door closed behind Litasse. No one in the room so much as looked her way. She swallowed the excuses she'd rehearsed; that she was humbling herself to serve them in the interests of discretion. Who knew where the exiles might have spies?

"Treachery!" Duke Garnot stared blindly out of the window, clenched fists striking the stone sill.

"Your Grace." Iruvain cleared his throat. "What of your wife and son?"

What had happened? Litasse dared not draw attention by asking.

Lord Cassat, Draximal's youthful heir, suddenly noticed her arrival. He sprang to his feet to relieve her of the tray. "Carluse Castle has fallen," he explained in low tones.

"Saedrin save us," she breathed, suitably appalled.

Lord Cassat was five years older than Lord Ricart of Carluse, and worth ten of Lord Ricart, in her father's estimation. Everything that Pelletria had learned eavesdropping on the dukes seemed to confirm it. For a young man untried in war, he had a singular grasp of strategy.

"Murdered." Duke Garnot choked on fury, not grief. "Those guilty of this treason will be hurled from my castle's heights and left for the buzzards on the plain below."

"As is only right and proper." Lord Geferin of Parnilesse didn't sound particularly distraught over his sister's death. "What of your daughters?"

There had been talk of a match between Duke

Orlin's second son and one or other of the two unwed girls remaining in Tadira's clutches.

Litasse took a step backwards to efface herself against the panelling. Tall with curly brown hair, Lord Cassat was handsome enough to prompt Iruvain's unwarranted jealousy and she certainly didn't want to draw Lord Geferin's licentious eye.

"They are held captive," Garnot spat. "Subject to Saedrin knows what outrage. Well, their sisters are married to loyal men who will avenge their lost virtue."

Was that so? Duke Garnot was still waiting for his vassal lords to rally to the boar's head standard, according to the letters that Pelletria was intercepting and reading before sending them on their way.

"Evord Fal Breven won't allow any abuse of your daughters, Your Grace."

The audience chamber door opened to reveal Ridianne of Marlier. Well, Pelletria could hardly have stood against her, Litasse allowed.

"They'll be accommodated with every comfort, like Duchess Aphanie and the Sharlac girls," the mercenary woman continued. "I imagine they'll be housed together."

"Do you?" Garnot scorned her assurance. "To see justice done, we must retake Carluse and—"

"Where is this Soluran heading next?" Lord Cassat interrupted. "Does anybody know?"

Ridianne was still standing in the entrance. "May I have a seat?"

How could Ferdain of Marlier take such a woman to his bed? She was gracelessly stout, her features coarsened by wind and weather. Her greying hair looked to have been cropped with blunt shears and she wore faded black breeches and doublet without a hint of shame.

Litasse could only assume she'd been more alluring in her youth, or infamously free with her favours. Ferdain of Marlier's marriage must have been even more of a sham than her own.

"As you wish, Madam Captain." Iruvain gestured grudgingly to the table.

"According to my sources, Carluse Castle fell two days ago," Ridianne said, harsh and uncompromising. "If Evord has been taking counsel with his captains while his men tend their wounds and resupply themselves, he will march on today or tomorrow."

"But where to?" Lord Cassat turned his frustration on the mercenary woman. "We cannot prepare till we know his intentions."

"Send scouts to find out," Duke Garnot ordered Duke Iruvain.

"The dog has a choice of three roads," Iruvain said testily. "North and east towards Ashgil, south and east towards Tyrle, or south and west towards Hengere. We will know before sunset tomorrow—"

Ridianne of Marlier interrupted. "We must march before sunset today."

"Shall we each pick a rune for a road and roll the

bones to guide us?" Iruvain was scathing.

"You can if you wish, Your Grace," Ridianne retorted. "I'd recommend more rational reasoning."

"If he takes the Ashgil Road, we can assume he intends to attack Draximal," Lord Cassat suggested. "Heading for Tyrle puts Triolle in his sights while taking the Hengere Road challenges Duke Ferdain."

"Each of which demands a different response," Lord Geferin said thoughtfully. "Guess wrong and we'll be fatally wrong-footed. Better to wait."

"Parnilesse can afford to wait." Polite, Lord Cassat was nevertheless firm. "Don't presume for the rest of us, my lord."

Duke Garnot grunted his agreement while Iruvain slowly nodded.

"Evord will head for Tyrle." Ridianne the Vixen had no doubts. "It's his first step to stamping on Triolle. He's not a man to leave a job half-finished and as long as you are here, Your Grace, Carluse cannot be considered beaten. He won't want to see Triolle and Parnilesse uniting with either Draximal or Marlier while he campaigns against the other, my lords. Why else do you think he has those Dalasorians of his camped around Ashgil, if not to stop your army following the straightest line to Carluse, my Lord Cassat? Conquering Triolle divides his remaining foes."

Litasse's mouth was dry. Iruvain wouldn't swallow that unpalatable truth.

"You are misinformed," Iruvain rasped. "Triolle can field five thousand men this very day."

"Excellent." Ridianne was unabashed. "May I suggest you march them to Tyrle? Leave now and you should arrive a day or so ahead of Captain-General Evord."

"I take it the fortifications are in good repair?" Lord Cassat asked thoughtfully.

"Naturally," Garnot snapped, wheeling around from the window.

"I can see sound arguments for moving Triolle's regiments there, Your Grace." The young Draximal lord addressed himself respectfully to Iruvain. "If this Soluran does plan on attacking Triolle—and Marlier's woman is right, keeping our forces divided is sound strategy on his part—we want to stop him short of your borders.

"If he moves on Draximal or Marlier instead—" he balanced that possibility on his other open hand "—we'll know all the sooner if you're headquartered in Tyrle. Then whichever dukedom he's intent on can make ready to meet him in battle. All the while, Triolle's forces can ally with either myself or Duke Ferdain's army and make ready to attack him from the rear."

"With Parnilesse's support," Lord Geferin interjected quickly.

"And Carluse's," Duke Garnot insisted, venomous. "My vassal lords are mustering my militia regiments as we speak."

"We can crack this Soluran between us." Iruvain smiled with relief. "Like a festival nut."

Was such optimism justified? Litasse wondered how strong Marlier and Draximal's armies might be.

Ridianne asked the question for her. "What strength can you field, Lord Cassat? How far from Tyrle are your forces?"

"We have five thousand foot and over a thousand cavalry," he replied promptly, "two-thirds of them paid men, the rest well-drilled militia." He hesitated. "At present, as best I can estimate, they will be some six days' march from Tyrle, though."

"March faster," Duke Garnot said tersely.

"I have about the same number under arms," Ridianne observed. "Some few hundreds more cavalry. We'll reach Marlier's border in seven days or so, Tyrle a few days after that if we force the pace."

"Parnilesse forces will arrive at much the same time," Lord Geferin said quickly.

Litasse saw the other lords pay little heed to his ingratiating smile.

"Can you hold Tyrle until then, Your Grace?" Ridianne asked Iruvain.

"Of course," Duke Garnot snapped.

Iruvain shot him an indignant glare. "Naturally we can."

"Draximal and Triolle together will have an advantage in numbers even without Marlier." The female mercenary thought for a moment, then nodded. "If you can entangle Evord in another siege and keep him occupied with skirmishes around Tyrle, I can cut off his retreat to Carluse, maybe even retake the town and castle there."

"You'll do no such thing," Duke Garnot said caustically. "Loot this Soluran's baggage train and consider yourself well paid. Do not plunder my domains."

"I'm assuming Evord's men will have picked Carluse clean," Ridianne retorted before addressing Lord Cassat and Duke Iruvain. "Consider the advantages of breaking the chain linking Evord's army to the Great West Road and the supplies he's receiving from Ensaimin."

"Cut off the snake's head and it dies," Lord Cassat observed. "She's right, and we should move on Ashgil as soon as Tyrle is secure. He's relying on those Dalasorians to keep the roads open for his wagons."

Lord Geferin said something Litasse didn't catch as the door opened again. A liveried lackey slipped in, coming to take away the tray of refreshments. He jerked his head infinitesimally towards the door. Litasse saw he'd left it a fraction ajar. Pelletria was beckoning through the crack.

The noblemen and Marlier's whore were all talking at once, their arguments growing heated. Litasse slipped out, unnoticed.

"What is it?" she demanded.

Pelletria raised a cautionary finger to her withered lips before hurrying towards the outer door. Litasse followed. By the time they reached the music room in the Duchess's Tower, she was burning with frustration.

"What is it?"

Pelletria locked the door. "Another courier dove from Karn," she said quietly.

"Well?" she demanded in a whisper. With just the two of them, there was no one to guard against ears pressed to the keyhole.

"A mage called Minelas is on his way." Pelletria's eyes were icy-bright. "He'll be here inside ten days."

"No sooner?" Litasse was aghast.

Pelletria shook her head. "A wizard cannot use magic to travel where he's never been."

"What manner of man is he?" Litasse's stomach hollowed. "What of the Archmage's strictures?"

"Karn says he has no patience with Planir the Black." Pelletria offered a coiled slip of paper taken from the lace at her cuff. "He's been using his magic all this past summer while corsairs have been raiding the Caladhrian coast."

"Without suffering any consequences?" Litasse still sought assurance.

"Perhaps Hadrumal turns a blind eye when magic is used to defend the innocent." A faint frown deepened Pelletria's wrinkles.

Litasse bit her lip. "Iruvain and the rest seem confident they can beat this Soluran. We may not need to take such a step." Had she been too hasty, blinded by her hatred of Garnot?

"It never hurts to have a second string for a bow," Pelletria observed. "Once this Soluran is defeated, having a wizard beholden to Triolle could still make all the difference to Lescar."

"I'll see my family restored to Sharlac before I see Iruvain crowned High King," Litasse said viciously, "and we'll ensure Carluse and all the other dukes pay for abandoning their alliances with my father."

How could she do that without a wizard's help? Desperate times called for desperate deeds. Very well, they would see what use they might make of this wizard, when he eventually arrived. There were more urgent matters at hand.

She moved to the window to stare across the open bailey towards the Duke's Tower. "Garnot keeps insisting his vassal lords are rousing militia to reclaim Carluse from this Soluran. Is there any word of that?"

"My man inside Carluse Castle says the Guilds now govern the town. They're raising their own militia to hold the walls against Duke Garnot's return." Pelletria came to stand beside her. "There are declarations nailed to every shrine door for three leagues around. They say no one owes fealty to Duke Garnot since he fled the battlefield at Carluse Bridge. No one is tearing them down."

"What of the lords who are wed to his daughters?" Litasse wondered. "Surely one of them must see Lord Ricart's death opens the way for his own son to stand as Garnot's heir?"

"I imagine they're waiting for the others to stick their heads above the parapet," Pelletria said. "If one gets a crossbow bolt in the face, that improves the odds for the rest."

"That's true." And it was as true for dukes as it was for lesser lords. Litasse smoothed her skirts. "I don't trust Duke Garnot. Can you get word to Karn, as quickly as possible? I want him to go to Tyrle, to join Iruvain's retinue, if that's where he takes Triolle's regiments."

"What's your concern?" asked Pelletria.

Litasse shook her head with slow exasperation. "I don't know. But Garnot of Carluse has nothing left to lose now. Hamare always said a man in such straits was never more dangerous."

CHAPTER TWENTY-TWO
Karn

**Tyrle, in the Lescari Dukedom of Carluse,
20th of Aft-Autumn**

As HE CAME up the stairs to the anteroom, a few men glanced his way. They lost interest when they saw his Triolle livery. These lounging mercenaries weren't interested in servants. It was the other men seated along the walls that they watched with veiled suspicion. If they were confident no enemy could scale Tyrle's formidable walls, they still didn't trust their allies.

Karn raised the lidded flagons of wine he carried as excuse for his presence.

"We'll take one of those." The commander of Duke Garnot's retinue snapped his fingers.

"Captain." Karn obediently handed a pewter jug to the closest man in Carluse black and white.

"We'll wet our throats too." Duke Iruvain's

captain gestured and one of his men took a flagon, stony-faced.

"Is one of those for us?" a balding man with a red surcoat over his hauberk asked from his seat by the door.

Karn knew him by the fetterlock blazon on his breast. Captain Jophen of the Locksmiths. He'd informed Duke Garnot that his promises no longer retained the company's services after the retreat from Carluse and offered his men's swords to Triolle. Now he sat with the hired captains who'd come up from Relshaz by sea and river, impervious to the contemptuous glances from Duke Garnot's militia commander.

"Of course." Karn had brought four flagons, enough for a sup or two for each waiting man, not enough to provoke the simmering ill will into conflict. That wouldn't serve his purposes. As long as all three contingents watched each other with baleful suspicion, no one paid any heed to him.

He handed the third flagon to a man wearing a Moonraker's badge before knocking on the inner door.

"Enter," Duke Garnot barked.

As he obeyed, Karn saw Duke Iruvain's jaw was taut with irritation. The younger man had had his fill of Duke Garnot's overbearing manner on the forced march north from Triolle.

"Wine, Your Grace, Your Grace." Karn bowed like a well-trained lackey.

"Thank you." Iruvain's expression lightened with recognition.

On Litasse's instruction, Karn had taken pains to ingratiate himself with the duke, once he'd persuaded the former under-steward to flee Triolle Castle with a purse of Tormalin gold and assurances that no one else would ever learn the man had pilfered ducal liquor to supply his brother's inn.

"Who sent us wine?" Duke Garnot growled.

Karn ducked his head, feigning nervousness. "Your reeve, Your Grace."

As soon as the two dukes had entered Tyrle, the man had turned over these fine offices above the town's main gate, as well as his own luxuriously furnished house. The pennies the man pocketed from every toll taken in the duke's name plainly added up to a tidy sum. That was hardly surprising. Tyrle commanded the road coming south from Ashgil: the main route carrying goods from the Great West Road to Triolle and to those towns in Marlier and Parnilesse too far from the rivers for merchants to take advantage of barges.

Duke Garnot stalked to the window overlooking the high road, where the reeve's clerks would have seen every trader's wagon, every laden farmwife or peddler bringing goods to the market. "Tell him I want him here at first light tomorrow."

"Very good, Your Grace." Karn polished the already gleaming silver goblets with a crumpled cloth.

"Have they made any move?" Over by the hearth where a modest fire crackled, Duke Iruvain had donned mail and plate as soon as the enemy arrived. Unlike the Carluse duke, he still looked ill at ease in his armour.

"No." Garnot was still staring out of the window.

Karn poured the wine. Frustration burned in his throat. Master Hamare would have sent spies out beyond the walls, identifying every enemy company. Duke Garnot and Duke Iruvain didn't even agree on the count of the forces opposing them, each obstinately holding to reports already several days old.

Iruvain accepted his wine with a nod of thanks. "Dusk will come early."

"What we want is more rain." Garnot looked up at the sky outside, grey as the pewter flagon.

Two days of blustery showers had finally broken the long dry spell. Not enough rain to soak the roads and bog down the Soluran's advance, Dastennin curse it, Karn thought. Still, lingering damp made the autumn cold more penetrating, nights in the open all the more wretched for their foes. That could be a few pennyweight in the scales once battle was joined, Karn judged.

Though Triolle's militiamen would be suffering the same chill in their hurriedly dug entrenchments underneath the walls. Might it not have been wiser to keep them within the town, sleeping more warmly under cover? But Karn hadn't been able to prompt Duke Iruvain into thinking of that for himself.

The duke thought of something else now. "What if they attack at night, like Sharlac?"

"The Soluran's no such fool." Duke Garnot scorned that suggestion. "They've been marching all day, probably through last night. We hold a town with defensible walls. They'll camp and send skirmishers to look for some weakness tomorrow and probably the next day too. Then they'll take a day or so to come up with some plan of attack, which we will naturally repel."

"By which time Lord Cassat and the Draximal army will be here." Iruvain joined him at the window. "And Marlier's bitch and her curs."

Karn knelt to quietly tend the fire. From what he'd seen of Tyrle, Duke Garnot's confidence was justified. The reeve had assiduously maintained the walls and the militia garrison seemed well drilled and loyal. Karn guessed the reeve had generously shared the cream that he skimmed from Duke Garnot's dairy.

Though solid walls and loyal guards hadn't saved Carluse Town. Karn's ears were pricked for any murmur of doubt. His daggers would silence such whispers. With Tyrle the last bulwark before the Soluran's army could threaten Triolle, Karn would see every last drop of Carluse blood shed before it fell.

A shattering crash shook the tower. Karn choked on soot cascading down the chimney. Cold wind flung it around the room. Wiping his streaming eyes, Karn saw the windows were smashed, mere fragments of glass still hanging in the strips of lead.

"Poldrion's black balls!" Iruvain crouched low, his face ashen. "What was that?"

"Siege engines." Garnot looked out into the dusk, heedless of the cuts flying glass had left on his face.

Mercenary captains and dukes' guards crowded in through the door, all shouting each other down.

A second crash deafened and silenced them in the same instant.

"Where was that?" Jophen of the Locksmiths demanded.

Karn realised that blow hadn't shaken the gatehouse nearly so violently.

"To the west." Carluse's black-browed captain hurried to the broken window. "The tower between this gate and the one on the Carluse Road."

"Are they intent on the walls or the towers?" Duke Garnot's question was lost beneath the crash of another strike, this time to the east.

A chunk of masonry fell from the gatehouse's battlements, landing amid shrieks in the street below.

"Trebuchets." Jophen was peering through a spyglass.

"Man-powered or weighted?" The Carluse captain was the first of several to ask.

Duke Garnot snatched the spyglass from Jophen. "Counterweighted," he growled. "Can't you hear?"

Karn saw every warrior's face harden. Men tired of pulling a siege engine's throwing arm down. A box of earth and stones didn't, and ropes and pulleys made light work of hauling the massive sling back down for reloading.

"But it'll be dark soon—" Iruvain broke off, colouring with mortification.

Amid the hubbub rising from the town, awkward silence filled the room. Another strike on the wall towards the Carluse Gate emphasised what the younger duke had just realised. Once trebuchets found their range, engineers need not see their target to bombard it. Missiles were slamming into the walls and towers to east and west. How had they found their range so easily?

Karn lost hold of that thought as more men raced up the stairs. In Carluse livery, in Triolle colours, wearing a handful of mercenary blazons, they all shouted at once, bringing reports from the walls and the entrenchments.

Karn did his best to ignore them. Why hadn't ranging shots landed short among the militia detachments out beyond the walls? Why hadn't some of those first few missiles flown too long, soaring over the walls to demolish houses inside the town?

Iruvain pushed an excited messenger away and seized Duke Garnot's elbow. "We must move from here. What if they start throwing sticky fire? Aldabreshin alchemy burned Emirle Bridge!"

No, it hadn't. Karn cowered by the hearth, apparently terrified, calmly enduring a fresh fall of soot. Wizardry had burned the border town to set

Draximal and Parnilesse at daggers drawn. Turning every eye away from the perfidy plotted by Vanam's Lescari exiles.

Karn believed Duchess Litasse when she insisted the Soluran had suborned mages. She said they'd admitted it when they murdered Master Hamare in the very heart of Triolle Castle. Whatever Duke Iruvain's suspicions, Karn would never believe Litasse had killed the spymaster. He had sworn she loved him and Karn knew the depth of Hamare's devotion to her. Even if he found all talk of love meaningless, Karn trusted Hamare's judgement. He'd trusted his life to it time and again.

Iruvain shook Garnot's arm. "They can see our standards flying here!"

"You want to strike your colours?" Duke Garnot shoved the younger man away. "To give those Soluran scum something to cheer and put the fear of Poldrion's shadow into your own men?"

Hamare had trusted Karn with his doubts about their duke. Iruvain had never been tested in battle as his father had been. Master Hamare had even contemplated fomenting some border skirmish, just to blood him, but the right opportunity had never arisen.

The floor quivered as more missiles struck the walls on either side of the gatehouse.

"Dastennin drown them," Iruvain spat. "If we'd only had more rain!"

Karn didn't waste time on futile regrets or curses for gods he'd abandoned as a child orphaned by war. He spat soot and disgust into the hearth.

Master Hamare would have sent spies to see what the Soluran's men were up to, as they idled around Carluse Town's walls. He'd have known they were plundering Duke Garnot's forests and his quarries full of stone, to build these siege engines and supply their missiles. Iruvain hadn't thought to, Litasse couldn't and Tyrle was going to pay a high price for that error.

The Carluse messenger was still talking as the echoes of more booming impacts died away. "They'll have the town ringed by dawn, Your Grace."

Duke Garnot rounded on the mercenary captains. "Get your thumbs out of each other's arses! Get every archer and crossbowman up on the walls. I want an arrow storm driving every engineer under cover and those accursed machines alight! Before the sun sets! Take every household's stores of oil and pitch. Kick in their doors if you have to. Don't come back till it's done!"

The mercenaries were already leaving, Garnot's bellows pursuing them down the stairs. He turned his attention to Duke Iruvain.

"Tyrle can hold until Draximal arrives. These walls are strong. It will take several days to make a breach anywhere and they cannot attack without overcoming our entrenchments. While they're held at the outer line, we can mass our reserves within the walls to defend the breach. Then the townsfolk must be ready to barricade it."

"You don't think those trebuchets will just pound my regiments into the mud?" Iruvain was shaking.

With fear or anger? Karn couldn't tell.

"Your regiments?" Duke Garnot was losing his temper. "Those mercenaries took my coin before they took yours."

"They thought better of that bargain," Iruvain spat, "once you'd led them to a string of defeats. What right have you to command here? With barely five hundred men still wearing your badge!"

In fact, only three hundred still wore the boar's head and only a hundred were sworn men-at-arms. Karn had made sure to ascertain that.

"Where are your vassal lords and your faithful militia?" Iruvain's voice cracked. "How long before these townsfolk turn against you, just as they did in Carluse?"

Garnot's slap across his face left Iruvain frozen with shock.

As Karn crouched motionless by the hearth, movement caught his eye. Two liveried youths stood in the doorway. One in yellow and green, one in black and white, both were aghast.

"What are you staring at? Find out what's going on!"

Duke Garnot slammed the door and strode back to the broken window as horn calls beyond the entrenchments prompted fresh terror in the streets.

"How dare you?" Iruvain whispered with low fury.

Garnot ignored him, peering through the spyglass. "What are those grassland scum doing?"

His evident mystification threw Iruvain on the back foot.

"What do you mean?"

"See for yourself." Garnot offered him the spyglass.

With both men's attention occupied by events outside, Karn crept silently towards the smaller window looking eastwards along the town's walls. Through the failing light, he could see mercenary horsemen wheeling and charging at the dark scars of the earthworks hurriedly dug in the grazing around Tyrle. He guessed they were launching lances and arrows at the cowering defenders.

Triolle's raw militia would be pissing in their boots. But the sworn men-at-arms wouldn't break, knowing darkness would soon force the horsemen back to their own lines. In the meantime, they'd keep their heads down. Archers on the town walls were already shooting at the enemy horsemen.

The bulk of their mercenary forces were safely entrenched beneath the walls, carefully placed to cover the militia's inevitable retreat back through the town's three gates. The Soluran had three men under arms for every two that Carluse and Triolle could claim, so these outer lines would have to be abandoned before their losses became too great.

On the other side of the scales, the mercenary cavalry Karn had recruited in Relshaz, with Triolle's silver and the promise of Carluse gold, were safely within the walls. They'd ride out to ensure that retreat didn't become a rout. Once everyone was inside the walls, the reunited army could hold off an enemy with twice the regiments. Even with these unexpected siege engines, Duke Garnot's plan for holding Tyrle remained sound.

As long as the walls held against this bombardment. Karn looked up dubiously as shards of plaster fell from the ceiling.

"Why aren't those cursed siege engines alight?" Garnot seemed to have forgotten his quarrel with Iruvain.

The younger duke seized his chance to point out the obvious answer. "They'll have wet hides draped over the wood."

Perhaps. Karn could see another possibility. Perhaps the Soluran's engineers could call up magic to quench flames as well as provoke them. That reminded him of his earlier question. Why hadn't the trebuchets' first shots landed short among the militia beyond the walls? Or flown too long? Because wizards were guiding their flight directly to the walls and towers?

Karn stiffened. Amid the resonant crashes, he'd heard a louder calamity.

Duke Garnot had heard it too. "What was that?"

The inner door flew open. "Your Grace!" The

youth was as white as the quartering on his Carluse surcoat.

Duke Iruvain rushed to the anteroom window, looking out over the town itself.

Under the westering sky, the town wall should have drawn a dark line between the Ashgil Gate and the Triolle Gate. An inferno raged instead, the tower ravaged like a lightning-struck tree.

Iruvain gasped. "Undermining!"

"How?"

Karn shared Duke Garnot's incredulous fury. Digging tunnels to a fortification's foundations took days. Packing the void with brush and hog carcasses, fired to burn away the props and bring the structure crashing down, took longer still. This had to be magic at work. No other explanation made sense.

"Your Grace, we must leave."

"What?"

"No!" Garnot's bellow overrode Iruvain's confusion.

Karn ignored the Carluse duke. "This is wizard's work, Your Grace. You must warn Draximal, at once."

They would fight this magic. Karn had seen to that, by enlisting that renegade mage. But they had to get out of here first.

"I'll kill any man who tries to flee." Duke Garnot drew the sword at his hip. "Our captains will rally their men, inside the town and without. We will repel this assault and hold fast!"

"We will be trapped like rats in a burning barn." Iruvain was too appalled to see his immediate peril. "Tyrle is lost, and Carluse with it!" He took a step towards the stairs.

Garnot's sword was at his throat. "You'll die before your cowardice costs me my dukedom!"

That was enough for Karn. He drew the narrow dagger sheathed lengthways inside his belt. No use against a sword, a joke against plate armour, it was sharp enough to penetrate Duke Garnot's eye, long enough to lodge in his skull.

Garnot clawed blindly at his brow. He bellowed with agony as his fingers struck the dagger's handle.

Karn wrestled the flailing sword from his hand and turned the blade on the young men-at-arms. The Carluse lad collapsed, decapitated, his blood spraying the disintegrating ceiling. The Triolle man shrieked in wordless terror as Karn buried the sword in his belly. Karn ripped the blade back, strewing entrails across the floor.

"Carluse! Treachery!" As Duke Garnot managed to call for aid, Karn stepped behind him, the sword-point slicing through his neck. Garnot fell in a crash of armour.

"He would have murdered you, Your Grace." Karn flung the bloodied sword away. "He had nothing left to lose."

Iruvain was staring numbly at the dead men-at-arms. "Why kill *them*?"

"Look at me." Karn clasped Iruvain's face between

his hands. He pressed mercilessly on the bruise raised by Garnot's blow and saw the pain cut through Iruvain's daze.

"Who knows what lies they'd have told, to blackmail you, to dishonour Duke Garnot's memory?" Karn stared unblinking into Iruvain's white-rimmed eyes. "Better no one knows he lost his head so thoroughly that he was ready to do murder, Your Grace. Now, we must ride to warn Draximal's forces. We must warn Lord Cassat that the Soluran has taken Tyrle through vilest sorcery."

It was a roll of the runes whether the Draximal column or Triolle's border was their closest sanctuary. But Triolle would be the Soluran's next objective and Karn wanted Draximal's forces drawn up along the border as soon as possible.

"We must rally the troops. We must hold the town—"

Iruvain tried to shake his head but Karn's vice-like grip defeated him.

"We must ride for Draximal. Lord Cassat will recognise you, Your Grace. Any other messenger could be a feint, bringing lies concocted by the exiles. You're the only one who can convince him to press on, to bring his army swiftly enough to save Tyrle."

Hamare always said it was best to offer the young duke whatever argument or explanation showed him in the best possible light.

"Yes," Duke Iruvain said slowly. "The captains here will know what to do. Sending other messengers to Lord Cassat will only cause more delay. It's my duty to go myself."

Satisfied, Karn armed himself with the dead men-at-arms' blades. "We cannot stop to explain ourselves, Your Grace. Stay close and let me fight our way through the panic."

He would have the advantage. He always did. Karn never suffered the qualms about killing that so fatally slowed most opponents. Dukes and nobles could talk about honour from dawn till dusk. He'd never understood it himself, any more than he understood what people meant by love. He just understood loyalty to those he trusted—Hamare, Pelletria and Litasse—and revenge on those who hurt them, even if he didn't yet know all their names.

CHAPTER TWENTY-THREE
Aremil

**Carluse Castle,
20th of Aft-Autumn**

HOW LONG BEFORE they received news from Tyrle? Had Tathrin even arrived? Aremil longed to know but he was just as reluctant to seek Tathrin out in a battle. Distraction could be the death of his friend. Or Aremil might find him in the midst of something neither of them wished to share.

A blush warmed Aremil's thin face. Had Tathrin any notion he'd seen him entwined with that whore in Relshaz? Aremil couldn't tell. Since he'd learned of Carluse's fall, Tathrin's thoughts had resounded with his indignation at not being forewarned of Failla's plan. Even her success did little to temper his ire towards Aremil and Reher, and even with Failla herself.

Ironically, whatever Aremil's former doubts, her courage and commitment to saving Carluse from a massacre had redeemed her in his eyes. Whatever else he wished Tathrin couldn't see through the inconvenient clarity of Artifice, he was glad his friend understood that.

Aremil sighed. It was his choice when to reach through the aether to Tathrin. Jettin had made it very plain he would initiate all Artifice. So when was the bold young adept going to tell him what those Dalasorian scouts based in Ashgil had learned of the Draximal army's progress? The army led by his unknown brother, heir to the father Aremil couldn't even recall.

He glanced up at the portrait of Carluse's heir still hanging on the wall of this castle chamberlain's office. Even in distant Vanam, he'd heard rumours of Lord Ricart's arrogance, as well as Iruvain's love of hunting and hawking in Triolle's marshes. Such passing comment had told Aremil that Lord Cassat was well regarded, his courteous manners approved, his intelligence admired. His visits to Toremal were considered a valuable education and some hinted he'd been welcomed into Emperor Tadriol's circle.

Aremil picked up a penknife to trim the quill he'd been using. He set it down again. His hands were shaking too much to be of use.

His faithful nurse Lyrlen always picked up gossip among Lescar's exiles, eager for news of the home she'd not seen for nigh on twenty years. Always discreet, for fear of drawing attention to Aremil, for whose sake she had left her family and friends. Aremil paid more heed to Vanam's scholars, to the quarrels and alliances around the university's halls, and to news of Guild machinations in the lower town. Why risk exposure by enquiring about Lescari affairs?

Would he have wanted to live with all the responsibilities that the trials of his birth had denied him? Even for the sake of the luxury that Lord Jaras, Lord Ricart and Lord Cassat enjoyed? Hardly, and two of those noble lords were now dead. He was alive, if crippled. His house in Vanam had all the comforts he had desired. More, Branca had taught him how much less many folk possessed and still considered themselves fortunate.

This self-indulgence was wasting time. Aremil sorted awkwardly through a sheaf of letters but his weak vision refused to make sense of their scrawl.

Had Lyrlen forgiven him yet? For ignoring her advice, her tearful pleas, when he had insisted on risking his precarious health making the journey to Lescar. So he could play his part in bringing this brutal war to innocents who'd already suffered so much.

Had his brother committed any great crime? Not that Aremil had heard. His gaze drifted to the window. But Lord Cassat would be risking his life whenever Draximal's army met Captain-General Evord's. Doing his duty, following the honourable course he'd been taught.

Would they have been friends, him and his brother, if they had known each other as boys, as men?

Would they have had anything in common? Would they ever have the chance to find out?

Aremil looked back at the flattering portrait of Lord Ricart. He'd never seen a picture of Lord Cassat. There was no reason why any likeness of Draximal's heir would have travelled as far as Vanam.

The timepiece on the wall struck the fourth chime of the night. How was the battle for Tyrle progressing?

"You didn't eat your supper." The Soluran lieutenant Dagaran entered with a perfunctory knock. "Are you unwell?"

"I've no appetite." Aremil shrugged his uneven shoulders. "The poppy tincture kills it."

That was true, as far as it went. The journey south from Losand over the rutted forest roads had been agony. His cramps had been slow to fade even after they had taken possession of Carluse Castle.

"You should ask what Master Welgren advises." Dagaran closed the door. "Perhaps he should remain here."

"The captain-general will have far more need of him in Tyrle," Aremil objected.

Dagaran nodded, his expression sombre. "True enough."

Now illness among their companies was adding to their losses, as well as desertion, injury and death. Aremil looked down at notes he'd made earlier, dried blots like drops of blood. Ten dead here, a score there, such neat, round figures in Dagaran's ledger. Yet militia or mercenary, every dead man was some mother's son, a father, someone's beloved. Brothers in arms grieved as deeply for each other as anyone did for dead kin.

Angry voices scattered his bleak reflections. Dagaran turned as the door flew open.

"Let me pass." Lord Rousharn stared at the Soluran on the threshold, astonishment momentarily overcoming his outrage.

"My apologies." The lieutenant bowed politely. "Your arrival was somewhat precipitate."

"Remove your hand," Lady Derenna said with icy precision.

Aremil saw Dagaran's warning glance at the man-at-arms unwise enough to seize her elbow.

"Their coach only just arrived," the man pleaded. "We offered them refreshment. I was going to send word but they came barging in—"

"Since my letters go unanswered, I thought it best." Lord Rousharn glowered at the papers littering Aremil's table. "I am still waiting for an answer to my proposal for a regency in Sharlac."

"You may go." Shaking the hapless man off, Derenna shut the door in his face.

Both nobles' garb was creased and dusty from their journey. Aremil noted she was still dressed with the elegance of rank that she'd scorned in exile in Vanam though.

"Explain Duchess Tadira's death and Lord Ricart's," Lord Rousharn demanded without preamble.

At least he was looking straight at him this time. Aremil shrugged. "They were casualties of this war. Regrettable yet unavoidable, like so many hundreds of others."

"They were murdered," spat Lord Rousharn. "Have the culprits been hanged?"

"No, and I don't imagine they will be," Aremil said tightly. "None of the castle garrison or household is prepared to identify those responsible."

Lord Rousharn stared at him. "And you accept that?"

"Would you like to see everyone who was present flogged till they talk?" Aremil queried.

"I would like to see justice," Lord Rousharn said angrily.

"As far as the folk of Carluse Town are concerned, justice was done," retorted Aremil.

"Justice or revenge?" The Sharlac nobleman wasn't yielding. "Do you deny that Duke Garnot's discarded whore urged these deaths?"

"I can and I do." Infuriated, Aremil glared at Lady Derenna, who had the grace to look embarrassed. "Failla risked her own life several times over to get into the town and then into the castle. She was urging the garrison to surrender, to save the town from being stormed and sacked by Captain-General Evord's army. She had Lord Ricart's sword at her throat when someone killed Duchess Tadira." He choked on spittle and fury.

Derenna laid a restraining hand on her husband's forearm. "We should speak to Failla, to get a clearer understanding of exactly what happened."

"Indeed." Lord Rousharn squared his broad shoulders. "Where is she?"

"She's tending those of her family, and others, who were confined in Duke Garnot's dungeons on Duchess Tadira's orders. Like the priest from Saedrin's shrine, her uncle. An old man, my lord, much respected, tutor to most of the merchants' sons in the town. He was beaten till he couldn't stand and then kicked half to death, merely for suggesting Tadira send an envoy to ask what terms might lift the siege." Aremil swallowed and drew a steadying breath.

"Then there's her cousin, a mere boy, a groom from the stables, thrown into a dungeon because someone accused him of trying to get word to his mother who lives in the town, him and several others. Nothing was proven, you understand. Duchess Tadira had no interest in justice. The boy was chained in darkness and filth without food or water for days. He survived by licking at the moisture running down the walls of his cell."

"Of course Failla must attend to them." Lady Derenna spoke quickly, seeing her husband had no answer. "Please let her know we'll see her at her leisure."

"I will." Despite his efforts, Aremil's voice shook.

Bodily, Vrist hadn't suffered much beyond a few bruises but the man he'd been shackled to had perished four days before the castle fell. According to Failla, Vrist was waking every night, screaming for fear of still being chained to the corpse.

When Aremil had told Tathrin, his friend's thoughts were thrown into turmoil. He was torn between desperate desire to race back to Carluse to console Failla and his redoubled determination to see every duke thrown down, so such cruelty could never be repeated.

Aremil waited for someone to speak, either Dagaran or one of their unsought visitors.

Lady Derenna cleared her throat. "Will Carluse's younger daughters be ready to travel by the morning?"

Aremil looked at Dagaran who quickly nodded. "They will, my lady."

Aremil's throat tightened. "As you may imagine, they are much distressed."

"Did they see what happened?" Derenna demanded.

"No." He found that scant relief.

What difference did it make to girls of twelve years old and nine? To be told that their mother and brother had been slain by the very garrison sworn to protect them, or to see it? As they found their home occupied by an enemy army. As half their servants fled and those whom Failla said couldn't be trusted were dismissed. Now they'd been told to pack only their most precious things and make ready to leave the castle where they'd lived all their days. To go to an unknown manor house, in an unknown dukedom, in the care of a woman as unsympathetic as Derenna. Well, they'd have plenty in common with Sharlac's widowed duchess and her daughters.

"Duchess Aphanie is still most distressed over the loss of Lord Jaras's ashes. Has there been any sign of the urn?"

Derenna's words made Aremil wonder if he was being unjust. Her face was genuinely troubled.

"I'm afraid not." Aremil hoped she believed his sincere regret.

"We have interrogated every mercenary company's quartermaster," Dagaran assured her. "All their baggage wagons have been searched."

Lord Rousharn stirred from contemplating Duchess Tadira's crimes. "What have you done with Lord Ricart's body? And his mother's? Don't tell me they were thrown on some common pyre?" he warned, menacing.

Aremil stiffened in his chair, refusing to cower. "Do you think I would allow such dishonour? They've been burned with all due ceremony and their ashes are interred in the shrine to Poldrion within these castle walls."

And both pyres had been unattended save by the mercenary surgeons who'd lost the roll of runes for the duty. Since then, according to Dagaran, none of the ducal household, none of the castle garrison, had made even the briefest of visits to the shrine. From fear of reprisal if they showed any sorrow or simply because the duchess and her son were reaping in death what they had assiduously sown in life?

"What are you intending to do with Carluse's daughters, and with Duchess Aphanie and her girls?" Lord Rousharn was still staring at Aremil. "In the longer term. Do you intend to ransom them, as befits their rank?"

Aremil struggled for an answer. "We seek peace and prosperity for all in Lescar, whatever their station in life."

"You spoke of setting Lescar's dukes aside. You argued they had forfeited all fealty with their excess. Many of us agreed." Lord Rousharn's voice roughened with anger. "Now one duke is dead, plus one duchess and two ducal heirs."

"We did not agree to summary executions," Derenna interjected.

"Is this Soluran's campaign just the prelude to general anarchy?" Lord Rousharn asked wrathfully. "Should all vassal lords expect to be thrown off our lands into beggary?"

"You know full well we have no such intent." It took all Aremil's resolve to speak in level tones. "Duke Moncan of Sharlac and Lord Kerlin died in battle, like Lord Jaras before them. As did countless others. We can show you the name of every dead and wounded man, humble and noble."

He nodded incautiously at Dagaran, prompting a shudder that twisted his shoulders. Lord Rousharn couldn't hide his instant of revulsion. Anger scalded Aremil.

Dagaran saw it and spoke up swiftly. "There's a great deal to discuss, but you must be weary from your journey, my lord, my lady." He ushered them inexorably towards the door, talking all the while. "In the morning, we have a favour to ask. Carluse's militia commanders naturally included vassal lords' sons. A number were captured and they're housed here as befits their rank. My lady Derenna, if you could explain your reasons for supporting our endeavour? And assure them they're free to return home once their wounds have been treated and we have their oath not to take up arms again. Of course, we're not asking a copper cut-piece for their freedom." He smiled with a shake of his head. "Such assurances may not sound so convincing from a Soluran."

Aremil didn't think Lord Rousharn was actually listening to a word Dagaran said. Not until he continued.

"As for regents for Sharlac and, indeed, for Carluse, if rumour accuses us of seeking to overthrow the established order, we should look for someone who could never have military ambitions. No one could think that of Aremil, given his infirmity." The Soluran glanced towards him, veiled mischief in his eyes. "And he is both nobly born and well qualified by virtue of scholarship."

Aremil saw Lord Rousharn was appalled at the idea of yielding to a cripple. "I'm sure we can find a great many possible candidates." He managed to conceal his own horror at the notion of taking on such responsibility.

Lady Derenna was quicker to gather her wits. "I see we have a great many things to settle. Doubtless the most rational course will be clearer to us all in the morning. Let's breakfast together."

She took Lord Rousharn's arm, though he hadn't offered it, and led him swiftly from the room. Dagaran closed the door behind them.

Aremil looked wryly at him. "I don't imagine I'll have much appetite tomorrow morning."

"A meal with that pair promises heartburn." The Soluran sat down. "But while they're here, we can keep them from throwing our plans off-kilter more easily than if they're in Sharlac."

"I'd hoped he'd forgotten that notion of a regency," Aremil admitted. "And thank you all the same, but I have no ambitions in that direction."

"I know, but the idea will help us keep him talking in circles for a while." Dagaran ran a hand over his cropped hair and for the first time, Aremil saw weariness on his saturnine face. "And it will be useful to have Lady Derenna arguing our case to Carluse's vassal lords."

"They'll probably agree just to stop her talking." Aremil sighed. "Do you suppose they're paying any heed to Reniack's broadsheets and ballads?"

Dagaran shrugged. "If they're not, their servants are."

The rabble-rouser had skilfully threaded new verses, humorous and obscene, onto familiar tunes. Aremil found these songs lodged in his brain like burrs in a donkey's coat.

Aremil considered what else Dagaran had said about their noble captives. "I understand we had to throw Lord Rousharn a bone, but what will the mercenary captains say when you tell them they can't ransom their lordlings? When they haven't even been allowed to plunder Carluse Town."

"They won't be best pleased. Let's hope they capture plenty of rival captains in Tyrle, and let enough of their sergeants escape to buy them back. In the meantime, we'll pay a retainer." Dagaran grimaced. "There wasn't nearly the gold we'd hoped in Duke Garnot's private coffers. Can you let Master Gruit know we need more coin?"

"I can." Aremil wondered what the wine merchant would make of that. Kerith always passed on Gruit's confident assurances that he'd gathered a fortune from his fellow exiles. But Aremil saw Kerith's anxiety that they would dip their bucket too often and find the well dry. Or was that just Kerith's parsimony? Aremil had seen the scholar was used to making the four silver pennies in a mark do the duty of a handful.

"Coin is least of our worries." Dagaran heaved a sigh. "We've been lucky with the weather thus far but I can't see it holding much longer, not beyond the turn of For-Winter. We'll be hard put to keep ourselves supplied once rain softens the roads, never mind sending wagons on to Tyrle. We must press on and win this campaign."

"We'll have taken a long stride towards that once we've secured Tyrle." Aremil looked down at his blotted notes. "Then it's on to Marlier or Parnilesse."

"Either dukedom with an army to equal our own." Dagaran looked grim. "We must defeat each one separately without taking too many losses. If they unite to face us ..." He shook his head. "Well, if any captain-general can win through, it's Evord Fal Breven."

"Indeed." Aremil could only hope the Soluran's confidence was well placed.

Dagaran leaned back in his chair, stretching his arms above his head, his boots wrinkling the rug. "Have you had any word from Parnilesse?"

"Not since the day before yesterday," Aremil said slowly. If Branca hadn't been as angry as Tathrin about what had happened in Carluse, she'd been appalled to think of Failla taking such risks. The sufferings of Failla's innocent relatives had horrified her and the potential consequences of the duchess's death troubled her gravely. Aremil had told himself he should give her some time to come to terms with it all.

"Perhaps it would be as well to find out if Madam Charoleia has discovered anything new about Duke

Orlin's plans?" Dagaran suggested.

Aremil nodded, trying to hide his unwillingness. "I'll see what Branca has to say, once we have news from Tyrle."

Just at that moment he didn't think he'd be able to hide his tangled fears for his unknown brother from her.

CHAPTER TWENTY-FOUR
Karn

The Second Battle of Tyrle,
21st of Aft-Autumn

THE CLOSER THEY drew to Tyrle, the closer Karn stayed to Duke Iruvain. No one questioned it. What other retinue did Triolle's duke have?

He was riding with the sons of Duke Secaris's most favoured vassal lords. Stern warriors flanked them all. The right to guard and guide Lord Cassat and his entourage was their reward for long and loyal service, instead of risking life and limb amid clashing swords.

Karn had heard the younger men speculating and the seasoned warriors weren't immune to curiosity. Why had Duke Iruvain arrived in the dead of night, one sole attendant at his stirrup, both spattered with blood, smeared with muck?

Lord Cassat had been roused from his canvas bed; candles making lanterns of the tents as word spread. Never mind the wearisome day just endured, they must march on through the night. Never mind that both moons were showing less than a quarter, the Greater waxing, the Lesser waning. What did that matter, sergeants demanded, rousing reluctant militia with kicks and curses, when the night sky was blanketed with cloud regardless?

Karn's horse tossed its head, uneasy as it smelled burning on the chill breeze. He wondered how fast and how far fire had spread through the town. The Soluran's wizard had doubtless helped it on its way.

The road approaching Tyrle ran through market gardens trampled by the attackers' boots, the stripped orchards scarred by greedy axes. Lord Cassat's retinue didn't slow.

Karn shifted in his saddle, frustrated. Advancing through the darkness, uncertain where enemy skirmishers might lurk, Lord Cassat and Duke Iruvain had kept their scouts close for fear of ambush.

If he'd had anyone else to trust to watch Duke Iruvain's back, Karn would had ridden ahead. Knowing the enemy was at Tyrle was one thing. Knowing how they had deployed their regiments, their archers, that was quite another. But Lord Cassat had only sent scouts ahead once they'd passed the last waymark.

"Will we pen them up till Marlier's Vixen arrives?" One thoughtful lieutenant turned to the older man at his side.

"Most likely," grunted the grizzled sergeant.

There was a flurry of activity ahead. Outriders swiftly challenged a gaunt man on a lathered horse. Karn spurred his mount closer to Iruvain.

"The siege engines have been burned," the man was saying as he was escorted in. "The traitors have taken the entrenchments, but the green grebe still flies from the Triolle Road Gate."

"Are you sure?" Iruvain's voice cracked with incredulity. "And Carluse?"

"The black boar flies at half mast," the man said, troubled.

Karn wished he could see Iruvain's face. Would he hold fast to what Karn had told him, after their desperate scramble through the confusion, escaping the town amid the mercenaries sent to reinforce the cowering militiamen in the entrenchments?

Duke Garnot had been the first to draw steel, so Duke Iruvain had no need to explain. Duke Garnot had forfeited all right to command when he had forbidden them to do their duty and hasten Draximal's army to Tyrle's aid. In the current crisis, it was best to say they'd left Duke Garnot alive. If the Soluran's curs were accused of his murder, let that stiffen Carluse resistance.

Iruvain had finally nodded acquiescence. Arguing the justice of Duke Garnot's death would merely distract everyone from saving Lescar.

Later, as they rode through the night, Iruvain had mused on his duty to protect Garnot's orphaned daughters. If his brother Lord Roreth were to wed either one, Triolle's influence could reach unbroken to Sharlac, once he asserted Litasse's claims to her father's dominions. Once this traitorous mob of exiles were defeated. Indeed, Karn had agreed. Privately he wondered if the unwed Lord Cassat intended advancing Draximal's interests through a Carluse marriage.

The young nobleman had more immediate concerns. "The siege engines have been burned?"

How had that happened, Karn wondered?

"Where are the traitors concentrating their attack?" Iruvain demanded.

"On the Ashgil Gate, Your Grace," the scout answered readily. "They've drawn up their forces along that road. They're renewing their assault on the breach in the wall between the Ashgil Road and the Carluse Gate."

"The forces inside the town pushed back that attack? And the Carluse Gate still holds?"

Karn shared Iruvain's shock. Though he had to allow it was possible that the mercenary companies, Carluse's remaining militia and Tyrle's desperate townsfolk had repelled the assault.

"Your Grace!" Another scout forced his horse through the outriders. "The town's defenders are attacking the earthworks!"

"Draw up our regiments for battle. Call the mercenary horse forward!"

Lord Cassat's urgent orders mingled with Duke Iruvain's questions.

"What banners can you see? Where are they coming from?"

Signal horns sent shivers down Draximal's long column. Karn heard sergeants bellowing at their men.

"Where do we take our stand?" Duke Iruvain looked for some vantage point to secure a clear view of the town.

"We lead from the front!" Lord Cassat drew his sword.

Karn wasn't so keen on that. He elbowed his way to Iruvain's stirrup as the ducal retinue spurred towards Tyrle.

"We were right to get out when we did, Your Grace," he observed as Iruvain looked around. "If Draximal's army had stayed camped for the night, Tyrle would have been irretrievably lost."

"That's true." Iruvain nodded. "That's very true."

Mercenary horsemen fanned out on either side of the road, Draximal's red and gold sewn beside their blazons. They soon outstripped the foot soldiers, exhausted after their night march. The best those valiant men could manage was a purposeful jog-trot.

Battle was already joined outside Tyrle. Halberdiers were advancing out of the Triolle Gate beneath yellow and green pennants. The towers behind them were smashed to rubble but there was no visible breach in the walls. Karn guessed the defenders intended reclaiming these entrenchments now that dawn had shown them the bulk of the enemy's forces was drawn up on the far side of the town. Who had seized command when they'd discovered Garnot was dead and Iruvain absent? Jophen of the Locksmiths? The Moonrakers' Captain Ruivar?

The Soluran's mercenaries were making a fight of it, already defiant on top of the earthworks.

"Ware arrows!" The leading horsemen swiftly passed the shout back.

Some of Draximal's youthful lieutenants inadvertently checked their horses. Karn stayed close by Iruvain's side. Even the most expert crossbowmen couldn't reach them at this distance.

The attackers exposed on the earthworks were well within range of the archers on the broken battlements. An arrow storm swiftly drove them back into the entrenchments.

They reached the blackened remnants of a trebuchet. Karn kicked his horse mercilessly as the weary beast threatened to shy at the pungent charred timbers. Whatever fire arrow had found that in the darkness must have been the purest fluke. Duke Garnot was welcome to that little victory as he waited for Poldrion's barge.

"They're running!" Standing in his stirrups, Iruvain shouted over his shoulder to Karn. His voice hardened. "Come on! Lord Cassat's not claiming the glory of saving Carluse!"

Draximal's lordly retinue was forging onwards through broken fences and trampled vegetable patches. Ahead, Karn glimpsed men scrambling out of the entrenchments. Those mercenaries weren't fool enough to be crushed between this hammer and the anvil of Tyrle's walls. He saw the mercenary horse veer aside to pursue them until they were recalled by peremptory horn blasts.

"We'll deal with those scum when we've secured the town!" Lord Cassat shouted to Iruvain.

The fleeing mercenaries were heading for their colleagues encamped along the Ashgil Road.

Iruvain shook his head, furiously. "As soon as they know we've reclaimed the Triolle Gate, they'll throw all his reserves into the assault on the breach!"

Lord Cassat was unshaken. "Then we must get into the town before them. Once we have Tyrle, we can hold it till Ridianne of Marlier arrives. Her troops can attack those felons on three sides if they stay camped out on the road. And our bowmen can skewer them from Tyrle's walls!"

All the retinue were listening intently to this shouted exchange. They cheered Lord Cassat's assertions.

Karn wondered if the young noble was right. If the enemy won through the breach, the streets of Tyrle would run with the blood of mercenaries, militia and bystanders. Lescar hadn't seen such slaughter as this, Karn thought distantly, since the battles across Marlier, Triolle and Parnilesse when he'd been a child. When everyone he'd known had died, even his own mother at his father's hand to save her from famine, rape or worse.

Ahead, the galloping mercenaries were threading through gaps in the hastily dug earthworks. Karn saw the militia who'd come out of the Triolle Gate beckoning the horsemen onwards.

Iruvain set his own horse to jump one of the outermost trenches. The tiring beast baulked and Karn's own horse reared away from the void. As the recalcitrant beast wheeled around, a curious noise rushed overhead. Karn saw flames erupting amid the marching companies still hurrying to catch up with Lord Cassat's charge. The militiamen scattered with yells of alarm.

He forced his horse back to face the town. The distinctive rattling thump of a trebuchet sounded again, within the battered walls. Another missile soared overhead, detonating in a fiery burst. Terrified horses fought their riders, intent on fleeing the flames. But now the town's so-called defenders were planting their halberds deep in the churned-up soil to impale the hapless animals. The deceitful archers on the walls were bringing down men and horses, aiming their arrows in earnest instead of harmlessly at the banks of turf.

He should have trusted his instincts. Tyrle had fallen just as Karn had foreseen. Those burned timbers hadn't been all of the trebuchets. These fires assaulting them were Garnot's final legacy, as the traitors made use of the pitch and oil the dead duke had demanded.

But the exiles' mercenaries had sprung their trap too early. Fewer than half the Draximal horsemen had been caught between the entrenchments and the wall. Once the trebuchets' reach along the Triolle Road was apparent, they could retreat and regroup. Karn wrenched his horse's head around, bloody foam dripping from its mouth.

He reached for Duke Iruvain's bridle, shouting, "We must rally to Lord Cassat's standard!"

Horsemen were galloping towards the youthful lord's banner from all directions. The advancing foot soldiers were halting a safe distance beyond the trebuchets' range. All the enemy's missiles did now was splash liquid fire around the entrenchments. The turf smouldered, merely throwing a rank pall of smoke over the Triolle Road.

Karn and Iruvain reached Lord Cassat's retinue to hear him sending gallopers to all his captains. "The Tunnellers' Sons are to draw up out of reach of those trebuchets. They must make sure no one comes out of the Triolle Gate to harry our flank—" He broke off as Iruvain arrived. "We nearly swallowed that poisoned bait!" he shouted with chagrin.

"Nearly but not quite!"

Karn understood Iruvain's relief. Now no one could accuse him of fleeing the town before it had fallen. Instead, getting safely away proved his noble prudence, rather than condemning him for arrant cowardice.

Let Iruvain console himself with his delusions. The dukes still had to win the day. Karn swiftly assessed the unfolding battle, now the exiles were holding the town.

"I want an assessment of those forces holding the Ashgil Road." Lord Cassat was sending his noble lieutenants hither and yon. "We will draw up along that cart track and advance on a broad front." He turned to Duke Iruvain, his gestures expansive. "We must force them back from the walls. Dividing their forces to lure us in is all very well but they'll see the error of their ways when we drive a wedge between them."

"Our united numbers will become a crushing advantage," Iruvain shouted back to show everyone he understood the tactical situation just as readily as the younger man.

Whatever companies the enemy had within the walls had little room for manoeuvre, Karn allowed. Once Lord Cassat's army disposed of the troops outside the walls, either by killing them or driving them off, they could set about a siege of their own and wait for Marlier's Vixen to arrive.

Draximal's regiments were already advancing steadily on the exiles' army ranged along the Ashgil Road. Experienced sergeants-at-arms held their men in check, saving all their strength for the murderous fighting to come. The solid ranks bristled with swords and polearms. The exiles' companies were more thinly spread, visible gaps between each regiment.

The Draximal line was longer. Companies on either flank began to curve around, threatening the exiles with a crushing embrace. Militia and mercenaries alike began drumming their weapons upon their shields. The menacing beat underscored ominous chants from different companies, all promising painful death.

Would the mercenaries who'd followed the Soluran through his victories hold their ground in the face of defeat? Would they cut and run? Enough gold to fight for was seldom enough to die for.

Lord Cassat was still sending messengers out as he rode. Close by Duke Iruvain's stirrup, Karn approved his stern orders for the Draximal horsemen. They were to cut down anyone fleeing the field.

Draximal's fire-basket banner flapped overhead, the blue ground mocking the grey sky. Cloth of gold had been used on the heir to the dukedom's standard, sparkling amid red velvet flames.

It fell in a garish blaze—real fire, not some devoted embroideress's semblance. The youth honoured with the burden shrieked as his clothes caught alight, his hair seared away. His horse screamed with uncomprehending terror, bucking frantically to get rid of this horror. Flung to the ground, the young noble writhed, unable to stifle the flames as he died before his skin could even blister.

Karn jumped from his saddle, not to help the youth but to save his own neck as his maddened horse dropped to roll on the grass. Whatever viscous, burning liquid had crashed amongst them had splashed the wretched animal.

"Lord Cassat!"

Whatever his other failings, Duke Iruvain was a peerless horseman. He mastered his frantic steed with one hand, reaching out to catch Lord Cassat as Draximal's heir toppled from his saddle.

"I can't hold him!" Iruvain yelled.

Karn ran up to take the youthful lord's weight, heedless of the stinking flames running down from Lord Cassat's ear to his chest. The grass underfoot was burning, flames licking up the inside of his boots. Ready hands surrounded him, all desperate to carry Lord Cassat out of danger. One of the noble lieutenants dispatched his thrashing horse with a merciful stab to the heart.

"Water!" Someone thrust a leather bottle forward, hands trembling.

"Soak some cloth!" Karn felt as if he'd caught the heat of an opening furnace. His eyes were sore, his skin tender. He saw they had reached unsullied grass. "Lay him down!"

The man with the bottle shed his cloak, spilling more water than he poured upon it. Karn snatched at the woollen cloth, ignoring his stinging hands. It was barely damp enough to quench the fire engulfing Lord Cassat. The young man was gasping, his expression more bemused than suffering.

"Water!" Karn shouted. "Pour it on!" Bronze flasks and humbler waterskins soaked Karn as readily as the stricken lord.

Lord Cassat choked, his face darkening as if he were being throttled. His arms flailed wildly and then dropped limp to the muddy earth. He lay dead, even as his frantic retinue poured water, yelled for aid, or desperately besought every god and goddess's mercy.

"Send for a surgeon!"

The milling Draximal nobles couldn't believe their heir was dead.

"Duke Iruvain!"

That shout amid the lamentations made Karn look up. He saw a rider aghast at the woeful scene still with sufficient wits to seek out a commander.

"Your Grace, the Dalasorians!"

Karn fought his way clear of the uproar around Lord Cassat's corpse. Following the rider's pointing hand, he saw lances piercing the pall hanging over the Triolle Road. So the grassland horsemen had been hiding on the far side of the town. The fires started by the trebuchets had served to conceal their advance. And the brazen calls of the Soluran's regiments were ordering a general assault from the other direction. They were charging forward from the Ashgil Road. Once again, Draximal's army was caught in a deadly vice.

High up on his horse, Duke Iruvain shouted, "Sound the retreat!"

Draximal's lieutenants stared at him with furious disbelief. They began shouting refusals, denials and vile insults.

"If we stand, we'll be attacked front and rear and, who knows, maybe from the flank as well." Iruvain appealed to the retinue's sergeants, men versed in the bitter realities of war. "Retreat and we live to fight another day. Fall back and we can hold the line between the river and the hills till Marlier's men and Parnilesse's arrive. But we have to retreat now!"

He was quite right. Karn grabbed the reins of a riderless horse and scrambled into the saddle. Master Hamare would have been pleasantly surprised to finally see Duke Iruvain showing something of his late father's mettle.

The sergeants-at-arms were following Iruvain's lead. Those lieutenants not understanding their peril were roughly shoved aside. Horns sounded and flags signalled. The Draximal forces were already standing fast, swiftly turning from assault to defensive formations.

Karn took a moment to assess the situation. If the militia's training held firm, as long as the mercenary captains recognised their companies' best hope of salvation lay in strength of numbers, the Draximal army should be able to leave this debacle in fair order. The odds were good that Iruvain would survive, to bluster and justify himself.

Karn had other concerns. Ignoring his scorched hands and face, he kicked his horse into a gallop. The beast was only too happy to leave the tumult behind.

Master Hamare would never believe Lord Cassat's death was some stroke of exiles' luck. No unseen trebuchet amid the debris of Tyrle's wrecked streets could have decapitated Draximal's army with such a precise strike. Not even with the most eagle-eyed spotter on the walls relaying instructions to an expert engineer. Karn didn't believe in luck, any more than he believed in the gods. The exiles' cursed wizards had encompassed this murder, no doubt about it.

Very well. Karn knew a wizard as ruthless. He would make sure Minelas was ready to defend Triolle with the most brutal magic he could command. Once he'd ensured Litasse was defended, he'd ride for Marlier and for Parnilesse. However quickly this Soluran could move his army, a single man on a horse was always going to be faster.

He'd ensure Lord Geferin and Ridianne the Vixen brought their forces to bear as swiftly as possible, whatever promises, lies or threats that took. These exiles, who'd murdered Master Hamare and disgraced Duchess Litasse, who'd so nearly been his own death, they weren't going to win this war.

CHAPTER TWENTY-FIVE
Branca

Brynock, in the Lescari Dukedom of Parnilesse, 23rd of Aft-Autumn

THERE WAS A lot to be said for woollen stockings and flannel petticoats, a sturdy gown and a frieze cloak. Despite the chill wind, Branca was pleasantly warm, even if so many layers threatened to make her as broad as she was tall. This was currently a further advantage. It was no time to look pretty, nor even passably handsome.

The town was full of expectant mercenaries and sullen militia. Every woman risked their lust or resentment. From maidens barely blooded by Drianon to inconveniently fresh-faced grandmothers, women were staying safely within doors as much as they could. Those forced to go to the market hid beneath hoods and bonnets.

Any woman relying on a son or brother's escort soon rued their mistake. Branca had seen youths too young to shave forcibly enlisted into Duke Orlin's army. A baker had stood his ground, brandishing his flour-caked cap at the recruiting sergeant. He'd been released, but Lord Geferin's decree had soon been cried through the streets. All the town's linen weavers, potters and every apprentice were needed to defend the dukedom.

Branca wondered if the recruiter's roving eye had noticed her sitting in the indifferent shelter of this wagonload of bricks. No one had come to claim it for two days. Was its owner reluctantly marching with Parnilesse's regiments, a family out in the brickfields frantic with worry, not knowing what had become of him?

She must find somewhere different to sit tomorrow. Though she couldn't readily think of anywhere offering such a good view of the bridge. Aremil needed to see the banners crossing the river. Tens of companies were crossing into Triolle's eastern fiefdoms. The procession had continued all morning, men and horses trudging over the long bridge supported by twenty stone pillars marching across the wide river.

Branca noticed each company leaving a prudent distance between themselves and the next. Above the ancient Tormalin foundations, an ugly patchwork of differing stone and mortar marked the collapse of various spans over the years. Flat-bottomed ferries were carrying those unwilling to risk the bridge. She'd seen all the wagons transporting supplies for Lord Geferin's advance entrusted to the boats.

A flurry of rain pattered against her hood. She ignored it, contemplating the river's low flow. No aetheric magic she knew of could stir the waters, despite the storm rune figuring so strongly in the enchantments she and Kerith had discussed. They still had no notion how to use Artifice with the ferocity the ancient texts promised. Branca might just be able to shove some aggressive militiaman away, maybe trip a galloping horse, though privately she doubted it.

Could a wizard summon up rain to swell the river and bring down the bridge? That wouldn't be using magic in battle but would it provoke Planir the Black's wrath? She feared it might. Regardless, storms could turn the roads to clinging mud that would hamper their forces as direly as the Parnilesse army. The last thing Captain-General Evord needed was delay. Every league the exiles' army advanced was another pennyweight in the scales towards their victory.

Branca shivered more with apprehension than cold. Aremil did his best to convince her that the campaign was going well but she was much more adept at reading his fears through the aether than he was at hiding them. Would brushing against Captain-General Evord's thoughts give her some more hopeful insight? Branca had never been so tempted to ignore the masters of Artifice's strictures, laid down in ages past and now reiterated in Vanam's scholarly halls.

Was it really so wrong to look behind someone's words into their unguarded thoughts? But what of the consequences for the adept as well as their victim? Branca still felt Kerith's lacerating guilt over forcing his will on Failla, uncovering her desperate deceits despite all her pleas. Perhaps those strictures sought to protect adepts.

But what if those subject to aetheric enchantments never knew what had happened? She knew Kerith was pondering those stealthiest of enchantments woven around the Sea Breeze rune signifying the subtle southern wind. Would any of them ever master Artifice so completely that they could read someone else's thoughts and change their mind, leaving them all unawares? If they could do that, couldn't they just possibly end this war without any further bloodshed? Jettin might revel in battle and blame the dead on Poldrion's whim but Branca was sick of slaughter, even seen through others' eyes.

Her growling stomach recalled her to prosaic concerns. It had been far too long since she'd eaten breakfast. Time to return to the inn and see what was offered for lunch. Trissa would be there, even if Charoleia hadn't yet returned.

From the shelter of her hood, Branca looked carefully around. Standing up, shoulders hunched like every other woman forced onto these streets, she mouthed the enchantment to brush aside curious eyes as she hurried over the litter-strewn cobbles.

"*Fae dar ameneul, sar dar redicorlen.*"

Past the dairy market and the stone pillar where bulls were tethered for baiting on high festival days. Lord Geferin's captains had turned the pillar into a gallows. Branca averted her gaze from the dangling corpse. Heralds had cried the man's crime through the streets, condemning him for rape and murder. Such villainy wouldn't be tolerated, they assured the townsfolk.

Branca didn't feel any safer. The man had been accused but he'd been given no chance to answer before Raeponin's shrine. Anyway, what consolation was a murderer's death to a victim? Man or woman, young or old, they were just as dead. She ignored an alley offering a quicker route between a tailor's shuttered shop and a shoemaker's. This was no time to take a byway, even in broad daylight.

The shoemaker leaned on his door, a hefty cudgel beside him as he balanced the chances of turning some coin against the risks of dealing with mercenaries. He ignored Branca. This was no time to strike up conversation with strangers.

Not when Lord Geferin's sergeants were hunting whoever was spreading such scurrilous rumours about Duke Orlin. Branca turned past the shrine to Dastennin. The Lord of Storms was widely revered in Parnilesse, with its long coast and the rivers defending both the dukedom's flanks. The door had still been removed, like that of every other shrine in the town. Zealous beatings and Lord Geferin's threats hadn't stopped the accusing letters nailed up during the night. So now even Saedrin's statue gazed solemnly through an open portal.

That was a tribute to Reniack's diligence. Branca wondered whereabouts the rabble-rouser was in Parnilesse. Jettin was consistently evasive whenever she reached through the aether to him. They were busy shoving spokes in Lord Geferin's wheels, that was all anyone needed to know. Branca saw the young adept's fearful recollection of those caught in sedition. They were nailed by their ears to pillories or trapped in a set of stocks to be battered with merciless stones. Several had already died. Thankfully, Reniack was well used to evading ducal wrath.

Beyond that, the veils around Jettin's thoughts were unexpectedly opaque. Branca wondered if that was why Kerith was so interested in mastering enchantments of piercing subtlety. He would want to know how Jettin had improved his aetheric understanding of magic, as well as finding out if the boy was hiding something.

Branca knew Kerith anticipated receiving the accolade of mentor once he returned to the university. Jettin wasn't looking that far ahead. Always ready to defend Lescari blood back in Vanam, his passions burned twice as bright now he'd returned to the land of his forefathers.

Branca crossed the Golden Carp's threshold. The broad inn of brick and timber served travellers who could afford comforts on the road as well as the prosperous merchants they came to meet. Its parlour served fine Tormalin wine to men and women playing thoughtful games of white raven or just enjoying quiet conversation.

Charoleia had entertained a discreet stream of visitors these past few evenings. Or rather, Mistress Halisoun had, her Parnilesse accent faultless, her hair a dowdy brown beneath her lace caps, thanks to Trissa's deft hand with a dye bottle. Her figure matronly, thanks to heavily padded stays, Mistress Halisoun had once been a governess. She still had a wide acquaintance among the musicians and dancing masters who circulated around noble schoolrooms. Parnilesse's lords and their ladies were adamant their children's accomplishments should equal their Tormalin neighbours'.

The parlour was empty, and so was the dining salon. Branca went swiftly up the stairs to halt surprised in the doorway of the bedchamber they shared. Trissa was briskly folding the last of their gowns into the travelling chest.

"Are we leaving?"

"As soon as Lord Usine's coach arrives." Charoleia was clearing the dressing table. "We'll travel as far as possible before dark today."

Branca wondered in passing what this local lord might owe Mistress Halisoun that made him so very eager to assist her. Never mind; getting safely out of the town was what mattered. She closed the door and shed her cloak. "Why such haste?"

"Lord Geferin and Duke Orlin have realised they'll be fighting inside Parnilesse's borders if they don't make a stand in Triolle." Charoleia stowed cosmetic jars in their padded coffer. "They're moving faster than I expected. Duke Iruvain's messengers must be flogging their horses to half to death."

"Some rain wouldn't go amiss, to slow their courier doves." Branca glanced through the window towards the tall tower where Brynock's reeve cherished the birds bred in Parnilesse Castle's lofts. They'd seen two and three fly at a time, each one carrying copies of vital news reaching this first foothold over the river.

"The Parnilesse baggage train will arrive within the day." Trissa folded a chemise. "The town will be choked with camp followers."

"If you think the streets are dangerous now..." Charoleia shook her head. "Women following the drum are five times as vicious as their menfolk."

Branca sat on the bed. "Where are we going?"

"To Carluse, by the straightest route we can find." Charoleia tucked silver-backed hairbrushes into the coffer's corners. "Since Parnilesse's army is doing the same, men and wagons will be nose to tail on the high road. But once we're beyond Pannal, we can take to the byways. Don't worry. I'll find a path to keep us well away from the fighting." She patted the brass-bound case that held her maps.

Branca didn't doubt the collection was irreplaceable. These weren't the broad charts she'd seen Nath drawing up when they'd all been together in Losand. Rather, the long strips of vellum that Charoleia prized followed each major road, noting the hazards, accommodation and settlements the traveller could expect.

She cast her mind back to Nath's maps. Pannal was a day's journey into Triolle, beyond the meadows so often submerged beneath winter floods. "Won't they ask our business, when we cross the bridge?"

"Lord Usine is sending a handful of men to guard us," Trissa assured her.

"He appreciates Mistress Halisoun's worth." Charoleia smiled pertly, then became more serious. "We shall have to shed them once we reach Pannal. We'll travel a good deal faster by horse and much less noticeably."

Branca bit her lip. "I don't know how to ride a horse. We walk, in Vanam, or hire coaches."

"Oh." Charoleia looked momentarily surprised. "No matter. We'll find you a well-tempered beast and we'll hardly be riding at breakneck pace. We just need to stay ahead of foraging quartermasters."

"Don't fret," Trissa encouraged her.

That was easy for her to say. She'd doubtless been riding horses all her life. As far as Branca was concerned, horses were unpleasantly large, wholly unpredictable and inclined to bite, kick or both, at the slightest provocation. But she'd be cursed before she'd make such a feeble admission to Trissa or Charoleia.

"Could you let Master Aremil know we'll be leaving here today?" Charoleia's gaze was sympathetic. "And do give him our fondest regards."

"How is he?" Trissa asked.

"Still very distressed." Branca's own tears threatened.

If she or Kerith or some other adept had been able to master the right enchantments, could they have stopped this war before Aremil's worst fears for his unknown brother had been so brutally realised?

Steeling herself, she went to the window, gazing unseeing at the mossy roof opposite.

"*Al daera sa Aremil sast elarmin as feorel.*"

It hardly took a moment's thought to reach him.

"*They've found his body.*"

His unguarded thoughts washed over her. She was instantly drawn into the echoing stone hall of Aremil's imagination. No semblance of sunlight shone through the coloured windows. Outside, all was dark, torches blazing along the pillared aisles within.

His crippled self sat motionless in the shadows while the reflection of the man he so desperately wished he could be paced impatiently back and forth. She was shocked to feel his distress coloured with fury.

He was incensed at Tathrin's unguarded instant of relief when he had heard Lord Cassat was dead. Aremil couldn't forgive his friend. Even if the battle for Tyrle, indeed both battles, had been the most savage, the most closely fought struggles of all their campaign thus far. Even if the balance could easily have tipped against them, if luck and Lord Cassat's leadership had inspired the Draximal army.

Branca gasped as she saw a young man's blighted face, his hair burned away, the skin blackened and cracked to show dull red flesh beneath. One eye was entirely gone. Consumed by fire or eaten by some scavenging animal? She couldn't escape Tathrin's horrified thoughts when he'd come to make certain this really was Cassat's body, finally reclaimed from the battlefield.

"They won't tell me if he was killed with magic."

Aremil's anger was swelling rather than receding. Branca wasn't sure what to say for the best.

"Reher only helped bring down the towers, didn't he? So the Mountain Men could scale the walls. Sorgrad wasn't even there."

She opened her thoughts to Aremil, to remind him of that uncanny magewoman with her grisly talents in Relshaz, who was already hunting down renegade wizards. Tathrin had insisted she'd warned Sorgrad off using his magic in battle.

"They arrived just before the battle. Ask Charoleia if he could keep his wizardry to himself once the fighting started!"

Branca saw the Mountain Man had sworn he was innocent. Tathrin wanted to believe him, to credit Sorgrad with that much decency. Aremil couldn't help suspecting the ruthless mercenary had used his magic to do deliberate murder. She shook her head, dizzy with all these layers of thought and memory blurring her mind's eye.

"What's the latest news from Tyrle? Is everyone all right?"

Branca's vision of Aremil's hall wavered as Charoleia took her hand. She snatched it away.

"A moment, please."

But Aremil was already answering. Branca's heart twisted as she felt his bleak relief at having something else on which to focus his thoughts.

"*There's a great deal to do before we can pursue Duke Iruvain. Our men must rest and tend their wounds. The muster rolls are being revised. It seems we've lost around five hundred men from our fighting strength.*"

Branca winced at a vision of the battlefield littered with the plundered dead and dying.

"*Duke Iruvain lost at least the same number when we took the town. More than eight hundred died beyond the walls with Lord Cassat. We've more than two and a half thousand prisoners. They must be escorted to Abray under guard.*"

Branca remembered what had happened after the first battles in Carluse. "Can't we enlist them in our own army? To make up our numbers?"

"*Some, but there are a great many companies we don't want anywhere near our own, troublemakers, brutes and the like. Not that our army can boast of any great virtue.*"

Aremil's rising anger drew her back into the stone hall. He was pacing again, the torches on the pillars blazing.

"*Some of our companies began looting Tyrle as soon as the walls were breached. They're being allowed to keep what they stole, as are those companies sworn to Triolle who decided to surrender. Tathrin says if they can carry their booty, they're allowed to take it with them.*"

Aremil couldn't conceal his outrage even as he explained the captain-general's reasoning.

"*Too many men have made a bad bargain taking a duke's coin. They'll be looking to cut their losses. If we let them keep what they can carry, to see them through the winter, they're more likely to keep on walking once they reach the Great West Road.*"

Charoleia took Branca's hand once more, insistent. "Do we know where Duke Iruvain is now?"

"Aremil? The Duke of Triolle—?"

For the first time, Branca saw the pacing facsimile of Aremil frozen as his true semblance sitting in the high-backed chair stirred.

"*All Tathrin can say is he hasn't reached Triolle Castle. Apparently Sorgrad has been scrying on Duchess Litasse, though he won't say why. As best as we can tell, Iruvain led near half the Draximal*" *army away in good order. Our scouts say about the same number of his own militia and mercenaries are already heading back to Triolle. They're the ones who saw sense and abandoned Tyrle during the night after the walls were first breached. Iruvain's been beaten, but not defeated.*"

He looked straight at her, visibly troubled.

"*Apparently a sizeable contingent of Draximal mercenaries have abandoned their allegiance completely. We're trying to find out where they're headed.*"

Charoleia took her hand once again. "Branca, the coach is here."

"I'm sorry, we have to go."

"*Go carefully.*"

"We will," she promised him fervently as his presence in her mind faded away.

She drew a deep breath.

"Well, what's the news?" Charoleia tucked a wisp of Mistress Halisoun's dull hair under her lace cap.

"I'll tell you in the carriage." Branca looked at her. "Would Sorgrad have killed Lord Cassat? With his wizardry?"

"He could have, though I doubt it. Does it matter?" Charoleia tied her cloak's ribbons and raised her hood. "Lord Cassat could just as easily have been killed by an arrow or a lance. War's a perilous business for men of all ranks." She frowned. "Did Aremil say anything about Ridianne the Vixen? How soon are her forces expected to reach Marlier's border?"

"My lady," Trissa warned as someone knocked on the bedchamber door.

"We can discuss it in the carriage." Charoleia handed Branca her cloak. "You can tell our friends from me, if something doesn't hobble Lord Geferin or slow Ridianne the Vixen's advance, Captain-General Evord's prospects will be balanced on a knife-edge. I'll put some thought to wedging a stone into Parnilesse's shoe. Tell Tathrin he and Sorgrad and Gren could do well to pay a visit to Marlier on the same errand."

Falling silent, Charoleia nodded and Trissa opened the door to admit the inn's porters, ready to carry their luggage down to the coach.

Walking beside Trissa, Branca followed Charoleia down the stairs. She didn't doubt Charoleia's assessment. She'd soon realised the woman could have been a mercenary captain to rival the finest company's tacticians if she hadn't scorned the hardships of such a life. No matter how many battles they won, it seemed they could never be certain of victory.

Not unless magic tipped the scales.

CHAPTER TWENTY-SIX
Litasse

Triolle Castle,
24ᵗʰ of Aft-Autumn

"HE'S HERE." KARN slipped through the music room's door.

Litasse caught a glimpse of the man behind him, the candles on the stair burnishing golden hair. The wizard had finally come? Her stomach hollowed with apprehension.

"Your Grace, may I present Master Minelas of Grynth?" Karn bowed with unusual formality. "Master Minelas, I have the honour to make you known to Her Grace Duchess Litasse of Triolle."

She studied him frankly, as Hamare had taught her. Perhaps a couple of years older than her husband, he wasn't as tall or as well muscled as Iruvain. Still, he wore boots and breeches with an ease suggesting he preferred riding to coach journeys. How far had he ridden? Beneath his dusty cloak, his midnight-blue doublet was creased and travel-stained.

"Grynth is in the far north of Ensaimin, Your Grace." The slender man was neither overawed by her rank nor discomfited by his dishevelment. "A town of wool merchants and mine owners, tucked between the mountains and the plain."

Which explained his lowland features and slender build coupled with such fair hair and blue eyes.

"So I understand." Litasse inclined her head with courteous reserve. In fact she had no notion where the place might be. The man had seen that in her eyes, hadn't he? She lifted her chin. "You've been living in Caladhria of late?"

"Indeed." Now the wizard withdrew behind courtesy, sweeping a courtly bow. "Your Grace, it is an honour to meet you."

"What have you been doing in Caladhria?" asked Litasse.

He shrugged with a hint of insolence. "This and that, Your Grace."

Litasse glanced at Karn, only to see his expression was studiously blank. Very well. He could tell her later.

"Could 'this' or 'that' have incurred the Archmage's displeasure?" she demanded of Master Minelas.

"That need not concern you. Let's discuss what you want me to do." The wizard smiled as she hesitated. "Don't worry. I'll keep your secrets, just as surely as I keep the secrets of those who retained my services in Caladhria."

Litasse supposed she would have to accept that. Of course, betraying her would mean he was condemning himself. That should keep his mouth shut.

"You don't look like a wizard." She spoke the thought aloud to see how he responded.

"Too young?" He was unperturbed. "No scholar's stoop beneath a moth-eaten velvet robe? No furrowed brow, eternally creased from pondering elemental mysteries? No soft hands stained with ink and alchemy?" He waggled his fingers, his smile curled with a suggestion of a sneer. Was he mocking her? "You think I should be studying in some windswept tower, far above the mundane appetites of lesser men?"

Scarlet fire flickered suddenly around Minelas's upraised hand.

"Oh!" Litasse was startled into an involuntary exclamation.

The mage gestured and the licking flames turned to brilliant blue, his fair skin quite unblemished.

"Those content with intellectual rewards are welcome to them. I believe the exceptional skills of the mageborn entitle us to tangible recompense and the bodily comforts they bring. How much do you propose to pay me?"

Litasse rallied. "That depends on what you can do."

"What do you want?"

He snapped his fingers. Incandescence flew across the room to kindle an unlit lamp. A breeze snatched music from the harpsichord and whirled the sheets around Litasse's head. Insistent gusts plucked at her skirts till she staggered.

"Would you like your enemies' tents burned over their heads? Or snatched away by a storm? Would it turn a battle in your favour if their charging horses lost their footing? Or if they were struck by lightning? Would you prefer I merely blinded the beasts?"

The papers fell to the floor in a flash that dazzled Litasse. She rubbed at her eyes but she still couldn't see. She rubbed harder, to no avail. She turned her panic into fury.

"Enough!"

Litasse's vision abruptly cleared and she saw Minelas folding his fingers around a sphere of white light.

"I take it that's eased your doubts." He smiled contentedly. "Leave me to decide how to secure victory for His Grace of Triolle. I'll wield something more subtle than fire and lightning as I gather Duke Iruvain has no notion you've enlisted me? That suits me very well, and besides, I have no desire to draw the Archmage's eye this way." He brushed blue sparks from his hands, ostentatiously fastidious. "You need only concern yourself with paying me. Gold coin," he added, "none of your lead-tainted silver. Five thousand Tormalin crowns."

So, unnerving though his magic was, he was as much a mercenary as any of those carrying banners for Triolle. That simplified their dealings.

"That's a great deal of money," Litasse observed.

"A fair price for Triolle's salvation." He looked at her quizzically. "Would you like me to turn a dish of water into a magic mirror and scry out the enemy's deployments in advance of your husband's next battle? Would you like me to lame their lancers' horses and weaken their archers' bowstaves?"

"Very well. You'll be paid when the exiles' army is finally defeated."

Smiling serenely, Litasse thought swiftly. Still claiming to be exhausted from his headlong flight back to safety, Iruvain wouldn't stir outside Triolle's walls until Parnilesse's army arrived, and Marlier's whore with her forces. That gave her a few days to find enough coin to content the wizard for the moment.

The entire sum was out of the question. Iruvain didn't have that much ready coin in the entire castle. But she could promise the wizard ten thousand crowns from Sharlac's coffers, to be paid just as soon as he helped reclaim her family's dominions. And promise that in good faith. She'd pay him, if he did all he claimed he could. What could he do in the meantime? Unravel whatever sorcery defeated the rebels? That bell could hardly be unrung.

Gasping, she clutched at her throat. She was choking. A strangling hand wrapped around her neck. Her fingernails dug into her skin. There was nothing there. Her vision blurred. Blood pounded in her head.

"No."

She heard Minelas's warning as Karn took a step towards him. Then the awful pressure yielded and she could breathe again. As she stumbled to the harpsichord stool, blinking away tears, she saw Karn looking warily at the wizard.

"I expect a thousand crowns on account before I lift a finger to help you," Minelas said calmly.

Litasse nodded, still nauseated.

There were a thousand crowns in Triolle's coffers. She knew Iruvain had promised the coin to his mercenary captains but she could still show it to the wizard. Getting the coffers away from the castle was his problem. Which he'd doubtless solve with magic. She had to stifle a hysterical giggle. What would Iruvain do, if he unlocked his strongroom to find all his treasure chests empty?

She saw Minelas was waiting for her answer, his expression irritatingly superior.

"Agreed," she said hoarsely.

Karn would have spoken but an urgent hand rapped on the door.

"Your Grace?" Pelletria hurried in. "Duke Iruvain is on his way."

"What does he want?" Litasse sprang to her feet.

"To discuss Lord Geferin's accommodations, supposedly." Pelletria gestured towards Minelas.

"He must not find him here."

"I'll hardly betray myself, woman," Minelas said, scornful.

Pelletria ignored him. "He's young and handsome and you've had no chaperone."

The wizard was good-looking. That simply hadn't occurred to Litasse, not when she still ached for Hamare's loss.

Minelas laughed. "So that's how the land lies."

"You know nothing of it." Litasse turned to Karn. "Take him to the guest chambers in the White Tower." The White Tower was largely given over to favoured servants and apartments for visitors requiring minimal courtesies but the wizard wouldn't know that.

"You've brought letters for Her Grace from Lord Leysen in Sharlac, if anyone asks," Pelletria told Minelas. "You don't know what's in them. You merely await a reply."

"Do I indeed?" The wizard looked inclined to argue. Then he nodded. "I'll be a scholar from Col, returning from Toremal where I've enquired into Aldabreshin alchemy."

His secretive smile irritated Litasse but there was no time for that. She clapped her hands. "Quickly!"

"This way." Karn led Minelas from the room.

Litasse watched him go. "Did some sneak tell Iruvain he was here?"

Did her husband really think she was some harlot who'd spread her thighs for any handsome stranger?

"He's no notion you've had any visitors but let's not take risks we don't have to." Pelletria began gathering up the fallen sheets of music.

Litasse knelt to help. "Lord Geferin's not expected for another five days. What does Iruvain really want?"

"I don't know." Stiffly, Pelletria stood up. "But there's something you have to tell him. I've had word from some of Master Hamare's enquiry agents back in Vanam. One of the chief instigators of this exiles' plot is Duke Secaris of Draximal's son."

Litasse didn't understand. "But Lord Cassat's dead."

"There was an elder son, a cripple," Pelletria said testily, putting the music back on the harpsichord. "We thought he was dead long since. It seems not. He's been living in Vanam all this while. No one thought him more than some lesser son of a minor noble sent away to die in comfort. But now he's been stirring up trouble, a few folk have been asking questions. Our man caught wind of it."

"He started this war? To pursue his claim on the dukedom? Or just for revenge?" Litasse was suddenly furious. "So all these high-minded proclamations about seeking peace and prosperity for Lescar, they're all lies!"

Her father, her brothers, they had died for *this*?

"He's one among a handful who set this in motion. Some may truly believe their path leads to a better future." Pelletria shrugged. "But now Lord Cassat's dead, Duke Iruvain and Duke Orlin should offer this unknown son his birthright as Draximal's heir."

"What will that achieve?" Litasse rose to her feet, brushing angrily at her gown. "Duke Secaris already set him aside, and if he's crippled, Draximal's vassals will never accept him."

"I don't suppose they will, any more than Duke Secaris would countenance it," Pelletria agreed. "We need only convince this poor fool he could reclaim the rank he was born to. How will his allies trust him then? How long could such dissent delay the Soluran's next attack?"

Litasse nodded slowly. "Long enough to see Parnilesse arrive here, and Marlier's woman and her troops."

Pelletria's head turned, quick as a bird. "That's Duke Iruvain's step."

Litasse sat at the harpsichord. Her fingers stumbled over the keys and she tried again, more harmoniously this time. Then Iruvain's lackey opened the door and she struck another discord.

"You won't entertain Lord Geferin with that mockery." The duke scowled. "How long have you been idling up here?"

He wanted to turn every conversation into a quarrel, ever since he'd returned from Tyrle.

"Everything is in hand," Litasse said meekly. "Lord Geferin will be suitably accommodated in the Oriel Tower. Duke Garnot's remaining retinue—"

"I want them out of my castle by sunset," Iruvain

said crossly. "Let them go cap in hand to whatever vassal lords care to claim their fealty."

"I will see to it, my lord." Litasse folded her hands in her lap. Not for the first time, she wondered what had happened between the two dukes in Tyrle. Iruvain refused to discuss it, only insisting it was the rebels who'd been Garnot's death.

Karn had said nothing at all, resolutely evading her questions, just as he refused to tell her what she wanted to know about Minelas. Litasse was getting a trifle tired of all this manly secrecy.

Iruvain was crossing the room to look out of the window. "I've sent word to Lord Geferin insisting he travel ahead of the main strength. He and I have urgent matters to discuss so he should be here within a day or so. Make ready but don't waste our time with some tedious banquet."

He wasn't just angry, Litasse saw, he was apprehensive, no matter how he tried to hide it.

"Is it the news from Carluse that concerns you?" she ventured.

He rounded on her. "What news?"

"About Duke Secaris's son?" She looked up at him, wide-eyed.

He took a step forwards, fists clenching. "There was nothing I could do to save Lord Cassat."

His face twisted with anguish. Disconcerted, Litasse hastened to explain.

"No, Duke Secaris had another son, a cripple who was sent away to Vanam. He's one of the men who enlisted this army to attack us."

"What nonsense is this?" Iruvain stared at her, his colour fading.

Litasse swiftly sought a plausible explanation. "There are serving women in Carluse Castle—"

"Servants' tittle-tattle," Iruvain spat with renewed wrath. "Just what Hamare would have me believe? How well has his so-called intelligence served Triolle? When we have exiles and mercenaries overrunning two dukedoms, their heirs and rulers dead!"

"Forgive me, my lord." Litasse studied the harpsichord's keys so he couldn't see the anger in her eyes. How dared Iruvain scorn Hamare, when he'd been the first to suspect the Vanam plot?

"Any number of liars and frauds will lay claim to Sharlac and Carluse." Iruvain dismissed them all with a gesture. "Doubtless to Draximal as well. It means nothing. When Parnilesse comes, we'll have the regiments we need to crush this Soluran's army." He nodded vehemently. "We'll see Sharlac and Carluse avenged, and Lord Cassat too. Then we'll hang these exiles like the felons they are, whoever they may claim to be. They'll rue the day they ever imagined they could throw down Lescar's dukes."

Iruvain's rhetoric was for his own benefit, not hers. He was afraid. He'd already been beaten once and he feared another whipping. And there was something more, Litasse could hear it in his voice. What might that be? Was it finding himself overruled by Lord Geferin, indebted to Ferdain of Marlier, as he had to turn to them to save his dukedom? His feebleness as Duke of Triolle would be laid bare for all the world to see.

She closed her eyes on stinging tears, of grief for Hamare and of dread she couldn't explain. She let the teardrops spill down her cheeks. She'd soon realised seeing her cry satisfied Iruvain's spiteful need to relieve his anxieties.

He looked around the music room, ignoring Pelletria standing silently in a corner. "You have my man Karn running your errands today, don't you?"

"Yes, my lord." Litasse wiped a careful finger along her damp lashes.

"I need him." Fresh malice lit Iruvain's eyes. "Duke Ferdain's whore has proved as unreliable as all your kind, my lady wife. She's marched his men as far as Marlier's border and now she squats on her fat arse there."

"I believe I can find Karn, Your Grace," Pelletria said quickly.

He turned his ire on her. "Then send him to me. Tell him I want the truth of what's happening in Marlier inside the next two days."

The duke strode out of the room, slamming the door behind him.

Litasse sat gazing after him. "What do you suppose that's all about?"

"Marlier's Vixen being so dilatory?" Pelletria looked thoughtful. "Or His Grace's foul temper?"

"Either. Both." Litasse turned to the old woman.

"What do you make of his mood?"

"Our friends among his servants say he sits up late into the night, long after he's dismissed his men. He paces and drinks till he falls asleep but he cannot sleep for long. Nightmares wake him sweating and crying out."

Once, Litasse would have felt some sympathy for her husband. She would have believed it her wifely duty to ease whatever burdens so oppressed him. No longer.

"That won't impress Lord Geferin," she said grimly. "And we do need Marlier's regiments to be sure of victory. Why has that cursed whore halted?"

"I've no idea," Pelletria admitted.

Rising to her feet, Litasse went to the mirror over the fireplace, to make sure her tears hadn't smudged her cosmetics. She caught her breath on a sudden thought. They had a new tool to hand, to find out what was going on anywhere else they might wish. She turned to Pelletria, suddenly gleeful.

"When you go to Karn, please give my compliments to Master Minelas and ask him to rejoin me here. Let's see if his exceptional skills can shed any light on what Marlier's Vixen's up to, and what's going on in Carluse Castle, and what's become of my mother and sisters!"

Pelletria understood at once. "I'll fetch your jewel case, the one with the diamonds. I imagine Master Minelas will need payment in advance for such extra duties," she commented sardonically.

"Let's see if his magic is sufficient to tell Aldabreshin glass from real gems." Litasse didn't care. The mage could take every gift Iruvain had given her if he proved useful now.

Pelletria frowned. "It'll be a challenge to explain how you've come up with such information, given His Grace's temper. But I'm sure we can think of something."

"I think we'll be amazed just how much Karn finds out on his way to and from Marlier," Litasse said confidently.

Though even riding all night, he'd be hard pressed to make the trip and return with news fast enough to satisfy Iruvain in his current mood.

CHAPTER TWENTY-SEVEN
Tathrin

Ridianne the Vixen's Camp,
Outside Skebban, in the Lescari Dukedom of
Marlier,
25th of Aft-Autumn

"QUICKSILVER'S BANNER," GREN remarked.

"And the Steelhands." Sorgrad inclined his head.

Tathrin was careful not to catch anyone's eye as he made note of both standards above the clusters of tents. An alchemist's alembic was embroidered in white and grey on a blue ground while a clenched fist of actual metal plates had been riveted to black cloth. There was still no sign of a dog fox skewered by Marlier's three swords.

Ridianne the Vixen's encampment was easily as big as Captain-General Evord's. It was far bigger than Skebban, the village clustered around the junction where roads from the south of Marlier headed north into Carluse and east into Triolle. Few folk wanted to live within a day and a half's march of those borders.

Apart from the insignia, Tathrin found it very familiar. Each company had claimed its own patch. Fighting men and women sat outside their tents, companionably stitching leather, polishing armour and sharpening swords. The scents of oil and woodsmoke mingled with the faint reek of latrines.

Quartermasters' minions tended their fires and ran errands for the cooks and the surgeon if their company was lucky enough to have one. The Steelhands did, Tathrin noted. He was grinding something in a pestle and mortar, just as Master Welgren did, joking with two old warriors retired to this safer life among the supply wagons. A handful of boys and girls played just beyond.

"There are children here." Tathrin was appalled.

Sorgrad shrugged. "What of it?"

"Why aren't they apprenticed?" demanded Tathrin. "Or learning their letters and reckoning somewhere safe?"

"You think everyone's as lucky as your Failla?" Gren laughed. "There's not one woman in ten on a muster roll who have someone to trust with their children."

"Or have skills beyond their swordplay to provide for a family," Sorgrad added.

"Should they drown their babies like unwanted puppies?" Gren taunted.

Sorgrad waved him to silence. "The Vixen keeps her own children close. That's why she lets others do the same."

Tathrin glanced at him. "What else do you know of her?"

"Enough to know she's unpredictable." The Mountain Man looked thoughtful.

They were into the inner camp now, passing between standards that blended Duke Ferdain's blazon with each company's insignia. Here, Marlier's three swords framed a serpent coiled ready to strike. There, the blades were ranked above a blue shield displaying a bulbous brown toad.

Tathrin found it incredible they'd advanced so far unchallenged. But Sorgrad had assured him a mere three men, dressed like any other mercenaries, could slip into the Vixen's camp.

Still safe within Marlier's borders, with her scouts confirming Evord's army was headed towards Triolle, Ridianne would expect each company to secure their own tents. As long as they did nothing to arouse suspicion, anyone seeing them would assume they belonged to some other company among the vast array.

That was all very well, as long as they could leave the camp as easily as they had entered it, once Ridianne knew who they were. Or had their luck just run out?

As Tathrin spotted the Vixen's standard, four heavyset mercenaries headed straight towards them.

All were fully armoured, with foxes' pelts mounted on their helmets as crests. The masks' hollow gazes stared above each warrior's watchful eyes.

"Keep your mouth shut, long lad," Gren advised softly.

Every mercenary Tathrin could see wore Ridianne's personal badge. They all stopped to see what transpired. This far inside her purview twenty swords would skewer a troublemaker inside the blink of an eye.

"We're here to see herself." Calm, Sorgrad threw his hood back. "To present Captain-General Evord's compliments."

Seeing his yellow hair, three of the men drew their swords. Tathrin didn't need Gren's warning look to keep his own hand well clear of his blade.

The fourth man, his jowls dark with stubble, shoved his helm back to reveal shrewd eyes. "I'll see if herself is interested."

As he disappeared into one of the tents surrounding Ridianne's standard, Tathrin saw more men and women gathering. He kept his expression as amiable as he could. Sorgrad placidly studied his fingernails while Gren looked around with a blithe smile that prompted a speculative murmur.

Sorgrad had assured Tathrin that word of so many Mountain Men fighting with the exiles' army would have spread through every mercenary camp. If nothing else, curiosity should prompt Ridianne to talk to them.

Perhaps, but Tathrin couldn't believe Ridianne would simply let them walk away if she declined to hear their message. He couldn't help wanting to see Sorgrad proved wrong just once. Though not today, he decided. Well, there was always Sorgrad's magic to save their necks. He swallowed the nausea that notion prompted.

To his relief, the grizzled mercenary swiftly returned. "Herself will see you."

His companions stepped back as he led them to an open space amid the ring of tents beneath the dog-fox standard. The Vixen was reclining on a chair softened with embroidered cushions beneath a prudent awning. Her booted feet rested on a stool and a little table at her elbow bore a silver flagon ornamented with vine leaves and a goblet. Turning a page in the book she was reading, she showed no sign of registering their arrival.

She trusted her men sufficiently to relax unarmoured, wearing a black doublet and breeches, good broadcloth even if the colour showed every smudge of dust from the road. Somehow Tathrin didn't imagine that concerned her.

Dress her in a sober gown and cover her cropped greying hair with a respectable shawl and she'd remind him of his mother's elder sister, not so much in her features as in the severity of her countenance. His aunt had been a beauty in her youth, just as Ridianne was reputed to have been.

Tathrin's mother said the love of his aunt's youth

had died in battle serving Duke Garnot's father, before they could wed as they'd hoped. According to the comments around his father's taproom, she had merely been too proud, too certain of her own worth to bend her neck to a husband's bidding. Left a spinster, she'd nursed Tathrin's grandparents through their last illnesses and now she occupied herself with the austere charities offered in Maewelin's name.

Ridianne had married; Tathrin knew that, to a Caladhrian lord, who had died leaving her with no child of her own. Caladhrian law bequeathed every stick and stone, every pot and penny of his property to his son, sole offspring of his first marriage. Had Ridianne been such a harsh stepmother, Tathrin wondered, to deserve being dismissed from her home as soon as her lord's ashes were cold, with only the mourning gown on her back?

That bumptious Caladhrian lordling had misjudged her. The tale was still told in all the taverns along the high roads. She'd cut short her russet hair and returned the next season with a troop of mercenaries to throw him down by force of arms. When he bought her off, she purchased a ruined manor house from Duke Ferdain, just across the River Rel from her erstwhile home. Within a few years, she'd earned her reputation as one of Lescar's most formidable mercenary captains.

Now she sat before him, placidly turning another page of her small green-bound tome. Tathrin looked around. He couldn't see her guards but they were there, no question. Who did she trust to overhear this conversation? The sons she was training to fight as hard and as fiercely as she ever had?

When did Duke Ferdain become her lover? Who had been the hunter and who had been the quarry in that chase? What did the duke's legitimate sons and daughters think of the bastards he'd openly acknowledged?

Ridianne cut his speculations short by marking her place with a strip of tasselled needlepoint. Setting the book down, she looked up, hazel eyes bright in her lined face. "You have something to say to me on Captain-General Evord's account?"

"We present his compliments." Sorgrad smiled with the easy charm Tathrin remembered from their first meetings in Vanam's drawing rooms.

"I'm flattered," Ridianne remarked drily. "Please assure him of my admiration in return." She reached for her book.

Sorgrad made no move. "Our captain-general is curious to know why you've called a halt here."

"You're Mountain born but that's no Mountain accent." Ridianne looked at him. "What's your business, when you're not carrying this Soluran's messages?"

"I turn a coin wherever I can, with sword, runes or white raven." He smiled ruefully "Though I prefer a feather bed beneath a weatherproof roof to a roll of blankets under the stars these days. I'm not as young as I was."

Ridianne snorted. "I'm ten years closer to Saedrin's door than you."

"Indeed." Sorgrad nodded sympathetically. "I'm not surprised you need a respite from the trials of your journey."

Tathrin saw Ridianne's eyes widen at this impertinence. To his intense relief, she laughed.

"I'll march you into the ground, runt, and not miss you till three leagues later. But I won't see our horses ruined through overwork." Ridianne kicked her stool away and sat up. "Why are you really here? To spy out our forces? Let me save you the trouble. I've a few hundreds more men on foot than your Soluran master and I have my own cavalry very well drilled. Your Dalasorians won't be the advantage you imagine."

"No," Sorgrad agreed readily enough. "But we'll still beat you bloody."

"So you say." Ridianne's lip curled. "Why should I trust your judgement? You haven't even told me your name or any company that you've fought with."

"Over the years, we've mustered with Arkady the Red, with the Brewer's Boys and the Ast Maulers, among others." The Mountain Man bowed politely. "My friends call me Sorgrad, and this is my brother, Gren."

Tathrin could see no sign Ridianne had ever heard those names before. Then again, most mercenary captains' expressions were as empty as a statue's, whether they were playing runes, white raven or ordering an errant swordsman hanged.

Ridianne suddenly looked at him. "Who are you?"

"Tathrin Sayron, my lady." The courtesy title was out before he could help it. Somewhere behind a leather tent flap, he heard a stifled chuckle.

"Sweet talking as well as straight talking." Ridianne smiled amiably. "A Carluse man, by your accent. Why've you joined these incomers to overthrow your liege lords?"

Tathrin met her gaze. "Duke Garnot's contempt for his people has forfeited any claim on their fealty. Too many humble Lescari suffer for the sake of noble quarrels that they have no part in. I seek a better future for us all."

"You come into my camp and say that to my face? You're either a fool or admirably brave." Ridianne laughed. "I've read those pamphlets your people have been strewing round the markets. I'd prefer more reasoned arguments and rather less high-flown rhetoric or low calumny."

To Tathrin's relief, she returned her attention to Sorgrad. "Perhaps your captain-general could fight me to a standstill, perhaps not. Either way, his regiments will be cut to shreds. Parnilesse can mop up the stragglers."

"Perhaps, perhaps not." Sorgrad pursed his lips. "I hear the militia Duke Iruvain salvaged from the field at Tyrle have fled to hide under their beds and he's locked himself up in his castle."

"A goodly number of the companies fool enough to take Lord Cassat's coin have thought better of that bargain," Gren chipped in.

Ridianne waved that away. "Parnilesse will bring their fighting cocks up to the scratch. No one gainsays Lord Geferin."

"That's what they used to say about Duke Garnot," Sorgrad observed. "But what good does it do you to have Lord Geferin crowing as cock of the walk? Even if our forces can only win a bloody victory over you alone, where does that leave Duke Ferdain? Without swords or allies to back him, he can only stand by while Duke Orlin proclaims himself High King, his heirs to follow. What future for your own sons then?"

Ridianne's face hardened. "You need not concern yourself with me and mine."

"I mean no disrespect." Sorgrad's contrition seemed sincere.

"Duke Orlin will not be High King." Ridianne shook her head. "Once I join forces with Lord Geferin, we will have double the men you can muster, including your Mountain kindred, the grassland horsemen and all the Soluran's regiments. You'll be smashed like wheat in a hailstorm and Marlier and Parnilesse will come to terms as equals."

"But you won't join forces with Lord Geferin," Sorgrad said apologetically. "You can't do that without fighting your way through us."

Ridianne angled her head. "If your captain-general fights us first, he cannot hope to defeat Parnilesse."

"So you suppose." A hint of complacency coloured Sorgrad's smile.

"You suppose otherwise?" Ridianne challenged.

"Much as I respect you, there are things I cannot say." Sorgrad spread his hands, entreating. "Why not come to terms with Captain-General Evord? What do you owe Parnilesse? It's barely a generation since Duke Orlin's father burned Marlier's crops."

Tathrin saw Ridianne's gaze lengthen to look past his shoulder. What were they going to do if she decided her sergeants could try beating their secrets out of them? He dared not turn to see who was stood there.

"You think Duke Ferdain would leave my head on my shoulders if I did that?" scoffed Ridianne. "When you people intend throwing him down along with every other duke? No matter." She leaned back against her cushions, deftly setting her stool upright with the toe of her boot. "You'll be beaten, whether by my regiments or Lord Geferin's. Your Soluran should sue for terms now, if he hopes to get home with his skin whole. But if he wants to die in Lescar, that's no concern of mine. Good day to you. Edlich!"

The black-jowled mercenary appeared at Tathrin's shoulder. "Captain?"

"We march at first light tomorrow." Ridianne reached for her book. "See these three fine fools safely out of the camp. We respect any herald's immunity."

The mercenary led them away. "Where did you leave your horses?"

"At the Peapod Inn, in Skebban." Sorgrad was looking around.

"The Pisspot?" Edlich laughed. "Don't risk a meal or you'll be squatting in a ditch and wishing for dock leaves before you reach the border."

Tathrin couldn't understand how mercenaries could be so friendly, even when they found themselves on opposing sides.

He realised they were taking a different route out of the camp and began gloomily looking for insignia. They may as well take some useful information back to Captain-General Evord. There was a circle of oak leaves around Marlier's three swords. Beyond he saw a brace of cups and then a goat's head with some sort of halter around its neck. He'd have to ask Sorgrad if he knew those companies.

What would Evord do now that Ridianne's intentions were clear? He couldn't help feeling downcast, even though this had been a wild roll of the runes.

"Look on the bright side, long lad," Sorgrad said quietly. "They didn't hang us from the nearest tree."

"I wasn't expecting to see Alsar's Eaglets here." Gren nodded towards an orange banner where a tawny bird spread finger-feathered wings.

Edlich grinned. "Captain Boon has a keen eye for a winning side."

"That he does," Sorgrad admitted.

They walked on in silence. At the edge of the camp Edlich let them go on unescorted. Tathrin glanced back now and again. Every time, he saw the mercenary still watching.

Not even bothering to pause in Skebban, they continued along the wide road between the stubbled fields. Finally, Sorgrad halted beneath the shelter of a sturdy oak.

"Time to go home?" Tathrin braced himself.

"Not just yet." Sorgrad rubbed his chin. "If Ridianne won't sniff at our hand, and Charoleia still hasn't found a way to hobble Lord Geferin, I think we'd better piss in Duke Iruvain's ale."

"What are you going to do?" Tathrin asked with foreboding.

Sorgrad searched his belt pouch for the silver bowl he normally used for scrying. "I've seen that renegade mage Madam Jilseth is looking for, in Triolle Castle."

"How long has he been there?" Tathrin was horrified. "Why haven't you told the captain-general?"

Sorgrad shrugged. "For the moment he's done nothing but eat and drink and idle his days away."

"Then why hand him over to Hadrumal?" Gren objected.

"Triolle can't bridge the gap between Marlier and Parnilesse if Duke Iruvain's answering for his crimes to Planir." Sorgrad raised a hand. "Now, don't say a word or Jilseth will hear you."

As he turned the little dish bottom uppermost, he plucked a twig from the hedge. It flared with magefire, casting a scarlet reflection on the polished metal. The light swirled into a circle framing an enchanted image.

Jilseth looked back through the magic, unperturbed by this interruption. "Sorgrad. I'd hoped to hear from you sooner than this."

"There's no profit in sharing no news." Sorgrad smiled at the distant magewoman. "Today, we have news."

"We know where your renegade is," Gren interrupted gleefully.

"Excellent," Jilseth said coolly.

Sorgrad matched her equanimity. "He's in Triolle Castle. Do remove him from this game of raven just as soon as you like."

"Once I've scried over the area." As Jilseth spoke, the magefire circle flared golden.

"You can't translocate anywhere close?" Faint concern creased Sorgrad's brow.

"That's no concern of yours." Jilseth's face loomed larger within the spell. "I confess, I'm surprised you've betrayed him. If there's no wizardry on Triolle's side, you've no excuse to use your own. Well, I'm glad you've finally seen sense."

"Don't presume to understand me in the least," Sorgrad said curtly. "Now, excuse me, we must continue on our way."

"Good day, then."

Before Sorgrad could end his spell, the fiery ring vanished to leave a sooty circle on the upturned silver.

"She could have said thank you." Gren wasn't impressed.

"Planir should teach her some manners." Sorgrad was scrubbing the black circle away with what looked like unnecessary violence to Tathrin. "Never mind that. Let's just hope she snares this bastard good and fast." He glowered at the blind surface of the bowl. "I don't want her—"

He broke off to shoot Tathrin a stern look. "Jilseth can think what she likes about me forswearing magic in battle. If we need wizardry to win the day against Marlier, Parnilesse or both, I'll use it. You'll need to help me convince Reher to use his talents too."

"I'll try." Tathrin wasn't convinced he'd succeed. It had been hard enough to persuade the smith to undermine Tyrle's walls. He'd been so furious at the havoc that followed, Tathrin had feared Reher was about to hit him.

Gren's thoughts were still elsewhere. "Why do you keep scrying into Triolle? And why don't you want this Minelas around your bold lass?"

If Sorgrad replied, Tathrin didn't hear it, as the white magelight swirled around to carry them back to Evord's camp.

CHAPTER TWENTY-EIGHT
Branca

**The Pannal High Road,
in the Lescari Dukedom of Triolle,
25th of Aft-Autumn**

THE ROAD FORKED ahead. Which way to go? One route must be the highway, but Triolle's roads were so ill-kept it was hard to tell which that might be. The roan mare sensed Branca's uncertainty, stopping on the crown of the road. The rain buffeted her but she didn't seek shelter. The highway margins were too treacherous with potholes hidden by autumn leaves stripped from the trees by the blustery winds.

"Where are we?" Branca wiped damp tendrils of hair from her face and threw back her hood. She was already cold and wet and the cloth only blinkered her and muffled her voice.

Charoleia was sheltering a vellum strip inside her cloak. They'd abandoned almost all their belongings when they'd slipped away from the inn where Lord Usine's men had escorted them. Charoleia had kept safe hold of her map case though.

Did she have an itinerary for every highway, the length and breadth of Lescar, Ensaimin and beyond, all annotated with her tiniest handwriting, if not in that sturdy case, then safely stowed in some distant dwelling? Branca wouldn't be in the least surprised if she did.

She shivered, chilled to the bone, stiff and aching. Staying in a horse's saddle hadn't proved the challenge she'd feared but she'd had no notion riding could be so tiring. She wriggled her feet inside her boots, trying to feel her cold toes.

"We're still twenty leagues short of Adel," Charoleia said finally, swiftly coiling the map.

"The castle on the lake?" Trissa's jennet stamped impatient hooves despite the encumbering saddlebags, their leather black with damp. She soothed the beast with a gloved hand. "We might make that tomorrow but this isn't a night for travelling any further, my lady."

"But what about those mercenaries we saw this morning?" Branca desperately contradicted the maid. As they'd been leaving the inn where they'd stopped for the night, two men had ridden into the yard. One wore a pied crow badge with the wreath from Parnilesse's banner in the bird's beak. The other man's shield displayed a leather bottle atop Duke Orlin's crossed halberd and sword. "I told you, those blazons were the first standards I saw cross the bridge."

"Scouts or couriers, either way they'll be at least a day ahead of Lord Geferin," Trissa assured her.

"They won't be travelling any faster than us in this weather." Charoleia looked upwards.

The Greater Moon was now at its half but that was no more use than the last paring of the Lesser Moon that accompanied it. The autumnal rain had brought unbroken clouds and dusk was already gathering beneath the hedgerows.

"If we continue along the high road, there's a village that should offer a tavern, not too far distant." Charoleia contemplated their choices. "But which one is the high road, do you suppose?"

"We may as well roll a rune," Branca said sourly.

"It'll be the one with proper waymarks." Trissa curbed her jennet's ill-tempered snap at Branca's mare. "If we don't see something inside half a league, we'll turn back and take the other fork."

"Indeed," Charoleia agreed.

Branca let her roan mare follow Charoleia's bay gelding. They were bound to take the wrong route, she thought wearily. Then they'd have to retrace their steps and be no further on for all that wasted effort. By which time night would doubtless have fallen with the day's showers settling into ceaseless rain. Always assuming one of the horses or Trissa's burdened jennet didn't lame itself.

Which was a wholly irrational set of assumptions, she chided herself.

"*Yes, it is.*"

His amusement warmed her mentally if not physically.

"Aremil!"

She hadn't even felt his touch on her mind through the aether. She must be more tired than she realised.

Hearing Branca's surprise, Charoleia reined her own horse back and reached for the roan mare's bridle. "Go on," she reassured Branca.

"*Where are you?*"

For a few moments, Branca struggled to hear Aremil. She couldn't have initiated any Artifice herself, so tired and cold and painfully unsure of herself on horseback.

"We're travelling towards Adel," Charoleia prompted.

"On the high road." Trissa pointed at a pale stone marker blotched with wet leaves.

The road ahead blurred and the trees beyond the broad verge reshaped themselves into the pillars of Aremil's hall. Branca's awareness of the reins in her hands, of the saddle beneath her aching rump faded. Fearing such loss of sensation would rapidly mean she'd lose her balance, Branca ruthlessly closed herself to all but the lightest touch of Aremil's Artifice.

"We're looking for a tavern for the night. We should reach Adel by tomorrow evening."

For a moment she felt his hurt at her rejection. Then his surprise washed over her, coloured with his own longing and faint echoes of Tathrin and Jettin's exultant charges in the campaign's first battles.

"*You've never ridden a horse before?*"

His surprise let her see something else.

"Aremil, what's wrong?"

"What's happened?"

As Charoleia asked what was amiss, Branca raised her hand. If she tried to juggle two conversations, she would surely fall off the mare.

"*Someone has told Lord Rousharn that I am Duke Secaris of Draximal's son.*"

Branca flinched at an echo of the Sharlac lord's enraged accusation. "It was Derenna?"

"*She says a trusted friend from Vanam wrote with the news.*"

Aremil's chagrin at being unmasked like this was riven by differing fears. Was it Lyrlen who'd betrayed him? Who else could it be? What would Duke Secaris do once he knew? What fate might befall his faithful nurse, when he was so far away, unable to protect her?

Branca shook her head to clear her thoughts.

"What has Derenna said?"

Travelling together through Sharlac, Branca had learned the noblewoman's commitment to the duties of her rank was as unwavering as her devotion to natural philosophy.

"*She says I have no excuse for refusing the obligations of birth.*"

Aremil's fierce irritation stung Branca.

"How dare she?"

She felt her outrage soothe him a little.

"What's happened?" Charoleia asked again.

"Derenna and Lord Rousharn know that Aremil is Duke Secaris's son." Branca closed her eyes to concentrate on the Artifice linking them. "How soon do you think word will spread?"

"*That's what I wanted to ask Mistress Charoleia, but find some shelter and tell me at your leisure. Dear heart, you're freezing!*"

Aremil's concern warmed Branca's thoughts, if not her fingers and toes.

"Branca." Charoleia's thoughts were elsewhere. "Ask him about the Vixen. How did Sorgrad and Gren fare?"

"*Not well. Or at least, well enough for them to return alive. But she's resumed her advance to Triolle.*"

Branca opened her eyes. "Marlier's army is still resolute."

"*Evord's army is still one step ahead. They'll be at the gates of Triolle Town in the morning. Duke Iruvain is still cowering in his castle. He's shown no sign of wanting another drubbing.*"

Branca repeated his words for the other women's benefit.

"Will the captain-general be able to drive Marlier's army away from Triolle before Parnilesse's army arrives?" Charoleia demanded.

"Tathrin says so."

Aremil was certain of Tathrin's opinion and Tathrin had total faith in Evord. Branca could only hope neither man's confidence was misplaced.

"They believe so."

"Well, that's good news, but can we discuss this when we're safely off the highway?" Trissa glanced back down the darkling road.

"Duke Iruvain will be sending a whole company of dispatch riders to hurry Geferin along, if he fears he's about to be besieged." Charoleia grimaced. "Let's find that tavern and get warm and dry. Then we can look for the least travelled byways to take us into Carluse."

Branca found the notion of being caught between the two hostile dukes profoundly unnerving.

"We have to go."

"Go safely."

Aremil was gone, leaving only the fading echo of his loving concern. The dwindling day seemed danker than ever, the wind sour with rotting leaves.

"If there isn't an inn, I'm sure we'll find a house to take us in." Charoleia released the roan's bridle and urged her own horse on.

The brief respite had reinvigorated their mounts. Jennet, gelding and mare all sought to nose ahead of their stablemates. Trotting jolted Branca horribly, renewing every ache. She gritted her teeth and endured it, Trissa close beside her.

Thankfully it wasn't long before lights ahead

pierced the gloom. A small tavern claimed one quarter of a crossroads where a byway cut across the high road. A brazier's cheerful flames illuminated the tavern's sign, a circle of homely horn cups.

An old man warming himself regarded them with astonishment. "You're out late, my ladies."

"Our coach has damaged not one but two of its wheels." Charoleia sighed with heartbreaking weariness. "Has our luggage arrived yet?"

"Luggage, my lady?" The old man was concerned. "We ain't seen no one since this morning and that was only stockmen."

"The men could have been delayed, my lady." Trissa frowned. "Or we might have passed them, if they turned aside from the road for some reason."

"Unless they took the wrong choice at the fork." Charoleia's voice faltered on the suggestion of a sob.

"Oh, my lady." Trissa reached out a comforting hand.

Seeing she had no lines in this well-rehearsed masquerade, Branca sat silently on her mare.

"We'll stop here for the night," Trissa said firmly, as befitted a privileged retainer. "I'm sure we'll have word of Fikal and Senn in the morning. We may even wake to find the coach repaired and waiting."

As she spoke, she was dismounting, handing the jennet's reins to the old man before helping Charoleia from her saddle.

The old man hurried to hold the gelding's head. "Ansin!"

"My lady." Trissa's tone as she turned to Branca was respectful, if not quite as deferential. Unseen by the old man, her eyes were lit with amusement.

Branca slipped gracelessly down from the mare. Standing on her own two feet relieved her aches only at the cost of new torments. The mare whickered at the sound of an opening door, catching the scent of a stable.

"We're not what you'd call an inn for quality," the old man said anxiously, doing his best to curb the gelding and the jennet who were both equally keen on hay and shelter. "But we can offer a clean bedroom and good food."

"That will be quite sufficient and most welcome ..." Charoleia's voice broke on her assurance.

Assuming the youth hurrying into the pool of light cast by the brazier was Ansin, Branca handed him the roan mare's reins.

He ducked his head dutifully. "We'll bring your bags in, my ladies, soon as we've got the horses settled."

"Thank you."

Charoleia and Trissa were already pushing open the tavern's door. Branca hurried after them and breathed a sigh of relief. There was no one to remark on their unescorted, unannounced arrival.

The room's sole occupant was a fat man relaxing in the inglenook of the broad fire at the far end of the room. Hastily rising, he hurried towards them, wiping broad red hands on his spotless apron.

"Your ladyships? It's a nasty night to be on the road. How can we be of service?"

As Charoleia repeated the tale of a broken-down carriage, Branca took the measure of the inn. The taproom was basic, offering wooden benches and tables and a row of casks racked against the far wall. The pewter candlesticks were polished, though, no trails of tallow spilling on the scrubbed tabletops. No cobwebs were tolerated even in the most deeply shadowed corners and the rushes on the floor were freshened with judicious herbs.

"Let me draw you some ale. I'll get my wife."

All sympathy, the tavern-keeper ushered them to a table and clapped his leathery hands. A startled girl with the flat round face and snub nose of a simpleton hurried through the door beside the great fireplace.

"Take these good ladies' cloaks and see them hung to dry," he urged her as he fetched a foaming jug and horn cups.

Trissa had already taken Charoleia's cloak and handed it over along with her own. Surrendering her own cape to the willing simpleton, Branca poured drinks for them all as the kindly man ushered the girl away through the inner door.

The first mouthful of ale merely cut through the dust in her throat. She savoured the second more appreciatively. "I warn you, three cups of this and I'll be asleep."

"We should all turn in early." Closest to the fire, Trissa spread her damp skirts over the bench.

"Ready for a prompt start in the morning."

Charoleia hadn't surrendered her precious map case with their saddlebags. She took a drink, nodded her own approval for the brew and sorted through the leather cylinders holding the maps. "Our safest course will be to skirt eastwards, along this lesser road." She spread a strip of vellum on the clean table.

Branca shifted to get a better look. "Yes, I see."

The door in the fireplace wall opened, with the sounds of a freshly roused kitchen beyond.

"Good evening, my ladies." The tavern-keeper's wife was as thin as he was round, a little woman with a freckled face in a brown gown. As her hands fluttered apologetically, Branca was irresistibly reminded of a thrush.

"With the weather and the rumours on the road, we weren't expecting callers, not beyond the men of the village wanting their ale. I can offer you collops in a cream sauce, with pease and fresh bread?"

"As long as we're not eating your own supper." Charoleia studied her closely.

"Oh, no, my lady," the woman assured her. "We killed a pig last market day."

"Then collops and pease will be most welcome." Charoleia smiled.

Chiming in with Trissa's agreement, Branca allowed herself to hope for sausage for breakfast. She took another draught of the fragrant ale and felt the day's tensions ebbing away. Now she just had to stay awake until their dinner arrived, and play her part in whatever story Charoleia had contrived.

"What's my role here?" she asked quietly once the tavern-keeper's wife returned to the kitchen.

"I'm Mistress Lanagyre," Charoleia said quickly, "unwed sister to a Triolle joiner, a man of some wealth but no Guild ambition. You'll be the daughter of my fondest friend, who is married to another joiner living in Pannal. You're coming to spend some time in Triolle in hopes of finding a husband. Naturally, our plans have been entirely overcome by events."

She didn't need to explain that Trissa was, as always, her loyal maid.

The tavern-keeper's wife proved as good a cook as her husband was a brewer. Fried slices of pork were succulent in a sauce flavoured with hoarded spices in their honour. Newly baked, the loaf was speckled with meal rather than the fine white bread Charoleia's guises normally demanded but Branca didn't care. It was what she was more used to eating. The pease pottage was equally fine, buttery with onion and the humble herbs that grew by the scullery door.

She was wiping her plate with a last crust as the goodwife bustled out of the kitchen with a plate of honeyed griddle cakes. "The girl's made up the guest bed with fresh linen and Ansin's took your bags up."

"You're a woman made in Drianon's own image," Branca said with fervent gratitude.

"You are indeed," Charoleia agreed, taking a cake a moment ahead of Trissa.

Despite dining so well, Branca found she had room for two or three but by the time the plate was empty, she could barely keep her eyes open.

"Now," Charoleia said briskly, "I'm going to call for my cloak and my horse and you're going to protest at first and then you're going to let me go in search of our errant coachmen. Tell our good host and his wife that I'm always this headstrong, but you're sure I'll come hurrying back, once I realise how cold and dark the night is. Make sure they don't send anyone after me, not for at least half a chime."

"Where are you going?" Alarm put Branca's weariness to flight.

"You say Lord Rousharn knows that Aremil is Duke Secaris's son?" Charoleia tucked a wisp of her dull dyed hair under her lace cap.

"I'd like to know how he learned that," Trissa commented.

"As would I," Charoleia agreed. "But that's a question for another day. Now, Derenna would probably keep her tongue behind her teeth but I've no such confidence in her lord. However, it'll take him a day or so to consult with his closest allies and longer still to decide what this might mean."

"What can you do about it?" Branca was confused.

"Now the word's out, it's as far beyond recall as a loosed arrow. So we'd better see the news spreads fastest where it'll do us most good." Charoleia's eyes brightened with mischief belying her matronly appearance. "Let's see if we can drive a wedge between Duke Secaris and Duke Orlin. We might just deprive Duke Iruvain of those Draximal troops he salvaged from the rout at Tyrle."

"Do you really think so? Could it make any real difference?"

Branca couldn't see how the loss of those regiments would be enough to guarantee victory for Evord. Not once the Parnilesse advance joined forces with Marlier.

"Where are you going?" Trissa demanded.

"Do you recall Lord and Lady Capalire, who were so grateful for our help in disentangling their son and heir from that fortune-hunting songstress?"

"I do." Trissa nodded with reluctant understanding.

"I don't," Branca snapped.

"Lady Capalire was one of the late lamented Duchess Casatia's most intimate friends," Charoleia explained. "One of her most trusted waiting-women is a Draximal spy. If I tell Lady Capalire that Duke Secaris's unknown son has been found, the woman will find a way to get word to Lord Geferin, I'm sure of it. He'll set his own dogs chasing that hare as well as sending word to Duke Orlin. That should cost him at least a day's delay."

Trissa looked uncertain. "Whatever mummer's tale you tell Lady Capalire, she won't let you ride back alone through the night. You'll have to stay there till morning."

"True enough." Charoleia thought for a moment. "So you two will realise that's where I must have gone, when our good hosts start worrying why I haven't returned. I'll be full of apologies in the morning and explain that's where our gallant coachmen had gone for help. And we'll be on our way with profuse thanks and a suitably generous purse."

Branca tried to pick her way through all this. "How does Mistress Lanagyre know this Lady Capalire? Or are you still Mistress Halisoun? What if these good folk here ask someone from the household about it all and they know nothing about a broken coach?"

Charoleia waved such inconvenient questions away. "Lord Capalire's men don't drink in wayside taverns."

Trissa had other concerns. "Are you sure we have time for this? We'll be that much later setting out on the road tomorrow. Those scouts aren't so very far behind us."

"We must make time," Charoleia said firmly, "otherwise Lord Geferin and Ridianne the Vixen will both arrive to threaten our friends while they're still waiting beneath Triolle's walls."

Chapter Twenty-Nine
Litasse

Triolle Castle,
26th of Aft-Autumn

"Your Grace, your husband." Pelletria slipped into Litasse's bedchamber, her face taut with concern.

Litasse's heart quickened. She slapped away the maid's hand brushing her hair. "Has Lord Geferin arrived?" Would that improve Iruvain's temper?

"No." Pelletria glared at the startled maid. "I'll see to Her Grace, Milda. Get about your duties."

The girl quickly gathered up the previous day's chemise from Litasse's bed and scurried away.

"He's had some news." Pelletria took up the brush. "But I can't find out what it is."

The frustration in her words was at odds with her gentle hands as she coaxed out tangles. Litasse's cap had signally failed to smooth her hair as she had tossed and turned through another sleepless night.

Down in the courtyard, the racket of the armed men crammed into the castle was relentless, night and day. That wasn't what kept her awake; she'd stopped paying it any heed. Now she listened afresh and heard a disquieting note of urgency. What was afoot?

She contemplated her half-dressed reflection in the mirror. It would take all Pelletria's skill with cosmetics to hide the bruises of weariness under her eyes. Despite the bright fire in the grate, she felt cold with foreboding.

Iruvain's heavy tread was advancing up the stairs. Litasse felt the brush tug her hair as Pelletria tensed.

He threw open the door. "Get dressed, quickly!"

"My lord." Litasse sprang to her stocking feet. "Has Lord Geferin arrived?"

"What?" Iruvain stared, uncomprehending. "No, and I'm not waiting here any longer. We're going to meet him."

Now it was Litasse who gaped. "My lord?"

"Get dressed, for travelling," Iruvain ordered harshly. He glowered at Pelletria. "You, pack no more than one horse can carry. You'll leave with the first contingent, under Lord Roreth's command. Don't forget Her Grace's jewels."

As he turned to leave, Litasse hurried across the room and reached for his arm. "I don't understand."

"We're going to take the Pannal Road and join forces with the Parnilesse army." He angrily shook off her hand. His eyes were more shadowed than her own. "That Soluran and his mob will be here by tomorrow. We must leave while we can, or be trapped within these walls."

"What of Marlier's army?" protested Litasse. "They're little more than a day away!"

Too late, Litasse remembered Iruvain hadn't told her that. She'd heard it from Karn, who had returned just before dawn. He wasn't supposed to have spoken to anyone but the duke himself.

"That laggard whore's nowhere near close enough to be useful." With his anger focused on Ridianne, Iruvain didn't notice Litasse's unsanctioned knowledge. "The Soluran will arrive here before she can bring him to battle."

"Then he can sit at our gates, and outside Triolle Town, and endure our arrows as long as he wishes," Litasse protested, "until the Vixen pins his regiments against the walls like wolf skins on a barn door!"

"I will not be trapped in another siege!"

Iruvain's voice rose from fear, Litasse realised, not from anger.

"My lord husband," she said carefully to hide her own unease. "No one can blame you for the fall of Tyrle. Duke Garnot—"

"Duke Garnot—" Iruvain turned away. Not before Litasse saw the tremor twisting his mouth. "You know nothing of it, woman, so keep your tongue behind your teeth. Be ready to leave before the next chime."

"No, my lord husband, this is folly." Litasse stood firm. "You cannot leave a defensible position where you can easily halt an enemy's advance. Not when you have allies approaching from both directions who will crack them like a nut on an anvil!"

"Do not gainsay me, woman!" Iruvain raised his hand and took a menacing step towards her.

"Beating me won't make it any less true." She raised her chin defiantly, even though her knees trembled beneath her petticoats. "We are safe behind solid stone walls. We have our own men-at-arms and militia defending this castle. Triolle Town's walls are guarded by trusted mercenaries, sworn to our own badge and Draximal's—"

"Draximal's?" Iruvain clenched his fist but punched only the empty air. Whoever his wrath was aimed at, it wasn't Litasse. "Do you know what Draximal's trusted mercenaries are doing, my lady wife?"

"No." She could say that with all honesty.

Iruvain ran a hand through his hair, leaving his normally ordered curls ragged. "Once Lord Cassat fell, the field outside Tyrle was chaos." He closed his haunted eyes for an instant. "I couldn't recall all his hired regiments, not after the Dalasorians hit us. The Draximal militiamen fled too, in all directions. We thought the mercenaries would rally them, see them safely back across the border into Duke Secaris's lands." He shook his head in despair. "But the hirelings slaughtered the militia. I've just had word of it."

"No!" Litasse protested, appalled.

"They've left bodies naked for the crows all along the Wyril Road, robbed and murdered." Iruvain's anger subsided into bleakness. "Honest men, loyal men, only trying to get home to their families. Because they knew Lord Cassat's muster had left only old men and boys to guard their homes. So now the loathsome curs are plundering every hamlet and village along the highway and killing anyone who stands in their way."

"That's vile." Litasse shared Iruvain's horror. "But Duke Secaris will see justice done, you know he will," she insisted. "There's no reason for us to leave these walls and our own loyal men—"

"Trusting in walls was Garnot's folly." Iruvain's ire abruptly rekindled. "I told you what happened at Tyrle. This Soluran has Mountain Men bringing who knows what ruinous skills from their upland mines. He has mercenaries well versed in whatever Aldabreshin alchemy can burn wood and stone. Duke Garnot should have learned the lesson of Emirle Bridge. I won't make that mistake, my lady wife. I won't sit here to become their next victim. Make ready to leave at once and don't oppose me again!"

He strode for the door. Litasse let him go. Down in the open bailey, men shouted, horses neighed and wagons rumbled over the cobbles.

Litasse sank onto her dressing stool. "What do you make of that?"

Pelletria was combing hairs out of the brush, her lined face thoughtful. She dropped a black tangle into the flames, to crackle and flare into nothingness.

"I think we should make certain it's really Draximal mercenaries murdering and raping along the Wyril Road," she said finally. "That wizard can earn some of the wine he's been drinking. It could just as easily be some of these rebels slipping their leash. Mercenaries are all as bad as rabid dogs, no matter whose collar they wear."

Litasse looked at her. "Do you honestly believe this Soluran would permit such atrocities?"

"No." Pelletria admitted. "But if we can find some news that might at least make His Grace wonder, that might just delay this folly of his long enough for the Vixen and her men to arrive. Or for Karn to return with some word from Lord Geferin to convince Iruvain to hold fast here." She sighed. "I don't like the notion of divulging Iruvain's plans to Parnilesse but I don't see that we have any choice."

"If Iruvain doesn't want folk to think him a coward, he shouldn't act like one." Litasse felt more of a pang at the thought of rousing Karn from the bed he'd so recently sought, exhausted. "Let him sleep till we've written our letter. Is there anything else we can do? We need something to put some backbone into Iruvain."

Pelletria looked searchingly at Litasse. "His Grace still hasn't come to your bed, not once, since he learned you'd lain with Master Hamare?"

"No." Litasse hadn't imagined she'd have cause to regret that. "Why?"

"He couldn't make you travel if we feigned the threat of a miscarriage," Pelletria said grimly.

"I suppose not." The old woman doubtless had the necessary herbs to make the pretence convincing. Litasse shivered.

"You're cold." That spurred Pelletria towards the bell pull. "We had better send for some travelling clothes and pack a chest. There's nothing to be gained by openly antagonising His Grace."

"How long do you imagine the maids and lackeys and whoever he leaves to garrison the castle will stay once their duke and duchess run away?" Litasse reached for the gold and scarlet gown laid ready for this morning. "Do you suppose he's thought of that?"

"I doubt it," Pelletria said frankly.

"Help me with this." Litasse stepped into the gown and turned so Pelletria could lace the back. "Master Minelas can scry and find out exactly where Lord Geferin and the Vixen are now. If they're close, we'll let Iruvain know somehow. Karn will think of something."

Litasse stood, tense with impatience as Pelletria found jewels befitting her rank. She reached for a fine wool shawl. "Let's see what help our guest can offer."

Walking across the open bailey, she contemplated the bustle with disfavour. "This looks more like a kicked ant's nest than resolute preparation for retreat," she said in low tones.

"Panic choking the roads with carts could actually help us," Pelletria mused. "If Iruvain's scared of being trapped inside these walls, surely we can argue being caught in the open would be ten times more perilous."

"He won't be delayed as long as his men have whips and swords to force a path," Litasse said with asperity.

As they reached the steps to the White Tower, a kitchen boy opened the door, precariously balancing a tray burdened with dirty dishes.

"Your Grace!" He nearly dropped the load as he attempted a bow.

Litasse saved a sliding bowl. "Please, don't let me delay you."

"Away with you." Pelletria glared at the lad.

"Your Grace." Ducking his head, he scurried off through the crowd of servants, men-at-arms and grooms harnessing quarrelsome horses.

"I see our guest has breakfasted adequately," Litasse commented tartly once the boy was out of earshot.

"He ate enough for two men thrice his size yesterday." Pelletria sniffed. "It's a wonder he stays so slender."

Did some magic ensure that? Litasse wasn't about to say such a thing aloud with so many people hurrying up and down the stairs.

"Let's hope he's dressed, Your Grace." Pelletria knocked on the wizard's chamber door. "He doesn't seem to be an early riser."

To Litasse's relief, Minelas was already fully clothed in a purple doublet and velvet breeches with amethyst-studded buckles at the knee. He was currently picking his teeth, intent on his reflection in a silver mirror. When he made no move to stop, Pelletria coughed ominously.

Minelas set the mirror down and replaced his toothpick in its ivory case. "Good morning, Your Grace. I have news. The Soluran and his army are within a day's march." He gestured towards the bowl on the washstand. "But the Duke of Marlier's forces are hard on their heels."

"I don't need you to tell me that," Litasse said impatiently. "Where are Lord Geferin and the Parnilesse army?"

Minelas's lips tightened. "Last night they camped about a day's travel south of a lake that boasts a castle on an island opposite a small town. I assume you know where that is?"

"Adel." Litasse was unimpressed. "Precisely where Lord Geferin's dispatches said to expect them. Once again, you tell me nothing I don't already know, Master Mage. What can you tell me of these massacres along the Wyril Road? Do you know who's responsible?"

She was sure she saw a flicker of surprise in the wizard's eyes before he smiled with irritating superiority.

"You never asked me to cast my eye in that direction, Your Grace. If you want me to search out such things, I will gladly oblige. You should be more specific in your instructions, and consider what such additional requests will cost you."

Litasse didn't need the warning pressure of Pelletria's hand in the small of her back. She could see that bandying words with the wizard was pointless.

"What else can you do," she demanded bluntly, "to defend this castle and Triolle Town?"

Minelas raised a finger. "According to the boy who brought my breakfast, Duke Iruvain has already decided to cede this ground to the Soluran. I see no reason to dispute His Grace's plan."

"That has yet to be decided," Litasse snapped. "Tell me, how would you defend us here?"

"With sufficient subtlety to leave your lord and husband unaware of my influence on his victory," he said loftily. "You may safely leave that to me, should the occasion arise."

Litasse felt her temper fraying. "What will you do, precisely? Will you slow their advance? Scatter their horses?"

"I've already explained the many ways I can turn a battle in your favour." Minelas shook his head. "There's no point in discussing it further. I can only make the crucial decisions once the enemy has arrived. I must see how they have drawn up their lines around the roads and the rivers." His smile turned condescending. "As for the specifics of my craft, explanations would mean nothing to you."

Litasse found her palms itching to slap his self-satisfied face. "I don't need specifics of your wizardly arts. I would like something more than evasions, though, when I ask you to explain your plans."

"If you'll be specific about my payment," he answered swiftly, "instead of fobbing me off with vague promises."

"I have no intention of paying for anything but results," she assured him.

His handsome features hardened unattractively. "Do you require another demonstration to convince you I can do all that I promise, and more?"

Blue light crackled with menace around his fingers.

"Your Grace." Pelletria moved to stand between Litasse and the mage. "If Lord Geferin is near Adel, perhaps you should accede to Duke Iruvain's retreat. The island castle is a stronghold that this Soluran could never storm."

Litasse saw that the old woman's eyes were intent with meaning but she couldn't fathom it out. "Perhaps," she said slowly.

"I could work far more readily there," Minelas said swiftly. "Water is so unpredictable, no one would look for explanations beyond bad luck when wind and wave turn against these rebels. I take it you don't want my presence revealed?" He smiled with renewed composure. "Such a move would also secure your safety, Your Grace."

The wizard's solicitude rang hollow in Litasse's ears. Fighting an urge to tell him so, she watched him cross over to his washstand and pass a hand over the bowl. An eerie green light reflected on his palm.

"What are you doing now?" she demanded.

"I will scry for more news of your allies." He looked up as if he were surprised to see her still there. "I will also look beyond the most immediate threats, to see what's happened along the Wyril Road, now I know that's what you want me to do. Come back later and I'll tell you what I've learned." He dismissed them with a gesture, peering into the glowing bowl.

Pelletria stiffened with indignation. "I will bring word when Her Grace has the leisure for you to attend on her."

"As you wish." Green radiance erupted from the water. Arcane light rippled across Minelas's face and the ceiling overhead.

There was nothing to be gained by pursuing this. What use was this supercilious mage? He was only bleeding her for the coin he so obviously coveted. The realisation was bitter as ashes in Litasse's mouth.

"Your Grace." Pelletria went to open the door.

Litasse didn't move. How was she to convince Iruvain not to run away from Triolle Castle? That was the most immediate problem.

"Your Grace," Pelletria said more urgently, her hand waiting on the door handle.

Of course. They dared not risk some passing lackey seeing Minelas's uncanny behaviour. Litasse quickly hurried from the room and Pelletria shut the magelight safely away behind the door.

"Where is Karn sleeping?" she demanded savagely. "I want him on the road in search of Lord Geferin before the next chime sounds."

"I'll rouse him, Your Grace." Pelletria gave vent to her own frustration. "And he can tell us just what that preening peacock was doing in Caladhria. It had better be something impressive."

Litasse nodded. "Unless it's something to convince us he could truly save Triolle, he can make his own way out of the castle and take his chances on the roads alone."

But cold fear undercut her anger. Minelas was a mage, there was no doubt of that. How could she dismiss him without him turning his wicked wizardry on her?

They walked down the stairs and out into the bustling courtyard. Wagons were being loaded. Burdened pack animals were already following each other nose to tail out through the bastion. Litasse saw cloaked and booted servants clutching meagre bundles of belongings. Those with family and friends among the castle's men-at-arms embraced in anguished farewells.

"We're not going to dissuade Iruvain, are we?" That realisation depressed her still further.

"Not if Lord Geferin's still no closer than Adel.

Besides, I've been thinking about what the ordinary folk would make of it, for everyone to see the duke go back on his decision, after this decree's already been cried through the town." Pelletria's eyes were hooded with doubt. "It could do more harm than good, especially if they already doubt his leadership."

"Then we had better do as we're bid and pack."

Despite all the people crowding around the castle bailey, Litasse walked back to her own tower feeling more wretchedly alone, more utterly powerless than ever.

Chapter Thirty
Branca

The Hollybush Tavern, on the Triolle High Road, 27th of Aft-Autumn

IF THE FOOD and the welcome in this inn weren't as fine as the hospitality they'd enjoyed at the Ring of Cups, Branca didn't care. After another two days in the saddle, she was even more stiff and sore. Anything was better than spending another night in the open, huddled beneath a hedge.

The tavern wife was already returning with a candle and an armful of towels. "There's a fire lit and warm water waiting, my ladies."

It was hard to tell if her expression was sour with disapproval at their travelling with so little luggage and no escort, or from fear of what might happen when the regiments arrived. Every village they had passed through was rife with rumour of the approaching Parnilesse army.

A lifetime's mistrust of the neighbouring dukedom wasn't so easily set aside, no matter what Duke Iruvain's criers had been declaring in the marketplaces, nailing his proclamations of welcome for Lord Geferin to the doors of the wayside shrines.

A wash and a comfortable bed would suffice, Branca decided. If a bath was available, she'd only fall asleep in it. Wincing, she followed the others up the narrow stair.

The largest guest chamber was at the end of this long building. As Trissa opened the door, Branca saw the walls were freshly whitewashed and the small windows under the thatched eaves sparkled in the firelight. Coverlets were invitingly turned down on a broad canopied bedstead with a truckle bed made up at its foot. While the bed hangings were old, they had been scrupulously darned. A faint scent of lavender hung in the air.

"Ring if there's anything you need." The tavern wife set down the candle and a silver bell on the table by the window.

"You've already done all we could wish for." Smiling, Charoleia ushered her to the door and closed it behind her.

Branca didn't dare sit on the bed in all her dirt, so she lowered herself onto a stool by the door. Stifling a groan, she began unlacing her boots.

Trissa was already unbuckling their saddlebags.

She clicked her tongue as she assessed the condition of their spare gowns and linen. "Let's hang these in front of the fire."

"Here, let me." Charoleia moved the fire screen back so the fabrics wouldn't scorch. "Branca, what did Aremil have to say?"

While the two other women had sought to allay the tavern wife's suspicions with their now well-rehearsed tale, Branca had seized the opportunity of a few moments alone in the privy to let him know where they were.

"Duke Iruvain has abandoned Triolle, both the castle and the town."

"Saedrin save us," Trissa exclaimed.

"It gets better. Since Duke Iruvain's not standing by his people, they're not inclined to stand by him. When Evord and the army arrived last night, the gates were standing open." Despite her weariness, Branca couldn't help smiling at the memory of Aremil's exultation. "Tathrin says the captain-general is negotiating with the guildmasters and with the captain of the garrison. He expects to breakfast in Duke Iruvain's dining hall tomorrow. So he'll hold Triolle before Ridianne the Vixen arrives."

"Barely," Charoleia observed. "But that should be good enough. So where are Duke Iruvain and his household? We don't want to run into them on the road."

"Sorgrad's been scrying and as best he can tell, the duke is heading for Adel," Branca said.

"The castle on the lake," Trissa said with sudden understanding.

"It's the most defensible place within reach." Charoleia nodded. "Iruvain must be thankful that more than one Duke of Triolle has found it necessary to lock up an errant wife yet keep her close to hand. Very well, we will stay well clear of His Grace and whoever's still clinging to his cart tail as long as we head east and north. It'll us take longer to get to Carluse, but with Marlier's army coming in from the west, that will be our safest course." She went to open her map case.

Branca's smile faded. "Aremil says we mustn't risk going anywhere near the Wyril Road. It seems those Draximal mercenary companies that fled the field at Tyrle are heading north, looting and killing as they go."

Aremil's thoughts had been grimmer than Branca could ever recall.

"What's the captain-general doing about that?" Charoleia frowned, concerned.

"At the moment, he's waiting for the Dalasorian lancers to find out exactly where they're headed." Branca shared her unease. "They could threaten Ashgil or they could march on Wyril itself."

"Can the captain-general spare troops to hunt them down?" Trissa asked doubtfully.

"Not given the quantity of cavalry he's already had to send to Abray, to make sure the mercenaries who surrendered to us are well and truly taken out of the game."

That was how Aremil had phrased it. But this was all so much more serious and more complex than a game of white raven, Branca thought bleakly.

"Are we sure these erstwhile Draximal mercenaries are truly running unchecked?" Charoleia's frown deepened. "It could be a ploy, to force Evord to commit some of his companies to a mere distraction."

"They've already considered that possibility. The captain-general certainly doesn't want to divide his forces any more than he's already had to. But all the evidence bears out the reports that these men are solely seeking their own enrichment and carnal pleasures."

At least Branca had seen something of Aremil and Tathrin's rapport had returned as they had wrestled with this new conundrum. That was the smallest of consolations.

"Lord Rousharn says we cannot allow such destruction to go unchecked," she continued. "Not when we need the commonalty's goodwill, or at very least, their reluctance to support their dukes."

"Regretfully, I'm forced to agree with him," Charoleia said grimly.

Branca closed her eyes on echoes of Aremil's furious argument with Lady Derenna and her husband. Lord Rousharn was insisting that Captain-General Evord must leave Triolle at once to pursue the plundering mercenaries. Lady Derenna was less inclined to give up such gains but nevertheless she insisted the brigands must be stopped and hanged from the roadside gibbets, to prove the exiles' good faith.

They had to face facts, Lord Rousharn said with insulting condescension. The weather was deteriorating as Aft-Autumn turned towards For-Winter. Captain-General Evord's army had fought a brave campaign but such efforts couldn't be sustained much longer. It was time for wiser counsel to prevail. Negotiation was their only rational course.

Derenna didn't quite agree, but she warned Aremil that the day for offering terms to Draximal could well come sooner rather than later, or to make a settlement with Duke Ferdain or even Duke Orlin, come to that.

Almost incoherent with fury, Aremil had remained adamant that the exiles in Vanam hadn't begun this awful war to come to terms with any of the dukes. They were going to overturn their corrupt rule entirely.

Branca opened her eyes at the muted rattle of vellum rolling up. She had nearly fallen asleep, she realised with some surprise.

"We'll make the earliest start we can tomorrow." Charoleia was briskly replacing her maps. "We'll take to the byways to skirt around Adel and then we'll head back to the high road to lose ourselves among the confusion there. Branca, ask Aremil to tell Tathrin that I want Sorgrad and Gren to ride out to meet us. Sorgrad's scrying will find us easily enough and I think the time has come to have some swords around us. Then we can decide if our best course is heading straight to Triolle or carrying on to Carluse. I think Aremil might welcome some help dealing with Lord Rousharn."

"Indeed." Branca saw relief on Trissa's face to equal her own.

There was a knock at the bedchamber door. What else had the tavern wife thought to offer them? Branca would have stood up but she was simply too stiff and weary.

Trissa opened the door but immediately recoiled, her hands raised in futile defence. A man entered, a short, lethal sword in his hand. He closed the door, pressing his back to it, effectively barring the way to anyone else outside and to the three of them within.

Branca sat frozen with a shock of recognition. It was Karn, the man who'd come hunting her and Lady Derenna when they'd been travelling in Sharlac with Welgren the apothecary.

"Lady Alaric." He smiled coldly. "Aren't you pleased to see me?"

After a barely perceptible pause, Charoleia closed the lid of her map case. "It's certainly a surprise. What's your business on this road?"

"Never mind that." Karn cocked his head. "Only you're not Lady Alaric, are you? You're a lying bitch, Mistress Lanagyre or whatever your name truly is. No amount of padding and dyed hair will hide that."

Charoleia didn't react to his vehemence. "We all travel under false names and faces. Now, say your piece and leave, before someone comes knocking to see why you're disturbing respectable women at their bedtime."

"Oh, the tavern wife knows I'm up here." Karn's smile was chillingly confident. "I'm your young ward's desperate suitor, come to beg your permission to pay my addresses."

"I'm impressed." Charoleia looked at him with apparent admiration. "How did you know to spin that yarn?"

"Don't think you can flatter me." He was unmoved. "You know as well as I do how readily someone will tell everything you need to know without even realising they've done so."

"True enough," Charoleia acknowledged. "How long have you been tracing our steps?" she asked with quick interest.

"I had no notion you were within a hundred leagues of here till I caught a glimpse of you on the road this afternoon." Karn laughed without humour. "You can thank Halcarion for that, or curse her as you see fit."

Branca was inclined to curses, even though she didn't believe in gods.

"You were carrying letters from Triolle's duke to Lord Geferin?" Charoleia guessed. "Or his lordship's replies?"

"Something like that." Karn scowled.

Charoleia nodded, satisfied. "So what business do you have with me, before you go on your way and we do the same?"

Karn shook his head slowly. "You've been meddling in my affairs, my lady."

"I have no idea what you're talking about." Charoleia seemed utterly mystified.

Branca guessed what he meant. She knew how Karn had come by the wound that Master Welgren had sworn would prove fatal. So much for the apothecary's wisdom. She concentrated on the woven patterns in the hearthrug. Neither of the other women's faces would betray anything, so she didn't want to inadvertently confirm Karn's suspicions if he happened to look at her.

"I've been in Ridianne's camp," he said coldly. "I've spoken to the men whose services you bought, to stick their knives in my back. I repaid them in kind," he added. "They're all dead."

After another tense moment of silence, Charoleia chuckled softly. Branca looked up, startled.

"Forgive me." Charoleia favoured Karn with her most charming smile. "A reliable sword is so hard to find at short notice. It's all in the roll of the runes, though. You know that."

"Was killing Master Hamare a fair fall of the bones?"

Looking sideways at him from under her lashes, Branca saw the first light of passion in Karn's eyes.

"Was sending whatever wizards you seduced or suborned into Triolle fair play?" he demanded. "To cut his throat and leave the duchess accused of his murder?"

Charoleia's face hardened and she took a step forward. "I'll admit to sending knives to hamstring you. I'd have wept if they'd killed you, believe that or not as you wish. All the same, it had to be done, to safeguard my principals' endeavours. You'd have done just the same in my shoes and well you know it."

Her voice thickened with anger and she took another step. "Don't accuse me of this other outrage, of murdering Master Hamare. What's all this wild talk of wizards? Were you even there when Hamare died?" She thrust an accusing finger at him. "Don't accuse me to relieve your own guilt. Countless things could have driven Duchess Litasse to such desperate straits. Was she—"

"Stop where you are." Karn wasn't watching Charoleia. While she had been advancing on him, Trissa had moved unobtrusively behind her, towards the foot of the bed, all the closer to the table by the window.

"Try ringing that bell and you'll be dead before you touch it." Karn showed her the throwing dagger in his previously empty hand. He raised his sword-point to threaten Charoleia. "Don't think you'll get close enough to stick me with whatever blade you've got in your petticoats."

Charoleia folded her arms, unimpressed. "You can't cut all our throats before one of us can scream."

"No," Karn agreed, unperturbed. "But I can still kill you all, however much noise it makes. And then

I'll kill whoever comes to see what's amiss. Don't think I won't."

Branca believed him without a doubt. But she could still call for help, she realised belatedly. If she could whisper the enchantments too softly for Karn to hear, she could alert Aremil to their peril. Where were Tathrin, Sorgrad and Gren? Too far to save them or close enough to come to their aid? She closed her eyes, the better to concentrate. She was so tired, so stiff, so scared. But she had to set all that aside, for all their sakes.

Charoleia was still challenging Karn. "How will you explain away so many murders?"

"There'll be nothing to explain if I kill everyone who's seen me here." Karn clearly saw no difficulty. "The locals can go beating the bushes for murderous mercenaries and good luck to them."

The tavern wife, the stable-hands and the amiable youth selling nuts in the yard, all slaughtered like autumn's pigs?

The horror of that notion shattered Branca's painstaking calm. Drawing a careful breath, she began looking inwards once again, searching for the peace that would enable her to reach through the aether. She was on the verge of finding the necessary composure when Karn's words startled her out of it again.

"You need not have all their blood on your hands," he offered.

"How so?" Charoleia asked cautiously.

"You're coming with me to Adel Castle," he assured her. "The only question is whether you arrive bound and gagged or riding your own horse in comfort."

"How could I turn a profit at Adel Castle?" Charoleia was politely sceptical.

"You'll tell us everything you know about this Soluran and his plans." Karn made it sound simple.

Charoleia looked thoughtful. "I might have some information to share, for the right price."

"You'll tell us everything," Karn said with sudden viciousness, "and be grateful to escape with your whoring hide. Then you'll tell me where to find those bastard Mountain-born mages so I can see Master Hamare's final account settled."

"No, I don't think that's going to happen," Charoleia said judiciously. "And you'll have nothing to show for your delay on the road if you kill us, will you?"

"Do you think that bothers me?"

Branca couldn't help it. She opened her eyes to see Karn raise his sword-point to Charoleia's pale throat. She recalled seeing him lash out at Lady Derenna with a metal rod, not caring in the least if he killed her. Her own heart was pounding. She could see the pulse in Charoleia's neck.

"One thing at a time, then. You agree to come with me now, you and your maid and the Vanam girl, and we leave everyone here alive." Unexpectedly, Karn smiled. "Cooperate and you can be looking for your chance to stick a knife in my back a second time, can't you?"

Charoleia smiled serenely back. "Wouldn't you do the same?"

"Oh, I would," he agreed. "So let's make sure you have other concerns to occupy you. Over there, both of you. Keep your hands where I can see them and don't move." He gestured with sword and dagger.

At Charoleia's nod, Trissa moved obediently with her to the far side of the bed.

That put them near the bell, Branca saw, but how could ringing that possibly help?

Then she realised Karn was looking down at her, as she sat on her stool.

"Did you think I'd forgotten you?" His cold gaze filled her with dread. "Lady Derenna's boot-faced young waiting-woman? You have the most unfortunate taste in friends. Stand up!"

Stiff as she was, Branca obeyed. Not fast enough.

Swiftly sheathing his dagger, he wound his hand in her hair and hauled her upwards. "I owe you an ill-turn. Letting that sawbones tend my wound would have saved me more pain than you can imagine. I might even have got back to Triolle in time to save Master Hamare," he snarled with sudden fury.

Charoleia stepped forwards. "What are you—"

"I said, stand still!" Karn menaced her with the sword he still held ready.

Tears blurred Branca's vision, of weariness, of the absurd pain of having her hair so cruelly pulled.

Summoning the calm for aetheric enchantment was utterly beyond her.

"You won't be stabbing me in the back again." Karn regained some measure of precarious calm as he addressed Charoleia. "You'll have your hands too full nursing your friend here."

As he wrenched her head sideways, Branca did her best to fight back. It was futile. All she could do was twist aside and close her eyes as he smashed her face into the solid oak of the door.

She collapsed onto the floorboards, dimly aware of the sticky warmth of blood trickling down her face. Then everything faded away.

Chapter Thirty-One
Tathrin

Triolle Castle,
28th of Aft-Autumn

"Should we fear knives in the dark?" Tathrin followed Sorgrad and Gren down the spiral stair of the bastion.

"That depends," said Sorgrad, shrugging, "on whether these servants and soldiers have stayed because they've nowhere to run to or because they're intent on defiance."

Gren was more certain. "Only some kind of fool would risk dangling from these battlements for a duke who's already fled like a scalded cat."

"Blind loyalty might find courage at the bottom of a bottle," Sorgrad countered. "Especially if they think Ridianne the Vixen has some chance of retaking the town for Iruvain."

Tathrin was glad of the steel plates between the

hardened leather of his jerkin and the linen lining. "Does she?"

"Let's find out." Sorgrad opened the door and led the way into the open bailey.

The castle clocks sounded noon's handful of chimes. Captain-General Evord was waiting, already mounted, his lieutenants gathered close. A groom led their own horses towards them. Tathrin tried to assess the man's expression but his hood was raised against the cold rain, leaving only his downturned mouth visible.

Captain-General Evord raised his hand to Arest, now commander of the castle's new guard. At the heavyset mercenary's shout, the inner gates opened. Evord's standard-bearer led them out, the cream and gold of the banner bright against the dull day.

Tathrin followed Sorgrad and Gren at the rear of the contingent. The outer gates opened and the leading riders rounded the sharp angle of the bastion's walls, crossing the wooden bridge that spanned the soggy ditch running down to the mere.

Away to their offside, the town's gates were solidly barred. Tathrin could see the battlements were still manned by Triolle men-at-arms, who had remained at their posts as the castle had been surrendered. They would not fight, their herald had said, but neither would they allow any of the mercenaries into the town. Had Evord been right to praise their loyalty to their fellow Triollese? Was he wise to allow them to keep their weapons, commending them to the local guildmasters' command?

"Wondering if that coat of plates will stop some treacherous crossbow bolt?" Gren teased.

"The captain-general can't spare the men to garrison a hostile town," Sorgrad said curtly. "Taking them prisoner's no option either."

Tathrin said nothing. He was too well aware how many of their Dalasorians were absent escorting recalcitrant mercenaries who'd been captured at Tyrle safely away to Abray.

Away to the other side of the road, the rain made a muddy slough out of grassland already trampled to dust by the mercenaries who'd taken Duke Iruvain's coin. That didn't seem to bother Ridianne the Vixen. She sat easily on her pied horse, her scarlet standard with its skewered dog-fox flamboyant behind her.

Tathrin did his best to count the helmets of her retinue. More men escorted her than rode with Evord.

"Is she capable of treachery?" he asked Sorgrad quietly.

"Capable, yes," the Mountain Man said. "Stupid, no. She won't start a fight out in the open like this."

Tathrin could only hope he was right. Beyond the contingent that Ridianne had brought to this parley, he could see the vast sprawl of her army. Smoke was already rising from impromptu cookfires as quartermasters took the opportunity of this halt to offer their companies a hot meal.

That was how to tell a good mercenary from an indifferent one, he recalled Sorgrad saying once. You hired the men who were warm, dry and fed whatever the weather or circumstances. From what Tathrin could tell, Ridianne's army met this standard.

To be fair, so did Captain-General Evord's. But his mercenary companies were now divided between garrisoning the castle and defending their own encampment on the far side of the town and the mere. Those outside the walls were a sizeable force but not equal to Ridianne's army.

Sorgrad was unconcerned. "She doesn't want to fight. Remember Saltebre."

"What happened there?" Tathrin demanded.

"It was ten or more years ago," Sorgrad explained. "Parnilesse paid Relshazri mercenaries to raid Marlier's southern districts. Ridianne brought them to bay. But rather than have everyone fight, she proposed a tourney between the captains of all the companies, her own included. Only every bout was to go to the death." He shrugged. "The army with most captains left standing was deemed to have won the unfought battle. It was hers."

"The Parnilesse captains agreed to this?" Tathrin was astonished.

"Rather than back down and look like cowards." Sorgrad chuckled. "She's a woman who knows how to take advantage of a man's vanity."

Gren was dubious. "Captain-General Evord won't

agree to anything of the kind. Any battle here's going to be a bloody affair."

To Tathrin's alarm, Sorgrad yielded a little. "You heard Evord give the captains their orders, in case they need to defend each other."

"You know she left her Marlier militia regiments behind at the border?" Gren persisted. "To make certain Duke Ferdain's defended if she gets herself beaten here."

Tathrin uneasily recalled those scouts' reports which had prompted lively speculation among Evord's lieutenants. Just what was the Vixen plotting?

"Captain-General." The Soluran inclined his head to acknowledge Ridianne. "You called for a parley?"

"I did." Ridianne nodded and at that signal, swords appeared all around her.

Evord's men instantly armed themselves.

"Treachery!"

"No." Ridianne answered a tense cry behind Tathrin with a chuckle. "At least, not the way you think."

"So I see," Evord said drily.

The swords surrounding the Vixen weren't menacing him. Instead, a third of the mercenary captains in her entourage now faced their erstwhile allies' weapons.

"His Grace Duke Ferdain of Marlier retains me to guard his borders and his interests as I think best," Ridianne said pleasantly. "I've come here at Iruvain of Triolle's bidding, only to find he's cut and run. Duke Garnot is dead, along with Lord Cassat, and all Lord Geferin has ever offered me is disdain and discourtesy. I'm beginning to think this game isn't worth the candle, for me or for Marlier."

At this distance, Tathrin couldn't be sure but he thought her glance shifted briefly to Sorgrad standing beside him.

"I take it there's some disagreement?" Evord raised a quizzical brow at those captains now raising their hands in surrender.

"Not disagreement. We just knew who not to bother asking, eh, Daifer?" Ridianne winked at a furious man whose white-rose badge was bracketed by the antlers of Sharlac's stag. He couldn't do much to retaliate since one of her men was unbuckling his sword-belt while another held a blade at his throat.

"My preferred captains and I have been discussing our options." She swept a scarred hand around the men encircling her. "You know Beresin Steelhand?"

"I do." Evord nodded a greeting to a tall, lean man riding forward from the rear of Ridianne's contingent.

He wouldn't be a man you'd easily forget, Tathrin saw. Some past battle had left a sword scar right across his forehead, cutting through one eyebrow and deep into his cheekbone. It was a wonder it hadn't smashed his beak of a nose, all the more prominent with his long black hair drawn back into a tail.

"Captain-General." He bowed courteously.

"Beresin has a list of all the companies prepared to fight with you against Parnilesse and whatever might remain of Triolle and Draximal's forces," Ridianne continued, "for the right price, of course."

"What do you propose to do with those companies disinclined to join us?" Evord asked.

As the Soluran spoke, a shift in the wind brought shouts and the clash of steel over from Ridianne's camp.

She shrugged. "I don't propose to do anything with them, once I've made certain they don't start a dogfight here."

"I see." Evord nodded. "Go on."

She nodded at the black-clad mercenary. "Send Beresin to me with your best offer by noon tomorrow. Bear in mind you cannot be sure of defeating Parnilesse without my assistance. But if you choose to try, we shan't interfere. We'll be marching back to Marlier. I take it you can get word to and from your principals, if you need to?"

For a tense moment, Tathrin wondered how she could possibly know of their Artifice.

Sorgrad murmured under his breath. "She knows a courier dove can reach Carluse before dark, even in this weather."

Ridianne was still speaking. "You might also ask your principals to consider what terms Duke Ferdain might expect, once Parnilesse is defeated. We would be interested to know, whether or not you decide to pay for our swords." Her face hardened slightly. "You should let your principals know that we all accept the fortunes of war, Duke Ferdain included. That said, Marlier has long been a friend to Draximal."

Tathrin couldn't quite follow this. Was she threatening some revenge for Lord Cassat's death or did she know about Aremil?

"She's heard he's Duke Secaris's son," Gren said softly. "Was that the pennyweight that tipped the scales?"

Sorgrad was sceptical. "Only if she seriously thinks he can lay claim to the dukedom as heir, which I very much doubt."

"Then I wonder how much gold it'll take," Gren mused, "to weight the balance in our favour?"

"You couldn't buy a barrel of ale with what's left in these strongrooms," Sorgrad growled.

"Hush." Tathrin silenced them both with a gesture.

"I've left Marlier's borders securely defended," Ridianne continued calmly.

"We've no intention of testing them." Evord seemed surprised she should think so.

And that, Tathrin saw, concluded their conversation. Each commander turned back with their respective escorts.

"Captain-General!" Sorgrad was already edging his horse forwards. "I know how to rid ourselves of any mercenaries who won't follow Ridianne."

Evord broke off giving instructions to a galloper. "How?"

"Duke Iruvain's mercenaries came up the River Dyal by boat." Sorgrad gestured towards the unseen wharfs. "Send them back to Relshaz the same way, in chains if need be. We have friends who'll persuade them not to look back," he said with a grin.

"I imagine the city's magistrates will be as keen as anyone to see this fighting ended." Evord looked quickly at Tathrin. "Have you heard from Master Aremil lately?"

Tathrin nodded. "I have."

Evord glanced at the lieutenants around him. "A moment, if you please."

As they obediently withdrew, Tathrin urged his horse close to Evord's. "I told Aremil of Ridianne's request for a noon parley. He'll contact me before the next chime."

"Tell him accepting her offer of assistance is our quickest path to ending this campaign." Evord looked intently at him. "With the weather so uncertain, we cannot afford delay. I must know what funds Master Gruit has on hand and whatever's been secured from Sharlac and Carluse's treasuries. Tell Aremil he needs some plan for dealing with Marlier as soon as the fighting's done." He paused, grim-faced. "And maybe for some approach to Parnilesse, if all we can do is give Lord Geferin's men bloody noses, even with Ridianne's help."

"Of course," Tathrin nodded.

"Come on, lad." Gren turned his horse's head back towards the castle.

Evord was already writing another set of instructions for a messenger to carry to Triolle Town. A second and a third waited to carry his orders to the mercenaries' camp.

As soon as they were back inside the castle, Sorgrad whistled for a passing groom and threw the man his reins.

"Let's find some peace and quiet." He contemplated the many-towered ring of the castle. "I reckon hidden ears are more of a threat than hidden knives. Master Hamare may be dead but his spies won't be."

"But I have to wait for Aremil to speak to me." All the same, Tathrin followed both Mountain Men to the chamber they'd appropriated, high in what he'd learned was the Chatelaine's Tower.

"Not if I bespeak Reher and tell him to tell Aremil we've got urgent news."

Well, that was one advantage of the blacksmith's refusal to leave Carluse, Tathrin reflected.

Sorgrad unlocked the door to reveal a chamber comfortably furnished with upholstered chairs, a marble washstand and a canopied bed. All the walls were richly panelled, so Gren had tested every handspan for the hollow knock of a hidden cupboard or secret passageway. He'd been disappointed to find nothing. Tathrin hadn't.

"Tell me if you hear any step on the stairs." With

Gren listening at the door, Sorgrad took a candle from the mantel. As he snapped his fingers, the wick flared with magefire. Sorgrad took up a silver salver that Gren had found somewhere and held it up to reflect the flame.

Tathrin took a chair, wondering how long he'd have to kick his heels before he heard Aremil's voice inside his head.

He scowled as Sorgrad spoke. He wasn't bespeaking Reher at all.

"Mellitha, good day to you."

Before Tathrin could protest, dizzying distress assailed him. He was on his feet before he realised it, his heart racing.

"*It's Branca. I can't find her.*"

"Aremil, what's wrong? Where's Failla?"

Aremil's anguish filled Tathrin with inexplicable fear for her.

"*Failla? She's here in Carluse. She's safe and well.*"

Aremil's bemusement momentarily overcame his concern. His sudden anger buffeted Tathrin. How dare he waste time asking after his own sweetheart when the woman Aremil loved might be—

"Aremil!" Tathrin couldn't tell if his friend broke off that thought because he realised how unjust he was or because the prospect of Branca's loss was too horrible to contemplate.

"*Don't, please.*"

As Aremil begged him not even to think the worst, Tathrin felt him rein in his tormented emotions.

"Forgive me. It's been a dreadful day."

Tathrin tried to thrust Aremil's anguish away. "She's with Charoleia and Trissa," he said aloud. "They'll keep her safe."

"Can you ask Sorgrad to scry for them?"

"Of course!"

As Tathrin cursed himself for a fool for not thinking of that himself, he felt Aremil's shaky amusement.

"I'm sure it would have occurred to you once I'd stopped filling your head with my worries."

Was that Aremil taking a determined breath, Tathrin wondered, or just his own imagination?

"So tell me, what did Ridianne have to say?"

Tathrin rallied sufficiently to tell him the essentials of the brief meeting.

"Assuming we can overthrow Parnilesse with her help, that will leave Ferdain of Marlier as the only remaining duke still holding his lands securely," he concluded.

"The only one with a living heir, or at least, with a son fit to succeed him. We're already discussing diplomatic overtures."

Aremil's familiar frustration with his own crippled condition was mingled with odd defiance. Tathrin heard faint echoes of irate shouting, by Aremil and Lord Rousharn.

"The prospect should be clearer once we've beaten Lord Geferin in battle," he ventured.

Aremil's thoughts rang with unaccustomed savagery.

"*Can Captain-General Evord do that?*"

Knowing his thoughts were open across the aether made Tathrin's reply easier. "We have a much better chance with Ridianne's companies. We need enough gold to make sure of them."

"*I'll see to it. Now, can Sorgrad scry for Branca, please?*"

Aremil's distress was so all-consuming that trying to restrain it snapped the Artifice linking them. Tathrin was glad of the chair beneath him as his knees gave way.

He opened his eyes to see Sorgrad and Gren both looking intently at him.

"What's happened to Charoleia?" Gren demanded.

"I don't know," Tathrin protested. "Aremil can't find Branca."

"Let's see if wizardry can outdo Artifice." Sorgrad was already pouring water from the washstand's ewer. The broad basin glowed with bright green light.

"Where is she?" Gren took a step away from the door.

"Watch the door." Sorgrad dropped ink into the water.

"What can you see?" Tathrin found the bowl blindingly uninformative.

Sorgrad set the ink bottle down. "Can you find any scent, any pomade?"

"What's the matter? Can't you find her?" Tathrin began searching among the oddments left on the mantel shelf by whoever had fled the room.

"No," Sorgrad said simply.

Tathrin hated himself as he asked the inevitable question. "Is she dead?"

How could he possibly hide that from Aremil? How could they have been so stupid, to let the women travel unescorted? So many mishaps could have befallen them on the road.

"I don't know." Sorgrad was oddly surprised. "I've never tried scrying for someone dead before."

"You do and I'll slap you," Gren growled from the doorway. "Trifling with necromancy."

Tathrin concentrated on the task in hand. Inexplicable though it was, it was still preferable to thinking about what might be happening to Branca. "I've found some shaving balm. Why—?"

"Some mages use ink, some use oils." Sorgrad poured the soiled water into the slop bucket. "Mellitha swears by perfumers' essences."

"Try looking for Charoleia," Gren suggested.

"I'm doing that." Sorgrad swiftly refilled the bowl and took the crystal vial. He poured a little of the sharply scented balm into each palm, as if he were about to soothe freshly razored cheeks. Instead he slid his hands into the water, heedless of his cuffs.

Tathrin watched tendrils of green light weaving around his fingers. The white ceramic bowl glowed emerald. Then the surface of the water clouded, hiding Sorgrad's hands. A floating image formed.

"Who's that?" he wondered, horrified.

"A dead man," snarled Gren.

"Madam Mage Jilseth's let us down," Sorgrad hissed.

Charoleia sat in a high-backed wooden chair. Her wrists were securely bound to the sturdy arms; another rope wound around her neck, forcing her head upright. All her bindings were bloodied, the skin beneath cruelly scored where she had struggled. Bruises were plain on her pale skin, a trickle of blood clotting one nostril.

A man stood by the chair, wearing an elegant green doublet with a gold-embroidered collar. Slender and disconcertingly blond, he was no Mountain Man, Tathrin quickly realised. He was a wizard though. Scarlet magefire danced on his palm. He touched his other forefinger to it, lifting free a petal of flame. His face mocking, he delicately brushed it against Charoleia's ringlets. Her hair burned with a crimson flash. She writhed against her bonds, fresh blood flowing.

"How much do you think she's told them?"

Tathrin was recalling Sorgrad telling him that sooner or later, everyone broke under torture. The Mountain mage didn't think much of it. You might hear the truth or you might just hear what the suffering victim thought you wanted to hear. Finding out which was which only wasted more time.

"He's a dead man!" Gren's fist came down to smash the bowl.

"No!"

A flash of lightning seared Tathrin's vision. Blinking, he saw Gren had been thrown clean across the room. Bemused, the younger Mountain Man lay motionless, staring at his brother.

"He's dead," Sorgrad spat with barely restrained violence, "just as soon as I've scried enough to take us there."

For an instant, the vision in the bowl vanished. Tathrin saw Sorgrad's fists clenched beneath the water, his knuckles white even through the bright sorcery. Then, to his mingled horror and relief, the awful scene reappeared.

"Where are they?" he asked hoarsely.

"Evord's scouts said Iruvain was heading for Adel Castle." Now icily calm, Sorgrad drew the spell outwards, mercifully shrinking Charoleia's tormented image.

"Trissa!" Tathrin gasped.

Charoleia's maid lay in a corner of the room, sprawled senseless. Her hair had almost all been singed away as had the sleeves of her gown, burns livid beside the rope scars on her wrists.

"There's that bastard Karn," Sorgrad breathed.

Tathrin couldn't conceive how the gaunt man could be watching this outrage so impassively. He looked up as a slithering noise distracted him. Still sat on the floor, Gren was running a whetstone along a dagger, his face murderous.

Sorgrad was still intent on his spell. "Let's see what we can see."

The image rippled and blurred and a new picture floated on the water. Tathrin saw the castle surrounded by empty turf, four-square on a rocky island shaped like a flat iron. Towers kept watch at the corners, with a squat keep pressed against the rear wall. A gate opened onto a path running to the island's pointed end. A wooden bridge hung from posts driven into the lake bed, stretching across the turbulent water to a smaller fortification on the shore.

Even before they reached that shore fort, anyone attacking the castle would have to fight their way through the swordsmen camped along the lakeside. Mercenary flags fluttered all the way to the walls of the town built where the lake emptied into a narrow river. Duke Iruvain had managed to join forces with Lord Geferin and Parnilesse's army.

No matter. Loathsome as being carried by Sorgrad's magic was, Tathrin didn't hesitate. "We can't wait for Evord to mount an attack on that castle."

"We'll have them out of there soon enough." Sorgrad was looking intently at an image of the keep's pitched, tiled roof now filling the washstand's bowl. "And that mage and that bastard Karn are dead men. Then it doesn't matter what Charoleia and Trissa have said."

Tathrin looked down at the scrying and frowned. "But where's Branca?"

CHAPTER THIRTY-TWO
Litasse

Adel Castle,
28th of Aft-Autumn

RAIN DRUMMED ON the tiles overhead. She looked out of the corridor's mean window, grimed with lichen. Never mind the town on the lakeshore; she could barely see the far side of the castle. Even Iruvain couldn't fret about the exiles attacking today.

She was only delaying the inevitable. Reluctantly Litasse approached the garret. She flinched at a shuddering gasp within but forced herself to open the door.

"Minelas!"

The wizard stood over the older of the two captured women. He wasn't content with searing away her chestnut hair any more. He had ripped her gown open to drop his magefire on her naked skin. Crimson flames slid down, slow as molten wax, leaving a blistered trail. The lace cupping the woman's breasts smouldered. The stink tainted the room, already airless with the fire in the hearth. Minelas had discarded his doublet, sweat sticking the shirt to his back.

Rising bile burned Litasse's throat. "Can't you see she's fainted?"

The woman's head would have slumped to her chest if not for the wizard's cruel bindings.

"Perhaps." Surveying his handiwork, Minelas absently snuffed the flame at his fingertip as if it were some ghastly candle.

As he smiled, Litasse was revolted to see his eyes dark and sleepy, his smile languorous with satisfaction. In the open neck of his shirt, blisters marred his own hairless chest. The linen hung loose at his waist and she saw one button of his breeches was undone.

"What are you doing?" As soon as she spoke, she regretted asking.

The wizard brushed back his sweat-darkened hair. "Finding out what she knows."

Litasse couldn't bear to look at him. She turned to the motionless figure in the corner. "Karn?"

"The bitch is neck deep in all the exiles' plots," he said doggedly.

"She wouldn't talk to save her maid!" Litasse tried not to look at the pitiful figure dumped like discarded laundry.

How long would the tortured maid's screams echo in her memory? And Minelas's mocking laughter as she fled the room, hands pressed to her mouth, her stomach heaving. Was the wretched creature still alive? Litasse was afraid to find out, for fear of drawing Minelas's attention back to the poor woman now her mistress had escaped him into unconsciousness.

Karn rubbed at his forehead, scowling. Litasse sympathised. A sick headache assailed her whenever she set foot in this ghastly eyrie.

"Let some fresh air in here," she ordered.

"Good idea." Karn forced open a casement with a grunt, the hinges squealing in protest.

Minelas stroked the unconscious woman's neck, tender as any lover. "That might bring her round."

Litasse went over to Karn and laid a hand on his forearm. "What do you think she can tell us that you don't already know?"

He looked at her, merciless. "She knows who killed Master Hamare." He glanced at Minelas. "When we find out, he can help us kill them."

Could that possibly be worth this depravity? Hamare would still be dead. Litasse turned unwillingly to Minelas.

"If she comes to her senses, ask her about Hamare's murderers. But nothing else." She smoothed her brocade skirts with nervous hands. "Lord Geferin's rooms are only two floors below."

Minelas drew a deep breath of the cold air now flowing through the window. "No one will hear a thing. No one will even know I'm up here."

Misgiving pricked Litasse. What would the mage do without anyone to see, with no one to hear him or his victims' cries? Sudden rage overwhelmed her.

"Is this all you can do? Torment helpless women? Where's this magical aid you promised?"

The wizard rounded on her so fast that Karn's hand went to his sword hilt.

Minelas laughed at the haggard man. "Do you really think you could save her?" He waved a hand at the foul weather outside. "What about that, Your Grace? Don't you appreciate my efforts in slowing the Soluran's army? He's up to his hocks in mud and his men are cold and wet and discouraged."

"So are ours. So are Lord Geferin's," snapped Litasse.

Minelas wagged a reproving finger. "I'll expect your apology, when I've riven Evord's forces with lightning and drowned his fallen men in the mire. And no one will suspect a thing, after so many days of storms."

"Karn! Come down to the Great Hall with me. Iruvain's sure to have questions about Ridianne, as will Geferin."

Choking on her disgust, Litasse left the room in a whirl of gold and lace. She stopped at the top of the stairs, still trembling.

"Your Grace?" Karn pinched the bridge of his nose, closing his eyes for a moment.

"You must get some sleep." Litasse hurried down the stairs. If only she could leave behind what she had seen so easily.

A pace behind, Karn grunted. "Maybe later."

"Ask Pelletria for one of her tisanes." Looking over her shoulder, Litasse tripped. She would have fallen headlong if not for Karn's swift hand.

"Your Grace?"

They had reached the landing below.

"Where—?"

The stairs they had descended were no longer there. Litasse stretched out a shaking hand to the lime-plastered wall. Instead of feeling its roughness, her fingertip disappeared. She snatched her hand back, gasping.

"How many men could he hide with an illusion like that?" Karn asked with new interest.

"I don't know." Litasse felt unaccountably soiled though there was nothing to see on her finger. A rush of noise escaped an opening door below. "Quick, before someone comes looking."

Panic goading her, she plucked up her petticoats and ran down the remaining flights. Karn was half a pace behind her.

"Your Grace." His hand on her shoulder slowed her as they approached the dining hall's doors.

Pelletria was wringing anxious hands beside them. "It's all right. Lord Geferin's yet to come down."

"Iruvain?" Litasse smoothed her hair, finding her palms were damp with sweat.

"Just taking his seat." Pelletria adjusted the set of her pearl necklace. "He's ordered only three places laid at the high table," she warned.

So Lord Roreth was still shivering out by the waterside, ostensible command of the bridge his reward for whatever he'd said to displease Iruvain.

"Very well." Lifting her chin, Litasse nodded to Karn to open the door.

Instead he looked back up the stairs, veiled warning in his eyes. "Your Grace."

"Your Grace!" It was Lord Geferin, followed by a youthful lieutenant from his personal guard.

The Parnilesse lord bowed low before taking both of her hands. He leaned forwards to brush a kiss on her cheek, unmistakable invitation in his eyes.

"My lord." Litasse dropped her gaze demurely.

Karn opened the door as, inevitably, Lord Geferin offered his arm. With no choice but to take it, Litasse smiled brightly as the Parnilesse lord escorted her down the hall's central aisle. She could still smell the mildew that afflicted the faded tapestries, even above the smoke of the candles and the aroma of sketchily washed bodies and inadequately dried leather. What a hovel this castle was.

Conversation continued all along the tables as she passed by. She found it impossible to untangle the words. Did she detect speculation or condemnation? Or did anyone care what she did with her favours, now that Triolle was menaced so sorely?

"Your Grace." Lord Geferin courteously ushered her up the dais steps.

She was sure his hand stroked her hip. Had Iruvain noticed? Unlikely. Her husband was tearing a slice of bread into tasteless fragments, his eyes unfocused in thought.

Thank Saedrin, he'd taken the central seat. Litasse walked briskly past him. Karn swiftly pulled out her high-backed chair as Lord Geferin's bodyguard did the same for his master. Karn poured damson-coloured wine into two empty goblets and topped up the one in front of the duke.

Iruvain took a drink. "Forgive me, my lord. This isn't quite the hospitality I should be offering."

"You'll soon be enjoying every comfort that Parnilesse can provide," Lord Geferin said easily.

"I'm sorry?" Iruvain's sharp reply was loud enough to startle those sitting closest to the dais.

Filling their mouths should stop their ears. Litasse gestured quickly to the castle's steward hesitating at the side of the hall. He clapped his hands and servitors hurried from the kitchen corridor, laden with platters of baked fish, and bowls of apples and parsnips tumbled in peppercorn sauce.

"Your Grace." Karn set a succulent haunch of roast venison on the table.

"Thank you." As Iruvain deftly wielded the knife, he looked sternly at Lord Geferin. "We'll be happy to visit Parnilesse once order is restored in Triolle."

Litasse nodded silent thanks as a lackey set down a dish of little marrows stuffed with minced mushrooms. Another brought a bowl of cabbage dressed with spices, apple and juniper berries.

Lord Geferin shook his head. "No, we'll be

heading back to Brynock just as soon as this foul weather breaks."

Iruvain stared at him, uncomprehending. "We'll be taking battle to this upstart Soluran!"

"If you wish to hand him your dukedom along with Sharlac and Carluse," Lord Geferin said calmly, "I shan't be following you, nor any of my men."

"Then why are you here?" Iruvain stabbed the carving knife into the table, heedless of the fine napery.

"To explain how you save your dukedom." Lord Geferin reached for the silver wine jug and refilled his goblet.

"By crushing these exiles between our army and Marlier's whore's!" Iruvain snarled, shoving the venison away.

"No." Geferin was infuriatingly calm. "We leave the Vixen to the roll of the runes. I imagine she'll run before she's beaten too soundly." He shrugged. "If she survives, we can reward her."

"What can we possibly gain by this folly?" cried Iruvain.

"Winter." Lord Geferin frowned at his empty plate. His bodyguard hurried to serve him a generous slice of meat.

"Winter?" Iruvain stared at the Parnilesse lord.

"This alliance, between these exiles and our own malcontents, between all these ragged-arsed mercenaries, these mobs from the uplands and the grasslands and Talagrin only knows where else, how long do you think it can endure?" Geferin chewed briskly as the boy served him with vegetables. "Their thieves' bargain won't hold until spring, you may be certain of that." He set down his knife and fork to trace lines across the tablecloth. "We retreat across the River Anock. We hold all the bridges. There's simply no way for this Soluran to cross into Parnilesse."

"Unless he marches north and comes at you through Draximal," Iruvain objected.

Geferin resumed eating, unbothered. "That's a journey which will take him deep into For-Winter and all the travails of cold and hunger. When he arrives, he'll find Secaris of Draximal's men ready and waiting to avenge Lord Cassat."

Iruvain shook his head. "Draximal's mercenaries have slipped their leash."

"No matter. Twenty companies of our own militia will still be waiting in those woods for the Soluran and his footsore band." Lord Geferin smiled. "Parnilesse has six thousand men under arms now. Every market day we hand out more halberds and helmets. How many men can you muster? Two thousand?"

"From Triolle? A few hundreds more than that," Iruvain admitted grudgingly.

Too sick at heart to eat, Litasse could only push the food around her plate.

Lord Geferin glanced at Karn. "You were Master Hamare's man? I take it you know the enemy's strength."

Karn stood impassive, hands clasped behind his back. "Of the order of five thousand men, my lord."

"So if we add the Vixen's army to our tally, the rightful rulers of Lescar can already muster two men for every one in this exiles' army. By the spring, we shall have half as many again." Lord Geferin paused to eat some mushroom-stuffed marrow. "While this Soluran has already exhausted his men with this foolishly fierce campaign. How many do you think will desert him over the winter?"

Iruvain's reply was a grunt as he drank more wine. Litasse saw his food was as untouched as her own.

"The Soluran cannot win this campaign if it runs into the spring," Lord Geferin said firmly through a mouthful of cabbage, "so we merely have to avoid losing it through the folly of joining battle too soon. We rally Draximal to our side as we mourn Lord Cassat's murder. We can seal that alliance by marrying one of my nephews to one of his daughters, or maybe that handsome brother of yours will take one of the lasses' fancy. We make common cause with Duke Ferdain—"

"After we abandoned his whore to her fate?" Iruvain protested.

Lord Geferin waved that away with his knife. "Ferdain has the gold to make good whatever losses her mercenaries may have suffered. Believe me, he won't pass up the chance to extend his holdings all the way up the Rel to Abray, when we settle Carluse's affairs." Pausing to drink some wine, he looked meaningfully at Karn. "All the while, we can sow dissent among these exiles and their allies. We may find no one left to fight, when spring arrives."

Iruvain scowled, spilling wine on the linen as he refilled his goblet. "We can break this Soluran if we meet him now."

"He won't even offer you battle once he sees that I've withdrawn." Lord Geferin laughed. "I don't know whose advice brought you here. Do you think your men will hold their ground along the lakeshore? No, and as soon as the Soluran cuts the bridge to this rat-trap, a mere handful of companies will pen you up here while his main force pursues me and mine." He began eating again. "He knows the only way to win this war is to defeat Parnilesse before For-Winter. You may rest assured I won't give him any such opportunity."

Twelve days until For-Winter. Could it really be so simple, wondered Litasse?

Iruvain stared blindly across the dining hall, brow furrowed.

Litasse noticed how many of the men and women below were watching the dais, expectant. They may not have been able to hear Lord Geferin, but they clearly assumed their overlords were agreeing some campaign.

Iruvain rose abruptly. "We'll discuss this further tomorrow."

"As you wish." Lord Geferin smiled. "But we'll be leaving by noon, me and mine."

Was that a threat? Before Litasse could decide, Iruvain disappeared through a door at the back of the dais.

"Well now, Your Grace." Lord Geferin slid into Iruvain's empty seat. "What sweetmeats has your excellent cook prepared this evening?"

"Forgive me, my lord." Litasse summoned up a wan smile. "But I have no appetite, even for such dainties. My woman tells me it's only to be expected, when I am so... fatigued." She let her hand slip to the enamelled buckle of her girdle.

"Oh." Lord Geferin withdrew a little.

"Why don't I have hot brandy and spice cakes sent to your room?" Litasse suggested.

"That would be very welcome." Lord Geferin rose and bowed courteously.

Litasse watched him depart down the hall's central aisle. As soon as the main door closed behind him, Karn deftly withdrew her chair. She swiftly followed Iruvain's path from the hall, not caring that her exit loosed every tongue in the hall.

The private chamber behind the great hall was empty. Karn closed the door. "Your Grace," he began cautiously.

"Lord Geferin can tell his duke that I'm pregnant if he wishes. He'll just look a fool when I'm not." Litasse stopped, gripped with sudden dread. "They killed their father, didn't they, Duke Orlin and his brothers? Once they have us both inside Parnilesse, how long before Iruvain breaks his neck out hunting?

Will he be safer if they think I carry Triolle's heir or not?"

"Your Grace." Karn looked at her, bemused. "Master Hamare never trusted Duke Orlin and Lord Geferin's without doubt a lecher, but they won't throw Triolle to these exiles by killing Duke Iruvain—"

But as he broke off, Litasse saw her own doubts reflected in his eyes.

"Not until the Soluran's defeated, at least," he went on slowly. "When the day comes to decide a new order for Lescar, though—"

"Never mind." Litasse pressed her hands to her face, her head throbbing. "Is he right? Is fleeing to Parnilesse the only way to win through in the end?"

"Yes," Karn said finally.

"Your Grace?" Pelletria hurried in from the stairs leading to the ducal apartments. "Where are you going?"

"I... I don't know." Litasse was too exhausted to think. No, that wasn't true. She looked at Karn. "Can we win this without Minelas? If we do as Lord Geferin says?"

Karn hesitated. "He might still prove useful."

Pelletria spoke up, unbidden. "He's been precious little use so far, just eating and drinking and demanding ever more coin."

"My father never trusted a greedy man," Litasse said slowly.

"I wouldn't trust any man who enjoys tormenting

captive women." Pelletria's voice shook with disgust.

"Can we be rid of him?" Litasse looked at Karn. "Without him taking some revenge?"

He shrugged. "As soon as I get behind him with a knife."

The emptiness in his eyes startled her. "Is there no way to—"

"Do you want to pay for his silence instead?" He looked steadily at her. "How much coin will that take, and for how many years? And if you refuse, I'm sure Duke Orlin would pay handsomely, to accuse Duke Iruvain of bringing magic into Lescar's wars."

Litasse closed her eyes, overwhelmed with guilt and despair. What had she done? How could she have been so stupid, thinking that bringing a mage into Triolle's affairs could possibly have been an answer?

Wringing your hands and lamenting will do no good. Karn is still waiting for your answer. We're all still trapped in this sodden castle. That despicable wizard is still indulging Halcarion only knows what base appetites up above. Well, at least you can do something about that.

"Kill him and throw his body in the lake." She shuddered. "Saedrin forgive me."

"Raeponin knows he's earned his death long before now."

She opened her eyes to see Karn's own gaze strangely veiled. She seemed to hear some strange echo of his words inside her own head.

Before Litasse could ask what he meant, Pelletria addressed more practical concerns.

"Make sure the body's well weighted. We don't want him washing up on the shore."

Litasse nodded. "As soon as it's done, you and I must be ready with bandages and salves, and poppy tincture, as much as you have. We will tend the women's hurts and then you must carry them far away, Karn. When they wake, they can only set their word against ours," she said desperately.

CHAPTER THIRTY~THREE
Branca

Adel Castle,
28th of Aft-Autumn

SHE WAS EXHAUSTED. She longed to close her eyes. No. Sleep would be fatal and not just for her.

"There are few more delightful places in Vanam." Charoleia surveyed the Physic Garden with a sigh of contentment.

"Few better for a discreet meeting," Trissa added with a smile.

"Or simply a peaceful walk." Branca concentrated on every detail.

They were strolling across the lawn. Over there, an outcrop of the upper town's granite was covered with creeping plants, tiny white flowers bright amid the ruffles of silvery leaves. Charoleia wore a high-necked green muslin gown and ivory combs secured her demure coiffure.

"One must always beware of ears lurking behind the trees." Trissa pointed at the carefully nurtured saplings, each one brought home from some distant land by one of Vanam's scholars. However far they travelled, it was said, scholars always came home.

Branca stopped dead. Would she ever get safely home?

"The sun is very hot today." Charoleia looked up at the cloudless sky.

"Indeed." Trissa rubbed the back of her neck. The sleeves of her primrose gown darkened to torn brown, burned flesh livid beneath.

"You're still stiff from riding so far," Branca said quickly. "Shall we sit? There's a honeysuckle arbour this way."

She ushered both women towards a gravel path shaded by leafy trees.

Trissa twirled the lacy parasol she now carried. "Do you walk here often?"

"It's a good place to think undisturbed." Branca replied with simple truth.

"Indeed." Charoleia fanned herself with the silver-mounted spray of white feathers that had appeared in her hand.

Branca knew she mostly came here to meet housemaids and coachmen and all manner of folk who sold her their masters' and mistresses' secrets. All Charoleia's secrets lay open to Branca now, and the choices that had brought her here. Here to the

Physic Garden, secure in the very heart of Vanam. That was what Branca had to remember.

"There's the new Apothecaries' Hall." She pointed to a roof just beyond the garden's wall. "Naturally the School of Physicians are now building themselves an even more splendid home."

"I must speak to Mentor Robarin, the anatomist." Charoleia was concerned. "He promised me—"

"That can wait. Truly, it can," Branca insisted. "Look, here's the arbour."

"How delightful." A smile lit Charoleia's face.

"What a wonderful scent," exclaimed Trissa.

Branca breathed more easily, seeing both women successfully distracted.

If Charoleia began thinking too deeply, recalling something she'd left undone, her thoughts could outrun Branca's fragile aetheric contrivance. If that happened, the older woman would surely wake to—

No. She mustn't even think about that. "Why don't we sit?" She indicated the wooden bench within the golden bower.

"Yes, let's." A faint frown creased Trissa's forehead. She rubbed her hands together as if they ached.

"Have you ever brought a sweetheart here?" Charoleia teased Branca.

Where had that thought come from? For an instant Branca recalled bringing Aremil here, the very first day they had met.

"You were testing him?" Charoleia stared at her, troubled. "Wasn't that cruel?"

"Perhaps, but I didn't know him then." Branca couldn't imagine doing such a thing now.

But she mustn't think about Aremil, not at all. If she did, she risked him finding her. If he reached through the aether when she was so tired, so scared, he could draw her into his own imagined sanctuary. Then Charoleia and Trissa would wake—

"You're tired," she said forcefully. "Why don't you rest awhile?"

Charoleia looked uneasy. "I'm sure there's something we should being doing."

"It can wait," Branca assured her.

"Just for a little while," Charoleia capitulated, covering a yawn with her fan.

Trissa's eyelids were already drooping. It was the thought of a moment for Branca to soften the bench with plump cushions. Soon Charoleia was drowsing beside her.

Branca waited until both women were soundly asleep before giving way to her growing fears.

How badly injured were they? Easing Trissa into this semblance of sleep was easier every time. Why did Charoleia never realise they kept tracing the same path through the gardens? If she had a grasp of even half her wits, she would never accept the absurdity of these boudoir furnishings or the foolhardiness of sleeping in the open like this.

Well, they were safe for the moment. That was enough. She had to find out what else was happening. Resolutely, Branca withdrew from the haven she'd woven with her Artifice. As her favourite corner of the physic garden dissolved, oppressive stone walls closed around her. She listened, tense, in case anyone was coming up this stair.

All she could hear was the rain drumming on the trapdoor above. Branca found herself promising Ostrin an offering, Dastennin too, just as long as this keep's roof proved sound. Only a leak into the rooms below would give anyone a reason to come up the garret stair, to brave the storm to check the lead and the tiles of the roof outside.

As she shivered in the cold, she winced. Saving Trissa from that foul man's beatings, defending Charoleia from his sadistic pleasures, meant Branca felt every blow, every burn, even though her own flesh remained unbruised. Every scream tore at her own throat. How much longer could any of them endure this?

But what hope of rescue was there? For her to reach out to Aremil, she must abandon Trissa and Charoleia to their torture, and risk her own safety. She must keep that man Karn from remembering that he had captured her too. His recollections constantly threatened to break the bonds she had woven to constrain him, when she realised he hadn't noticed her come to her senses, intent as he was on berating Charoleia for her treachery towards Hamare.

If he saw Charoleia and Trissa while her own thoughts were elsewhere, Branca knew he'd remember exactly how he'd used her to compel their obedience. Then there'd be nowhere to hide. This cursed castle was too small for anyone to escape a determined search. Should she use aetheric concealment to slip through the main gate and hide somewhere outside? Where, on this barren rock? Even if she did find some stunted shrub, she'd soon be wet through as well as chilled to the bone. Who would help Trissa and Charoleia if she died from exposure?

Besides, Branca wasn't sure how far she could go before her aetheric hold on their senses would slip. The further away that frightening man Karn and his unpredictable duchess were, the harder it was to nudge their thoughts along the paths she wished. Reaching down to the dining hall, to read Duke Iruvain's feelings and those of that Parnilesse lord, was harder still.

Branca's stomach growled. So many of Lord Geferin's thoughts centred on his dinner. That was pure torment while she was wracked with hunger and thirst. How long before such pangs overcame her mastery of Artifice? Mentor Tonin had once told her of imprisoned adepts who'd been left in hunger and filth to make sure that their bodily discomfort frustrated all their enchantments.

At least Lord Geferin's lust for Litasse was straightforward, desiring her naked body responding to his caressing hands. Minelas's appetites were a noisome confusion of pleasure and pain, shot through with exultation at his own daring and unnerving fear as to where his yearnings might lead him.

Gritting her teeth, Branca reached through the aether into the room below. Putting Trissa and Charoleia's wits beyond harm was one thing. She still had to save their unconscious bodies from as much abuse as she could.

Minelas was hesitating over Charoleia. The entertainment of searing her flesh had palled. Now he wondered if he could rouse her with a subtle spark of lightning. He wanted to strip her entirely, to see her writhe beneath his crackling fingertips. Savouring the anticipation, he was thinking how he might justify his actions to Litasse. The longer he could hoodwink the silly girl, the more time he would have for his well-deserved and woefully misunderstood pleasures.

Were all wizards so revoltingly self-centred? Well, his utter absorption with his own satisfactions did make some things easier.

Bracing herself, Branca turned Minelas's thoughts from the present to the past. He had all too many memories of abused and helpless whores. There had been that curly-headed maid in Col. The old woman selling her for each chime of the day had sworn she was a virgin. The child was nothing of the kind, but she was young enough to never have encountered anyone like Minelas. He'd indulged himself, fore and aft, his control like iron. Then he'd had her kneeling before him. Her terrified face glistened with tears. Soon it would be sticky with—

Branca left him to his erotic reveries, his hand absently seeking his own flesh instead of abusing anyone else's.

If they ever escaped this awful place, a bath would cleanse them all. Trissa and Charoleia's hurts could be soothed. Branca just hoped there was some aetheric enchantment that could scour her soiled mind clean.

She leaned her aching head against the cool stone. Aremil had learned how to rise above his infirmities, above the ceaseless pains that nagged him. The least she could do was ignore her own suffering. Maybe she could search for him at dead of night, when everyone was asleep? She wouldn't have to constantly search their thoughts, twisting their intentions: Litasse, Karn, Minelas.

Once, long ago, in Vanam, she'd seen a trickster at the Summer Solstice fair. In the middle of a circle of canes, he had set a fine white plate spinning on each one, one after another until he had ten, twenty, more, all dancing at his command. As they had slowed and tilted, he had darted from one wobbling cane to another, quickening them once again.

Branca hadn't thought of that jongleur in years. Why remember him now? Because she was frantically trying to keep so many things in play? When would her turn come to gather up all the spinning plates, letting the canes fall where they might? She couldn't let a single plate break, not even the last.

She sat up with a jerk. Had she fallen asleep? She couldn't risk that, even for an instant. She should keep moving instead of sitting still. Standing up, her knees failed her. She fell backwards, her numb rump landing hard on the stone steps.

Light-headed, she barely noticed the pain. Tears trickling down her face, Branca hugged her knees. Hunger was a physical ache in her belly. Her tongue was sticky and foul. She had to find food and drink. She'd be no use to anyone if she collapsed in a faint.

Carefully, she wiped the tears from her cheeks and unlaced her boots. Aetheric enchantments were all very well but unshod feet would be quieter. She rose more slowly and this time the dizziness receded. She walked cautiously down the dark stair, one hand on the cold wall, making sure of each footfall. Slipping and breaking an ankle would be the death of them all as surely as her being captured.

She murmured the concealing enchantment as she peered warily around the corner towards the door where the other two women were imprisoned with Minelas in the garret. He'd have shot his pathetic little bolt by now. But the afterglow should leave him content long enough for her to sneak down to the kitchens. If there was any luck left in the world, he might even drowse for a while.

"Fae dar ameneul, sar dar redicorlen."

She walked quietly along the corridor. A single candle lantern shone at the top of the garret stair, its flame strangely sickly. She picked her way down the steps to the landing below. There was no one to be seen. All the servants must still be in attendance on the duke and duchess.

"Fae dar ameneul, sar dar redicorlen."

Speed was of the essence. She walked quickly towards the lesser stair spiralling down through the corner of the keep. All she needed was some bread, a sup of milk or ale. One hand steadying herself against the curving wall, she hurried downwards.

"Fae dar ameneul, sar dar redicorlen."

"Who are you?"

Branca stared at the old woman who'd rounded the spiral to bump into her.

"What are you doing up here?" The old woman's grip tightened on her hand.

"Fae dar ameneul, sar dar redicorlen," Branca breathed.

"What's that you say?" The old woman shook her crossly.

"I came, with the duchess—"

Why had Mentor Tonin forbidden any talk of those enchantments rumoured to hide falsehood behind a semblance of truth?

"You're no Triolle maid." The old woman's face wrinkled suspiciously.

Of course, she was the duchess's waiting woman, who'd been deftly turning away questions downstairs when Litasse had come up to see Minelas.

"No, I came to serve the duchess," Branca said desperately. "From Parnilesse—"

"Not with that Vanam voice, you didn't!"

Branca's lies foundered on a shock of recognition. This was the old woman who had menaced Failla. Pelletria, that was her name. She'd threatened to hand Failla's baby over to Duke Garnot of Carluse.

"You're some exile spy!" The old woman still had hold of her. She raised her other hand to slap Branca's face.

Branca blocked the blow with her forearm. She wasn't ready for the rush of fear that assailed her.

The old woman was terrified, for herself, for Litasse, even for that cold and empty man Karn. She detested Minelas, and feared him too, but her dread was more that their treachery would be uncovered. That somehow the wizard would escape Karn's knife. Her only concern for Charoleia and Trissa was apprehension lest their bodies be discovered. They had to die as soon as Minelas was dead. There was no other way to bury this secret. She would send them to Poldrion with an excess of poppy tincture and convince Litasse that their injuries had carried them off, Maewelin forgive her.

Forget me. Forget us all. You don't know who we are. You never saw us here.

In a panic, Branca shoved the woman away.

Never see us again, you murderous bitch!

The old woman's hold broke and she fell backwards. The curving wall caught her before she could tumble far and she slumped in a dusty black huddle, gasping with pain.

Horrified, Branca went down a few steps. Old women were brittle. Had the fall broken some bone? She hadn't meant to hurt her, truly, just to make her forget.

The old woman choked and her head lolled sideways. Branca was reaching for her. Now she snatched back her hand, appalled. Blood trickled from Pelletria's nose, from her sightless eyes. Was she dead or merely stricken? Had Branca done this somehow or was it some unforeseen apoplexy?

What did that matter? Dead or dying, she was blocking the stairs. Branca could probably lift her but how would that help? Where could she take her? She couldn't answer the simplest question as to who she was or why she was in the castle. How could she explain away an old woman's body in her arms? Branca backed away up the steps. All she could do was hide. She turned and ran back for the garret.

As she reached the narrow stair to the roof, slipping on the damp stone, a scream shrilled through the castle, followed by another and another. Crouching on the topmost step, Branca belatedly realised she was weeping.

Tears couldn't save her. What could she do now? Wasn't it possible the old woman had fallen? Could she persuade Litasse to mourn such a tragic accident?

Now she heard shouts, urgent and angry. She couldn't make out the questions but their intent was unmistakable. Doors slammed, booted footfalls echoing through the halls.

It was no good. She couldn't master her Artifice. Summoning the calm to find Litasse's thoughts amid the storm of emotion rioting through the castle was simply impossible.

Despair redoubled the throbbing in Branca's head. Even if she could touch the duchess's thoughts, how could she hope to persuade her that this death didn't matter? That her only ally's murder was no real concern?

Branca hid her face in her hands, hunching to muffle her sobs in her skirts. She couldn't hide the truth from herself. She hadn't meant to but she'd murdered that woman. Now she could only wait to be caught.

CHAPTER THIRTY-FOUR
Tathrin

Adel Castle,
28th of Aft-Autumn

"DON'T FALL OVER the parapet." Gren held his arm cruelly tight. "And don't puke on my boots, or I'll make you lick them clean."

Tathrin was grateful for the pain. It made the nausea recede. Drenching rain slapping his face helped some more.

"I'm all right." He knew that was a lie when he opened his eyes. He was still horribly dizzy. But he could walk and that would suffice. He took a step and his foot slipped, hobnails scraping uselessly on the mossy tiles. He threw himself heavily onto the pitched roof rather than risk a lethal fall.

"Let's hope no one heard that." Sorgrad knelt by a trapdoor, sliding a knife blade into the crack between the hinges.

Tathrin expected him to lever it open. Instead the Mountain Man brushed a hand over the dagger and the hinges twisted into broken, hissing metal.

"Come on."

Sorgrad hauled the trapdoor up and Gren jumped through. Both had their swords ready. Tathrin drew his own blade and followed. Blue light flared in the darkness.

"No!" Sorgrad's shout cut through Gren's obscene curse. "Don't kill her!"

Gren's sword scored a pale line on the wall. "*Sheltya*," he spat at the cowering woman he'd nearly decapitated.

The Mountain adepts, whose Artifice he feared so? That made no sense. Then Tathrin recognised her.

"Branca?" Relief overwhelmed him.

"I thought—" she sobbed.

"Look after her." Sorgrad thrust her into Tathrin's arms.

"Where are they?" Gren jumped to the bottom of the narrow stair.

"That way?" Sorgrad looked back up at Branca. "What's all the noise?"

Tathrin could hear rising commotion below.

"I... I..." She couldn't speak for weeping.

"Who cares?" Gren disappeared. Sorgrad followed.

"Branca, please." One arm around her waist, Tathrin half-carried her down the steps, his sword in his other hand.

A splintering crash drowned out the shouting. Gren hadn't waited for Sorgrad's magic: he'd kicked in the garret door. Tathrin dragged Branca after them. However dangerous it might be at Sorgrad's side, it was safer than any alternative.

Before they reached the threshold, Gren was flung out of the room. Landing hard, he skidded along the floor on his back. Spitting curses, he fought a crackling tangle of white light.

Barely slowing as he ran, Sorgrad stooped to rip the magic away. Swirling the sparkling skein around his hand, he threw it through the doorway and followed. Already back on his feet, Gren was half a pace behind.

Tathrin held Branca at his back as he peered around the door jamb. He saw the light-haired man from Sorgrad's scrying. Minelas.

"Whoever you are, you'll regret this!" hissed the renegade mage.

"Eat shit and die," Gren retorted.

Minelas flung shards of lightning towards both men. Sorgrad threw a ball of fire the size of his fist. It scattered the murderous magic in all directions. Tathrin ducked as sparks struck smoking fragments from the plastered walls.

"Is that the best you can do?"

Minelas's derisive laugh was cut short as Sorgrad's magefire rebounded from the far wall. The renegade barely turned it aside with a flare of blue light that left purple smears all across Tathrin's vision.

Blinking, he saw Charoleia, helplessly lashed to that chair, and Trissa, collapsed in the corner. Minelas stood between them all and the women.

"You think I'd break sweat for scum like you?" Sorgrad wrapped the taller wizard in crimson flame.

Minelas ripped it to shreds with sapphire talons. "I see you're not man enough to face me alone."

Gren had been about to thrust his sword through the fire. Cobalt magelight leaped from Minelas's fingers to the tip of the blade. The tempered steel exploded in a razor shower.

"You think that'll save you?" Ignoring the cuts to his face, Gren had daggers in both hands before Tathrin had stopped blinking.

"How many knives do you have, little man?" taunted Minelas. "I have more magic."

"So have I." Sorgrad's gesture sent the lethal metal splinters buzzing towards Minelas's head.

The taller mage threw up his hands and they flashed into white sparks. The room reeked like a blacksmith's forge.

Tathrin saw flying metal had cut fresh scores across Charoleia's cheek. He looked back down the corridor. Whatever caused the uproar below, no one had come up here. Not yet.

"Stay here," he ordered Branca.

His chance came when Minelas blinked into invisibility. Sorgrad tore a gout of ruby fire from the blaze in the hearth and threw it at seemingly empty air. The renegade's concealment went up in smoke.

He wasn't laughing now, as he vanished again. An instant later he reappeared, menaced once more by Sorgrad's magefire. Tathrin ran crouching along the wall.

"You dare—?"

Whatever outraged magic Minelas launched, Sorgrad blocked its path with a veil of searing flame. Tathrin felt it scorch his hair. Never mind. He had reached Charoleia, and Minelas couldn't turn his back on either Mountain Man and live.

Gren was circling around, lobbing insults, ready to throw a dagger through any opening. Minelas did his best to ignore him, trading furious handfuls of magefire with Sorgrad, cobalt and crimson consuming each other. The room was stifling.

Tathrin sheathed his sword and pulled a knife from his boot top. "It's all right." Though he didn't know if Charoleia could hear him.

"I'll see to Trissa." Branca was slapping at her skirts to snuff out sparks.

He hadn't meant her to follow. Then again, she'd hardly be safer in the doorway. Tathrin sawed at the ropes securing Charoleia's wrists, the knife slipping perilously on her clotted blood. Tathrin wanted to look up, to see what was happening inside the room and beyond. He didn't dare. If he killed Charoleia by accident, Sorgrad would surely kill him, and he'd deserve it.

"She's alive." Crouched over Trissa, Branca's voice broke between relief and a sob.

Tathrin risked a glance and winced as Gren dodged a lightning bolt at his feet. Sorgrad threw out a hand and the hearth spat scarlet fire at Minelas. The taller mage snared it with his own magelight. Purple light flowed back down the flames and killed the fire dead.

Charoleia's wrists were free. Tathrin felt for the beat of her blood amid the lacerations. There it was, stronger than he expected. Heartened, he eased the knife under the rope around her neck. A dowdy brown curl fell to the floor. No matter. She'd be wearing a wig till summer to hide Minelas's ruin of her hair.

Branca screamed. "Look out!"

She was staring through the broken door. Karn was running up the corridor, a naked sword in his hand. Duchess Litasse stood frozen in shock at the top of the stair. Her tear-streaked face was as pale as Charoleia's.

"You kill that bastard. I'll gut the other." Gren abandoned Minelas in favour of this new prey. Karn charged to meet him.

"The duchess!" Tathrin shouted.

She was turning to flee, to summon all the castle's swords.

A gale rose up from nowhere. Dust swirled down the corridor to envelop Litasse and she was dragged bodily into the room. Karn snatched at her hands, but the whirlwind was dragging him inside too.

Sorgrad blocked the broken doorway with a curtain of flame. Tathrin could feel its heat clear across the room.

"You think I need a spark?" the Mountain mage taunted Minelas. "That you're the only one who can wield elemental air?"

"Jack of all trades." The renegade mage launched a spear of blinding light at his head. "Master of none."

Sorgrad dodged the murderous lightning. It left a black scar down the wall.

"Loose Charoleia." Tathrin handed Branca his dagger. She began cutting the final rope, muttering under her breath as she glared at Minelas.

Drawing his sword once again, Tathrin stood between the three women and the rival combatants: between Gren and Karn, between Sorgrad and the renegade mage.

Taller and armed with both sword and dagger, Karn could use neither advantage. Gren had come inside the reach of the longer blade to menace him with stabbing strokes. He'd already drawn blood, a rusty smear on the yellow sleeve of Karn's livery. Karn's drawn face was murderous.

Where was Minelas? Tathrin couldn't see the wizard at all. Had he fled?

"No you don't!" Sorgrad gestured at the dead hearth and black ashes billowed into the room.

Abruptly, Litasse screamed, falling towards the deadly fire that filled the doorway. Sorgrad swore and a gust of wind shoved her into the wall instead.

Minelas reappeared, outlined by swirling cinders. Tathrin saw his hands still outstretched, where he'd pushed Litasse at the flames. He fell to his knees, yelping with pain as the ash enveloping him glowed white hot.

"How does it feel?"

Tathrin barely recognised Branca's voice, so harsh with hatred. The dagger hung loose at her side, her unblinking eyes fixed on the renegade mage.

Minelas tore at his hair, at his clothing, with frantic hands. "No! I beg—" He collapsed to the floor, keening incoherently.

Gren's blades were locked with Karn's, neither able to steal an advantage. "What's that he's feeling?" the shorter man asked with interest.

"A taste of what's he's inflicted." Branca broke off to chant something insidiously lyrical and Minelas screamed.

Sorgrad looked through the veiling flames into the corridor. "I'm all in favour of vengeance but we must leave."

Tathrin braced himself for the blinding nausea of Sorgrad's spell. Instead the floorboards shook like a rickety bridge. He fell to his knees, barely avoiding Trissa's feet. Charoleia toppled insensible from her chair and he lunged to save her from a brutal fall.

As Litasse lost her footing, Sorgrad turned his own fall into a tumbler's roll and saved her from the fire in the entrance a second time.

Gren seized his chance to grapple with Karn.

Before either could recover his balance, they fell together, close as lovers. Gren was on top of the taller man, seizing his wrists and slamming his hands into the floor to make him drop sword and dagger. Then he clamped deadly fingers tight round Karn's throat. Karn punched Gren hard in the ribs, twisting his hips to throw him off.

"Enough!"

The slender figure in the middle of the room threw back her black cloak's hood. It was Jilseth.

"Behind the fair, Madam Mage, but good day to you regardless." Sorgrad tried to bow but lacked all his usual grace.

Tathrin saw Litasse try to stab the Mountain mage with a slender dagger she'd got from somewhere. She could only manage a feeble gesture. Gren had fallen sideways, away from Karn. They clawed at each other with murderous intent only to slump to the floor, exhausted.

Jilseth scowled. "I said, enough."

Across Tathrin's lap, Charoleia's weight dragged at his arms. He wanted to lay her down, for her ease and his own, but he could barely move. It wasn't as if he were bound, more like being caught in some invisible net. He could barely shift his hand a finger's length along his thigh.

Amber magic hauled Minelas upright and pressed him against the wall.

"There's your turncoat." If Sorgrad couldn't bow, his smile was as charming as ever.

Jilseth was unimpressed. "You'll be answering to Hadrumal too."

Tathrin found it hard to swallow. Was that the magewoman's wizardry or his own dread constricting his chest? What punishment could he expect? Even if he hadn't used magic himself, he was hardly an innocent here.

He heard a fluid whisper beside him. It was Branca, attempting Artifice.

The magewoman narrowed her eyes at the adept. "I think not."

Branca's eyes widened as her words were stifled. Tathrin opened his mouth to object and found he too was mute.

"Watch out," Sorgrad warned.

The Mountain mage's words were muffled and distorted, as though Tathrin's head was underwater. To his intense relief, his hearing cleared as Litasse broke the silence with a hoarse whisper.

"I never meant him to go this far."

"You think that's any excuse?" Jilseth's contempt was chilling.

"I was going to kill him," Karn growled, prostrate on the floor. Tathrin saw the man's arms flex as he tried, and failed, to raise himself up.

Jilseth was implacable. "That merely compounds your offences against the Archmage's authority."

"I had no notion what he was," cried Litasse.

"You purchase the services of a man who's abandoned every oath he has sworn?" Jilseth's voice warmed with anger. "Who's taken corsair gold and used his magic to enslave Caladhrian peasants, and you're surprised he's a vicious brute?"

"He's done—?"

"What?"

Where Litasse looked uncomprehending at Jilseth, Sorgrad's eyes sharpened with interest.

Jilseth was having none of it. "Don't pretend you don't know."

"Karn!" Angry colour smudged Litasse's ashen cheekbones. "What is she talking about?"

"What does it matter?" The Triolle man was genuinely perplexed.

"Don't listen to their lies," Minelas shrieked.

Branca thumped her fists against the floorboards. There was no sound even though she pounded hard enough to bloody her knuckles.

"Let her speak." Sorgrad tried to take a step. "For pity's sake, before she breaks her hands!"

Still scowling, Jilseth gestured and Branca gasped. Her voice shook as she spoke.

"A Caladhrian coastal baron, Lord Halferan, offered Minelas gold, land, every favour in his gift, if he'd defy the Archmage and help defend his fiefdom. Lord Halferan's people have suffered time and again, raided by corsairs hiding among the northernmost Aldabreshin islands."

She paused, her distant eyes fixed on some horror only she could see. Cowardly it might be, but Tathrin desperately hoped she wouldn't share it.

"So he took Halferan's gold. Then he went to the corsairs and proposed his own bargain. If they paid him more than Lord Halferan, he'd lead the baron and his men into an ambush so the corsairs could kill them. Then he'd claim Lord Halferan's fiefdom with a forged grant of guardianship. As long as the corsairs shared their plunder, they'd have a safe harbour. While he took all Lord Halferan's rents and revenues for his own."

Gren chuckled. "Don't usually see wizards with that kind of cunning."

Branca's gaze bored into Minelas. "But no amount of coin could sate your real greed, could it? It's never been about the gold, not truly. That just buys victims for your perversions and willing hands to stifle screams and bury bodies."

"You know nothing—" He flinched and looked fearfully at her.

"I didn't know!" Litasse protested desperately.

"So you say." Jilseth clearly disbelieved her. "You were still ready to bring magic into Lescar's wars."

Litasse's knuckles whitened as she clutched the hilt of her dagger. "Only because they did it first!"

"Excuses from the schoolroom?" Jilseth's lip curled. "Archmage Planir will want something more compelling."

Sorgrad angled his head. "She'll answer for her crimes before the whole Council of Mages?"

"As will you," Jilseth assured him. "You've your own tally of offences to settle. That was your thumb on the scales at Tyrle. Don't imagine that I don't know it."

"What are you? Some merchant's daughter? There's no honour in battle so you take every advantage you can. Never mind. Hadrumal has no claim on me." Sorgrad tried to shake his head, muscles taut in his neck. "But does Planir believe he can swear the whole Council to secrecy, when a Duchess of Triolle stands accused? Hearth Master Kalion will insist Emperor Tadriol be informed. You know that as well as I do. Knowing Kalion, he'll write to every Tormalin prince whom he feels should know. Flood Mistress Troanna has a great many friends in Caladhria. How does Planir propose to silence her?"

"They will respect the Archmage's authority," Jilseth insisted.

"The Duchess of Triolle can't just disappear from a guarded castle in the middle of a lake without some hue and cry. Someone will say magic's to blame, especially after Emirle Bridge." Sorgrad looked unblinking at Jilseth, his blue eyes icy. "How will you silence her, or Duke Iruvain, when you hand her back? Or will you imprison her on Hadrumal for the rest of her life?"

"No!" Litasse exclaimed, appalled.

"Don't be ridiculous," Jilseth said quickly.

Sorgrad managed a tight smile. "So, we're agreed. Word will get out. And what will Hadrumal say, when Her Grace explains she only sought to counter the magic first loosed at Emirle Bridge?"

"That was your magic," Jilseth snapped.

"Quite so." Sorgrad was unabashed. "But who will believe that? It's so much more likely to be Draximal or Parnilesse's doing. Once Triolle admits to hiring a renegade mage, who's to believe the other dukes weren't doing the same? Who'll believe they won't all go and search for some compliant wizard? Now that they know there really are wizards who'll defy Planir for gold? Duke Ferdain has deep pockets and he's caught between fire and flood. Whether Evord defeats Parnilesse or Lord Geferin wins the day, Marlier's on the back foot."

"Save your rhetoric for the Council," Jilseth advised, scathing.

"You came to suppress any use of magic in Lescar's wars, and any word of such magic getting out. But don't you see? Punishing us just ensures every dirty secret will be dragged into the open." Sorgrad's face hardened as he looked at Minelas. "How far do you think the stink will reach, when all that scum-sucker's victims are unearthed? How will that enhance Hadrumal's reputation?" He glanced at Karn. "You'd have done better to leave well alone and let my brother cut the bastard's throat. Him or anyone else with a knife and a conscience."

"The Archmage decides a renegade's punishment." White light blurred Tathrin's vision as Jilseth raised a hand.

So did Sorgrad. "No, he won't."

To his fearful surprise, Tathrin found he could move. Not easily, but enough to lay Charoleia down and grip his sword hilt. Gren and Karn both snatched daggers from the floor, rising to their knees before they froze once more. Tathrin felt the sorcery weigh him down again.

Sorgrad looked at Jilseth, unsmiling. "You can't hold us firm with your magic and still carry us all to Hadrumal. You won't hold any of us with your magic if Minelas and I both attack you."

"You'd ally yourself with this murderer?"

Tathrin heard the apprehension undercutting Jilseth's anger.

"Isn't he just a mercenary, just like me?" Sorgrad's gaze slid to Gren. "The same as all our murderous friends?"

He smiled at Minelas and Tathrin saw hope rise in the repellent wizard's eyes.

"You cannot—"

Jilseth's words were lost in a crack of violet light. Tathrin was free. Gren and Karn were both on their feet.

Only Karn had moved to drive Sorgrad away from Litasse. Sorgrad barely had his sword ready in time.

So Gren was free to plunge his dagger into Minelas's belly. He ripped the blade upwards from the mage's waist clear to the collar of his shirt. The wizard screamed, clutching at his spilling entrails. Falling forwards, he collapsed to writhe shrieking in a stinking pool of blood.

Gren stooped to silence him with a dagger through the back of the neck and regarded his handiwork with satisfaction. "That's everyone's problem solved."

"Don't," Sorgrad advised Karn. They stood with their swords locked, muscled arms tense. "I don't want to kill you. Gren, keep away."

Tathrin halted a pace in front of Branca, Charoleia and Trissa. His sword was ready though he had no idea what to do now.

"You killed Hamare." Karn's hatred for Sorgrad was implacable. "I owe you his death."

"You just try collecting," Gren invited, circling with his dripping dagger ready.

"Step back," Sorgrad told him. He didn't take his eyes off Karn as he addressed Litasse. "I believe we've gone some way to settling that account, Your Grace."

"Did you have to kill Pelletria?" she asked, desolate.

"Bastards." Karn shifted his feet, forcing Sorgrad around to block Gren's deadly intent.

Pelletria? Tathrin didn't understand. What had the spy who'd forced Failla's unwilling treachery have to do with any of this?

"Her blood's not on our hands." Sorgrad held his ground against Karn's move to unbalance him.

"But she—" Litasse began, despairing.

"What's that noise?" Branca trembled.

Tathrin heard the approach of pounding feet.

"Those are Triolle men-at-arms, Madam Mage. The illusion that hid these stairs died with Minelas—" Sorgrad broke off to frustrate Karn's attempt to twist his sword free of their deadlock. "Do you want to explain yourself when they arrive?"

"This isn't over." Jilseth vanished in a golden flash, leaving only the lingering echo of her ominous promise.

"No!" This time Litasse checked Karn.

"This isn't over." The gaunt man stared into the Mountain Man's eyes.

"No, and nor's this war." Sorgrad didn't blink. "The next battle should decide it. Why don't we meet there like honest men and settle our scores without distressing Her Grace?"

Branca plucked at Tathrin's elbow, her voice choked with tears. "We have to get Trissa and Charoleia to Master Welgren."

"Sorgrad?" he begged. No one else could save them. If it wasn't already too late.

The Mountain wizard's eyes fixed on Litasse, his expression unreadable. "Until next time, Your Grace."

Then the white heat of the Mountain Man's wizardry swept Tathrin and everyone else across countless leagues in the blink of an eye.

CHAPTER THIRTY-FIVE
Aremil

Carluse Castle,
35th of Aft-Autumn

STEP AFTER PAINFUL step, however long it took. Gripping the handles of his crutches as best he could, trying not to lean so heavily that the wood dug painfully into his armpits, Aremil swung his inadequate legs forward. He tensed as he let his feet take his weight. There was no rain today, but after three days of deafening thunderstorms, the lawn of this inner ward was sodden. He had to keep moving or his crutches would sink into the grass.

At least the inner ward was sheltered from the buffeting winds. He had nearly fallen headlong in the outer court. The full force of autumn's weather couldn't have come at a worse time. How was Captain-General Evord's army faring? What was happening in the other towns? There'd been no dispatches from Triolle or Losand for two days. Every courier bird must be hiding in a tree, every sodden messenger walking a lamed horse to shelter.

He struggled doggedly onwards. At least there was no one to see his ungainly progress. Almost all of the garrison, with any townsman, any prentice youth who could wield a halberd, had marched to join Evord's army. Their wives and daughters were tending the wounded. Those too old to fight enforced the guildmasters' authority, led by Master Ernout the priest.

Supplementary edicts drafted by Lord Rousharn were piling up on Aremil's desk. They could wait for his approval, or more likely his rejection. He'd waited long enough for this chance. It had been seven interminable days since Tathrin had appeared in a blinding flash of magelight, supporting Branca. Sorgrad had been carrying Charoleia while Gren cradled Trissa's limp form.

His thin chest heaving with exertion, Aremil reached the stone flagway surrounding the keep. He looked up at Garnot's erstwhile sanctuary, a turreted conceit of ornate windows and wrought-iron balconies. The duke had never expected to defend this against armed assault. Well, he was gone to answer to Saedrin for his pride and tyranny, or to whatever oblivion truly lay beyond death.

It was almost enough to make one hope that there truly was an Otherworld, Aremil thought savagely. That somehow Duke Garnot knew his private apartments had been turned over to Master Welgren for an infirmary. That his fine Aldabreshin silks were now stained with blood and pus. That nurses rinsed rags foul with piss and shit in his priceless Dalasorian bowls. The only people paying heed to the painted walls and marble inlays were men and women wracked with fever or head wounds, who wove the frolicking gods and goddesses into their own delirium.

Aremil went resolutely on, fighting the villainous ache in his limbs. Duke Garnot's masons had built a broad stair of shallow stone steps right up through the centre of the keep. Aremil didn't know if he could tackle it unaided. He had to try, if this was the only way to see Branca. He had to know what had happened to her.

Tathrin had related their shocking encounter with the renegade wizard, the Hadrumal magewoman and Duchess Litasse. Face to face, Aremil couldn't tell if Tathrin was unable or unwilling to explain Branca's acute distress. Ruthlessly quashing his scruples, he'd looked deep into his friend's private thoughts. All he'd found was bemusement to equal his own, and fear that some second emissary from the Archmage would appear to punish him along with Sorgrad and Gren.

Aremil couldn't care about that. Not when Branca brushed aside his every attempt to reach her with Artifice. This wasn't just her usual reserve veiling her private thoughts. There was something desperately wrong and he had to find out what it was. Setting his crutches on the bottommost step, he began the laborious climb.

"My lord?" A nurse, a girl from the town, halted on the stairs, startled.

"Master Aremil." He tried not to vent his irritation on the girl. Serafia, that was her name. "I make no claim to any title."

For all his insistence, too many people followed Lord Rousharn's lead, deferring to him as Duke Secaris's son. Aremil still wanted to know who'd spread that news.

"Master Aremil." Serafia bobbed a dutiful curtsey. "Master Welgren is still with Mistress Charoleia."

Aremil declined to correct her assumption. After all she had suffered, he could hardly refuse to visit Charoleia on her sickbed. "I shan't stay long."

He let the girl escort him through the fine reception rooms on this landing. As he made his way carefully between the pallets, he allowed himself to hope Charoleia would be asleep. Then he need not linger.

Few curious eyes followed him. Most of the patients were lost in their misery. The most dangerously wounded were brought here, those with injuries to the face and neck. The arrow wounds exasperated Master Welgren the most. Where he could, he extracted the steel heads, washing out the deep cavities with wine and packing them with lard-soaked linen. Where such surgery couldn't be risked, he could only remove the splintered shaft, leaving the steel and striving to keep the wound from suppurating.

Aremil tried not to breathe too deeply amid the mingled smells of suffering and nursing. "Isn't Mistress Branca here?"

He'd sent daily notes, first asking, then begging her to visit. Her scrawled replies always promised she would, just as soon as Master Welgren could release her, just as soon as the storms had passed by, just as soon as she'd had some rest. She'd still not come. Aremil didn't believe she would. So he must act.

"She's upstairs." Serafia knocked softly on the door at the end of the room. "Master Welgren, it's Lord— Master Aremil."

Welgren opened the door, his genial face surprised. "Ostrin save us. Did you come all this way unaided?"

"Aremil, come in." Charolcia's voice was clear, if perilously weak.

Welgren stepped backwards. Aremil negotiated the narrow entrance of what had once been Duke Garnot's presence chamber, now Welgren's private refuge. He had insisted both women receive his personal care.

Polite greeting died on Aremil's tongue. Beneath the ancestral portraits decorating the dove-grey walls, one of the two beds was empty.

"She died in the night." Charoleia was as wan as the bandages swathing her head. "She never woke."

"There must have been some injury we couldn't see." Shaking his head, Welgren returned to the marble table where his instruments and notebooks lay neatly arranged. "Some slow bleeding of her organs or perhaps within her skull." He sighed heavily.

Failla sat on a stool, a clean apron covering old stains on her dun gown. "We've no notion what mischief the magic might have done bringing her here."

"We don't know that it caused any harm." Charoleia's violet eyes flashed with something of her old fire. "You're to say nothing of the kind to Sorgrad. Without him we'd both be dead." Tears sparkled on her cheek as the scudding clouds parted and sunlight fell through the many-paned windows. "He and Gren will mourn Trissa as sorely as anyone." She closed her eyes and turned her face from them all.

"Forgive me, I won't disturb you further." Aremil began retreating. "Please accept my sincerest condolences."

"Let me help you." Failla rose swiftly to open the door.

"Thank you." Aremil went back to the stairwell as quickly as he could.

Unexpected grief clawed at his heart. Trissa was dead. Though he'd barely known her. He'd never really paid her much heed. They'd exchanged a few words as he'd come and gone from Charoleia's house in Vanam but he'd had scant reason to talk to Lady Alaric's maid.

He halted, blinded by unexpected tears. Now he could never get to know Trissa. He'd never learn what had brought her and Charoleia together. Had she ever looked for some life beyond their travels and deceits? Did she have a family waiting anxiously for news? Would anyone care she was dead, beyond scoundrels like Sorgrad and Gren?

Wretchedness overwhelmed him and he wavered on his crutches. Trissa was dead, like countless others, fallen in battle or succumbing after days of drawn-out pain. If Poldrion truly existed, he must be filling ledger after ledger with names. The queues for his ferry across the river of death must be hundreds deep by now.

Hundreds deep or thousands? Doubtless Dagaran could supply the precise figure, for their army at least. Would Saedrin call him to account for each and every death? And for those killed fighting for Sharlac and Carluse and Triolle, mercenaries and slaughtered militia, helpless to refuse their lords' commands? Aremil's throat closed with anguish and he struggled to draw breath.

"Here, let me." Failla steadied him with a hand at his elbow and deftly wiped his eyes. Just as she wiped her child's running nose.

Aremil could only submit to her ministrations. He couldn't decide which disgusted him more: that he

hated her for such kindness or that he hated himself
for his weakness.

"It was good of you to come," she said quietly.
"Who brought you the news? I was about to find
you myself."

Aremil saw no point in a lie. "I didn't know. I
came to find Branca. She won't visit me."

"She is very busy."

But Aremil saw something of his own frustration
reflected in Failla's eyes.

"It's more than that, isn't it?"

"I don't know. She won't say. She won't talk to
anyone."

"She'll talk to me." Aremil gripped his crutches,
ready to tackle the next flight of stairs. "I won't
leave till she does."

"A moment, please." Failla bit her lip. "Have you
spoken to Tathrin?"

Aremil nodded. "This morning. I'll tell him about
Trissa as soon as I can."

He hoped whatever unease Failla saw in his face
looked like tiredness or grief. He didn't want her
thinking he begrudged her and Tathrin the comfort
they had taken in each other's bodies, before
Tathrin, Sorgrad and Gren had ridden to rejoin
Evord's army.

Aremil hadn't meant to intrude on Tathrin's
precious memories. Not when they redoubled the
ache in his own heart. Then he realised Failla's
thoughts were all with Tathrin.

"Where are they now?" she asked desperately. 'What's the plan of campaign?"

"They've been sitting out the thunderstorms in whatever shelter they can find." Aremil shivered with sympathy for Tathrin's tribulations. "They'll be marching for Pannal as soon as they can."

"Are Duke Iruvain and Lord Geferin still making haste for Parnilesse?"

Everyone in the castle knew that was their aim. Everyone knew once the enemy crossed the bridge at Brynock, any chance of ending this war before winter was lost.

"They've been as badly hampered by the storms as our own men. Evord's scouts say they're moving more slowly, with their coaches and wagons bogging down in the mud and all the Duke of Triolle's household clinging to their coat-tails. Tathrin says Evord's leading regiments will close with their rearguard just this side of Pannal."

"If the weather holds." Failla looked through a window at the tumultuous sky. "And all we can do is sit and wait."

"I know," Aremil said heavily.

Tathrin's thoughts were full of the upcoming battle. He was horribly afraid that Lord Geferin's army would somehow escape them, that all their efforts would have been in vain. Then the dukes would prevail and their rule would once again sweep across Lescar. All who'd stood against them through this year of upheaval would pay for their defiance with their lives. All Aremil could do was remind his friend not to borrow trouble before Poldrion's demons demanded their due.

A moan from the reception room drifted through the stairwell.

"I had better go." Failla managed a wry smile.

"It's best to keep busy." Aremil managed a weak smile and slowly climbed to the next floor.

Should he be taking his own advice? Would forcing Branca to talk to him just make matters worse? One way or the other, he would soon know.

The door to Duke Garnot's great bedchamber stood ajar. He pushed it open with one crutch. "Branca?"

"Aremil?" Startled, she looked up from papers strewn across the vast bed.

Moving this canopied heirloom, where generations of dukes had been begotten and born, was impossible. It had been easier to fill the space around it with elegant furniture stripped from the guest apartments.

"Branca, I've been so worried—"

"I've no time to spare today," she said quickly, looking down at her papers again. "I'm drawing up everything I remember about the use of Artifice in healing. I've asked Mentor Tonin to look through Vanam's archives, and to contact any other adepts—"

"Branca, stop it!" Aremil swung himself into the room and shoved the door closed with a jab of his crutch. "Why haven't you been to see me?" He gasped as cramp seized him. Hastily sweeping some books to the floor, he half-sat, half-fell on a padded velvet chair.

Branca stepped back from the bed. "What possessed you to risk yourself coming here?" She twisted her apron with anguished hands.

"Why won't you see me?" he asked desperately.

"Just leave me alone." She fled to the far side of the room.

"Don't you dare turn your back on me!" Aremil tried to stand up. He failed. The pain in his useless legs was nothing to the torment of being unable to reach Branca. Furious, he threw his crutches at the tapestried wall. Fabled Dukes of Carluse rode with gods and goddesses: Talagrin, Trimon and Larasion. All were tall and beautiful, strong and lithe. Every embroidered gaze mocked him for a helpless cripple.

"No!" Branca turned around, hands pressed to her tear-stained face. "Don't think that!"

Some spark leaped through the aether between them. He caught a glimpse of her inner turmoil.

You can't love a murderess.

"Branca, dear heart." Aremil didn't know if he spoke the words aloud or through the Artifice. "Gren killed that wizard. I saw it all through Tathrin."

"No, you don't understand—" Branca choked on a sob.

Her anguish shredded the veils wound around her thoughts.

I was so tired, so scared. I'd been doing all I could to save Charoleia from his cruelty, to soothe Trissa's hurts—

"Trissa's dead?" She looked at Aremil, aghast.

"No one told you?" How could he have known?

Then it was all for nothing, everything that I did—

Branca fell to her knees, hiding her face in her hands.

"Without you—" Aremil recoiled as she tried to sever the Artifice that linked them. No. He wasn't going to let her.

"You helped Charoleia and Trissa withstand that vile torture. They gave nothing away of our plans, of our Artifice!"

"Who cares about any of that?"

An aetheric echo of Branca's despair pierced him like a knife. Her self-loathing cut him still deeper.

I killed that old woman. The one who forced Failla to help her. I didn't mean to, I swear it. But she would have handed me over, to Karn and to that wizard. I was so alone. I was so scared. I only meant to push her away!

Aremil saw Pelletria's brutal fall. He heard the crunching snap of her thigh, of her neck. He heard Litasse's scream of desolate grief.

Shaken to his core, he held out helpless hands. "You didn't mean to do it. No one can blame you!"

How could he possibly comfort her?

"You can't!" She sprang to her feet and disappeared through a side door hidden by a tapestry.

"Branca!"

He reached desperately for his closest crutch. It was too far away. Serve him right for indulging in childish tantrums. Very well. He would crawl like an infant if he must.

Before he could lower himself to the floor, the main door opened.

"Aremil?" It was Failla.

"Help me up." Scarlet with embarrassment, he gestured at his crutches.

She swiftly collected them. "Lord Rousharn is looking for you."

"Tell him to go piss up a rope!"

Gren's obscenity escaped Aremil before he realised.

"Gladly." Failla's laugh startled them both. "But if you don't forbid this he'll act on his own authority."

"What's going on?" Aremil looked desperately at the closed door hiding Branca.

Failla turned serious. "We've had word of those mercenaries that fled from Tyrle."

"Into Draximal?" Aremil looked blankly at her.

"They've sacked Wyril." Failla looked sickened. "Now they're calling every brigand loose in Lescar to join them and set up a new dukedom."

"What does Lord Rousharn say to that?" Aremil knew he wasn't going to like her answer.

Failla glanced apprehensively over her shoulder. "He says we must recall Evord's army and send our regiments to contain them, while the Dalasorians drive off any mercenaries coming to join them.

Then—" she broke off as heavy footfalls echoed up the stairwell.

Lord Rousharn strode into the bedchamber, a black frown knotting his brows. "Why are you hiding up here?"

"I'm not hiding." Aremil stood up as straight as he could.

Lord Rousharn glared at him. "After these storms, we've no hope of victory this side of Solstice. We must cut our losses and reach a settlement like rational men. I have letters ready for Duke Orlin and Duke Secaris. You must sign them with your proper title and acknowledge the responsibilities of your rank."

"There's no rank I wish to claim," Aremil said tightly, "and how dare you usurp my authority?"

"Duke Orlin and Duke Secaris will see reason." Lord Rousharn continued as if Aremil hadn't even spoken. "Duke Ferdain's borders are secure, even if his whore's run wild. Our first task is to put down this mercenary rabble that you fools have loosed on the land." He shook his noble head, revolted. "We can offer reparations, for the sack of Wyril at the very least. I have friends at court in Tormalin. Emperor Tadriol will send envoys to ensure everyone negotiates in good faith."

"Emperor Tadriol can mind his own mutton. As can you!"

Aremil's shout finally silenced Rousharn.

"What did you just say to me?" His surprise turned to wrath.

Aremil gripped his crutches. "You will send no letters to Orlin or Secaris or to any other noble between Caladhria and Toremal." He swallowed hard, forcing himself to speak calmly and clearly. "If you send any orders to our army, I'll have Dagaran lock you in a cellar. You have no authority in this endeavour. You will not undermine Captain-General Evord when we are within a hair's breadth of victory."

"You're as weak in the head as you are in the legs." Lord Rousharn turned to go.

"Don't you dare—"

The door's slam cut through Aremil's furious shout.

Failla looked anxiously at him. "He'll send those letters with or without your signature."

"Run and find Dagaran," Aremil said grimly. "Tell him to lock the gates, to the castle and the town. No riders are to leave without a sealed docket from me."

He'd disliked Lord Rousharn before. Now he hated the man, for making him act like some tyrant duke just to stop the fool wreaking havoc.

Failla disappeared. He heard her running down the stair. Laboriously crossing the room to the door in the panelling, he found Branca had locked it against him.

"You must have heard all that. I have to talk to Welgren and to Dagaran." He rattled the handle in frustration. "Please, open this door. I can't bear to leave you like this."

There was no sound from the hidden room, not even Branca's weeping. With fury at Rousharn still ringing round his head, he'd no hope of summoning Artifice to reach her.

Aremil fought an urge to smash the panelling with his crutch. The last thing Branca needed was his anger. The last thing he needed was to fall and be injured, leaving Rousharn to cause more uproar.

"My love, I have to go. I will be back as soon as this nonsense is settled."

He forced himself away, every step agony of mind and body. Reaching the stairs, he teetered on the verge of returning, to beg her to open to the door, to let Lord Rousharn do whatever he pleased. How could he let Branca think he'd abandoned her?

Then he recalled Tathrin's pain at leaving Failla. He felt all his friend's fears for his family, his guilt at leaving them to face whatever perils this war brought down the highway. All that anguish still hadn't stopped Tathrin. He'd never doubted what he must do.

Aremil was so used to being one of those left behind. He'd never fully understood Tathrin's torment. Not till now. Gripping his crutches, he carefully headed downstairs. They had one final chance to win this war. They must bring Parnilesse and Triolle to battle. He could not let Lord Rousharn's folly make a mockery of all the countless deaths it had cost to get this far.

Chapter Thirty-Six
Tathrin

Pannal,
in the Lescari Dukedom of Triolle,
1st of For-Winter

Another dawn. Another looming battle. The grass crackled with frost, the ruts in the road hard as stone. Every russet leaf was rimed with white. In the fields and copses, men were rising with groans and curses, their breath like smoke. Steam rose from the flanks of horses being roughly brushed to warm their blood.

Tathrin supposed he should be thankful he could see just how cold it was. For the past two days they'd trudged through fog as thick as fleece. Every standard-bearer had struggled to see the rearguard of the company ahead.

There was no true smoke to be seen. Overnight fires had burned down to grey embers and breakfast would be cold ale and whatever bread and meat the men carried. They'd outstripped all the quartermasters and their wagons. Only the farriers and surgeons kept pace with the army now.

Tathrin saw Captain-General Evord talking with his lieutenants. The Soluran nodded, before taking a bite of something. Whatever he ate, it betrayed no wisp of warmth. The captain-general never enjoyed anything he denied his army.

Was that wise? Could any general, even one of Evord's talent, win such a crucial battle on barely half a night's sleep and no hot food? When every company in his regiments had just marched countless leagues in this vile weather? When nearly two swordsmen in every three had already fought battles in Sharlac, Losand, Carluse and Tyrle? Only Ridianne of Marlier's three thousand men were wholly fresh.

Tathrin wanted to believe Captain-General Evord when he said their numbers now equalled those of Parnilesse, that it was the quality of the troops that would prove decisive. He still couldn't shake off the doubts that plagued him. Lord Geferin led six thousand unblooded militiamen as well as the motley regiments Duke Iruvain had salvaged from Triolle and Draximal's scattered armies.

"We should have stopped sooner," he muttered.

Aremil had been appalled to find them on the road so late the night before, when he'd reached through the aether to ask for the latest news.

"Marching keeps the blood flowing." At his side, Gren was huddled into a blanket slung across one shoulder and belted around his hauberk. "If we'd stopped any sooner, some of us wouldn't have woken this morning."

"I suppose so."

The temperature had dropped like a stone when the skies had finally cleared, showing the last miserly quarter of the Greater Moon and the inadequate swell of the Lesser.

Tathrin shivered. He wasn't just cold. Every stitch of his clothing was damp, right through to his skin. Even oiled-leather cloaks hadn't been proof against the downpours. He'd welcome even a candle to warm his hands.

Though he wasn't about to reach for the one Sorgrad had just kindled. Shielded from curious eyes by himself and Gren, the Mountain mage was looking intently into the image reflected on the back of his silver bowl.

"You're certain the skies will stay clear?"

If they didn't, Tathrin didn't know what they would do. Relieved, he saw Mellitha, the prosperous magewoman from Relshaz, nodding.

"I've bespoken Velindre. You'll have blue skies today and tomorrow and then more rain will come up from the Southern Sea. Now, you follow the roll of the runes, Sorgrad," Mellitha continued sternly. "Captain-General Evord will win a fair fight, or he won't. Magic must not tip the scales, do you hear me?"

"I do," Sorgrad assured her.

"I'm a mother of four, Sorgrad. I know full well that hearing's one thing and obeying's quite another." Mellitha leaned into the spell. "You've had all the leniency you can expect from Hadrumal, by way of thanks for ridding us of Minelas. Don't try the Archmage's patience again, you or that blacksmith."

Reher? So that secret was out. Perhaps it was as well the blacksmith had insisted on staying with the farriers. Though he hadn't exactly refused to use his magic. He'd just told Tathrin he'd stick to what he knew best, his face unreadable behind his beard. Later Tathrin had seen him among the supply wagons, laying a broad hand on each of the barrels filled with bundles of arrows. Was he doing something to improve the quality of their steel heads?

"We'll just be carrying messages like the rest of the gallopers. Trust me." Sorgrad smiled as he snuffed the candle and Mellitha's face disappeared.

Tathrin relished the silence. Long might it continue. Carrying messages through the battle would be perilous enough without Aremil distracting him and sympathetic though he was, he didn't want to endure his friend's anguish over Branca today. He really hoped he wouldn't hear Aremil's voice until the battle was wholly over.

"Who's Velindre?" He was so cold his jaw was stiff.

"A wizard woman with an affinity for clouds." Sorgrad looked thoughtful. "If she says that's how the weather will play out, we can believe it."

"We only need one clear day." Tathrin recalled the final dispatch that Evord had sent to every company as they made their hasty camp the night before. "If we don't bring them down before nightfall, they'll be over the bridge to Parnilesse."

"Not if there's no bridge left to cross." Gren grinned at his brother. "You could see to that."

"I wouldn't be so sure." Sorgrad pointed to a puddle glazed with ice.

Startled, Tathrin shuddered. "Jilseth?"

The misty image of the black-clad magewoman's face slid away leaving only emptiness.

Gren scowled at the rising rim of the sun. "Can she still snoop if all the puddles melt? Or if we stamp on them?"

"I wouldn't take that wager," Sorgrad said frankly. "Velindre could see to it the ice lingers where they want it and she and Mellitha are very close friends."

"So the Archmage doesn't forbid their spells?" Gren challenged. "That's hardly fair."

"Fairness doesn't concern Planir," Sorgrad reminded him.

"Will you—" Tathrin couldn't bring himself to ask if Sorgrad intended using the sly magics that had tripped Duke Garnot's army.

The Mountain mage understood him regardless. "It depends how desperate the day becomes."

Horn calls were ringing through the crisp air as men and women began moving with swift purpose.

"Time to mount up." Sorgrad clapped a gloved hand on Tathrin's shoulder and exclaimed, "Lad, you're chilled to the bone!"

Tathrin could already feel dry warmth spreading outwards from the Mountain Man's touch. "Thank you."

He knew he sounded grudging. He couldn't help it. Was Sorgrad going to help every other cold swordsman? Hardly. Even if he wanted to, such comfort would doubtless fall foul of the Archmage's edict.

Sorgrad was paying no heed to Tathrin's gracelessness. Gren had already trotted off to meet the groom leading three horses towards them.

"Can we really do this?" Tathrin climbed into his saddle. "Can the captain-general win the day?"

"If he can't, no one can." Sorgrad looked grim.

"Do you know where the enemy's drawn up?"

If Tathrin had barely slept, he didn't think Sorgrad or Gren had even closed an eye. As scouts returned throughout the night, the Mountain Men had been at Evord's side. Like the youthful lieutenants, they'd promptly carried the captain-general's observations and instructions the length and breadth of the army.

"Our advance regiments were snapping at their heels last night, so they had to find somewhere defensible to stop." Gren looked far more cheerful than his brother. "There's a stretch of low ground ahead." He nodded as they all urged their horses to a trot. "The main road follows on down the westerly bank of this river and crosses a couple of streams coming down the valley side. Lord Geferin and Duke Iruvain took a byway heading to a ford. They all camped on the eastern bank last night, on a coppiced hillside with thicker woods behind."

"So they had shelter and probably rabbits to eat? While we've got streams and a river to cross before we have to fight uphill?" Tathrin couldn't see the least cause for optimism. Even if the streams were a trivial obstacle, this tributary running into the Anock was swollen with the recent rain.

Gren chuckled. "They had to stop and camp before the Parnilesse militia got a sniff of Pannal and the bridge. They're as cold and wet and hungry as any of us and they're far less used to such hardships. If just one company had broken for hearth and home, the rest would have followed like panicking lambs."

"Perhaps, but they didn't." Sorgrad's horse's hooves rang on the frozen road. "And Lord Geferin has found ground that'll hamper our Dalasorians."

"Maybe, but they've had no time to dig pits or plant stakes, and he'll have no more luck than us bringing his own horsemen into play." Gren wasn't going to be downcast. "And Captain-General Evord will make best use of our archers and crossbowmen, you'll see."

Ahead, the captain-general's retinue broke into a canter. On either side of the road, their mounted forces advanced in measured fashion, stirrup to stirrup. The foot regiments were marching at double pace. They must be as eager as anyone to see this campaign over. Would that be enough to outweigh their wounds and weariness? Despite his faith in the Soluran, Tathrin felt hollow inside.

All too soon he saw the fork in the road. The exiles' cream and gold banner led them away from the byway to the ford, heading across the fields of stubble along this side of the shallow valley.

Someone had scouted out a good vantage point as the weather cleared last night. The retinue gathered around Captain-General Evord had an ominously clear view of the enemy now swiftly assembling. Further down the valley, militia regiments under banners of yellow and light green and the ragged remnants of Triolle's mercenaries had come back across the river to occupy the main road to Pannal. Their ranks were drawn up tight on the far side of a little bridge that carried the highway over one of the streams running down to the river. As Tathrin had feared, both the stream and the tributary flowed swift and dark.

"See." Gren pointed out a second bridge crossing another stream a few plough lengths behind the Triolle militia companies. "Lord Geferin doesn't trust anyone who ran away from Tyrle. He's making sure they can't rout by putting them in that pocket."

"They're vulnerable on this side of the river, aren't they?"

Tathrin was watching Marlier's cavalry troops now sweeping past, barely hesitating as they splashed through the streams running down to the river meadows. As they advanced, they would soon menace the militia holding the ground between the two little bridges carrying the main road along this western side of the valley. His spirits rose a little.

"Won't Ridianne the Vixen's men just drive them into the river?"

"Hardly." Sorgrad nodded towards a sizeable contingent of Parnilesse cavalry now appearing in support of the Triolle mercenaries and militiamen on Lord Geferin's far-left flank.

Tathrin saw foot soldiers behind them, their mercenary banners adorned with black and green pennants.

"Those Parnilesse horse will charge just as soon as Marlier's horse make a move," Gren predicted, "with their mercenary foot soldiers ready to take on any of the Vixen's men who're unhorsed."

"Those Triolle mercenaries and militia will deny us the bridges and the highway for as long as they can," Sorgrad said thoughtfully. "Duke Iruvain will have sent Duchess Litasse on to Pannal. No Triolle man will want us catching her. Let's hope the Marlier horse don't realise that and go after her though." Sorgrad gestured across the valley. "If we're going to win this, we've got to cross that river and strike the Parnilesse line as hard as we can."

"Where is their line exactly?"

This wasn't like the battles for Carluse. Across the river, to the north, Tathrin could see troops of horsemen wearing Parnilesse black and green, over beyond the byway running east to the ford. He guessed that marked Lord Geferin's right flank. But the gently rising slope straight ahead, between those cavalry troops and the bridges on the highway, was a mass of coppices, the ground between them dense with gorse. A few of the trees were still defiantly green; most were now red, orange and yellow. Leaves brought down by the recent storms lay thick on the grass, fading to dull brown. Tathrin could see mercenary banners here and there but any clear view of the enemy's dispositions was impossible.

"There's his lordship, and His Grace." Gren's sharp eyes picked out two moving standards breaking cover at the southern edge of the scrubby woodland.

Tathrin followed his pointing finger. Even at this distance, Triolle's green grebe was unmistakable on its yellow field. Parnilesse's crossed sword and halberd were indistinct black lines on the flag's blue ground, the oak wreath a green smudge. He watched as the enemy commanders' flags wheeled around before coming to a halt.

"Where's the Vixen?" he asked suddenly.

"Over yonder." Gren pointed to the far side of Evord's command troop.

Tathrin caught a glimpse of Ridianne's red and silver banner. Surrounded by her own retinue, she was close enough to receive the captain-general's dispatches without delay, while still enjoying a clear view of her cavalry as they advanced on the Triolle mercenaries and militia who held the bridges along the road, as well as the Parnilesse horse on their left hand.

Tathrin saw the Marlier mercenary foot soldiers drawn up below Ridianne's standard. All her regiments formed the exiles' right flank. The bulk of the companies who'd fought this long campaign held their centre and left flank, their resolute lines reaching all the way back to the fork in the road. To the north of the fork, Tathrin could just glimpse the bold pennants of the Dalasorian lancers. He twisted in his saddle, struck by a sudden realisation.

"Where are the Mountain Men?" He had no idea.

"Waiting in reserve," Sorgrad chided. "Evord won't risk all this on one throw of the bones."

"How many companies do you suppose Lord Geferin is holding back?" Tathrin wondered aloud. It really was going to be a long and bloody day, wasn't it?

"Sausage?" Gren offered him a greasy link that looked like a dead man's finger.

"No, thank you." Hungry as Tathrin was, the thought of eating made him nauseous.

"Try this." Sorgrad pressed a currant cake into his hand. "You'll be no use to anyone if you swoon like a maiden."

To Tathrin's surprise, the spicy scent was inviting. Once he'd taken a bite, he quickly finished the cake.

"What now?" he said indistinctly through the crumbs.

On either side of the river, the two armies' massed ranks of foot soldiers were still shifting their ground. Tathrin could see Evord's archers and crossbowmen making ready to lead their advance. He couldn't see what riposte the Parnilesse army might make to such missiles.

"White brandy?" Sorgrad offered his flask.

Tathrin waved it away, reaching for his own leather-wrapped bottle of water. "I'll keep a clear head."

"How long do we have to wait?" Gren was impatient. "If we don't ford the river, they can cut and run at dusk and that'll come too cursed early now."

Sorgrad smiled thinly. "The captain-general won't allow that."

He nodded north, where the Dalasorian lancers were advancing towards the river, not bothering with the byway to the ford. The first troops urged their horses into the swollen waters. Tathrin recalled what that lancer had said before chancing the hidden ford below Carluse: there were no bridges in the grasslands. Nor any waiting lines of deadly halberds. How could they be so fearless?

As the Dalasorian horses plunged across, churning up dirty foam, Tathrin saw the Parnilesse horse were moving. How could the Dalasorians hope to reassemble before the Parnilesse cavalry struck?

Tathrin felt his own heart quicken as the black-and-green-clad riders broke into a purposeful canter. The Dalasorians were still scrambling onto the bank in disarray.

A horse's scream cut through the clamour rising along the valley. Yells followed, from men and beasts, of shock and pain. Tathrin saw the Parnilesse charge slowing.

"I don't believe anyone told Lord Geferin that we have mounted archers." Sorgrad raised his brandy flask in mocking salute.

Tathrin realised the Dalasorians' bowmen and -women had stayed on this side of the river. Their recurved bows were sending flight after flight of arrows clean over their lancers' heads. It didn't disrupt the Parnilesse charge completely but it won the Dalasorians time enough to close up their ranks, spurring their horses on.

The arrows ceased as the first riders met. The lancers' longer reach was murderously effective. Parnilesse riders fell amid the trampling hooves. Their second rank whipped their mounts on, charging to their comrades' aid. Swords already drawn, they hacked at the wooden lance shafts before attacking the grasslanders savagely.

Tathrin's grip tightened reflexively on his horse's reins. He'd seen how their own mercenaries could be handier with a sword on horseback than some of the Dalasorians. They were used to riding into battle with the clear intent of fighting dismounted.

The second rank of Dalasorians now riding into the furious mêlée were unable to use their lances decisively. It was impossible to see who was gaining the upper hand.

Tathrin's horse quivered as a galloper raced past with a dispatch for the captain-general.

"They won't get across the river," Gren said scornfully. "The Dalasorians haven't all joined in."

Tathrin saw the third rank of troops who'd crossed the river were still waiting to move. That must surely tip the balance in their favour, now all the Parnilesse horse were embroiled in the fighting.

"The Wyvern Hunters will be ready if they do." Sorgrad stowed his flask in his belt pouch.

Tathrin saw the captain-general's messenger arrive at the Wyvern Hunters' banner. Arest was soon leading the eight mercenary companies guarding the army's left flank closer to the river.

Gren was laughing.

"What's so funny?" Tathrin couldn't see anything amusing. In the mounted battle raging between the Dalasorians and the Parnilesse horse, men were killing and dying. Captain-General Evord's foot regiments were moving down into the centre of the valley. Ridianne of Marlier's mercenaries were wheeling slightly to advance towards the bridges that the Triolle mercenaries and militia held, denying them the highway.

"Those mounted archers, they're riding right around that skirmish." Chuckling, Gren was still intent on the cavalry battle at the northern end of the valley.

"That's Sia Kersain's banner," Tathrin realised, indignant. "What are they doing?"

Sorgrad stood in his stirrups to see the clan lord lead three troops of fresh lancers straight past the fight, not slowing to aid his fellow Dalasorians. "Let's hope he has some cunning scheme agreed with the captain-general."

"If he hasn't?" Tathrin demanded.

"Then he doesn't think we're going to prevail." Gren shrugged. "So he's decided to make some profit on the day. They'll be going after Parnilesse and Triolle's baggage wagons."

"Or making sure none of the Parnilesse horse escape," objected Tathrin. He could already see some of the black-and-green-clad riders struggling to break clear of the fighting.

A whistle interrupted him.

Gren slapped his grey horse's neck. "Time to earn our oats."

Tathrin wondered why he didn't feel scared. Riding through the thick of battle would be perilous in the extreme. But anything would be better than sitting up here, a mere helpless observer.

He followed the brothers to the captain-general's standard. Evord was dispatching messages in all directions. News from every regiment was arriving at the gallop.

"Ridianne's compliments," a rider with a Marlier accent said breathlessly. "Our cavalrymen are taking arrows from the Parnilesse mercenaries down by the river. Shall our mounted archers attack them?"

"No," Evord said promptly. "Tell the mounted bow captains to send a single arrow storm into the Parnilesse horsemen. Tell your cavalry captains to charge as soon as the last shafts are in the air."

"Captain-General." Sorgrad raised a hand to show Evord they awaited his orders.

The Soluran spared Tathrin a brief smile. "My compliments to Beresin Steelhand and he's to hold those Parnilesse mercenaries off our mounted troops until they break Lord Geferin's horse." He wrote quickly on a scrap of paper and handed it over.

"Captain-General." Tathrin offered a salute before stowing the paper safely inside his jerkin. Once the cavalry were engaged on both flanks of the field, battle would be well and truly joined.

Saedrin send he'd arrive safely to repeat Evord's words himself. He didn't want to fall victim to an arrow, waiting for some sharp-eyed company captain to send a runner to retrieve the written message from his body. Sending aid for a wounded galloper would be a secondary consideration.

On his way towards Evord's right-hand regiments, he spurred his horse past Ridianne the Vixen and her retinue. She was just as busy, taking charge of her side of the battle.

CHAPTER THIRTY-SEVEN
Karn

The Battle of Pannal,
in the Lescari Dukedom of Triolle,
1st of For-Winter

HE WAS GLAD Lord Geferin had taken command.
The Parnilesse lord understood the need for swift
decisions in the midst of a battle. If such choices
proved wrong, then action to salvage the situation
was still possible. Hesitation invariably proved fatal.
Karn knew that, if Duke Iruvain didn't.

Lord Geferin had chosen the best ground available
once it was clear the Soluran's army was close
enough to attack their rearguard in the morning.
He'd wasted no time calling a halt for what remained
of the night. He hadn't bothered explaining why
still attempting to reach Pannal and the bridge was
folly. Ignoring Duke Iruvain's protests, he'd sent his
lieutenants and his orders to all the captains.

He'd paid no heed to which ducal symbols were interwoven with mercenary badges or to militia colours, black and dark green or paler green and yellow. When Duke Iruvain had protested, Lord Geferin had told him bluntly this battle was now a Parnilesse concern. Duke Iruvain had flown into a rage, storming off to his tent.

Was Duchess Litasse's safety a Parnilesse concern? Karn could admire Lord Geferin's military prowess but he didn't like the way the nobleman looked at Her Grace on this journey. He'd insisted on sending a company of his own blue-sashed men to escort her carriage to the bridge. Karn had heard him order their captain to take her to Parnilesse Castle and with Pelletria dead, the duchess had no one she trusted with her.

But she had ordered him to remain with Duke Iruvain. She didn't trust Lord Geferin either. Let the runes roll where they may, she had said bitterly. If her husband fell fairly in battle, so be it and he could make his excuses to Saedrin. But Karn must make sure Iruvain didn't fall to a Parnilesse knife in the back. Litasse told Karn she dreaded finding herself widowed at Lord Geferin's mercy, her claims on Sharlac merely one of her assets.

Karn supposed that was reason enough to keep Duke Iruvain alive if he could, for the moment at least. He watched a mounted messenger negotiate the narrow paths winding between the clumps of trees on the valley's side. Reaching more open ground by the river, the man lashed his horse into a gallop. He forced his horse to swim the river and cut behind the first bridge between the weary remnants of Triolle's forces holding the road. His blue sash bright over his black and green livery, he swiftly carried fresh orders to the Parnilesse mercenaries holding their far-left flank.

Karn didn't think they'd be troubled any time soon. The Parnilesse mounted mercenaries had halted the charge by Marlier's cavalry and the Dalasorian lancers supporting them. They were fighting hand to hand, horses biting and kicking. The Dalasorian horse archers supposedly supporting Marlier could only vacillate some distance behind. Any arrows risked killing friends as readily as foes.

The Triolle mercenary companies holding the road had no such concerns. Their bowmen were sending flight after flight of shafts into the Marlier foot soldiers. The Vixen's rabble were already advancing more slowly than the exiles' mercenaries on their left hand. How far would their battle line bend before Lord Geferin could try breaking it?

How were their horsemen faring on the other end of the battle line? Karn looked northwards, towards the byway that cut eastwards to the ford across the river. From this vantage point Lord Geferin had chosen, on the southern edge of the coppiced woods, Karn could just make out the fierce fighting between Dalasorian lancers and the Parnilesse mounted regiments. Lord Geferin's horse were holding their own.

Karn contemplated the Soluran's regiments steadily advancing to the river. He wasn't at all sure which mercenary companies now fought for the enemy. Without Master Hamare to coordinate Triolle's enquiry agents, the reports reaching Duke Iruvain had been fragmentary and confusing. Worse, Lord Geferin made scant use of his scouts and shared little of their news with Duke Iruvain. Karn wasn't impressed.

At least the Parnilesse lord had insisted his own retinue and Duke Iruvain's assemble as one on the battlefield. Duke Iruvain chose to interpret this as belated respect for his superior rank. Karn suspected Lord Geferin simply wanted Iruvain on a short leash. Karn had no qualms about cutting them both free if needs must. In the meantime, he could unobtrusively edge his horse close enough to the Parnilesse lieutenants to hear the gallopers' reports.

Lord Geferin raised a hand to silence a man who'd raced along the Parnilesse lines as the exiles' foot regiments began fording the river.

"Tell the Flintstrikers' captain to fall back to the woodland. That will frustrate any attempt by their lancers to charge." The Parnilesse lord spoke distinctly, so his clerk could write his words down. "He must hold the line of the byway to make sure we're not outflanked."

Karn was relieved the Parnilesse lord was alert to the potential threat of those lancers. Better yet, the Flintstrikers' Captain Shalmay was one of the most quick-witted commanders wearing Parnilesse colours.

"Tell the captains of the Inchra militia to come forward out of the woodland," Lord Geferin continued. "They're to hold their ground on the Flintstrikers' right or they'll answer for their cowardice to me," he added ominously.

Karn hoped that would stiffen their resolve, if the shock of battle struck hard. Parnilesse's militias might be fresh but they'd not yet been tested like the survivors of Carluse and Tyrle. Well, Lord Geferin's wrath was deservedly feared. Even the rawest unblooded recruit should prefer standing against Dalasorian lances to facing that.

"They're crossing the river!" All Duke Iruvain's attention was on the centre of the battlefield. He beckoned and Karn hurried to his side.

"My compliments to Lord Geferin," he said through gritted teeth. "Might his archers care to follow Triolle's excellent example?" He pointed to the mercenaries behind the first bridge where the high road crossed the two streams. Their arrows were dropping Marlier's swordsmen to the muddy ground, slowing their advance still more.

"Your Grace." Karn dutifully bowed his head and rode for Lord Geferin. He waited until two anxious messengers had delivered fresh news and departed with their instructions.

"What is it?" Lord Geferin's gaze slid towards Duke Iruvain.

Karn chose his words carefully. "His Grace of Triolle is wondering when the archers in our central ranks will curb the exiles' advance."

Lord Geferin's lip curled with amusement. "You may thank His Grace for his concern. He can safely leave ordering this battle to me. Each mercenary captain's company is doing just as I wish. As they will continue to do," he added with a curious smile. "Duke Orlin's coffers of gold are safe in Parnilesse, unlike Duke Iruvain's lead-tainted silver now being counted by those exiles in Triolle Castle." He spoke loudly enough to be heard by everyone close at hand.

Karn's warning glare curbed the indignation of the closest Triolle lieutenants, Lord Roreth chief among them. He wasn't about to see victory handed to the Soluran because Iruvain's fool of a brother started a fight with Lord Geferin's personal guard. Besides, the Parnilesse lord wasn't wrong. Triolle had no coin to buy anyone's loyalty.

He bowed to Lord Geferin's unheeding back. "I will take your assurances to His Grace."

As Karn rode up, Duke Iruvain didn't appear to have heard Lord Geferin's insulting remarks. Huddled in his fur-lined cloak, he was still intent on the battle.

"What did he say?" he demanded

"The archers in the centre of our line are responding." Karn gestured towards the battle. Let Iruvain flatter himself that was on his account.

Parnilesse bowmen were now taking full advantage of the cover the scrubland offered as they loosed a hailstorm of arrows at the Soluran's foot soldiers. The exiles' archers were hanging back behind the advancing companies, replying as best they could. But they were sorely exposed in the wet meadows and dodging Parnilesse arrows made their own volleys horribly ragged. They hadn't been able to fashion nearly enough of the woven lath shields that archers usually favoured.

The enemy's mercenaries knew they would only frustrate the Parnilesse bowmen by closing the gap between them. They pressed forward only to find themselves mired. An unnoticed brook threaded all along the foot of the wooded slope and turned the meadow almost to swamp there.

"That water must be near freezing." Iruvain turned to Karn with sudden surprise. "Aren't you cold? You're not even wearing a cloak."

"I've a padded tunic under my hauberk." Karn rarely paid heed to such things. He'd survived harsher weather than this as a starving child.

Satisfied their centre was holding, he looked briefly to the north. The Dalasorians were gaining no ground against the Parnilesse horse. Better yet, the Soluran's foot troops were now advancing past that skirmish. If the Parnilesse horse could break through, they could cut right around behind the enemy's line.

Karn looked back towards the bridge. The Marlier mercenaries were now returning more consistent bow fire but they hadn't advanced by so much as a plough's length. Presumably some company captain was alert to the dangers of the second cavalry battle that was still raging at that southern end of the field. If the Parnilesse horse broke through there, Marlier's foot soldiers would have to wheel around double-quick to avoid being stabbed in the back.

There was no denying Lord Geferin's skill as a general. Which made it all the more urgent Karn decide what to do for the best, as soon as the battle was won.

Karn looked at the Triolle mercenaries and their militia regiments securing the high road on the far side of the river and the second bridge over the stream. How quickly could he and Iruvain gather up those men and take to the highway ahead of the Parnilesse lord and his retinue?

"Your Grace," he said quietly. "Once the day is won, we should make every effort to catch up with Duchess Litasse and her escort. Lord Geferin can clear up the mess here."

"And hand him all the glory, inside Triolle's borders?" Duke Iruvain objected. "Why such haste just to reassure Litasse?" he hissed with contempt.

"You have shown admirable restraint, every time his lordship has exceeded his authority," Karn said carefully. "I don't believe you need humour him by accepting Duke Orlin's hospitality. There are other refuges open to you both, just until Triolle's reclaimed," he added quickly as Duke Iruvain frowned ominously. "One of those might suit you better than Parnilesse Castle. After all, we'll be hunting fugitives through both halves of winter, until you've brought peace back to your people."

"Yes, we will." Iruvain tried to look as if he had thought the same all along.

"Lord Geferin may like to think defeating this Soluran today will end this exiles' revolt." Karn lowered his voice, confiding. "Your forbearance in not pointing out his folly is commendable, Your Grace."

"What refuge are you suggesting?" the duke asked slowly.

"Why not travel north to Draximal Castle?" Karn looked guilelessly at him. "Duke Secaris will surely wish to hear the true tale of his son's last moments, to honour your valour on that terrible day."

Iruvain's face twisted with misery. "Unless he blames me for Lord Cassat's death."

"Your Grace, a hundred men can say that's not so," protested Karn. "Besides, think of Her Grace. Doesn't she deserve some respite amid friends? Duke Secaris was an ally of Duke Moncan since before her birth."

Iruvain looked thoughtful. "There's every chance he'd welcome her for her father's sake."

"With Duchess Litasse there, so close to the dukedom's borders, and Duke Moncan's eldest surviving child besides," Karn mused, "do you suppose Sharlac's vassal lords would rally to her, if she begged them to rescue her mother?"

Iruvain nodded with grim satisfaction. "That would give Duke Orlin and his ambitious brother pause."

A flurry of horn calls interrupted them.

"What's happening?" Iruvain scanned the battlefield, alarmed.

Karn made a more measured assessment. "Northwards, Your Grace, look."

Beyond the byway, the Dalasorians had put Parnilesse's mounted mercenaries to flight. Companies of mercenary foot soldiers had crossed the river to emerge from a crease in the land, following up this advantage.

"His precious cavalry are in full flight!" Iruvain was clearly torn between satisfaction at this setback for Geferin and a degree of apprehension.

"It's not as bad as it seems." Karn watched the mounted mercenaries turning tail for the north, keenly pursued by the lancers. "They're leading those Dalasorians away from the battle and those enemy foot soldiers will be hard put to threaten our flank."

The grassy meadow between the newly visible enemy mercenaries and the woods where the Flintstrikers lay in wait with the Parnilesse militia was now a morass of mud and blood, of dying men and horses, a formidable barrier to any advance by the Soluran's forces.

But Duke Iruvain was looking at the southern end of the battlefield. "See, there! Is Marlier about to break?"

Parnilesse fortunes were wholly in the ascendant. The Marlier cavalry were fleeing southwards, routed. Horsemen in Parnilesse black and green mercilessly pursued them. The Dalasorians could only retreat towards the dubious safety of their original position on the far side of the valley.

The abrupt end to this cavalry skirmish left the right flank of Marlier's mercenaries wholly exposed. Those Parnilesse mercenaries who'd been waiting behind their mounted allies by the highway were already moving forwards. The Triolle mercenaries were making ready to advance too, their archers still raining down murderous arrows. Marlier's bowmen were replying as best they could but Karn could see the rest of the foot soldiers wavering.

"Ferdain's whore must be regretting her treachery," Duke Iruvain said with vicious satisfaction.

Karn remembered Lord Geferin's smile, so smug and secretive, as he boasted of Duke Orlin's gold. He studied the battle lines. Were Marlier's regiments about to retreat, rather than rout? An astonishing possibility struck him.

"Unless Ridianne has been taking Parnilesse coin all along, in order to secure our victory by turning her coat in this battle."

Duke Iruvain gaped at him. "Do you really think so?"

Chapter Thirty-Eight

Tathrin

The Battle of Pannal,
in the Lescari Dukedom of Triolle,
1st of For-Winter

HE PATTED HIS horse's foam-flecked neck. The bay gelding was sweating though Tathrin's fingers and toes still ached perversely with cold. His arms and thighs burned with the effort of controlling the horse amid the chaos.

Thankfully the snorting beast was calming down. He'd been able to give it its head as it thought it was fleeing the noise and the stink of battle. The ride up the incline towards Evord's standard had slowed its wild gallop and he'd been able to get it in hand.

The captain-general was surrounded by riders from all over the battlefield. Their horses were muddied to the hocks, a few splashed with blood, their eyes rimmed with white. Some were led away, their riders offered fresh mounts brought up by the farriers.

Tathrin wondered how long he and the gelding would have to catch their breath. How long had he been riding to and fro with Evord's concise, precise instructions? He was surprised to see the sun had risen barely a chime's measure since the battle was joined.

His mouth was horribly dry. Was that fear or the cold, dry air? Uncapping his water bottle, he took a measured swallow. It would be days before anyone could drink from these streams or the river down in the valley. Dead men and horses jostled in the swollen currents and an evil log jam already choked the shallow arch of the first little bridge.

Where were Sorgrad and Gren? Looking around, he couldn't see either of them.

"Tathrin!" A lieutenant beckoned him forward.

"Tell Pata Mezian's men they're not to engage the Parnilesse horse again." Evord was concluding his instructions to a Dalasorian woman. "The archers are to hold them off until the lancers can regroup, along with any of the Marlier cavalry who return." Ink spattered his fingers as his pen blotted the scratchy paper. "I'll send word when I want them to attack. For the moment, they must hold the end of the Marlier line. Do you understand me?"

"As you command." The Dalasorian took the paper and blew on it to dry the last shining words. Tucking it deep in her glove, she galloped for the south.

Tathrin would have moved forward but Evord summoned a youthful mercenary wearing the Vixen's badge on his black surcoat.

"Take this to Captain-General Ridianne. She must hold the valley floor. Whatever dispositions she chooses, her men must not advance beyond the river or any further down the high road. Nor must they retreat." Evord paused to look at the seething ranks below. "We have more archers than the enemy. Tell her to promise her bow captains whatever she must to inspire them."

"My lord." The man spurred his dappled horse towards the pierced-fox standard, now quite some distance further along the slope.

Evord finally raised his hand. "Tathrin!"

"Captain-General." The throng parted to let him through.

The Soluran was already writing on the next leaf of his leather-bound memorandum book. "Take this to Captain Chanis of the Wheelwrights. He's to advance to stand with the regiment led by Nyer's Watchmen in the centre. Then the Wheelwrights are to lead that whole left-flank regiment along the byway. I want them to circle around and attack the northern face of that woodland. Nyer's Watchmen will be pushing the Parnilesse line back into the coppices from the centre. I want the Wheelwrights ready to take them in the side."

"As you command." Tathrin quickly searched the northern end of the battle for the brown wheel on a red banner. There it was, solidly planted behind a wall of shields. The regiment led by the Wheelwrights had already forded the river and were now holding a prudent distance behind the carnage of that cavalry battle. Panicked horses rampaging through their ranks could be as lethal as any swordsmen.

Where were Nyer's Watchmen? Tathrin couldn't see their black flag with its white lantern at first. Then he saw them, leading the advance in the centre, trying to avoid the worst of the bogginess around that thrice-cursed, unsuspected brook.

"Tathrin?" Evord sounded amused.

Tathrin saw the captain-general was holding out the written copy of his orders.

"Forgive me." Stowing the paper in his jerkin, Tathrin gathered up his reins.

"No, wait. You need to hear this, all of you." Evord summoned a lean rider in a Shearlings' surcoat. "Reskine, take this to Nyer's Watchmen. They're to cross that brook and take the battle into the coppices. I want Parnilesse's mercenaries driven right back into those woods. Tell Captain Fethin to send the same word all down our line."

He looked around at the waiting gallopers as he handed over this second note to the young Shearling. "That's a general order but just for our regiments, not for Captain-General Ridianne's men. They have their own tasks. Make sure everyone understands that."

"Yes, Captain-General." Tathrin wasn't at all sure he understood. He could see the same uncertainty on several faces.

Evord wrote yet another note. "Tathrin, once you've spoken to Captain Chanis, see if you can gather up any Dalasorian lancers who're still interested in a fight. Invite them to clear the Parnilesse militia out of that northern face of the wood. If they can start any kind of panic, so much the better." He smiled. "Warn Captain Chanis to expect them."

"Yes, Captain-General." Tathrin took the second piece of paper and urged his bay horse northwards along the slope.

His shoulders itched. It seemed suicide to turn his back on the noisy battle in the valley, even though he knew no Parnilesse arrow had a hope of reaching him.

Movement caught his eye and he saw the thin sunlight gleaming on golden hair. Wherever they'd been lurking, one of the regiments of Mountain Men was now making haste down the road. Despite their successive losses through the campaign, they were still a formidable fighting force. Were Sorgrad and Gren with them? This was no time to wait and see. Tathrin had orders to deliver.

Crossing the road, he cut through a triangular field of yellowing grass to reach the byway. The track was badly rutted and with the sun rising, the frost was melting. He slowed as much as he dared. The last thing he needed was to lame his horse so far from any hope of a remount. Tathrin could see Dalasorian horses loose amid the aftermath of the cavalry battle but he wouldn't wager a bent copper cut-piece on his chances of catching one.

On the far side of the river, some of the Wheelwrights were busy plundering the dead of the Parnilesse horsemen. More were looking impatiently towards the main battle, slamming their swords on their shields, bellowing encouragement to their friends or abuse at the distant foe. The breeze ripped their words to shreds.

The clamour irked his horse and the bay gelding tossed its head, snorting. Tathrin's insistent hands only roused its rebellious instincts. It stamped and made a half-hearted attempt to rear. Leaning forwards, Tathrin used his heels, forcing it on towards the ford where the river cut through the byway.

Two men in Parnilesse black and green, breeched and booted, leaped up from the bushes. Tathrin's hand drew his sword before he even thought of it. He slashed at the man thrusting a long blade up at his belly. Some fraction of his mind was relieved to see the second attacker was more intent on grabbing the horse's bridle. He hacked again at the first man's jabbing sword, unable to reach the bastard with a killing blow from so high up in the saddle.

The gelding reared right up, front hooves flailing. Tathrin gripped desperately with his knees. If he lost his seat on its back, he was dead. The second man recoiled but only for a moment. He dodged forwards as the horse dropped back down onto all fours. The horse snapped at his snatching hand but he hooked his fingers inside its leather cheek strap. The gelding tried to rear again, wrenching its head aside. Now the Parnilesse horseman used all his weight to hold it down.

Forced back a pace, the first swordsman still watched for his chance. He stepped in, his sword lightning fast. The point drove deep into Tathrin's gut, slicing through his leather jerkin. He gasped as the steel plates behind the leather were driven hard into his belly. His sword came down on his attacker's head. Sorgrad's endless, repetitive lessons meant Tathrin's arm knew how to respond even if his mind was reeling with shock. The steel blade smashed through the man's temple, shattering his cheek and his eye socket. He fell backwards screaming through the crimson ruin of his broken jaw.

Tathrin's horse shrieked and recoiled from the spraying blood. He nearly lost hold of his sword. More by luck than judgement as the panicked beast fought him, he landed a blow on the second horseman still clinging grimly onto the bridle. There wasn't much force to the strike, only enough to leave a deep gash in his forearm, not cleaving right through his wrist.

The man fell away all the same. Tathrin saw a bloody wound in his thigh where the gelding's frantic hoof had caught him. Whatever damage the horse had done, the man couldn't run. He stumbled away, one bloody hand clutching his wounded arm.

"We'll get him for you!"

A handful of the Wheelwrights were running across the ploughed soil to the river, swords drawn. Three plunged into the water, hallooing as if they hunted a deer.

Tathrin let them pass and forced his horse into the water, looking around warily all the while. Cold, turbulent water tugged at his boots. The horse snorted, calmer as the river washed the blood from its chest and flanks.

"Are you hurt, lad?" demanded the first of the men waiting on the far bank.

"Do we have orders?" shouted a man in a russet surcoat.

"For Captain Chanis." Answering their questions saved Tathrin from having to think about what he'd just done.

The first man approached the bay gelding, his voice soothing. "Come on, lad, let's be having you." As he took firm hold of its bridle, he hissed between his teeth. "Your boy took a nasty cut."

Horrified, Tathrin saw blood trickling down the horse's forequarter. He couldn't decide which appalled him most: that the beast was hurt, or the realisation that he was the one who had wounded it as he hacked at the Parnilesse man's arm.

"You have orders? Let's have them!" Now Captain Chanis was hurrying forwards, his standard-bearer at his side. His company gathered itself in readiness, a shiver spreading through the ranks like wind through wheat.

Shoving all other considerations aside, Tathrin handed him the paper and repeated Evord's orders. "I'm going on to see if the Dalasorians can muster some lancers to help you."

Captain Chanis shook his head. "Halcarion help you with that."

He didn't waste time on further conversation, making haste back to his men. As runners from other companies approached, he shouted brisk orders to send them haring back.

Tathrin sat on the motionless horse. Its head drooped miserably. Stripping a glove from one shaking hand, he reached hesitantly under his jerkin. He flinched as he found a painful bruise, and his fingers were still horribly cold. But as best he could tell, his skin was intact. The armoured jerkin had saved him.

Saved him to kill a man. He could still see every detail of the dead man's ruined face, smashed to pulp as he ripped his sword free. He didn't need to look around to know exactly where that corpse lay. He didn't want to look around, for fear of seeing the wounded man who'd fled being hacked to pieces by the pursuing Wheelwrights.

But he knew what Sorgrad would say. This was a battle. Men died. Better him than you. Gren would be even blunter. Go and spew up, find a whore to get you thinking with your cock instead of your head or get so drunk you can't think at all. Do whatever you must, but get over it and fast.

Tathrin couldn't imagine doing any of those things. He still felt sick, a pain in his guts that had nothing to do with the bruise spreading across his navel. He had killed a man. He'd blooded his sword before, at Emirle Bridge, but he'd been able to kid himself he'd only inflicted wounds in all the confusion. He'd killed one of Wynald's Warband in Losand, but that mercenary had been out to kill him. Those poor bastards hiding by the river had only sought a horse to escape their own death. And Tathrin hadn't even killed that man cleanly. What agonies had he endured in the endless moments before his last breath, choking on his own blood?

No. He couldn't think about what he'd done. Not now. He had a job to do. Rigid with the effort of not looking backwards, Tathrin concentrated desperately on the advancing regiment's prospects.

He couldn't see any enemy forces able to stop them attacking the northern flank of the woods now that the Parnilesse horsemen were broken. The companies of foot soldiers in the centre of the battle were already splashing through the brook. The archery companies were holding back to shoot straight over their heads, turning the lie of the land against Lord Geferin's men now. Their merciless arrows were driving the Parnilesse men back to take cover in the scrubby woods. Yelling triumphantly, the foot soldiers pressed on up the slope.

Further down the valley, he could see the Marlier regiments were now fully engaged with those mercenaries who'd fought for Duke Iruvain. Neither side seemed to be gaining a single stride of ground in the fight for the road. The Triolle militia were still solidly arrayed between the two little bridges.

Beyond that, Tathrin had no idea what was happening. He couldn't see anything past the rise in the land where Captain-General Evord's standard flapped in the wind. He could only hope the Dalasorians on the Vixen's right flank were still holding off the Parnilesse cavalry and the mercenaries backing them. Well, Captain-General Evord was trusting Ridianne to manage her half of the battle, even if Tathrin couldn't see her banner any more.

He could see Lord Geferin's blue standard with its black and green blazon. Tathrin held his horse still for a moment. He'd just realised something crucial. The Parnilesse lord had an excellent view of the mayhem around the bridges, where Marlier's forces threatened Triolle's mercenaries. But if Lord Geferin were to look northwards, he would only see as far as the field where Tathrin now stood. The undulating slope cluttered with copses and brambles would completely block his view of the northernmost face of the battle. Lord Geferin and Duke Iruvain would have absolutely no idea what the Wheelwrights and Nyer's Watchmen were up to. Not unless some runners brought them news.

Unexpected exhilaration warming him, Tathrin spurred his horse towards a knot of Dalasorians who were busily rounding up loose horses. "Where's your clan lord?" he yelled.

One replied in his own tongue, incomprehensible. Another waved Tathrin towards a group clustered around a scarlet and yellow pennant.

"Rega Taszar!" Tathrin waved as he recognised their captain.

"Good day to you." Grim weariness sat oddly on the Dalasorian's youthful features. He was splashed with blood but as best Tathrin could tell, none of it was his own.

"Captain-General Evord's compliments," he said swiftly. "Can you gather your lancers and force an attack into those woods?" He pointed. "As quickly as you can. The captain-general wants to drive the Parnilesse flank back before Lord Geferin can learn what's amiss. Hunt down anyone making a break to carry him news."

Rega Taszar frowned. "Don't you think it's time for them to earn their bread?" He nodded towards the Wheelwrights who were now rapidly advancing, with the massed ranks of the regiment following. He gestured towards his countrymen who were tending their own wounds and those of their horses. "Haven't we done our duty?"

Tathrin flinched as he saw a Dalasorian cut the

throat of a broken-legged horse. He hardened his heart. "I'm just bringing you the captain-general's orders. What reply would you have me give him? What would you have me tell Sia Kersain?" Would putting the burden of refusal onto Rega Taszar tip the balance?

The young Dalasorian captain sighed. "We will do what we can. But after today—" He broke off with a shake of his head, shouting to his companions in their own tongue. Swift horn calls rang through the clear air

Tathrin's horse shied away. The bay gelding was wounded, exhausted and badly unnerved. He let it turn away, but once they reached the byway, he kicked it remorselessly into a canter. It could rest soon enough. Once he returned to Evord's retinue, he could demand a remount.

Riding back, he had a clear view of the valley. The battle was rapidly gaining pace, growing ever more deafening. In the centre, archery duels had given way to hand-to-hand slaughter. Nyer's Watchmen and the companies following them were pushing right into the scrubby trees. He couldn't see which side had the upper hand but Evord's men weren't being pushed back. That had to count for something.

Further along the dank valley bottom, everything was changing. The Marlier regiments were forcing their way forwards, step by bloody step, out of the sodden meadows. They left countless dead behind but they weren't stopping now.

Tathrin couldn't tell which corpses were Ridianne's mercenaries or Parnilesse's. Wet and muddy, their motley surcoats and jerkins were indistinguishable at this distance. But he could see the black and green liveries of Parnilesse's militia regiments clearly though. Their banners were wavering horribly in the face of the Marlier mercenaries' relentless approach.

Down by the bridges, where the high road crossed the streams running into the river, more of the Vixen's swordsmen were laying into the mercenaries flying Triolle colours. Given all that those companies had suffered, the defeat at Tyrle and their long, confused retreat to Triolle and on to Adel Castle, Tathrin was astonished to see them hold their ground so doggedly.

Behind them, however, the Triolle militia in their pale green and yellow were already visibly retreating. The first companies had already reached the second bridge. Nothing stood between them and headlong flight along the highway.

That was all well and good, but as Tathrin rode closer towards Evord's standard, he saw serious cause for concern. Those Marlier companies closest to the Soluran's regiments were following their lead into the woods. The Vixen's regiments attacking the Triolle forces were forcing their foes away from the treacherous ground by the river. As a consequence, the middle of the Marlier line was thinning dangerously.

Tathrin could see Lord Geferin's standard amid a cluster of mercenary banners. He was rallying every company not yet inextricably engaged. Was he preparing an attempt to break through the Marlier line? It looked horribly like it to Tathrin.

He saw the pale heads of the Mountain Men jogging down the road. Captain-General Evord must have anticipated this. The uplanders would reinforce that weakness in their line. As long as they could get there in time.

What would happen if they didn't? Tathrin still couldn't see what was happening on the far side of the rising land. He remembered the Parnilesse horsemen had been regrouping after their first punishing assault on Marlier's cavalry. Were the Dalasorian horse archers still holding them off?

If not, if Lord Geferin could break through the line and the Parnilesse cavalry followed his lead and attacked, more than half the Vixen's companies, the men who were desperately trying to force their way through to the bridges to take the high road, would find themselves with enemies on both sides.

Tathrin saw Duke Iruvain's standard. He was rallying the Triolle militiamen. His heart pounding, he rode towards Captain-General Evord's banner. What orders would the Soluran give Tathrin to ride out with next?

CHAPTER THIRTY-NINE

Karn

**The Battle of Pannal,
in the Lescari Dukedom of Triolle,
1st of For-Winter**

THEY MUST RALLY the Triolle militia. They had to hold the road and that second bridge long enough for the Parnilesse attack to break the Marlier line. There was still no sign of that whore Ridianne giving way.

The river was foul with bloody carcasses. Karn had to kick them aside as he forced his horse across. As the shivering animal scrambled up the far bank, he rapidly assessed the battle.

Could they still win this? Their best swordsmen had begun this battle already weary and they were tiring fast. Their worst troops were still fresh enough to run away as fast as their legs could carry them. What else could you expect from pox-ridden militiamen?

"How dare he?" Duke Iruvain raged. "Ordering me here and there, as if I were some sergeant-at-arms?"

"Your Grace, this battle is balanced on a knife edge." His sword drawn, Karn placed his horse between Iruvain and the Triolle mercenaries who were still holding their ground.

He wasn't going to be caught unawares if some Marlier swordsman came running to murder the duke. The youthful nobles serving as Parnilesse and Triolle's lieutenants would be no protection. They were milling about in confusion as the entangled retinues separated. Karn looked briefly for Lord Roreth but couldn't see where he was.

He risked a quick glance over his shoulder. Good. Iruvain's presence seemed to be bolstering the livery-clad militia. If they weren't advancing, they weren't retreating any further.

Unlike the Parnilesse regiments in the centre of the battle. They were still falling back amid the copses and brambles, all cohesion lost. Unable to draw up in a solid line, they were beginning to panic. If the enemy couldn't see them, they couldn't see each other and take heart knowing friends stood with them. Instead, they feared every bush hid a foe and shrank still further back.

What was going on? Had Lord Geferin had any recent reports from his right flank? Karn scowled. Down here in the valley bottom, all he could see were the enemy archers, unable to ply their trade, now busy amid the fallen stranded by the tide of battle. The exiles' wounded were swiftly carried away towards their surgeons. Parnilesse's helpless men were stripped of their helmets, the better to land a crushing blow to finish them off, their bodies swiftly looted.

Could he get a clearer view if he moved away?

"Men of Triolle! To your duke!" Iruvain stood in his stirrups as his standard-bearer swept the great green grebe to and fro. "To your duke! Let us drive these exiles and thieves from our precious home. They cannot defeat us! They only fight for coin and plunder. You fight for your families and the land that you love!"

Karn closed his ears to Iruvain's exhortations. Such speeches might sound very fine declaimed by festival players. Here in the din of battle, he doubted anyone heard half the duke's words.

He looked south and west. The battle was going better there. The beleaguered Triolle mercenaries need only hold a little longer. The Parnilesse horsemen who'd successfully rebuffed Marlier's first cavalry charge had finally regrouped. They were launching an attack of their own, hooves thundering as they broke from a canter into a gallop.

The Parnilesse horse would cut deep into the Marlier flank. Those cursed Dalasorian horse archers were doing their best to stop them but most of their arrows were falling short. Some men fell, a few beasts stumbled, but the Parnilesse charge didn't falter.

"You sons of noseless whores!" Karn gripped his reins as a fresh mounted force crested the shoulder of land behind the rebels' gold and white standard. They spurred their steeds straight at the Parnilesse horse. Dalasorian lancers.

Where had they come from? The Soluran must have held them in reserve. Worse, they'd rallied the remnants of the Marlier cavalry that Karn had thought hopelessly scattered. Stirrup to stirrup, mingled troops of lancers and mounted swordsmen were charging straight down the hill at the Parnilesse horse. Appalled as he was, Karn had to admire such riding.

"They've seen them. They've seen them!" Iruvain reassured his threadbare retinue, palpably relieved.

Amid ear-splitting horn calls, the Parnilesse riders swerved away from their intended victims to meet this new assault. The two mounted lines met with a shattering crash.

"Now you see our strategy!" Duke Iruvain pointed to the far side of the river where three companies of Parnilesse cavalry still remained, backed by a sizeable contingent of foot soldiers. "Now we will commit our reserves, mow down those grassland scum and then we scatter the Marlier line!"

Karn watched those distant standards closely. Lord Geferin had already sent three messengers to demand those mercenaries cross the river and press home the attack on the Vixen. Karn still couldn't see them moving.

He saw a single rider leaving the cluster of the captains' standards. But the horseman wasn't riding for the bridge, towards Lord Geferin and the Parnilesse lord's retinue. He was fording the river, swerving right around the fighting between the Parnilesse horse and the newly arrived lancers. He was heading straight for the cream and gold of the exiles' commander's banner.

The rider must be some galloper from the Soluran, sent with a message for those Parnilesse mercenaries. Karn recalled what he'd heard of Duke Garnot's first battle with the exiles. Captain-General Evord had spent long years fighting Lescar's battles. He had plenty of experienced captains on his side, who knew how to exploit all the rivalries and grudges of hired fighting men. What had the Soluran said?

"What are they doing? Are they coming back to the bridge?" Arriving at his side, Duke Iruvain watched the contingent south of the river begin a purposeful retreat.

"Perhaps." Karn didn't think so.

"We must clear the road!" Iruvain began shouting. "Make way! Make way! So our brave allies can get through. They must bring all their strength to bear as they reinforce our line!"

Karn saw the distance between the road and the retreating Parnilesse forces widening rapidly. They were leaving.

"Triolle! Stand!" Iruvain's voice cracked with outrage.

The liveried militia could see the Parnilesse reserve were deserting. That made up the waverers' minds. As those men began moving down the road away from the battle, militiamen who might have stood firm found themselves left exposed. Looking uncertainly at each other, they began walking backwards. The Triolle retreat towards the bridge began gathering pace.

"Signal a rally to my standard!" Iruvain raged at his closest lieutenant.

Karn ignored the ineffectual horn calls. Those Triolle mercenaries still doggedly holding their ground would soon realise no one guarded their backs. The Marlier regiments would see it too and that would give them fresh heart. The best Triolle's forces could hope for now was a defensible retreat to hold the second bridge.

He searched for Lord Geferin's standard. There was no sign of it leading any attempt to break through the enemy line. Those cursed Mountain Men had arrived to reinforce that transient weakness and Marlier's troops were fighting with renewed vigour. Parnilesse mercenaries were enmeshed in the slaughter.

Karn looked further up the valley. He still couldn't see the blue banner with its crossed sword and halberd. Was the Parnilesse lord hidden by the trees? Karn could see their own forces gaining no ground. Worse, the exiles were thrusting deeper into the woods.

"You will be pilloried! You will be flogged, and your wives and children!" Iruvain was yelling impotent threats after the fleeing militiamen. "You will be thrown naked into the gutters to starve, with every member of your families!"

Lord Geferin had placed too much reliance on the slope, Karn concluded. He'd trusted too readily in the cover offered by the trees and brambles. He had been too focused on the battle with Marlier down in the valley bottom. Every time he'd seen a possible route to victory, all his attention had been seduced.

What had actually happened on their far-right flank once the Dalasorians had broken the Parnilesse cavalry on the byway? Hadn't it occurred to Lord Geferin to wonder at the lack of reports from those regiments supposedly holding the northern face of the woodland? Didn't he think that might mean there was no one left in command to send him a runner?

Sudden uproar shook the air. Down in the valley bottom, Karn saw the Triolle mercenaries who'd fought so long and so hard were throwing up their hands in surrender. Men dropped to their knees, casting weapons aside. Standards were dipped so their streamers of green and yellow could be torn off and stamped into the mud.

There was no one to stop them. No one to offer them hope of reinforcement. Beyond all that chaos, the Parnilesse horsemen were still locked in vicious combat with the returning Marlier cavalry and the Dalasorians' reserve.

"Your Grace, we must go." Karn reached for Duke Iruvain's bridle.

"How dare they?" The duke gaped at the abject scene. "How dare they?"

"Your Grace!" Karn wrenched at the horse's head. "The tide of battle has turned against us here. Lord Geferin may yet prevail but we must get you to safety."

Their immediate situation was grave but escape was still possible. Not all of the Triolle mercenaries had surrendered. Enough were still fighting to slow Marlier's men's advance. The rest of the enemy were emptying their new prisoners' pockets and squabbling over the plunder. None of them had yet seen the tempting prizes of Duke Iruvain's retinue.

"Very well." Iruvain belatedly realised their peril, his irate colour fading. "Which is our safest route?"

"The high road," Karn decided. "We must catch Duchess Litasse and her escort. I don't recommend heading for Parnilesse now, Your Grace."

"Not when Lord Geferin will surely find some way to blame me for all this." Iruvain looked dubiously at the second bridge.

Triolle militiamen were shoving others aside in their desperation to flee. There were fist-fights and men grappling on the ground.

"You, go ahead and clear the road!" the duke shouted angrily at his standard-bearer. Several of the young lieutenants immediately obeyed, drawing their swords and spurring their horses.

"Your Grace, we can just go around," shouted Karn.

Though going southwards meant crossing the road and the second of these infuriating streams. Shallow though the waters were, even that slight delay might cost them dearly, if the Marlier mercenaries saw them running. Those men would already be calculating the ransoms they'd extort from the captains who'd surrendered to them. The chance of capturing Triolle's duke would look as good as gold in their hands.

The Parnilesse contingent who'd declined Lord Geferin's summons were also riding away in that direction. Karn didn't relish the thought of encountering them. Iruvain's retinue would be utterly outnumbered and again, the duke himself would be a prize worth capturing. Unless those scum decided it was safer to simply kill every witness to their bad faith. What was one more dead duke of Lescar?

He looked northwards. Risking the mayhem unfolding in the woods was unthinkable. That left the narrow gap between the coppiced slope and the river. That was their only clear route away from this carnage.

Could any enemy companies pursue them if they went that way? No, the evenly matched battle between Marlier and Parnilesse still raged in the centre. The Mountain Men were intent on a contingent of Triolle mercenaries who'd somehow escaped capture thus far.

Then Karn saw the cream and gold standard of the exiles moving slowly down the far side of the valley. Captain-General Evord's command company was escorted by a regiment of lancers, another of mercenary cavalry and a second sizeable contingent of those accursed Mountain Men. Ridianne the Vixen's scarlet and silver standard led her retinue to meet them.

"Your Grace, we must ride due east." He pointed. "Once we're sure we're not pursued, we can cut back towards the road."

"Very well." Iruvain spurred his horse. His personal guard and some of the young lieutenants, Lord Roreth among them, drew close.

As they pushed back across the river, fighting through the noisome corpses, Karn kept half an eye on the bridge. Some of the Triolle militia were looking their way, shouting and waving. Were they accusing Iruvain of deserting or begging for his help?

Safely on the eastern bank of the river, he chanced a longer look. So that was what the militia were shouting about. A contingent of Marlier mercenaries had seen their chance to snare a duke. They were running full tilt down the road.

Good luck to them, Karn thought distantly. He and Iruvain and most of the ducal retinue were mounted on comparatively fresh horses. A morning standing watching a battle had been no great trial. Their pursuers were on foot and exhausted.

Iruvain wasn't so sanguine. He shook Lord Roreth by the shoulder and pointed to the chaos by the bridge. "Tell them to hold and I'll ennoble every man and boy among them!"

"What?" The younger man gaped at him, pallid with fear.

"Do as your duke bids you!" Karn slashed his own whip at the rump of Roreth's horse. The startled beast sprang forwards, the young man helpless to hold it. Several of the noble lieutenants followed him without thinking.

Satisfied the Marlier mercenaries would have rich prizes to squabble over now, Karn lashed Iruvain's horse to a canter. "Your Grace, think of the duchess! We must ride to her aid!"

Whatever Iruvain said in reply was lost amid the disorder. Using his whip and elbows, Karn forced their way to the front of the other riders. They soon escaped the treacherous ground of the water meadows for the firmer grass of the chase between the woods and the river. He forced his horse to a gallop with brutal heels.

"Ware!" Someone away to Iruvain's left started yelling. "Ware foe!"

"Parnilesse! Parnilesse!"

Panicked militiamen in black and green burst out of the scrub. Iruvain instinctively reined in, with the rest of the riders slowing in confusion.

"Report!" Karn shouted promptly.

Instinct brought a sergeant-at-arms to run alongside his stirrup.

"It's murder, my lord," the man gasped. "They sent their northlanders through the woods. Their foot soldiers followed, to take us in the flank. Our lines are all broken. We had to run or we'd have been surrounded and cut to pieces!"

"Then save yourselves." Karn gathered his reins.

"My lord!" The sergeant grabbed at his boot. "Take me up! I have children—"

Karn kicked him in the face. The man fell back clutching his broken nose. Outraged, a man swung his halberd to hook Karn out of his saddle. His retaliating swordstroke splintered the shaft but didn't break it. No matter. His backhand cut ripped deep into the militiaman's shoulder, forcing him to drop the weapon with an agonised cry.

All around, Duke Iruvain's retinue spurred on their horses to escape such clutching hands. Karn used the flat of his blade and, here and there, the edge on men and horses alike to secure his place behind the duke.

"Ware to the left!"

The shout came again and so did the answering cry.

"Parnilesse!"

"Geferin!" Iruvain jerked on his reins.

His horse jibbed so hard that Karn's mount ran into its shoulder. The two horses reared up, fighting their bridles, long yellow teeth snapping at each other. Karn smacked his outraged steed hard between the ears to cow it.

It was indeed the Parnilesse standard, with a sizeable number of militia pennants and a few mercenary banners besides. Lord Geferin might not have achieved whatever he'd sought in those woods but he was holding this hastily assembled regiment together. They were retreating swiftly but in good order.

"Do we join forces, Your Grace?" A rider in their vanguard shouted back over his shoulder.

Karn saw other lieutenants already turning their horses to do that.

"No," he shouted before the duke could answer. "We're mounted and too many of them are on foot. They'll only slow us down!"

"Onwards," Iruvain roared. "Lord Geferin can make shift for himself!"

They swept past the motley Parnilesse regiment. Signal horns called, militia flags waved and Lord Geferin's standard waved an unmistakable summons. Iruvain ignored all their appeals. They quickly left the broken edge of the woodland behind, riding across open fields. There were no crops or herds to hamper them in this wintry season.

How soon could they cut back to the faster going of the road? Where was the next safe place to cross the river? Karn couldn't see anything useful past the riders crowding ahead of Iruvain.

"Ware horsemen!" One of the foremost lieutenants was pointing north.

Karn had to fall back to get a clear sight of this new threat. Dalasorian lancers, all unbloodied, their horses showing scant sign of toil. Where by everything sacred and profane had they come from?

Where were they going? The Parnilesse force was closer but far more threatening. Lord Geferin's men had already seen this unexpected menace. They were closing ranks, presenting a bristling palisade of halberds to impale any lancers' charge.

That left Duke Iruvain's retinue the easier prey, but they were already well ahead of the lancers. Even if they were pursued, they should still get clear away.

In the very instant Karn thought this, a horse ahead stumbled on freshly ploughed furrows. Its fall brought down three more. Duke Iruvain's guards scattered in confusion.

"Your Grace!" Karn risked a glance to see if the lancers were galloping to profit from their mishap. To his intense relief, he saw they were already attacking the Parnilesse militiamen.

"We must make for the duchess, and Draximal! If Triolle is lost for this winter, there's still Sharlac to reclaim!"

Iruvain wasn't listening. As his horse whirled around, he had seen the lancers' assault. His face slackened with horrified surprise.

"Geferin's standard." He looked at Karn, appalled. "It's fallen. What's happened?"

Even by Iruvain's standards that was a singularly pointless question.

"Your Grace, I don't know." Karn snapped his whip at Iruvain's steed. This time the grey was ready and he barely avoided being bitten. "One way or another, the news will reach us. Do you want to hear it safe in Draximal or locked inside your own dungeons?" he challenged the duke.

Scarlet in the face, Iruvain wrenched his horse's head around and galloped away.

Karn followed hard on his heels, to make certain he didn't waver. The remnants of the retinue were still in utter disarray. Some hesitated, shouting, looking for someone to lead them. Some were already galloping off, grimly intent on their own salvation. Seeing Iruvain fleeing, ones and twos followed, here and there a handful joining them.

Karn ignored them all. They were no longer his concern. With Lord Geferin fallen or captured, by whatever accursed luck that had happened, the Soluran had won the battle. Parnilesse and Triolle were now defeated as thoroughly as Sharlac and Carluse. Draximal was a spent force after the disaster at Tyrle and, abandoned by the Vixen, Marlier had no hope of raising an army to challenge these exiles.

The Soluran had waged a brilliant campaign. Very well. This war wasn't over. There were other ways to fight, with words and with all the subtle arts that Master Hamare had excelled in. Karn hoped Duchess Litasse would prove herself his old master's worthy pupil. And if that bastard Minelas had achieved nothing else, the renegade mage had deprived the exiles of their intelligencer, that treacherous bitch Lady Alaric or whatever her real name was.

Whatever else might happen, Karn was determined he and Litasse would still have their revenge on those Mountain-born assassins, whatever their arcane talents. One thing Minelas's death proved was that wizards were as vulnerable as anyone else to steel in the gut.

CHAPTER FORTY
Aremil

Carluse Castle,
6th of For-Winter

THE KNOCK WASN'T the one he longed for. It was welcome nonetheless.

"Come in!" Aremil reached for his crutches.

"No, don't disturb yourself," Tathrin protested as he entered.

Too late. Aremil was already on his feet, tucking one prop under an arm to hold out a hand to his friend.

"It's so good to see you." He meant it with all his heart.

Better yet, face to face, Tathrin couldn't see all the reasons for his relief. Nor would he be burdened with Tathrin's exhausting hopes and fears. Aremil longed for a respite from Artifice's intimacy.

"You look tired." Concern furrowed Tathrin's brow.

As Aremil withdrew his hand, he felt the calluses on Tathrin's palm. His friend was no longer a scholar. He tried for a light tone. "I'll wager the shadows under my eyes are equal to your own. Have you looked in a mirror recently?"

"No." Tathrin grinned as he fingered his stubble. "But are you sure you're quite well? You had that cough." He looked at the modest fire in the hearth. "Are you keeping warm?"

"Master Welgren was satisfied my chest was clear before he left for Triolle. He wouldn't have gone otherwise." He sought to turn the conversation. "Are Sorgrad and Gren not with you?"

"They've gone to see Charoleia." Tathrin looked anxious. "How will they find her?"

"Well enough," Aremil said slowly. "Master Welgren wouldn't have left if her hurts weren't mending. She says this is by no means the worst she has suffered."

"Saedrin save us."

Aremil saw his own appalled reaction reflected in Tathrin's brown eyes. If that were true, just what was Charoleia's true history?

The younger man sighed heavily. "I'll call on her later, if she's not too weary."

Aremil saw strain deepening the creases that this past year's sun, wind and sorrow had carved in Tathrin's face.

"She doesn't blame you for Trissa's death."

"I know." Tathrin's nod was wholly unconvincing.

Artifice itself wouldn't persuade Tathrin not to blame himself, Aremil reflected. For being too slow, too late, for not even being the one to kill Minelas. The only thing that stopped him castigating himself was dwelling miserably on the man he had cut down on the battlefield at Pannal. Even as he told himself he'd had no choice, Tathrin was still revolted by what he had done.

Failla stuck her head around the door. "I've asked the steward to send you some wine."

"Thank you." Tathrin's glance at Aremil involuntarily betrayed him.

"Please, join us." Aremil gestured towards the settle by the fire and returned to his own chair.

If nothing else, Failla's presence would save Tathrin from having to repeat their conversation. Anyway, Aremil had no real secrets from her these days.

"Failla has proved invaluable," he told Tathrin with a smile, "rallying support from the Guilds and the common folk of Carluse."

"I'm glad of it." Tathrin's hand strayed to hers. "Reher will be back to help too, any day now."

Aremil saw this was no news to Failla. That was hardly surprising. Tathrin's desire to see her had grown with every league on the road from Pannal. He must have sought her out as soon as he entered the castle. Still, he'd come straight here after that. Aremil could see Tathrin's boots and breeches still bore all the grime and creases of the road.

"How are things, in Triolle and Tyrle?"

Tathrin leaned back, still holding Failla's hand. "The town of Pannal surrendered without a fight, so we took the most seriously injured there. The walking wounded came back to Triolle."

"What does Master Welgren make of their chances?" Aremil didn't regret his inability to ask the apothecary himself. The last thing he wanted was to endure such pain and loss through the aether.

Tathrin sighed. "He says the toll is sure to rise. So many still linger with cruel wounds and many of those will fester."

"It would have been worse if the battle was in summer." Failla gave his hand a reassuring squeeze.

"True enough." Tathrin managed a brief smile for her. "There were men taken alive off the field a full night and a day after the battle. Can you believe it? Welgren says the cold staunched their wounds before they could bleed to death. He's hopeful for some."

Aremil glanced at the parchment where Dagaran had totalled the latest deaths, the numbers already calamitous. More than a thousand dead on each side. The pyres were still burning, the land for leagues around stripped of firewood, the houses of those who'd fled from both armies demolished for their doors and rafters. There were already reports of deadly flux striking villages along the banks of the Anock, where the unwary or foolhardy had drunk the waters polluted by the dead.

"If we paid a terrible price for our victory," he said grimly, "Triolle and Parnilesse paid as heavily."

More heavily, if Dagaran's numbers were correct. As of this morning, one hundred and sixty-three corpses tilted the balance against the dukes. Would Raeponin call that justice? Aremil had more cause than ever to be grateful he didn't believe in such gods.

"Their mercenaries suffered more losses than their militias." Tathrin frowned. "That so many of the common men fled doubtless helped us to win. The other side of that coin is they're still out there with all their swords and halberds."

"But without their leaders," Aremil pointed out. "And isn't Captain-General 'Evord encouraging them to go home and defend their families?"

"Talagrin knows, we can't defend all the towns and villages." Tathrin was still troubled. "Our offer to save Lescar from ducal rule looks like a basket of bad apples topped with wax ones, for a trickster to sell on market day. Our presence in Triolle is resented far more openly than it is here or in Sharlac."

"Duke Iruvain was never so feared as Duke Garnot," Failla said thoughtfully. "Nor did he prompt such uncertainty and anger as Duke Moncan, when he withdrew into his grief for Lord Jaras."

"What's the latest news from Ashgil?" Aremil hadn't heard anything for two days.

"It's securely held." Tathrin's face cleared a little. "Pata Mezian's Dalasorians made excellent speed from Abray, once they delivered the prisoners from Tyrle into Caladhrian hands."

"I'll make sure Master Gruit knows, the next time I talk with Kerith." Aremil's relief was tempered with recollection of his last conversation with the scholar. "Do you know how many prisoners were taken at Pannal?"

"Not beyond a guess." Tathrin frowned.

Aremil sighed. "Master Gruit tells us the guildmasters in Abray, and the Caladhrian lords, won't stand for us sending them any more prisoners. Far too many have turned to banditry along the Great West Road. Caladhrian militias are hanging any brigands they catch, and doing a fine job by all accounts. But we'll see such vagabonds driven straight back into Lescar from now on."

"Can you ship your captives to Relshaz?" Failla looked at Tathrin. "Like Ridianne sending away those mercenaries that she didn't trust to follow the captain-general?"

Tathrin grimaced. "Have you heard how many of those have already been sold into slavery in the Archipelago?"

Aremil was appalled. "This wizard woman, Mellitha, she told you this?"

Tathrin looked uncomfortable. "Relshazri laws are stern, Sorgrad says. It's easy to make a misstep, especially if you don't know the city."

Aremil knew Tathrin still had his doubts about that wizard woman. Outright fear of the other one, Jilseth, was a dark shadow at the back of his mind. Well, hopefully she was long gone back to the Archmage now the final battle had been won without any illicit magic's assistance.

Aremil was more concerned with another woman. "Have you any fresh news of Ridianne?"

"She marched the remnants of her regiments back to Triolle and they all took boats down the Dyal and along the Marlier coast to Capast." Tathrin looked grim. "Her men took appalling losses."

Aremil hardened his heart. "Then Duke Ferdain won't be able to attack us before spring."

"Aremil!" Tathrin was shocked. "She proved a worthy ally."

"Maybe so, but Duke Ferdain's still our foe." Aremil was unrepentant. "Master Gruit and Kerith say he's been writing to his Caladhrian allies all up the River Rel. They think some of the mercenaries we've sent up the Great West Road have been turning south."

"Marlier's camps always offered mercenaries a safe haven for the winter seasons," Tathrin protested half-heartedly.

Failla looked faintly sick. "Then we'll be fighting again, come the spring?"

"Unless we can find some way to avoid it." Aremil wasn't going to lie to her.

Tathrin rallied. "But the task we set ourselves is nearly done. We've rid Lescar of three dukes and none of the rest can field an army against us."

Failla was still pondering the problem of their mercenary captives. "Is there anywhere else we could send prisoners? Where else do they go in the winter?"

"Carif," Aremil said dourly.

Tathrin sounded less certain. "I've heard rumour that's where the mercenaries who fled the field at Pannal have gone."

"Ready for Duke Orlin to come recruiting in the spring," Aremil said grimly.

"I don't imagine his militiamen will get any choice about re-enlisting." Failla sounded bitter at that thought.

"I don't suppose he'll tolerate the Carifate's claims to self-rule any longer." Tathrin looked thoughtful. "The mercenary companies may well find their choice is to take to their ships or bow their heads to Duke Orlin's yoke."

Aremil remembered the one hopeful straw they could clutch at. "Parnilesse still won't have Lord Geferin to lead their army."

"What happened to him?" Failla seized her chance to ask Tathrin.

Aremil had heard the question whispered all around the castle since the first news of the nobleman's death.

"He died of bad luck more than anything else." Tathrin managed a rueful smile. "Sia Kersain was determined to keep his son out of danger. So when the Dalasorians first charged the Parnilesse cavalry, he ordered Sia Nanas to lead a separate company right around the far side of the woods, to hunt down stragglers and runaways. Sia Nanas wasn't best pleased, but he doesn't ever disobey his father."

Tathrin shook his head, still disbelieving. "He and his men stumbled on Lord Geferin and Duke Iruvain both, fleeing for Pannal. Sia Nanas's archers let loose. I don't imagine they intended much beyond startling their horses. But an arrow skewered Lord Geferin's thigh, pinning him to his saddle. Welgren says the arrowhead cut the great blood vessel. He bled to death before anyone could get him off the horse."

He looked at Aremil with a question of his own. "How's news of his death been received in Parnilesse? What has Jettin had to say? What's Reniack making of it?"

"Has Duke Iruvain fled to Parnilesse?" Failla looked expectantly at Aremil.

"To answer you both, we don't yet know." He glanced at the unhelpful parchments on his desk. "I've reached through the aether time and again and I cannot make Jettin hear me. He hasn't used his own Artifice to send me news, not for ten days or more now."

"Is he injured or captured?" Tathrin was alarmed.

Aremil wished the answer were so simple. "No, I can feel his presence though the aether. He's just being wilfully deaf."

"Could Branca—?" Tathrin broke off, self-conscious. "No, forgive me. Failla said she's been nursing Charoleia night and day."

So Failla had given him all the castle gossip, Aremil reflected. And however hard he tried to hide his worry and his chagrin, he assumed Tathrin knew Branca was still avoiding him as assiduously as she had since her rescue from Adel Castle.

He saved Tathrin from his embarrassment. "Branca has tried to reach Jettin, as has Kerith, but he's refusing all overtures of Artifice."

Kerith had told him so and passed on that same message from Branca. That she had reached through the aether to the scholar rather than talking to him herself had hurt Aremil more than anything else.

"What do you suppose is going on in Parnilesse?" Tathrin wondered uneasily.

"We'll find out soon enough." Aremil looked at a letter he'd dearly love to throw into the fire. "Lord Rousharn insists we send envoys to all the remaining dukes now that we've won this campaign. He has a list of men he recommends and he wishes to know when Captain-General Evord can provide suitable escorts. Sooner rather than later, if the captain-general pleases."

"What does the captain-general say to that?" Tathrin asked cautiously.

"I imagine he'll agree. Dagaran seems to think so. What harm can talking to them do, after all?"

"What do you suppose they'll say?" Failla wondered.

"Who knows?" Aremil looked at an unopened letter, its wax seals unbroken, beneath the latest one Rousharn had sent him. Once Evord agreed to send envoys, he would have to open that and tell the Soluran its contents. He would have to read whatever his unknown father had written.

Should he tell Tathrin about the letter? Should they open it together? If he couldn't share this with Branca, Aremil couldn't think of anyone else he would rather trust.

A knock broke the awkward silence.

Failla sprang up. "The wine."

But it was Dagaran, the Soluran lieutenant.

"A letter for you, Master Aremil." He read aloud from the enveloping outer parchment. "'From His Imperial Majesty Tadriol the Provident, Third of that Name, on behalf of the Convocation of Princes of Tormalin'. It's addressed to Lord Aremil of Draximal," he added.

"Who told him to call you that?" Tathrin was baffled.

"I don't know." Aremil could guess. "Please, open it," he asked with foreboding.

Dagaran used his belt knife to cut through the florid seals. He shook free a letter threaded with golden ribbon, a lead seal dangling from the end "This looks very official," he commented.

Aremil's back tightened with cramp. "Please, read it."

Dagaran cleared his throat.

"'On behalf of the Convocation of Tormalin Princes, honouring my election as their Emperor and my oath to manage our Empire's relations with all powers beyond our borders, I demand that you answer for the following outrages against the Dukes of Lescar and the people they have ruled with the full sanction and fealty of their vassals and the commonalty.'" He paused for breath.

"Go on," Tathrin invited.

"'Firstly the murder of Duke Moncan of Sharlac and his heir, together with the wanton destruction of Sharlac Castle and the barbarous imprisonment of his duchess and daughters.

"'Secondly, the murder of Duke Garnot of Carluse, his duchess and his heir, and the subsequent theft of his castle and property.

"'Thirdly, the murder of Duke Orlin of Parnilesse—'"

"He means Lord Geferin, surely?" Aremil looked at Tathrin, who nodded.

"The reports reaching Toremal must have got garbled on the way."

"No," Dagaran said slowly. "His Imperial Majesty is very precise in his accusation. 'Thirdly, the murder of Duke Orlin of Parnilesse, of his duchess, his heirs and his daughters and the destruction of Parnilesse Castle through fire and the subsequent massacres in Parnilesse Town.'" He looked up from the parchment. "I don't believe that's a mistake."

"What has happened?" Failla was appalled.

"What's Reniack done?" growled Tathrin.

No wonder Jettin was wrapping himself in the darkest cloak of Artifice he could muster. Aremil swallowed. "We had better find out, and quickly. Dagaran, what else does the Emperor say?"

The Soluran continued, "'In the light of this last and most heinous wrong, we are now minded to accede to the pleas of Duchess Aphanie of Sharlac. We hereby offer sanctuary to her and her daughters. You will surrender them to us, through the good offices of her castellan, Lord Rousharn—'" He broke off to look wryly at Aremil. "So that's the moth in the closet."

"Never mind him." Aremil gestured impatiently.

"'Should you fail to see the duchess and her daughters escorted to our borders with all due courtesy, your incivility will be swiftly punished.'" Dagaran paused once again. "I think he means all of us will suffer, rather than you personally."

Before Aremil could respond, he continued reading. "'Should you launch any further attack on Duke Ferdain of Marlier, on Duke Secaris of Draximal or on any of their vassal lords or the towns and villages under their protection, your aggression will be punished.'"

"Does he say how?" Tathrin asked slowly.

Dagaran shook his head. "Why do you ask?"

Tathrin grimaced. "Wouldn't he threaten to send in his legions, if he'd already made firm alliances with Marlier or Draximal?"

"Perhaps." Aremil wasn't sure. He looked at

Failla. "We had better see if Charoleia is up to advising us on how best to find out."

"And Sorgrad." Tathrin's lips narrowed. "He can scry and find out what's gone on. He's surely been to Parnilesse some time."

"Does he know Reniack well enough to scry for him?" wondered Failla.

"We'll find out," Tathrin assured her.

Dagaran frowned at the parchment. "There's more."

"Go on." Aremil wondered what could possibly be worse.

Dagaran cleared his throat. "'We demand the surrender of Duke Iruvain of Triolle and his duchess Litasse. You may rest assured you will be held to account for whatever injuries or insults they have suffered as your captives.'"

"Why would he think we're holding them prisoner?" That made no sense to Aremil. Lord Rousharn knew full well Triolle's duke had escaped the battle. He felt cold. "You don't think Reniack and his rabble could have caught them?"

"No." Tathrin rubbed his chin, calluses rasping on his stubble. "Sorgrad's been scrying for Litasse."

Aremil stiffened in his chair. "What?"

"He doesn't know where she is, exactly," Tathrin said sheepishly. "All he's seen is some hunting lodge and camps in the backwoods. But she's no captive, her or Iruvain."

"Let's hope they reach wherever they're going and appeal to someone who can tell Emperor Tadriol." Aremil leaned back. "Are we accused of any more crimes to bring Imperial wrath down on our heads?"

"No, that's all." The Soluran folded the parchment. "Barring a farewell as florid as the greeting and a request that you send your reply as soon as possible." He jerked his head in the direction of the gatehouse. "The Imperial courier who brought this tells me he has orders to wait until he's given one."

"Then we had better prepare it," Aremil said sardonically.

"I knew we had a lot of loose ends." Tathrin looked sombre. "I didn't imagine this tangle."

Failla's sudden laugh made them all look at her.

"I'm sorry." She pressed the back of one hand to her mouth. "It's just my mother always used to say, the true test of embroidery isn't how it looks from the front. It's how neatly it's finished at the back."

"Indeed." Aremil reached for his crutches. "Let's see if Charoleia's awake and able to advise on our needlework."

Dagaran opened the door to reveal a startled lackey carrying a silver tray with a wine jug and goblets.

"You've missed the festival, haven't you?" Tathrin seemed glad of someone to vent his anger on.

"Bring that to the inner keep," Aremil ordered the hapless servant.

Sorgrad would doubtless welcome the wine. Then he could use the tray for his scrying.

The battles might be over but there was evidently more still to be settled than he had imagined.

CHAPTER
FORTY-ONE
Litasse

Calsinn Strand,
in the Lescari Dukedom of Triolle,
6th of For-Winter

"YOUR BREAKFAST, YOUR GRACE." Karn entered and set the tray on the parlour table.

Fresh from the oven, the rolls smelled wonderful. Litasse noted the butter and preserves were served in crystal dishes, surely the innkeeper's wife's most treasured possessions. If only everyone was showing such loyalty.

"Where's Milda?" The girl had served her yesterday.

"Gone." Karn wiped a smear from the pewter goblet with a napkin. "Do you want small beer or wine?"

"Small beer, please." Litasse preferred watered wine but beer would surely be more palatable than any vintage found in this sorry excuse for a village. The barrels had probably washed up on the shingle bar. As for the water, her bedroom ewer smelled so brackish, she wasn't about to risk anything from a well hereabouts. The thought of being struck down with sickness or worse wasn't to be contemplated.

It was bad enough she had worn this chemise for three days now. Would she end up wearing her linen unwashed from one market day to the next, like some commoner's wife? She tried to recall how many of her gowns had been lost when the barge carrying their few salvaged possessions had foundered in the River Anock.

If the vessel *had* foundered. No wreckage had followed them down the current. Had the crew deserted them in the night, throwing the militiamen into the river? Or had they all forsworn their oath so they could split the booty with the watermen?

As Karn poured the light ale, she listened for footsteps in the hall, for voices elsewhere in the inn. There wasn't much to be heard.

"How many of the household are left now?"

Karn paused to tally them up. "Another seven have gone since yesterday."

"Every rune rolls one upright face." Litasse tore open a soft roll. "Fewer mouths to feed."

Flippancy was a mistake. A brittle note in her voice betrayed her. She spread butter and damson jam with vindictive thrusts of the bone-handled knife.

"I heard more fighting last night, didn't I?"

"His Grace's retinue fell out with some lads from the salt-marshes, over something and nothing. Your people are loyal," Karn assured her.

"I imagine Duchess Sherista thought so, until they broke down her door, cut off her head and stuck it on a pike." Litasse bit into the soft bread to stifle her fears. "Have you seen any more of those broadsheets?"

"No, Your Grace."

Litasse wasn't satisfied. He could well be hiding them to spare her more horrors. "What about travellers from Parnilesse? They could be bringing their murderous lies here."

"They could," Karn agreed. "I'm alert for any whispers."

Litasse could be certain of that. But Karn was only one man, much as she trusted him. He was the only one she could trust. Iruvain was a broken reed.

She had dreamed of Hamare last night. They had turned their backs on the dukedom without regret and sailed to make a new life in Col. She had woken with her face wet with tears.

"Where are we going to go, Karn? Where are we going to be safe?"

He walked to the window, his lean face thoughtful. "We have to make a decision before the weather is too foul for sailing. I recommend making for Relshaz. That takes us along Triolle's coast and Marlier's. If we're forced in to shore, we stand some chance of finding friends."

Litasse was dubious. "You don't think the Tormalin Emperor would be a better friend than Relshazri magistrates?"

"Emperor Tadriol's protection would be preferable," Karn admitted. "But making for Solland means navigating the full length of the Parnilesse coast, never mind safely rounding Cape Carif."

Litasse shivered. "Those mercenaries must be looting and plundering the length and breadth of the dukedom without Lord Geferin to bring them to heel."

Karn nodded. "If we make landfall anywhere along that coast, the best we can hope for is capture and ransom." He didn't have to describe the worst that could happen.

"Who would pay that," Litasse wondered bitterly, "while that Soluran thief hoards our coin?" She managed to finish the roll but had no appetite for another. "What was Iruvain thinking, coming south? We could have found sanctuary in Draximal only he's too proud to accept it, because it would be offered for my sake and Sharlac's, not his."

"A swift escape was our first priority," Karn reminded her. "A boat down the river was faster and safer than risking the roads. His Grace was right to fear that the mercenaries who fled the battle would turn bandit."

And that was before they had heard of the calamitous upheavals in Parnilesse. Litasse forbore to argue, though with ill-grace. "I hope we do get forced ashore when we sail for Relshaz. He can choke on the humiliation of going cap in hand to Ferdain."

"We may well find Duke Ferdain welcomes His Grace as an ally," Karn said thoughtfully. "Marlier's Caladhrian allies are far more likely to muster an army if two dukes appeal to them."

Litasse allowed herself a little hope. "Or three dukes, if we persuade Duke Secaris to uphold my claims to Sharlac."

The door to the parlour swung open. She jumped up, her hand going to the dagger concealed in her skirts. Karn was already between her and the entrance, his hand on his sword.

"There you are!" Duke Iruvain greeted him with an unexpected smile. "We must rally the men and start hiring horses."

"Your Grace." Karn bowed his head.

"We're going north." Iruvain spun around to point through the windows.

"To Draximal?" Litasse didn't know whether to be relieved or apprehensive. Karn was right about the perils of the roads.

"What?" Iruvain didn't seem to have noticed she was there. "Don't be a fool, woman. We're heading for the Anock Hills." He began pacing back and forth. "We'll hide out and rally the faithful men of Triolle. We can harry these usurping scum through the winter. Then we strike out in force as soon as Aft-Winter turns to For-Spring. We head west, to

Ashgil." He gestured expansively. "We drive a wedge between Carluse and Sharlac. Once we divide these filthy dogs and their horse-lovers, we turn south to retake Triolle!"

"That's a bold plan, Your Grace," Karn said cautiously.

"It's arrant folly!" snapped Litasse. "You think you can raise an army and start afresh, after a winter of living under hedges like a bandit, starving in the cold and the rain?"

Iruvain rounded on her. "No one will starve. Those hills teem with game. No one will be living like a bandit. We have friends and—"

"You don't think this Soluran knows all your hunting lodges," Litasse demanded, "now he can ask your stable-hands and kennel master?"

"They will never betray me." Iruvain's good humour vanished like morning mist. "Unlike you, my faithless wife."

He raised his hand. Litasse refused to flinch. He stepped closer, his colour rising.

Litasse smelled the wine on his breath. Unwatered wine, this early in the day. "You're drunk," she said with contempt.

"You're a whore," he snarled.

"What has that to do with anything?" She didn't care any more. "You were a fool not to listen to Hamare. If you'd only heeded him, you might still be—"

His back-handed blow cut her short. Reeling away, Litasse ripped the dagger through the slit in her skirts. She had the vicious point at Iruvain's belt buckle before he realised what had happened.

"Do that again and I'll gut you," she said coldly.

"You won't get the chance!" Iruvain lunged for the dagger.

Sober, he might have succeeded. Drunk, as Litasse recoiled, the blade sliced deep into his palm.

"Bitch." He stood staring at the gash, at the welling blood.

"Your Grace." Karn pressed the napkin from the breakfast tray to the wound. "You must see the surgeon. You cannot risk a disabling wound with everyone relying on you."

Shocked, Iruvain nodded slowly.

"This way, Your Grace." Karn tied the linen tight to staunch the bleeding and led him to the door.

Trembling, Litasse watched them go. Her eyes met Karn's as he glanced over his shoulder. Was that gaze a warning? What did he mean for her to do? As the door closed, she dropped the dagger and collapsed into her chair, shuddering with violent tears.

She had drawn a blade on her husband. Iruvain couldn't ignore that. The sorry remnants of their household and his retinue must all be within earshot too. He couldn't pretend it had never happened, not with a scar across his palm to remind him. Everyone would see it, each and every day.

What allies did she have among these ragtag servants and swordsmen? None that she could think of. Some seemed more trustworthy than others, but how long would it be before she woke to find every last one had fled in the night? Litasse thought her heart would burst. Pelletria's death was a physical ache in her breast.

No. She couldn't break. If she did, she would be utterly lost. She must take stock of her situation. She couldn't rely on Iruvain's protection or even his forbearance any more. Her status as duchess was no shield. He had nothing to lose by repudiating her now. How could Triolle's duke be any more humiliated, after fleeing headlong from the battle that saw the loss of his dukedom?

She had no protector now that Hamare was dead. She had no home, not as a wife nor as a disgraced daughter. Her father was dead, her mother and sisters captive. Those few confidants she might have called friends were dead or scattered to the four winds. They had no idea what had happened to Triolle's vassal lords. Who had come to terms with these exiles? Who defied them? They didn't even know what had befallen Lord Roreth.

Her unseeing eyes focused on the fallen dagger. Stooping, she picked it up. If Iruvain came looking for vengeance, she had better be ready. The only question remaining was did she wait for him to throw her in the gutter or should she strike out now to fend for herself?

It was that Mountain Man's dagger. The one who'd killed Hamare. Who'd come to kill Minelas though his fellow had actually done the deed. Litasse admitted she could hardly hold that against them.

Her expression hardened. If Hamare's killer thought that levelled the scales, he was sorely mistaken. If she ever got the chance, she would still make him pay. She would make them all pay. Wherever she fled, she would make it her business to find out who'd encompassed this ruination of Sharlac, of Triolle, even of Parnilesse and Carluse.

She had Karn. He had no real tie to Iruvain. He knew some of Hamare's old contacts. There would surely be some of those in Relshaz. Together, could they make use of such knowledge?

Litasse slowly wiped Iruvain's blood from the steel. Throwing her soiled kerchief in the fire, she watched the muslin flare before it fell into ashes. She had nothing left to lose. Vengeance was all that remained to her now.

DUKEDOMS OF LESCAR

EXILES AND REBELS

Tathrin: Originally from the Lescari dukedom of Carluse, apprenticed to Master Wyess, a fur trader in Vanam.

Aremil: A nobleman crippled from birth living a retired, scholarly life in Vanam.
Lyrlen: His loyal nurse.

Reniack: Originally from Parnilesse, born to a whore in the mercenary enclave of Carif. A rabble rouser and pamphleteer.

Lady Derenna: A noblewoman exiled from Sharlac when her husband,
Lord Rousharn of Nolsedge: fell foul of the duke.

Master Gruit: A wine merchant of Vanam originally from the dukedom of Marlier.
Courra and Sibetha: Servants in his Abray household.*

Failla: Previously mistress to Duke Garnot of Carluse.
Anilt: Her daughter.
Lathi: Failla's cousin and Anilt's foster-mother
Serafia: Failla's cousin and mother to the orphaned Kip.
Derou: Their aunt and Ernout's sister.

Ernout: Priest of Saedrin at the shrine in Carluse town and Failla's uncle.
Master Settan and Master Findrin: Guildmasters of Carluse town, conspiring with Ernout to relieve local people's suffering.
Jerich Sayron: Innkeeper at the Ring of Birches. An ally of the Guildmasters and Tathrin's father.

Reher: A mageborn blacksmith originally from Carluse.
Milar: A Carluse innkeeper and ally of Ernout and the Guildmasters.

Branca: A student at Vanam's university, born of Lescari blood. Adept at using the ancient enchantments called Artifice.
Kerith and Jettin: Also Adepts, also of Lescari origins,

Mentor Tonin: A noted Vanam scholar engaged in unravelling the secrets of Artifice.

Charoleia: An intelligent and beautiful information broker.
Her aliases include Lady Alaric, Mistress Larch, Lady Rochiel,
Mistress Horelle, Mistress Halisoun, Mistress Lanagyre.
Trissa: Her maid. Extremely discreet.

Nath. An itinerant mapmaker with links to Charoleia.
Welgren. A travelling apothecary with links to Charoleia.

Sorgrad and Gren. Mountain-born brothers. Mercenaries long involved in shady dealings the length and breadth of Einarinn.

Evord Fal Breven: Captain General of the Exiles' Army.
Dagaran Esk Breven: His principle lieutenant, also from the ancient Kingdom of Solura, to the far west of the Great Forest.

Sia Kersain: Dalasorian Clan Lord and commander of the
northern grassland lancers.
Sia Nanas: His son.

Rega Taszar: A Dalasorian clan lord.
Pata Mezian: A Dalasorian clan lord.

Alrene and Thyren: Commanders of the two regiments of Mountain Men.

Mercenary companies hired by Captain General Evord include:

The Wyvern Hunters
Juxon's Raiders
The Gallowsfruit
The Tallymen
The Longshanks
Vendist's Spearmen
Nyer's Watchmen
The Shearlings
The Sundowners
The Wheelwrights

THE DUKES OF LESCAR

CARLUSE
Insignia: a black boar's head on a white ground.
Colours: black and white

Duke Garnot.
Duchess Tadira: Born sister to the Duke of Parnilesse.

Lord Ricart: Heir to the dukedom.
Veblen: Duke Garnot's bastard son, killed in battle two years ago.

Corrad: Carluse Castle's horse master.
Vrist and Parlin: Grooms.
Zarene: A maidservant.
Sergeant Banel and Sergeant Haddow: Officers of the castle garrison

TRIOLLE
Insignia: a green grebe on a pale yellow ground.
Colours: green and yellow

Duke Iruvain: Succeeded his father Duke Gerone less than a year ago.
Litasse: His duchess, born daughter of the Duke of Sharlac.
Pelletria: Her attendant and confidante. Also an enquiry agent. Previously confidante of the late Duchess Casatia.
Valesti: Litasse's previous lady in waiting.
Milda: An insignificant maidservant.

Lord Roreth: Duke Iruvain's brother and heir.
Lady Mazien and Lady Erasie: Noblewomen of Triolle.

Hamare: Litasse's lover, Triolle's spymaster and erstwhile scholar of Col's university. Now dead.

Karn: An enquiry agent. Born in Marlier and orphaned as a child.

Minelas of Grynth: A renegade wizard, latterly employed in Caladhria to defend Lord Halferan's lands against Aldabreshin corsairs.

SHARLAC
Insignia: a russet stag on a green ground.
Colours: brown and green

Duke Moncan: Slain in the battle for Sharlac Castle.
Lord Kerlin: Second son and heir, slain in the battle for Sharlac Castle.
Lord Jaras: Heir to Sharlac previously killed in battle by Veblen of Carluse.

Duchess Aphanie: Mother of Litasse of Triolle, now widowed.

DRAXIMAL
Insignia: a golden brazier on a blue ground.
Colours: red and gold

Duke Secaris.
Lord Cassat. His heir.

MARLIER
Isignia: three silver swords on a scarlet ground.
Colours: silver-grey and red

Duke Ferdain.
Ridianne the Vixen: His mistress and captain of his
mercenaries.

PARNILESSE
*Insignia: a green wreath overlaying a black sword
and halberd crossed on a blue ground.*
Colours: green and black

Duke Orlin.
Lord Geferin: His brother.
Duchess Sherista: Wife to Duke Orlin.

Mercenary companies serving the dukes of Lescar
include:

Wynald's Warband (defeated and disbanded after
the battle for Losand)
The Moonrakers
The Red Hounds
The Slippery Eels
The Locksmiths
The Tunnellers' Sons
The Quicksilver Men
The Steelhands
Alsar's Eaglets
The Flintstrikers

OTHER INTERESTED PARTIES

TOREMAL
Tadriol the Provident, Emperor of Tormalin, Third of that Name.

THE WIZARD CITY OF HADRUMAL
Planir the Black: Archmage.
Jilseth: Magewoman and enquiry agent.

RELSHAZ
Mellitha Esterlin: Magewoman and tax-collector.
Egil the Toad: Information broker.
Downy Scardin: Introductions agent.

CALADHRIA
Baron Dacren, Baron Lynast, Lord Kishote and Lord Vapanet. Noblemen with border interests along the river Rel and a voice in the Caladhrian Parliament. Master Cardel and Master Bohad: Senior guildsmen of Abray.

SOLURA
King Solquen IV.

ABOUT THE AUTHOR

Juliet E McKenna has been interested in fantasy stories since childhood, from Winnie the Pooh to *The Iliad*. An abiding fascination with other worlds and their peoples played its part in her subsequently reading Classics at St. Hilda's College, Oxford. After combining bookselling and motherhood for a couple of years, she now fits in her writing around her family and vice versa. She lives with her husband and children in West Oxfordshire, England.

SOLARIS BOOKS

Founded in 2007 as an independent imprint, Solaris set out to publish a mix of innovative and traditional science fiction, fantasy and horror, by new and familiar authors alike, and to fill the gap between large-scale mass-market publishers and the small genre press. In two years, we've published gritty, hard-SF and high-octane adventure, creepy horror and swashbuckling fantasy. We've discovered new gems like the hugely successful Gail Z. Martin and snagged old favourites like Brian Lumley and Eric Brown. We've published seven anthologies, including new science fiction and fantasy, steampunk, and stories inspired by H. P. Lovecraft and Edgar Allan Poe, with contributions by some of the best-loved and most recognised names in science fiction. As of 2009, Solaris has been part of Rebellion, and are confident that they can only go from strength to strength in the future.

More than anything, Solaris exists to publish fantastic books by great authors, and to bring to your attention, as a reader, a plethora of exciting new stories and novels.

http://www.solarisbooks.com/

CHRONICLES OF THE LESCARI REVOLUTION
IRONS IN THE FIRE

"If you're not reading Juliet McKenna, you should be."
Kate Elliott, author of the Crown of Stars and Crossroads series

JULIET E MCKENNA

UK ISBN: 978 1 84416 620 6 • US ISBN: 978 1 84416 601 5 • £7.99/$7.99

The country of Lescar was born out of civil war. Carved out of the collapse of the Old Tourmalin Empire, the land has long been laid waste by its rival dukes, while bordering nations look on with indifference or exploit its misery. But a mismatched band of rebels is agreed that the time has come for a change, and they begin to put a scheme together for revolution.

 WWW.SOLARISBOOKS.COM

Follow us on Twitter! www.twitter.com/solarisbooks

"Attractive characters and an imaginative setting combine
in an excellent, fast-moving quest novel."
— David Drake, author of the Lord of the Isles series

GAIL Z. MARTIN

THE SUMMONER

Book One of the
CHRONICLES OF THE NECROMANCER

UK ISBN: 978 1 844164 68 4 • US ISBN: 978 1 844164 68 4 • £7.99/$7.99

The world of Prince Martris Drayke is thrown into chaos when his brother murders their
father and seizes the throne. Forced to flee with only a handful of loyal followers, Martris
must seek retribution and restore his father's honour. If the living are arrayed against
him, Martris must call on a different set of allies: the living dead.

 WWW.SOLARISBOOKS.COM

Follow us on Twitter! www.twitter.com/solarisbooks

GAIL Z. MARTIN
DARK HAVEN

Book Three of the
CHRONICLES OF THE NECROMANCER

"A fast-paced tale laced with plenty of action."
— SF Site on *The Summoner*

UK ISBN: 978 1 844167 08 1 • US ISBN: 978 1 844165 98 8 • £7.99/$7.99

The kingdom of Margolan lies in ruin. Martris Drayke, the new king, must rebuild his country in the aftermath of battle, while a new war looms on the horizon. Meanwhile Jonmarc Vahanian is now the Lord of Dark Haven, and there is defiance from the vampires of the Vayash Moru at the prospect of a mortal leader. But can he earn their trust, and at what cost?

 WWW.SOLARISBOOKS.COM

Follow us on Twitter! www.twitter.com/solarisbooks

UK ISBN: 978 1 844166 17 6 • US ISBN: 978 1 844165 84 1 • £7.99/$7.99

When he mysteriously finds himself drawn into a world of his own devising, bumbling writer Rod Everlar is confronted by a shocking truth - he has lost control of his creation to a brooding cabal of evil. In order to save his creation, he must seize control of Falconfar and halt the spread of corruption before it is too late.

FALCONFAR

Arch Wizard

"A master of fantasy world-building. His imagination and artistry are wondrous indeed." Margaret Weis, New York Times best selling author

ED GREENWOOD

BOOK TWO

UK ISBN: 978 1 906735 63 0 • US ISBN: 978 1 844167 64 7 • £7.99/$7.99

Having been drawn into a fantasy world of his own creation, Rod Everlar continues his quest to defeat the corruption he has discovered within. With the ambitious Arlaghaun now dead, he sets off in pursuit of the dark wizard Malraun, only to find that he has raised an army of monsters and mercenaries in order to conquer the world...

 WWW.SOLARISBOOKS.COM

Follow us on Twitter! www.twitter.com/solarisbooks

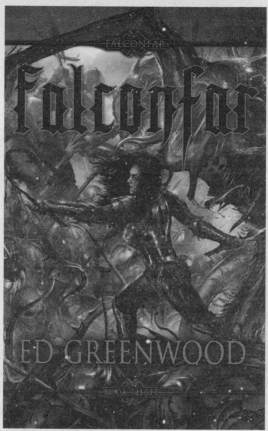

UK ISBN: 978-1-906735-60-9 • US ISBN: 978-1-906735-61-6 • £17.99/$17.99

With the evil wizards Malraun and Narmarkoun seemingly defeated and Malraun's tower falling about his ears, Rod Everlar, the science-fiction writer drawn into a world of his own creation, now faces his greatest challenge. As Falconfar descends into war, Rod must find the power and the knowledge to fight the first Archwizard, the most feared of the Dooms: Lorontar.

 WWW.SOLARISBOOKS.COM

Follow us on Twitter! www.twitter.com/solarisbooks

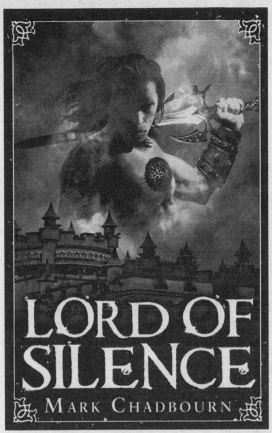

LORD OF SILENCE

MARK CHADBOURN

UK ISBN: 978 1 844167 52 4 • US ISBN: 978 1 844167 53 1 • £7.99/$7.99

When the great hero of Idriss is murdered, Vidar, the Lord of Silence, must take his place as chief defender against the terrors lurking in the forest beyond the walls. But Vidar is a man tormented — by his lost memories and by a life-draining jewel. With a killer loose within the city and a threat mounting without, he must solve an ancient mystery to unlock the secrets of his own past.

 WWW.SOLARISBOOKS.COM

Follow us on Twitter! www.twitter.com/solarisbooks